E

Elizabeth Pewsey was born in Chile and educated in
Calcutta, London and at St Hilda's College, Oxford. She
has worked as a civil servant and publisher, and now
lives in Wells, Somerset, with her husband and two
children. UNHOLY HARMONIES is the third novel in
the Mountjoy series, following CHILDREN OF CHANCE
and DIVINE COMEDY, and the fourth and latest is
VOLCANIC AIRS.

SCEPTRE

*Also by Elizabeth Pewsey*

Children of Chance
Divine Comedy
Volcanic Airs

# Unholy Harmonies

## ELIZABETH PEWSEY

**SCEPTRE**

First published in 1996 by Hodder and Stoughton
A division of Hodder Headline PLC
A Sceptre Paperback

British Library Cataloguing in Publication Data

Pewsey, Elizabeth
   Unholy harmonies
   1. English fiction – 20th century
   I. Title
   823.9'14 [F]

   ISBN 0 340 64911 9

Printed and bound in Great Britain by
Cox & Wyman Ltd, Reading, Berkshire

Hodder and Stoughton
A division of Hodder Headline PLC
338 Euston Road
London NW1 3BH

# For Naomi Harries,

*who kept the forces of chaos at bay*
*thus enabling these books to be written*

Dire.

How can I think my own wedding is dire? thought Justinia. And then, I wish this beastly little clergyman wouldn't call me Justy. No-one calls me Justy except family and close friends. Which he certainly isn't. She felt stifled in the magnificent Edwardian lace wedding dress she and her mother had chosen with such care. Why hadn't she slipped quietly into a register office? Why were they standing here in the Cathedral, with all too many friends and relations watching this man with his smirk and his primary school English lead them through a parody of the marriage service? Why had Digby insisted on the most modern and banal version for their wedding? Why had she given in?

She could feel eyes looking at her. Virginia Luthier's eyes. Cool, formidable Virginia, who had so plainly thought that she shouldn't marry Digby. Her cousin Lydia, surprised that she preferred Digby to all her previous and quite different boyfriends. Magdalena, worried that her Mountjoy temperament wouldn't settle down easily to life with Digby. Why hadn't she listened to them? Why had she let her mother persuade her to have this full-blown wedding, to which all her doubting friends and family felt obliged to come? Why was she getting married at all?

The priest droned on in his chatty way, and Justinia flashed a quick glance at the man standing at her side. Her doubts and irritation vanished. She loved him. She loved him totally and completely. She loved the way he stood, the way he looked, his hands, his thick, slightly wavy dark hair that sprung back from his wide forehead. She loved talking to him, she loved doing things with him, and most of all, she loved being in bed with him. That was the answer to all the questions.

"Justy and Digby are now well and truly married," the priest said with a fatuous little laugh. "So how about a round of applause for them?"

The stunned congregation drifted down the cathedral steps behind the bride and groom. The page boy, released by the photographer, had run across Tom Quad to the fountain and was making faces at the statue of Mercury.

"What an appalling wedding service," said Virginia to Magdalena.

"I suppose young people prefer a modern affair," said Magdalena, not sounding very convinced.

"Nonsense," said Virginia. "Simple bad taste. Digby chose it, so Celia told me. The man must have tin ears, dreadful language. As bad as his name. How can anyone be called Digby FitzOdo?"

"Not his fault, his name." Magdalena was doubtful.

"She's a fool to marry him on any count," went on Virginia. "Celia shouldn't have put such pressure on her to do so."

Lydia, emboldened by the obvious admiration of one of the guests from Digby's side of the church, spoke up in defence of her cousin. "She's very much in love with him."

Virginia looked at Lydia for a moment, her straight brows and severe eyes unyielding. "That's not a basis for marriage. Choose better when your time comes, Lydia."

"It's because he's an outsider," said Lydia defiantly. "The Mountjoys never think anyone is good enough for them."

"Good enough isn't the right expression, Lydia," said Magdalena in a calm voice. "You make it sound snobbish and silly. Justinia has a lot of character, as do most of the Mountjoys. If you have a lot of character, particularly if you're a woman, you need to be extremely careful when you marry."

Rebuked, Lydia fell back to join her friends and pretended to ignore the young man who had just joined them.

"May I introduce myself?" he said with an attractive smile. "I'm Angus. You're Lydia Holbeck, aren't you? You're at St Frideswyde's, I saw you at a do at my college the other evening. I'm at Balliol."

"Hello, Angus," said Lydia, forgetting all about the rather too adult conversation she had just been having with Virginia and Magdalena. Good, she thought. At least there'll be someone interesting at the reception; light relief from my doom-laden family.

"Why Oxford?" said Virginia. Spurning the spindly folding chairs, she stood and surveyed the throng of people.

Magdalena, herself elegant in lemon and black, thought how good Virginia looked in her black and white, and what a terrifying woman she was.

"Digby was at Christ Church. And it could hardly be held in Italy," she pointed out.

"Why not?" asked Virginia. "Better climate, better priest, no doubt, and probably livelier company."

"Probably not," said Magdalena. "Celia's never gone in for lively company."

"She shouldn't have shut herself away in that place when Hugo died. I know he loved it there, but she should have stayed in England, provided some kind of a home for Justinia."

"She was nineteen, and already up at Cambridge. I think once they go off to university, they don't mind what their parents do."

"In my experience they do mind; they expect their parents to be on hand to supply a bed, food, money, and even, occasionally, a shoulder to cry on."

"Celia would be more likely to cry on Justinia's shoulder than the other way around."

"Such a silly woman," said Virginia with a sigh, looking across to where Justinia's wraith-like mother was talking to Mountjoy. As always, her dark, soulful eyes seemed to be about to brim with tears. "I can't think why Hugo ever married her."

Magdalena laughed and helped herself to another glass of champagne as a waiter hurried past. "Of course you can. She was incredibly beautiful, and simply oozing sex appeal. If she didn't mind the fact that he was nearly thirty years older than she was, why should he? It was a good marriage, as marriages go."

"For a Mountjoy, an amazingly good one," said Virginia

tartly. "Sorry, Magdalena, it's quite different for you and Mountjoy. You're both grown up, for one thing, and you'd both been married before. Mountjoy's wild days are behind him, but I was surprised when Hugo became so domesticated."

"Marrying Celia calmed him down. And then Justinia, he felt the responsibility, and of course, he adored her, underneath all that ferocity."

"Everybody did," said Virginia. "She was a charming child. Still is charming, which is lucky for her, because charm outlasts looks – although I must say, she's grown into a real beauty. What a waste, marrying Digby."

"He is very attractive." Magdalena was definite.

"Do you think so?" Virginia looked at Digby with an appraising eye.

"It's his energy. And he pays attention to you, when you talk to him. Listens, focuses. That's a knockout, in a masculine man like him."

Virginia shook her head. "Not my type. Not only because he's years younger than me, he never would have been my type. And I don't think he's Justinia's type." She gave Digby another cool glance. "Still, one consolation, it won't last."

Magdalena looked startled. "Hardly the place and time to say that, at the wedding."

"Exactly the time and place. Let's hope they don't immediately have children, that complicates matters so."

"Not for the Mountjoys," said Magdalena wickedly.

Virginia gave one of her rare smiles, which transformed her face. A passing Digbyite eyed her with admiration, but was quickly seen off by a swift, piercing glance. He went off to find easier prey while Magdalena and Virginia sipped the champagne and watched Justinia, her face alight with happiness as she lolled against Digby.

"Anyway, Justinia wants to go on working, she's very keen on her job," Magdalena said. "Although it seems strange to me that such a vital, exotic creature could be happy working in museums, all among the dead things."

"I don't know," said Virginia. "I've seen maenads on the sides of Greek vases which distinctly remind me of Justinia."

"A maenad?" said Magdalena. "Justy? Oh, I do hope not. Think of the trouble it would cause. I don't think that would go down well with Digby at all."

"It won't," said Virginia definitely. "Just you wait and see."

"Justinia, how nice. What are you doing in Eyot?"

Oh, no. Pauline Norris. Justinia looked around as though some means of escape might suddenly appear.

"Hello, Pauline," she said in what she hoped was a friendly voice.

"Isn't it ridiculous? We both live in Unthrang, and hardly see each other, and then we bump into each other in Eyot. Of course, I'm so busy, it's hard to keep up with my friends."

I'm not a friend, thought Justinia.

"Shopping?" said Pauline, her sharp eyes boring into Justinia's big leather bag.

Justinia's defences went up; she's not going to prise anything out of me, she said to herself. Uninteresting though the contents of her bag were, she wasn't revealing them.

"Such a busy time, when one's moved into a new house, especially when there's a lot of work to be done," Pauline went on in her relentless way. "I expect you're picking up swatches of fabric, wallpaper samples. Really, I quite envy you."

"Toothpaste," said Justinia resignedly. You always gave in to Pauline, quicker and easier, really, to get it over with.

"You should support the local shops," said Pauline instantly. "Of course, Nigel and I do a big shop at Sainsbury's, well, you have to, don't you, one appreciates the variety . . . But things like a tube of toothpaste, well, we'd always go to Morton's in Unthrang for that."

"It's a special kind of toothpaste that Digby uses," said Justinia. "Morton's don't have it, so I have to come to Eyot for it."

"Special toothpaste? Does Digby have trouble with his teeth?

Bad gums, perhaps?" Her bright eyes, eager for information, searched Justinia's face.

Justinia was giving nothing away. "He just likes the taste," she said.

"You mustn't let men get away with their little foibles," said Pauline with a sharp laugh. "How long have you been married?"

None of your business, thought Justinia crossly.

"It's nearly four years, isn't it? And now this splendid house you've bought, I expect you'll soon be shopping for things for the nursery."

Justinia gave her a ravishing smile, thinking of the packet of contraceptive pills sitting in the bag with the toothpaste.

"A good idea, to start a family," Pauline persisted. "After all, with Digby up in London and you here . . . Well, men can get lonely, in that way. That's where children make a difference; they're a great tie for a man."

"Digby is too busy to be lonely," said Justinia firmly.

"Ah, I didn't mean anything, you know, you mustn't take offence. But I've been married quite a while, and of course, I'm older than you, and I know what men are like. Naturally, you feel sure that Digby wouldn't look at another woman, but perhaps you ought to know . . ."

"Justy!"

Rescue.

"Lydia, I'm sorry I'm late, I was just chatting to Pauline. You know Pauline, do you?"

"Yes," said Lydia without enthusiasm. "How are you, Pauline?"

Pauline longed to know Lydia better, since her husband was such a very distinguished composer. In truth, Lydia was one of the few people who could make Pauline feel uneasy, so with a few final remarks she excused herself and went on her way, hoping to meet someone else so that she could mention her chat with Lydia Praetorius; an old friend, you know, wife of Alban Praetorius, the composer.

"What was all that about?" asked Lydia. "Why were you making faces at me? What are you doing in Eyot? Why aren't you beavering away in the museum? Why were you talking to ghastly Pauline?"

"Lunch," said Justinia. "Let me take you to lunch, I feel in need of refreshment."

"All right," said Lydia. "But a quick one, although I long to chat. Alban's gone to London for the day, so I have masses of things to do while his back is turned."

"A lover?" asked Justinia with interest, as they joined the queue at the food counter in Horatio's Bar.

"Of course not," said Lydia, laughing. "Cleaning his studio, throwing out all the food he's been hoarding in the fridge – you know how he hates to throw anything away – that kind of thing. Very wifely. Very domestic. How's Digby?"

"Fine," said Justinia.

"So why aren't you in London, working? Have you taken time off to fix the new house?"

"I've given up my job in London," said Justinia. "Too difficult, now that we've bought this house in Unthrang. It's too far, and it's very stressful, hurtling down for Monday morning, and then fighting one's way back on Friday night."

"Won't you be bored?"

"Probably, but once the house is straight, I'll see if I can find a job here, in Eyot. Plenty of museums about, there must be something I can do."

"Not the same as the British Museum."

"No," agreed Justinia, squeezing her chair up to a little round table in the corner.

"Is Digby in London very much these days?"

"He's there today," said Justinia. "Usually, he goes into his office here, but he goes up to London once or twice a month."

"Business booming?"

Justinia nodded, her mouth full of luscious linguine. "This is good. Yes, it's all doing very well. People travelling more and more, at least the kind of people he arranges travel for."

"A select group, are they?"

"I wouldn't say select. Targeted. Particular types of business, and he's getting into other kinds of group travel: orchestras and so on."

"Lucrative?"

"Mmm, not too bad."

"You could work for his company. You know a lot about music, don't you? Do you still sing?"

"A bit. No, I wouldn't like to work for Digby, best to keep one's private and professional lives separate."

"I expect you're right. And Digby's probably difficult to work with, he's very bossy, isn't he? Still, don't let him get too involved with his work. You don't want to find yourself stranded out in Unthrang."

"While I languish into motherhood?" asked Justinia.

"No need to bite, such an idea wouldn't occur to me. I don't think you could languish. You look as though you could with your dreamy eyes and pre-Raphaelite hair, but that doesn't deceive anyone who knows you."

"Do you think Digby knows me?"

Lydia was sitting back, relaxed and peaceful, but she shot Justinia a very sharp glance from under half-closed eyes.

"I don't suppose he does. Men seldom do, they're constantly being surprised by their wives."

"Do you surprise Alban?"

"Nothing surprises Alban. He's far too wrapped up in himself and his music to be surprised. Annoyed is the furthest he'd go, and that only if it was something that directly affected his comfort or his work."

"You're very lucky, you know," said Justinia thoughtfully. "Being married to a musician."

Lydia looked hard at her cousin. "What an extraordinary thing to say. I'm married to Alban because he's Alban, not because he's a composer."

Justinia explained. "You live in a musical world. I don't. I think I should like to have been a musician, you see."

"Yes, you were very musical, weren't you? That lovely voice, I always thought you were destined to be a singer."

"It would have been difficult. My parents didn't approve of music as a career, and it didn't seem sensible to train at the time."

"Musicians never bother about those things," said Lydia with chilling directness. "They just go ahead and do it, because they have to. Not because it's sensible or convenient."

"No, well," said Justinia, "I never had the drive, so I suppose my mother was right. I have a degree, and qualifications for museum work; much more practical and useful."

"Yes," said Lydia. "And Digby isn't fond of music, is he?"

Justinia laughed. "Not at all. Likes what he calls a jolly good tune, which means one that he can whistle a few bars of, and that's his lot. I took him to the opera once or twice before we were married, but I can't say he took to it."

"There's a good Music Society Choir here," said Lydia. "Alban's brother Simon runs it. They're forming a Chamber Choir, too, the Eyot Camerata. Go and audition, you'd enjoy it, and you'd meet people."

"I've already met a lot of people," said Justinia darkly. "Unthrang is full of people."

"Interesting people?" asked Lydia.

"No, I don't think so. There's Pauline, of course."

"Ugh," said Lydia. "Well she and Nigel must be the worst of it."

"I suppose so. There's a strange old woman who lives in a big house with a tower. She's called Zephania Zouche, I'm told; I haven't met her; she keeps herself to herself and wears a strange flat hat. Then there's a woman, a young woman, called Roxane, who lives in a lovely seventeenth-century house on the green, Juniper House. I think she lives alone, but the woman at the shop told me that she lets the house out, and that a family are coming for the autumn."

"Then there's Sadie, she's all right; a widow I think – at any rate, there's no husband about. She lives in a funny little yellow cottage on the other side of the green. The vicarage contains the vicar, who's hearty and modern and evangelical. He gets on very well with Digby; Digby likes anything that's up-to-date. That's about it. Oh, and Sylvester is living in Crag End, while Midwinter Hall is having its works done."

Lydia looked pleased. "Sylvester? Well, never a dull moment if Sylvester's around. What about Lily? Is she with him? Is Gabriel in residence?"

"Lily's there, I think Gabriel is abroad. Anyway, those are all the ones I've met so far."

"There must be more than that. No country wenches to tempt Digby's roving eye?"

"Roving eye? What do you mean?"

Lydia shook her head, startled at the vehemence of Justinia's voice. "Calm down, it was an idle phrase, no more. Have some pud."

"Sorry," said Justinia, as a passing waiter waved a hand towards a table laden with ruinous and creamy things. "It's just Pauline was making some silly remarks. Why does everyone suppose that if you've been married for more than five minutes and you don't have children, then your husband must be off having affairs?"

"Which Digby isn't."

"No, he isn't," said Justinia, stabbing at a quivering crème caramel. "He isn't that sort, and besides, we're still in love, strange though that must seem."

"Doesn't seem strange to me," said Lydia. "Now, stop fretting and eat up. I'll be seeing Simon this evening, I'll ask him about his choirs. You're a soprano, aren't you?"

Justinia nodded. "I'd like that, as long as it's a convenient evening; Digby doesn't like me being out when he's at home. But he often works late, so it shouldn't be a problem."

They parted affectionately, Lydia promising to come and see the house. "And I'll bring Alban, too; although he always grumbles about my horrible Mountjoy relations, I think he's got rather a soft spot for you. Says you're too damn beautiful to miss."

Justinia laughed, and the tension which Lydia had noticed all through lunch vanished from her face.

I can't return the compliment, Justinia thought as she made her way through the tourists in the crowded streets towards the car park. Digby isn't very keen on any of my Mountjoy relations; I wonder if he knew what they said when we got married. Oh well, we've proved them wrong, our marriage is a success, more than you can say for some of them.

"Shock Sale," said the screamer in the window. "Swimsuits from France, ridiculous prices."

Justinia hesitated, eyed a particularly appealing costume which looked good even on the twig-like physique of the dummy in the window, and pushed open the door of the shop. Roxane had invited her to swim in her indoor pool at Juniper House. "It doesn't get enough use; you'd mostly have it to yourself."

Thinking that she would be glad to get out of the Old Rectory and that she could do with some exercise now she was no longer going to work every day, Justinia had searched in vain for her swimsuit. It had been lost or mislaid in the moves, first from her flat in London to Digby's larger one, then to their London house, and now up here to Unthrang.

A tiny, vivacious assistant emerged from behind the counter. "Is it a swimsuit you're after?"

Justinia smiled and said it was.

"Lovely, they are. From France, genuinely, not one of these signs some shops put up just to attract customers. We wouldn't do that. Did you see one you liked in the window?"

"Yes," said Justinia, pointing it out.

"Beautiful, these colours." The assistant fixed dark, sparkling, expert eyes on Justinia. "Thirty-six, is it? This should be all right."

She escorted Justinia to a minute changing room, pulling the curtain across with a flourish. "I'll go and check if we have other sizes, or perhaps you'd like to try on one or two different models."

Her heels clicked smartly as she went back into the main part of the shop, while Justinia took off her jacket and began to undo her shirt.

"I'll help you with your bra," said the assistant, coming back with an armful of brilliantly coloured costumes. "Lovely ones you've got, are they natural?"

Justinia laughed. "Yes, my own."

"Smashing," said the girl with a sigh. "I've got practically nothing up top myself, all artificially bolstered, that's the advantage of working in lingerie. But you'd be surprised at what some women have done, they go to America for it. Very realistic, but too firm. I only asked because you've got such a small waist, lucky you to have a figure like that."

Justinia pulled on the swimming costume, which turned out on inspection to cost an alarming amount, even in the Shock Sale, but the assistant's admiration was wholehearted and Justinia knew that Digby would appreciate it. As she was starting to get dressed again, the assistant reappeared, whisked away the costumes, with coos of delight at the one that Justinia had chosen, and delivered some wisps of underwear to the little table in the changing room. "Look lovely on you, these would," she said winningly. "Get your lover really excited."

"Lover?" said Justinia. What was this, why was everybody talking about lovers today?

"Must be a lover," said the girl. "You're married, you've got rings on, a good one too, it must have cost, that one. But the way you look at yourself, you're thinking of some man admiring you in that costume, I can tell."

"And why shouldn't it be my husband?" said Justinia, laughing.

"Never is," said the girl wisely. "Someone else's husband, perhaps, but not your own."

"Well, you're wrong." said Justinia, looking at the pile of lace. "It is for my husband."

"Never mind," said the girl with great cheerfulness. "Looking the way you do, it won't be for long, must be any number of men willing to have a fling, you with a figure like that, not to mention your looks. I see them all in here, women wanting to look sexy for their lovers, then ten minutes later, their husbands are in here – buying pretties for their mistresses of course, not for their wives."

"You're very cynical," said Justinia, hunting for her cheque book.

"Come back soon, when that lover turns up," said the girl with a wicked look as Justinia left the shop. "Tell me all about him, I shan't breathe a word!"

# 2

Sylvester sat in the front garden of Crag End, surveying the green. Lily brought him a tray of tea.

"Wonderful place, this," said Sylvester genially. "I'm going to enjoy it here. Warm enough to sit out now, and when it gets colder, I'll still be able to keep in touch with what's happening from my room."

"You won't be sitting out here for much longer if what Jack Lewthwaite says is true."

"Ah, your farmer friend has been out with his seaweed, has he?"

"He says this fine spell is going to break with a Helm."

Sylvester sat up, much interested. "A Helm? Truly? Now, that would be a piece of luck, just the time when we're staying here. It must be what, seven years since the last one?"

"Yes, seven years."

Sylvester looked up at the great fell which dominated the skyline. "Looks utterly peaceful to me, I think Jack's just trying to alarm us."

"We'll see," said Lily, going briskly back to her kitchen. Sylvester sat and looked again at Hell Fell. A few wisps of cloud, no, nothing was going to disturb this fine autumn weather. Crag End was one of several houses set round the wide green, which reflected the Anglian origins of the market town of Unthrang. A beck ran along one side, with little wooden bridges leading across to the front gates of the houses set on the other bank. Further along from Sylvester was an ancient church; quite small, since the population of the town had never been large. And behind, a backdrop to the peaceful scene, loomed the fells.

Sadie came out of her yellow cottage, and Sylvester waved to her to come over.

"Have some tea," said Sylvester, getting up and pulling out a chair for her. "Lily!"

"No need to shout," said Lily, arriving instantly with another cup and a plate of interesting-looking biscuits. "These are for you," she said to Sadie, putting them down beside her. "Sylvester's not to have one, you know what a struggle it is keeping his figure down to a reasonable size."

Sadie laughed. "I'd be glad of the tea, but I'd better not have a biscuit; trying to keep my own figure in good order."

"Kind of you to say that, but it's rubbish," said Sylvester. "You're too thin, if anything; lost a lot of weight since Charles buzzed off, haven't you?"

"It's no fun cooking just for me," said Sadie. "I can't be bothered, so I don't eat that much."

Sylvester looked at her pleasant, undistinguished face, her medium length greying hair and her rather shapeless clothes, and felt slightly irritated. He realized, though, that nothing she could have done would have stopped her husband from running off with the milkman; after all, if you were that way inclined, it didn't matter how your wife looked, it would make no difference.

Sylvester still didn't quite understand the milkman. "Wholly uninteresting specimen," he had remarked to Gabriel; however, each to his own taste, and certainly Charles's departure – with the milkman – to a new life in Liverpool had been highly dramatic. Charles was happy with his milkman, no doubt. Sadie, on the other hand, was definitely not happy, Sylvester thought, noticing the tiredness around her eyes which told of insomniac nights.

"Eat up, Lily will be offended if you don't have one of her biscuits," he told her. "I must say, I like Unthrang, plenty of to-and-fro-ing here."

Sadie bit into her biscuit. "Talking of to-ing and fro-ing, there's Digby; wonder what he's doing here at this time of day."

"Who's that with him?" said Sylvester, as Digby escorted a thin, dark woman to his front door.

"Interior designer, from London, since you're so inquisitive about your neighbours," said Lily, who had come silently out of the house. "And that's going to set the cat among the pigeons. Justinia, who's got a sensible head on her shoulders, doesn't want any fancy designer from London coming and covering everything with sludge-coloured paints and peculiar bits and pieces. Digby, on the other hand, doesn't trust Justinia to do it; says her taste is too eccentric."

"Ah," said Sylvester. "That sounds like the Justy I used to know. Obviously, marriage hasn't changed her."

"She seems pleasant enough," said Sadie. "If rather conventional. Not that I've said more than a few words to her. Digby's quite a powerhouse, though, isn't he? All that energy, and doesn't he make a lot of money doing whatever he does?"

"Travel," said Sylvester absently. "Yes, he's very good at it, raking in the loot."

"Must be a tiring man to live with. Still," and Sadie sounded sad, "better a tiring man than being alone."

"Better no man than living with one who's hankering after the milkman," said Sylvester briskly.

"True, but unpleasant."

"Truth is. Where *is* Justinia? I haven't seen her this afternoon."

"No, she was going into Eyot, I met her in the shop this morning, and she mentioned it."

"So he's sneaking this designing person in while Justy's not about."

"Looks like it," agreed Sadie. "Rather unwise."

"Very unwise, knowing Justy."

Inside the house Digby was in his element, full of vigour and enthusiasm as he showed off the house to Genevra. Attractive man, thought Genevra, as she noted down his commands and comments in an elegant black notebook.

"This room I want as a playroom," announced Digby, as they reached a goodsized room at the end of the house. "It's later than the rest of the house, you can see that it's been added on. Just right for the children, they need a place downstairs as well as their nursery."

"I didn't know you had children," said Genevra.

"I don't, but now we're settled here, we will have them. My

wife's given up her job, you see, it's too far for her to commute to London, so it's a good time to start a family."

"Where is she today?" asked Genevra, as she followed Digby upstairs, scribbling furiously in her little book. Generally, she worked with the wife; husbands took a token interest and paid the bills, but it was the wives who decided how everything should be. You could see that Digby might not be that kind of husband, though; he didn't look the acquiescent sort.

He led the way into their bedroom, a big, low-ceiled room.

"There isn't enough light in here," said Genevra at once. "You must have another window." She hung out of the single small window. "Perfect. There's room at this gable end for a huge window. It faces east, so you'll have a magnificent view of those hills." She looked round at the newly plastered walls, and the gleaming, polished floor. "Pity the builders didn't do it when they were doing the rest, it's bound to make a bit of a mess."

She moved on along the landing, taking notes in her little book, talking of billowing muslin curtains, the newest paint finishes, the country look. "I'm surprised you moved in here before it was done, it's much easier to decorate and furnish when a house is empty."

"Yes, I entirely agree," said Digby. "But Justinia – my wife – had an absurd idea that she was going to do the house up herself, and she was very keen to move in as soon as possible."

"Of course, very natural," murmured Genevra. "Now, furniture. What are you planning to keep?"

Digby hesitated, but only for a minute. "Not much. Justinia's a great collector of junk, as you can see, always poking round in strange shops. She has bizarre taste." He pointed to a strange table which was supported on the back of a grinning dragon. "That kind of thing, for example."

"Hmm," said Genevra. Hideous, of course, but in her experience you didn't throw out a client's possessions, not if you wanted recommendations to their friends.

"Those kind of items can be charming in their way, they need a little attention of course, nothing serious; they are essentially for fun, pieces like that. Is your wife having her own room? Because possibly her things could be grouped in there; a house should, after all, reflect the individuality of its owners."

What rubbish, she thought, with slight weariness. It pleased clients, though; most of them were dull through and through, without a shred of individuality, but the duller they were, the more they liked having their individuality praised and considered.

"No, she doesn't need a room of her own. I'll have a study of course, I often bring work home, and I'll need telephones and so on."

Genevra pushed back the bracelets on her wrist, and bent over her notebook. A rule flashed out, and Digby watched respectfully as cabalistic figures were jotted down. Nice hair, he thought. It was very dark, almost black, and hung long and straight from a central parting. Genevra wore it off her face, and she flicked the hair off her notebook and over her shoulder. Good figure, too, nice short skirt, pity Justinia felt she looked ridiculous in short skirts.

Genevra felt his scrutiny, smiled at him and clicked away to another room.

"What about the piano?" she asked as they came downstairs again. "It's very big."

"It's my wife's," said Digby without enthusiasm. "Belonged to her mother, doesn't look good, in my opinion. I could get her a new baby grand, that would be better."

"Ask her about that," said Genevra tactfully. Definitely an authoritative man; but she liked a man who was firm and knew his own mind. "Is your wife very musical?"

"Oh, she sings a bit, choirs and things. It'll have to stop now we're up here, it's not the same as in London, and besides, she'll have other interests, people do in the country, don't they?"

Genevra, who would sooner take up residence in an ants' nest than live outside London, agreed politely. "And this is your room?" she said, as Digby opened the door to a handsome square room overlooking the green.

"Yes, this is going to be my study. I'll have the TV in here, I like to watch sport, not that I often have time. Justinia might like a TV in the bedroom, she doesn't seem to watch much television."

Probably never gets the chance, Genevra said to herself. She wondered what his wife was like. A bimbo, who had married him for his money? That didn't go with pianos and singing and dragon tables. A quiet, reserved person, perhaps, who would be grateful to live with a man who made the decisions and so clearly knew what he wanted. Or maybe someone as vigorous and attractive as Digby himself; a woman with her own life and interests, who wasn't bothered by home and husband. That didn't seem likely, either; Digby certainly struck her as being the possessive type. A languid blonde, maybe, concerned only with her appearance and lunching with friends.

Justinia, who chose this moment to arrive back, came as a shock. Genevra hadn't imagined this Edwardian beauty with huge dark eyes, wavy dark-gold hair and an astonishingly sexy figure; wish I looked like that in a belt, was Genevra's immediate thought.

Justinia smiled delightedly at Digby. She was much of a height with him, since he wasn't a tall man, and she was tall for a woman. "Digby! I thought you were in London."

Digby wasn't the man to be at a loss. "Good, you're back, Justinia," he said. "I'm sure we could do with a cup of tea."

Justinia smiled enquiringly at Genevra. A business colleague of Digby's, she thought; why didn't he tell me he was bringing someone. "Of course," she said, throwing her bags on to a nearby sofa and heading for the kitchen. Digby gathered up her things, raised his eyebrows at Genevra. "Very untidy, my wife," he explained, and went after Justinia.

She was singing to herself as she reached up for the tea caddy, and Digby caught her round the waist.

"Don't do that," she said. "I'll drop the tea. Pass me the pot."

Digby pushed the pot across the table towards her, and perched on a stool.

"Genevra's a designer," he began.

"Is her name Genevra? What an extraordinary name. Does she work for you, what does she design, brochures and things?"

"No, she isn't a graphic designer. She's a very well-known interior designer."

Justinia put the teapot down on the tray. Her eyes darkened with suspicion as she looked across the table at her infuriating husband. Interior designer. He couldn't have . . . She looked at the firm jaw, the level eyes, the relaxed way he held himself and knew that he could. Not only could, but had.

Without a word, she carefully put two cups on the tray together with a sugar basin. Then she went to the sink, rinsed her hands and wiped them on the towel. She walked to the kitchen door, opened it and went out, closing it firmly behind her.

"Oh, shit," said Digby.

"Justy!" said Sylvester. He rose, nodded to Sadie, and swept Justy inside. "If you want to explode, better to do it indoors; don't want the whole town to know about it."

"I'm not going to explode," said Justy. "I need somewhere, however, to collect my thoughts."

"It's the designer," said Sadie, nodding at Sylvester. "I told you so."

Justinia snorted. "Designer, indeed. A lot of unliveable-with ideas born out of a strange, unrealistic notion of what The Country is like. And Digby falls for it! She's got designs on him, as well, if you ask me, she was sizing him up as much as the walls."

"Have some tea," offered Sylvester.

"It would taste of gall," said Justy. "Why on earth has Digby done it? We agreed, no designers, I was going to do the house up, gradually, as we settled into it. You can't move into a house like that and immediately do it over, you need to sink into it."

"What were your ideas for doing it up?" asked Sadie.

"I'm not sure. It's a very clerical house, don't you think? The ghosts of all those vicars who lived there, they've left an atmosphere."

"You don't mean crosses and altar cloths, do you?" said Sylvester, alarmed.

"Not exactly," said Justy. "But definitely not earth-coloured walls and dusty green beams and painted furniture."

"Good gracious, no," said Sylvester. "Digby can't want that."

"No knowing what Digby wants," said Justinia gloomily. "It's what that creature does, though; the penny dropped when he said Genevra - you can tell what she's like from her name, can't you? I know several people whose houses she's done over; most of them are suffering from depression now, hardly surprising, who wants to live in a dinge of authenticity?"

"The Georgians loved bright, vulgar colours," said Sadie helpfully.

"Yes, and so do I," said Justinia. "I'm not keen on simplicity myself, I like houses with life in them."

"Perhaps Digby considers you and he will supply that," said Sylvester.

"Doubtless, together with the patter of feet of beautiful children, all gifted and achieving . . . " said Sadie wickedly.

"I don't remember Justy being quite like that when she was little," said Sylvester. "Mountjoy children tend to be a bit different."

"Yes, and Digby wasn't like that, either," said Justinia. "I know this, because his mother told me. He had tantrums, really appalling rages. Right into his teens."

"When his will was crossed, I expect," said Sadie, thinking of her own utterly self-centred children.

"Probably."

"Be glad he doesn't have tantrums now," said Sylvester, looking on the bright side.

"I think he would, except he knows I'd laugh at him, and in any case it wouldn't fit in with being perfect."

"Perfect?" said Sadie, interested.

"He likes everything to be perfect," said Justinia. "Him, me, the car, the house . . . hence the designer. But we agreed," she finished, her voice rising as she remembered what Digby was up to.

"You agreed, and he went right ahead and did what he wanted and what he'd always intended to do," said Sadie.

"Our marriage isn't like that." Justinia was defensive. "We discuss everything, and then we work out a solution which pleases both of us."

"Oh, yes?" said Sadie sceptically. "And where do these discussions end? In bed?"

Justinia turned her big, dark eyes reproachfully on Sadie. "You're laughing at me."

"She's not," said Sylvester. "She's got a point there. That's how men like Digby operate."

"He's not a man like Digby, he is Digby, and he's my husband, and I happen to love him very much." She saw the looks on their faces. "He's very kind," she added defensively.

"Good," said Sylvester. "I'm all for domestic bliss. Who decided you should jack in your job - quite a future you had ahead of you at the museum, didn't you?"

"It was a joint decision."

Sadie raised her eyebrows.

"Don't do that," said Justinia, crossly.

"Do what?"

"Look at me like that. You look exactly like my cousin Virginia."

Sylvester laughed. "No-one could look like your cousin Virginia. She's unique."

"She disapproved of my marrying Digby, and she looked at me like that," insisted Justinia. "Well, she was quite wrong, as it's turned out, because Digby and I are extremely happy together."

"Then back you go, give the designer person a drink and be nice to her; admire her plans for the house, paying special attention to the nursery, and make Digby a happy man."

"I don't like you, Sylvester," said Justinia with dignity. "You've become very hard."

Sylvester laughed, a big, rich laugh to match his size. "No, Justy, I haven't, but you're grown up now, and there's no point in platitudes and coochy-coos. Digby needs sorting out, or he's going to make your life a misery. Much better to get things straight now, otherwise you'll bottle it all up and then one day you really will explode."

"I never lose my temper now," said Justinia. And then, "Nursery? Who said anything about a nursery? I'm not pregnant, nor am I planning to be."

"No?" said Sylvester wickedly. "This will be another pleasant discussion you can have with Digby, and then, as with the others, you'll end up in bed."

Justinia shook her head, and then, her humour getting the better of her, began to laugh.

"There," said Sylvester. "That's right, you have to see how amusing it is to us oldies."

"Speak for yourself," said Sadie. "Seriously, Justinia, think several times before you happily settle down to being a doormat. I know you can talk and be a spitfire here, but you'll face years of misery if you end up doing exactly what Digby wants, always, because he beats you down with sheer force of character, and because he holds the purse strings."

"It's not like that," said Justinia, subdued again. "We share."

"You won't have much to share if he's earning all the money, and you've given up your job," said Sadie callously.

"Money isn't everything."

"No, but lack of it reduces you to a horrible dependency," said Sadie, thinking of her own endless tussle with the lawyers to hang on to her house, which Charles felt was rightfully his. "My husband wants to come back here - to my house - and live here with his boyfriend, and since the house is in his name, which was entirely due to my dewy-eyed ignorance and trust when we got married, I've got a fight on my hands to keep a roof over my head."

Justinia looked at her thoughtfully, hearing the real anguish in her words. "We own the Old Rectory jointly," she said. "I put the money I got from my father into it. That's why Digby can't actually lay down the law about what's to be done."

"A signature on a contract won't help you sort out that one," said Sadie. "What you're talking about is trust and respect for another person. I'm looking at the other end of the tunnel, when you've agreed to all kinds of things out of love or simply to have an easy life, and then suddenly, you're left with nothing."

A sudden chill made Justinia shiver. She got up. "Thank you, Sadie, you are kind. Sylvester is more or less bound to listen to my moans and groans, because he's known me for years, but you've got enough problems of your own without having to think about anybody else's."

Sadie laughed. "Welcome relief, makes a change. But honestly, ducks, do watch out. You won't be twenty-six for ever, and life and chains have a way of catching up on you."

Justinia thought happily how wrong Sadie was, how wrong all the gloom-and-doom mongers were, all her bloody family except her mother. At least her mother had known how right Digby was for her.

She gave Digby a final caress and slid out of bed. Digby lay back, watching her, his hands clasped behind his head. Fit, alert, and desperately to be lusted-after, thought Justinia, her heart melting. She went round to his side of the bed and gave him another long kiss. "Love you," she said happily. "Do you know how devastating you are? I could spend all night and all day in bed with you, and we're an old married couple."

Digby laughed, and pulled her down on to him, blowing into her neck. Justinia pushed herself away and ruffled his thick, curly hair. "Look," she said, "a few grey hairs, just here on your temples, you're going to be even more madly sexy than you are now."

Digby didn't mind the odd grey hair, he knew well that steel grey hair suited men of his type, and would add gravitas to his drive and energy.

"That Genevra woman fancied you," said Justinia unwisely.

"Nonsense," said Digby. "Too thin to fancy anyone, small breasts, didn't you notice?"

Justinia was pulling a long cotton T-shirt over her head.

Digby frowned. "Why are you wearing that? It isn't very elegant."

"No, but it's comfortable."

"I bought you the others. I would have thought you would want to wear them to please me."

"It's only to sleep in."

"It's the principle of the thing."

Justinia looked at Digby's mouth, now set in firm and forceful lines. "Okay, you're the boss," she said. "I'll put on one of yours."

"I've got a much better idea," said Digby. "Don't put anything on, come back here instead."

"Mmm," said Justinia.

Justinia looked out of the window and saw Roxane walking towards the market place. She was dressed in her usual improbable eighteenth-century way in a long, loose jacket and narrow trousers, with her hair pulled back in a huge, black silk ribbon. She matches her house, thought Justinia, opening her front door and going out to meet her.

"You're out early, Roxane."

"Posting a letter. Then I've got to get to work on the house, the new people are coming today."

Justinia was puzzled. "New people?"

"Tenants. Only a short let; I think because, although he wants to move up here, he's been offered a job or something, his wife won't have any of it."

"That's a shame," said Justinia. "It's difficult when you can't agree about big things like that."

"Or the little things," said Roxane, flicking a glance at Justinia. Everyone knew that Justinia had to toe the party line at home.

"Otherwise," her informant had told her, "Digby kicks up a tremendous stink. Apparently, he's very courteous, but implacable. She hasn't got a hope, simply has to go along with whatever it is he wants."

It doesn't seem to be doing Justinia any harm, thought Roxane as she slid the envelope into the post box. She doesn't look at all oppressed or depressed.

"If your house is going to be let, then you won't want me to use the pool."

"The pool doesn't go with the house," said Roxane. "Come and have a cup of coffee, if you've nothing else to do."

Justinia looked pleased. "I'd like that. I'd better nip back and lock the door, though."

"No need," said Roxane. "Anyone gets within twenty yards of your house and they'll be spotted by sixteen people."

"I know. I wouldn't bother, but Digby likes me to lock it. Better safe than sorry, he says."

"How boring and unnecessary of him," said Roxane laconically. She led the way through her gate, but instead of going up the shallow steps to the front door, followed a path off to one side.

The path didn't lead to the back door as Justinia had expected, but ran towards the rear of the house, alongside a high stone wall. "Where are we going? I thought you lived in this house," she said, surprised.

"No, I let the main house out," said Roxane. "I live here, in what used to be the old stables. "She went through a wide archway and into an enchanting cobbled yard. "Huge stables," she explained. "Far too big for the house, but an ancestor was horse mad. He owned a lot of land behind here, and could have built himself a bigger house, but he never did."

"Well, he built wonderful stables," said Justinia, looking in awe at the classical pediment and columns that adorned the centre of one block of the stables. "When did you convert it?

"A couple of years ago, when my father died. I knew I couldn't go on living in the house, it was far too big when he was alive, and hopeless for just me. I sold some land, which paid the tax and some of the bills and left me a bit to convert this part of the stables. I could have sold the house, of course, but I didn't want to, it's been in the family a long time. So I rent it out, and it does quite well. It more or less pays for its upkeep."

Roxane led the way past a semi-circular fountain with a griffin's head and across the yard to a low, red brick building on the other side of the courtyard. She pushed open a wide door and stood back for Justinia to go in. "This is the pool. Built by my great-grandfather; his doctor told him that bathing would be good for his gout. He was very corpulent, and didn't care to expose himself in public, so he decided to build his own pool."

Justinia gazed in silence at the ornately tiled and decorated pool. Dolphins, nymphs, tritons and greater gods and goddesses swarmed in happy abandon around the edge of the oval pool, gazing recklessly into the turquoise water. She peered into it; the colour came from thousands of tiny mosaics, set in intricate patterns.

"Astonishing light," she said, looking upwards. Sunlight flooded in through a band of windows set high up in the wall, just under the slope of the roof.

"My great-grandfather was an astonishing man. The story about gout was mainly for his dutiful wife and the children, and he used the bath house to entertain his mistress. Or mistresses, I gather there were several."

"All at once, or one after the other?"

Roxane laughed. "Usually two at the same time, he was a generous man and liked sharing himself around."

"Didn't the neighbours complain?"

"The nearby ones, from the Manor and the Rectory as it was then, when the vicar still lived there, led fairly interesting lives of their own, so they weren't going to complain. I expect the rest of the town gossiped about it, same as they do now; they must have loved having something like that to get their teeth into."

## 3

Justinia followed Roxane out of the bath house and back across the yard. Roxane's kitchen bore traces of the two large loose boxes it had once been, with hay baskets still fixed in two corners.

"Real coffee, I don't have any decaffeinated, I'm afraid," said Roxane as she put the cup down in front of Justinia. "I mention this because my informants told me that you FitzOdos are health freaks. The coffee at the Old Rectory, they say, is always decaffeinated. Don't look surprised, people take a lot of interest in you, being newcomers."

"Offcomers, I suppose," said Justinia wryly.

"Hardly; you're a Mountjoy, no Mountjoy could be an offcomer in this neck of the woods. No doubt you have hordes of relations up here."

"Too many," said Justinia, "but I don't know them very well. I was brought up in Italy, you see. Still," and she found the recollection cheering, "I've found one cousin I like."

"Who's that?" Roxane stirred her coffee idly, making the slight froth on top drift round her spoon.

"Lydia Praetorius. I bumped into her yesterday, when I was shopping in Eyot. I knew her when she lived in the south."

"Ah, Alban's wife," said Roxane. "I've heard about her, although we haven't met. Good. Family and friends can be useful to have about, you never know when you may need allies."

"This coffee is delicious," said Justinia, keen to change the subject. Allies? Why should she need allies. What was the battle?

"But Digby wouldn't like it. The coffee, I mean," said Roxane, waving her spoon at the pot.

"Digby's very health-conscious. He disapproves of caffeine. I have my own supply of wicked coffee hidden at home, I couldn't go without it."

"Stick to your guns," advised Roxane. "Glug the caffeine, spread on the butter, tuck into the red meat, do you good."

Startled at how much Roxane seemed to know about her domestic arrangements, Justinia took a thoughtful sip from her cup. "It's very different from London here, isn't it?"

"Yes, it's very different, but there's quite a lot going on, if you care to find it."

"Here in Unthrang?"

"Here in Unthrang, and Eyot isn't far away, if you want more scope."

Justinia didn't like to enquire scope for what, so she asked about how Roxane could afford the swimming pool. "If you don't mind my asking, because they cost a lot to heat, and the water has to be filtered and so on, doesn't it?"

"I have the money from the house, and I work as a freelance illustrator," said Roxane. "The pool is my one extravagance. And I have one or two friends who come over to use it on a fairly regular basis; they help out a bit. No," she added quickly, "I don't expect you to pay anything, locals don't. I only ask the ones I want, and I wouldn't dream of charging. The tax man would pounce, just think."

"Does Pauline use it?"

Roxane's face darkened. "She does, dreadful woman, she jumped me into saying yes, and I've regretted it ever since. Still, she can only make it on Wednesday afternoons, because she's so busy organizing things, people, endless committees, and good deeds all round. Her boys come sometimes, I don't mind them, I feel sorry for them, and they love it here."

"So if I steer clear of Wednesdays afternoons . . ."

"Ah, I see you've got Pauline's measure. I can tell you a dispiriting truth, however: you can't avoid her. She's relentless, and she's certainly not going to let you and Digby go."

"Not a hope," said Justinia. "Nigel was at school with Digby and they play squash together at the club in Eyot, that kind of thing."

"Must have been a dreadful school, to produce Nigel," said Roxane, just restraining herself in time before adding "and Digby."

"Quite a good school in the eyes of the world. Digby likes to go back for the old boys' match and so forth. Lovely place, superb grounds, but I still feel sorry for the boys. Digby loved it, though, or he says he did. Nigel must have, too, because his boys are due to go there."

"And yours too, I expect, when you have them."

Justinia frowned. "No. I was desperately unhappy at boarding school, every minute. Fortunately, I got ill, so my parents had to take me away; goodness, how I loathed it. But I wouldn't make any child go away to school unless they really wanted to."

"Won't Digby decide about the children's education?"

No, he won't, thought Justinia, although with a small frisson of alarm as she remembered just how many things Digby did seem to decide about.

"Still, plenty of time to worry about that when it happens," said Roxane cheerfully. "Now, I must throw on a smock, take my mop and bucket, and make the house respectable for this Lucius Elrick and family."

"Want a hand?" asked Justinia.

"If you've nothing better to do."

Lucius and Merle approached Unthrang in stony silence. "Only about a mile on from here," Lucius volunteered, but Merle resolutely kept her gaze fixed on the road and pretended she hadn't heard.

"There," he said, as they drove through the narrow street leading to the town gates. "'A notable and unusual feature of this historic market town,' as the guidebook puts it. Lovely houses, and look at the flowers."

"I'm not interested in bloody flowers," she muttered under her breath. Her heart sank as she took in the market place dappled with afternoon sunlight, the two pubs, the neat row of shops, the beautiful Georgian houses ... "Twee," she said furiously. "Like the setting for some ghastly period detective series on the BBC." A creature of crowded streets and busy places, she had no wish to exchange city anonymity for a gossip-ridden little town in the middle of nowhere, as she told Lucius.

"How do you know it's gossip-ridden?" he said reasonably,

taking the road out of the square that led to the green where Juniper House should be.

"Because people who live in boring, petty places have boring, petty minds, and that means all they have to talk about is each other."

"Quite a lot of that in the offices of *New Living*, I would have thought."

"Professional chat is hardly the same."

"Here we are. Heavens, the photo didn't do it justice, what a marvellous house!"

Merle made no attempt to get out of the car, but sat where she was, staring in contempt at the house.

"That shell over the door, and those windows! The house itself is earlier, though, I should guess. Seventeenth century, wouldn't you say? What a gem!"

"Can you stop enthusing in that incredibly irritating way and go and find this Mrs Bumpkin, who presumably has the keys."

"Roxane Simme wrote that she would be in the house to the rear. Now I wonder how we get there? Do you suppose we drive round?"

"I haven't the slightest idea," said Merle. "Ask that huge yokel who's lumbering this way."

Lucius got out of the car. Then, "I don't believe it," he shouted, and began to run towards the man, much to his wife's astonishment.

"Sylvester," he cried. "What on earth are you doing here?"

Sylvester stopped in his tracks, startled, and then his face lit up as he recognized Lucius.

"Lucius, it's been a long time! I might ask the same of you, after all I live in these parts, but what brings you to Unthrang?"

"I've rented this house for a few weeks," said Lucius. "To get the feel of this area, because I've been offered a job up here."

"I know about that," said Sylvester. "I was hoping I'd see you, but if you're going to be a neighbour, that's much better. Is that your wife?"

"Yes, do come and meet her," said Lucius, and then saw that Merle was standing in the doorway of Juniper House, talking to another woman. They both disappeared inside.

"Get yourself settled, and then come over for a drink," said Sylvester. "Crag End, the one almost opposite yours."

"No chance," said Merle, flinging herself down in a sofa. "No bloody way am I going to go over and make polite chit-chat to one of your tedious ex-university chums. Go yourself, I shan't mind, I've got a stinking headache, and all I want to do is go to bed. If you want to hob-nob with peasants, you'll have to do it alone." She shut her eyes.

"You didn't listen," said Lucius. "He isn't a peasant, Merle. You must have heard of Sylvester Tate."

Merle opened one eye. "The cellist?"

"Yes."

Merle opened her other eye and sat up. "What's he doing up here? Is he on holiday? Or staying at a fat farm, perhaps," she added maliciously.

"Sylvester may be large, but he hardly qualifies for a fat farm. He lives up here."

"Lives up here?" Merle echoed, her voice rich with disbelief. "An international concert artist live here? In the back of beyond, counties away from London?"

"He's lived up here for years." Lucius frowned, trying to remember. "I thought he lived in a village, though, I don't remember Unthrang. Anyway, he'll enlighten me, I expect."

Merle closed her eyes again. "Well, he must be mad to live up here, it could ruin his career."

"Are you sure you don't want to come?"

"No, I don't."

Lucius leant over the back of the sofa and kissed her forehead. "Take an aspirin, then, and get to bed."

"You know I never take aspirin," she said in resigned accents. "Just go, Lucius, and leave me in peace."

"Who are these tenants, then?" said Justinia.

"Thank you, Digby," said Roxane, taking the glass of wine.

"Are they interesting people?" Justinia continued.

"Don't be nosy, Justinia," said Digby reprovingly, as he handed her a mineral water with a twist of lemon in it.

Justinia looked at her drink. "I'd like a glass of wine, please, Digby."

"Mineral water's better for you."

Justinia swiftly drank the mineral water. "There, I've done myself good, now I'll have a glass of wine. Wine is good for you, too; good for the soul."

Digby's face showed what he thought of that one, but he wasn't going to argue with Justinia in public. He didn't much like the look of this Roxane, too long-limbed and too much at her at ease, and she didn't look very admiring. Digby was used to being admired by women, so much so that he rarely noticed it. He noticed the lack of it, however, and trusted that Justinia and Roxane weren't planning to become too friendly. He hadn't wanted Justinia to ask her round this evening.

"We know nothing about her, you need to be more careful, Justinia, you know how unsuitable many of your friends turn out to be."

"Unsuitable? Unsuitable for what?"

"Well, they don't fit in with our other friends, being odd, and it makes life difficult."

"I find your friends odd," said Justinia defiantly.

"You argue like a child."

You treat me like a child, thought Justinia. "Roxane isn't odd at all. She illustrates children's books, her family have lived here for generations, she visits old ladies in Eyot twice a week for tea, and she has invited us to use her swimming pool."

"Very well," said Digby. "She's come down in the world rather, if she has to let out her house and live in the stables. I don't know how she can afford a pool, I don't suppose for a moment it's properly maintained. I wouldn't advise you to swim there."

"It's a delightful pool. You should see some of the pools and places I used in Italy, and I survived."

"I shall continue to use the pool at my club," said Digby.

"Lucius seems a sweetie," said Roxane. "A tall, gangly type, with specs that slide down his nose. Hair receding a bit, but bags of charm. Mrs is a bit of a cold fish, though, nothing but grumbles, definitely doesn't want to live up here."

"Are they planning to buy a house here?" said Digby.

Of course, it isn't nosiness when he wants to know about them, thought Justinia, downing her wine more swiftly than he would approve of.

"Possibly," said Roxane. "He's given up his job, he's a theatre administrator, I gather, or something like that. A new board of management came in, and they didn't see eye to eye, so they parted company. Quite amicably, I think, and I expect he got a good pay-off. Now he's been head-hunted for a post in Eyot, to do with the festival and he's keen, but Merle, that's his wife, doesn't want to leave London."

"It's a music festival," pointed out Justinia, interested. "Not theatrical."

"Yes, but he knows about music, he read music at Cambridge. Oh, and he knows Sylvester, because they were up at Cambridge together."

"Did he know Sylvester was here?"

"No, cries of surprise and exclamations in the street when they saw each other, that made Mrs cross as well. Everything makes her cross."

"How did you learn all this?" said Justinia.

"He's very chatty," said Roxane. "Sylvester had invited him over for coffee and brandy last night, so I went too; what a pair of gossips they are, Lily got quite cross with them."

"Who's Lily?" said Digby, filling up Roxane's glass.

"Mine, too, please," said Justinia.

"Sylvester's housekeeper. She's amazing, full of pep. You often drop in and have a chat, don't you Justinia? Lily's terrific value."

Digby wasn't sure if he wanted Justinia chatting with anybody's housekeeper, he was clearly going to have to be careful about the people she got to know in Unthrang. She should stick with Pauline and Nigel, they were bound to have some reasonable friends. Digby knew that if you got into the wrong circle when you were new in a town, then it was very difficult to extricate yourself from unwelcome friendships.

Roxane looked around the bare plastered walls and made the mistake of asking what they were going to do with the room. Digby was in his element, out came plans and samples, sketches of a fireplace bought by Genevra from a French abbey, beams, settles and designs for window hangings. Fired with enthusiasm, he began to show her Genevra's ideas for the other rooms. Bored, stunned by the banality and unoriginality of the fashionably bland and minimal style which was Genevra's hallmark, she came to life when he triumphantly flourished a drawing of the huge window which was going to be put into the bedroom.

"Bedroom?" said Roxane. "Which room is that?" She knew all these houses, and, indeed, as she had suspected, their bedroom was the one at the east end.

She laughed. "Oh, you can't have a window there."

Digby was taken aback. "I beg your pardon? I hardly think the planning people will object. And it won't overlook anyone."

"It's not the planning permission, it's the wind."

"The wind?"

"The Helm."

"The Helm!" said Justinia, her attention caught. Digby noticed that her glass was full again, and he shook his head slightly at her. She took no notice. "I'd forgotten about the Helm. Of course, Unthrang would get the Helm."

"It's an east wind that blows through the town," Roxane explained to Digby. "It sweeps across the valley, all the villages get it as well. It's a special and terrible wind, it whooshes over Hell Fell and gets trapped, so it blows round and round in a kind of tunnel. It can last for several days. It's quite an experience, because not only is it so strong that you can hardly stand up in it, but it roars; sounds like a train."

"Oh, come now," said Digby.

"No," retorted Roxane, "I'm not making it up."

"There's another one in Cumbria," remarked Justinia, "but the one here is regarded as being more severe."

"How often does this wind blow?" asked Digby sceptically.

"Depends," said Roxane. "We haven't had one for seven years, but you can get them two or three times within a few months. Spring and autumn are when the Helm blows."

"I really don't think it need affect my plans for a window in my bedroom," said Digby. "With modern building techniques, it isn't going to be a problem."

"Others have thought that before you," said Roxane cheerfully.

"With disastrous results. Look at the houses in Unthrang, and in all the nearby villages. You won't find a single one with doors or windows facing east."

Digby's face showed his disbelief, but he knew better than to argue with locals about their town. Legends grew up so easily, and strange, out-of-date notions took on the force of law.

Justinia had moved over to the piano, and was glancing through the papers which Digby had laid out for Roxane to see. She held one up, and pointed at it.

"What's this?"

"It's this room, the sitting room."

"I can see that, but why is there a baby grand in it?"

Digby shifted uncomfortably. He knew he had right on his side, it was wholly unreasonable to expect him to put up with a large and slightly battered piano in his sitting room.

"It was supposed to be a secret," he said in a slightly sulky voice. "I wanted to get you a new piano."

"Oh," said Justinia. "But this is a piano. My piano. An extremely good one, moreover, which has been shipped over from my mother's house at great expense."

"Yes, I appreciate that, but I hadn't realized it was going to be so big. After all," he said, exasperated, "you don't need a big piano, you're not a professional musician or anything like that. Thank God," he added, smiling affectionately at her. "I would find it very hard being married to a professional musician."

"You can save yourself the money," said Justinia coldly, not trusting herself to look at him.

Why doesn't that woman go? thought Digby, glancing at Roxane.

Roxane had no intention of going; she suspected that, if she left, Digby would walk all over Justinia. Perhaps not, though; clearly the piano represented more than a piece of furniture or even a fine instrument to Justinia. Sentimental value? She knew Justinia's father was dead, perhaps it had belonged to him. Unlikely; from what she'd heard none of that generation of Mountjoys had ever shown the slightest interest in music. "Better to discuss it later," said Digby.

"There's nothing to discuss," said Justinia. "If you don't want the piano in here, I'll put it in the room at the end. Calimpal &

Klimper are bringing Sylvester's piano over from Midwinter Hall, so I'll arrange with them to move mine at the same time."

"There are other plans for that room," said Digby.

"I've seen," said Justinia. She took up the drawings for a delightful children's playroom and looked at them thoughtfully. "Charming, but premature, don't you think? Do what you like with the rest of the house, but I'm having that room, and Genevra what's-her-name isn't going to set foot in it."

With that, she tore the drawings neatly in two and deposited them in the bin. Then, still without looking at Digby, she returned to her chair and swallowed the rest of her wine.

She'll change her mind once she's got children, thought Digby. "All right, I can appreciate that you think you'd like a room of your own," he said calmly. He could retrieve the drawings from the bin later; Genevra would understand. "Jolly good idea, to put the piano in there."

Roxane's slightly droopy eyes looked from wife to husband and back again. Not the last battle, by a long way. It didn't seem as though they'd got much sorted out in the four years they'd been married. It was a source of constant amazement to Roxane, marriage; the more she saw of it, the less she was tempted to try it.

"Lovely wine," she said, getting up. "Thank you, Digby."

"Must you go?" said Justinia.

"Duty calls, charity work, you know; one of my old ladies likes a visit on a Saturday evening, sets her up for Sunday. See you soon."

Digby escorted her to the front door, and then came back into the sitting room. He sat on the arm of Justinia's chair, and ran a hand over her head. "Bed," he said. "As soon as I've taken these glasses into the kitchen." Digby hated mess.

"Too early for bed," said Justinia unenthusiastically.

"Not that kind of bed," said Digby.

"No," said Justinia, firmly. "I am not coming to church with you this morning. In fact, I've decided I don't ever want to go to St Quivox's again."

"What's wrong with St Quivox's?"

"Oh, Digby, it's ghastly. All that waving and clapping, ugh.

People wreathed in smiles and hugging and kissing; it's horrible. And then the Rev Wroot will start twanging on his guitar, and all those women with short hair and round ecstatic faces will sing uplifting hymns."

"I like the hymns there," said Digby huffily. "Good tunes."

Tambourine tunes for the tone deaf, thought Justinia resentfully. Fine, since that's what he likes, but I am not sitting through another one of those services, not for Digby, not for anyone.

"It's a good place to get to know people, the local church," said Digby persuasively.

"Not the kind of people I want to know," said Justinia. "And if you're worried about my immortal soul, don't be; I'm going to drive into Eyot and go to Matins at the Cathedral."

"I suppose all your Mountjoy relatives will be there."

"Most unlikely, they're a highly irreligious family. Mind you, Valdemar's son is a chorister there, unless his voice has broken, so perhaps Valdemar or Magdalena might go."

"I thought Valdemar didn't have any children, only step-children."

"Well, he does. Thomas is twelve now, he was a page at our wedding, you must remember."

"Yes, I remember Tom. I didn't realize he was Valdemar's son. Nobody said."

Nobody knew, thought Justinia. "Thomas," she said aloud. "He's never called Tom."

"Valdemar only married Magdalena about five minutes ago. Was he married before?"

"No," said Justinia unhelpfully. Better not to mention Valdemar's other children, it would alarm Digby and confirm his prejudices about the Mountjoy family.

Digby disliked Justinia's Mountjoy relatives, they scared him with their total lack of interest in the rest of the human race, and their unconcern for what other people thought about them. Thank goodness Justinia took after her mother: feminine, anxious to please and perfectly amenable to reason. "So who is this boy's mother?" Digby persisted.

"My cousin Hortense."

Digby ran through what he knew about Justinia's family; he

had a very retentive memory for people and families. A horrified look came into his face.

"His half-sister?"

"Mmm," said Justinia, brushing her eyebrows into neatness and order.

"That's disgusting."

"He's a charming boy."

"That's hardly the point."

Justinia sighed. "Look, it's old history, now. It happened, there's nothing you can do about it, so stop fretting."

"Valdemar's not fit to be out," said Digby angrily. "And then marrying his aunt!"

"Aunt by marriage."

"When his uncle was barely in his grave."

"Mountjoy died at least a year before Magdalena and Valdemar got married."

"Well, I think it's revolting."

"Fine," said Justinia. "If I see Valdemar, I'll tell him."

"You'll do no such thing."

"The bells are ringing for your service," said Justinia. "Hurry up, or you'll be late. I'll be back about one o'clock."

## 4

Justinia slipped into her seat in the Cathedral just as the choristers were filing in. No Thomas, she thought, and then she saw him, not in chorister robes, but in his ordinary clothes. He was sitting opposite her, next to Valdemar, who at that moment looked up, saw Justinia and nodded at her.

Justinia found her place in the prayer book and as she listened to the music, her tumultuous thoughts calmed, she forgot Digby, forgot Genevra, forgot everything except the entrancing sounds. The Te Deum wrenched at her heart as it always did; the setting was Britten, and she was lost in admiration of the boys who sang the difficult music with such skill and assurance. I must come often, she thought, rising to her feet for the Creed, heavenly music, day after day, sung whether anybody's there or not.

The reading from the New Testament was the Parable of the Talents. The vaulted choir, the ancient stalls, the soft morning light shimmered and dissolved, and she was in a high bare room, with green and cream walls.

School, she thought, with something like panic. There beside her was Pamela – whatever had happened to Pamela, who had so wanted to be an actress? Her father had threatened to whip her if she ever set foot on a stage, he was a dour, religious man, Justinia remembered.

It was a Scripture lesson, and Justinia could see Miss Lechlade, the Scripture mistress quite clearly, with her thin, austere face and uncompromising mouth, standing very straight in front of the big blackboard.

"This parable, girls, is not about money. This parable is about the gifts which the good Lord has given each and every one of you, and it tells you how hard your future will be if you do not use those gifts to the full. Some of you have gifts of the human spirit, of kindness and love. Others may have intellectual gifts, or gifts of music or art. Use them, girls, because not to do so is a sin, and life itself will punish you for burying your talents. Now, for homework you may . . ."

Lost in a place she hadn't seen for sixteen years, Justinia only came back to the present as the voices in the choir rose in the closing bars of the anthem. She felt drained and miserable as she sat unheeding through the prayers and stood for the final hymn.

The man sitting next to her could sense her misery, what had brought on this change of mood? He had noticed her at once, not only because he had seen her in Unthrang, and had thought then how good she was to look at, but because she had had an air of buoyant happiness about her when the service had started, which had now vanished completely.

He followed her out of the choir, and saw a tall, dark man leave the group of people he was in and come across to her. He knew that face, it wasn't one you would ever forget.

"Hello, Val," the girl said, as she brushed cheeks with the tall man. "How are you? Where's Magdalena? Why wasn't Thomas singing?"

"Magdalena is at home with the twins," said Valdemar. "Thomas, come and say hello to Justy."

"Hello, Thomas," said Justinia. "I haven't seen you since you were a page at my wedding. Don't you sing any more?"

He grinned. "I do, but I'm an alto now, so I'm no further use to Mr Praetorius."

"Do you mind?"

"Not at all. I sang in the choir for nearly six years, that's more than enough."

"I can see that," said Justinia. "Half your childhood."

"Exactly," said Thomas. "Besides, it's crisis time in the choir, not enough money, ill-feeling all round, Dean and Precentor at daggers drawn, lay clerks snappy, much better not to be involved."

Valdemar laughed, and told Thomas not to exaggerate.

"I'm not," said Thomas darkly. "Val, I think there's a man over there who's trying to catch your attention."

Valdemar looked round. "Who? Good Lord . . ." He strode across the choir entrance, causing several stragglers to step hastily out of his way, and greeted the man who had been sitting next to Justinia. "Lucius, this is the last place I'd expect to see you."

"Why?" demanded Lucius. "Much more surprising that you should be here, considering what a pagan you've always been. After all, I sang in a cathedral, once, long ago, just as you did."

"Of course, St Paul's, wasn't it? Justy, let me introduce Lucius, who's a friend from a long time ago. Lucius, this is Thomas, my son, who's recently finished in the choir here."

"Didn't I see you in Unthrang?" said Lucius to Justinia.

She smiled at him. "Probably, because I live there, and you must be Roxane's new tenant."

Valdemar gathered them all up. "Where's your wife, Lucius, or don't you have one any more?"

"She stayed in Unthrang, had some work to catch up on."

"Fine," said Valdemar. "We'll wait for Simon, ah, there he is. Go and tell him we're here, Thomas, and then you must come back to the castle for lunch, you've never met Magdalena, have you? You too, Justy, of course, that goes without saying."

Justinia, swept along as usual by the charm and commanding personality of her cousin, protested that she had to get back to Digby.

"What on earth for? Dull as can be, your husband. Ring him up, tell him you'll be back later. You too, Lucius, your wife can do without you."

Lucius was quite happy to go to the castle, since Merle had told him to get himself some lunch out. She was going to work for most of the day and didn't want to be interrupted.

Thomas materialised at Justinia's elbow. "No point in arguing, cousin Justy, you know what Val's like. Besides, I know Magdalena will be pleased to see you."

Simon Praetorius, still in his red organist's robes, greeted Lucius. He wasn't surprised to see him, since he was on the committee which was appointing the new director of the Eyot music festival. "Give me a ring, Lucius, tonight, and we'll get together, talk the whole business over. Bye, Val, must catch the Dean," and he strode off, his surplice flapping over his arm.

\*　　\*　　\*

Justinia knew that Digby would be in an immense sulk by the time she got back. She hated it when he was like that and had to be coaxed back to good humour and flattered into bed, and so she had lingered at Mountjoy Castle, feeling guiltier and guiltier as the afternoon wore on. How much I like it here, though, she thought, watching the sun slanting down on the great copper and flame-coloured trees beyond the castle lawns. Even the fact that Virginia Luthier was spending the weekend at the castle hadn't marred her visit. Her bracing intelligence and character had been stimulating rather than intimidating, although there had been an uncomfortable few moments over the roast beef when Virginia had interrogated her about exactly what she did with herself all day in Unthrang, and hadn't been impressed with the answers.

"Much better to find yourself a job," she'd said uncompromisingly. "I don't suppose Digby does like your working; whatever gave him – or you – the idea that you were put upon this earth to make his life easier? I've never had any trouble of that kind with Ralph, he would find me very boring if I hung around at his beck and call."

Virginia's admirable husband was presently in America, where he went every few months to recover from Virginia. He didn't mind, as he told his friends; life with Virginia may be wearing, but it's never dull. He also appreciated his wife's growing reputation as a structural engineer; one of the partners in Valdemar's firm, her standing in her own field was on a par with his. "And Val's one of the best in the world," said Ralph with obvious pride in Virginia's success. "Not to mention the money these engineers earn, almost as good as the law."

Justinia had never spent much time with her father's family, and her mother had no known relations, but she was welcomed into the family group. Most of its members would not have ranked anywhere on Digby's scale of responsible citizenry or good business contacts; they were the kind of people he automatically stigmatized as "peculiar."

At least he isn't a snob, thought Justinia, as she drove slowly through the back lanes towards Unthrang. It doesn't matter to him that they live in a castle, and that my baby cousin is Lord Mountjoy; he just dislikes them because they don't fit in with his very straightforward view of life.

Was she, Justinia, practical? She could be, look how well she organized exhibitions at the museum. That was a gift she had from her mother, who had been an excellent organizer, although she disguised it well under cover of her appealing great eyes and graceful ways. Probably Digby didn't want her to be practical, he had married her because he had fallen in love with her, and didn't, when it came to the crunch, think that she would turn out like the Mountjoys. Good thing he never met my father, thought Justinia gloomily; he certainly wouldn't have married me if he had.

A car behind tooted at her to hurry up; reluctant to get to Unthrang any sooner, Justinia drew into the side, to let the other car pass. The driver hooted again as he went past, and waved out of the window at her. Justinia frowned, and then realized it was Lucius. Her spirits rose, he was excellent company, and it would be good to have him as a neighbour, even if was only for a few weeks.

Saved!

Digby wasn't alone. Pauline and Nigel were there, goodness, what luck; Justinia would never have thought that she would be glad to see them. They had jolted Digby out of his ill humour, partly because they had been impressed to see Justinia with Valdemar at the cathedral. "He's her cousin, isn't he?" said Pauline. "Of course, I know he has a terrible reputation, although they say he's calmed down since he got married. He was talking to the Lord Lieutenant just before Justinia came out, we know him, of course, a very nice man."

"Were you at the service?" said Justinia. "I didn't see you, I'm sorry."

"No, we didn't go to Matins today, we always go to Eucharist, and then there's Evensong as well, so we tend to give Matins a miss. We were there in the north transept after the service, to pick Gavin and Peter up."

Digby, who could see that Justinia was puzzled by so much churchiness, explained that Pauline and Nigel's two boys were both in the choir.

"Lucky them," said Justinia. "Heaven, all that singing."

Pauline and Nigel didn't see it quite in that light, since they regarded the choir as a form of privileged early music training, rather than as a pleasure in itself.

"Where are they?" said Justinia, looking around.

"At home, with the nanny."

The conversation turned to the new occupants of Juniper House. Pauline had been busy ferreting out what facts she could.

"Merle is quite famous," she said. "She's Merle Elrick, she writes for *New Living*, you must have read her column, all about country lifestyles."

Justinia was surprised to hear that. "Oh, how strange; her husband was saying at lunch how much Merle loves London, and she doesn't want to live in the country, or anywhere but London."

"Oh, you must be mistaken," Pauline said confidently. "She couldn't write so knowledgeably about it if she hated the country."

Justinia was glad when Digby invited Pauline and Nigel to stay for supper, and when, after a few half-hearted protests, Pauline popped back home to say good night to the boys and Nigel disappeared into Digby's study to watch sport on the television.

Digby had saved up some harsh things to say to her at bedtime; Justinia sat, brushing her hair, letting the words wash over her. "Sorry, darling," she murmured automatically.

"Well, never mind. Hurry up with your hair and come to bed."

For once, Justinia was pleased when Digby's car roared out of the garage and down the road at half past seven; how to annoy the neighbours, she thought. Digby was naturally an early riser, and he always liked to be at his office extra early on Monday morning. "To deal with anything that's cropped up over the weekend," he said, giving Justinia a kiss as he left.

I'll go and have a swim, Justinia said to herself, taking out her new costume and padding along to the airing cupboard for a towel. She wrapped herself in the huge towelling robe that Digby hated; he preferred her to wear the pretty things he had bought for her. She let herself out of the house and sloped across the road. Digby would have disapproved, out of doors in a dressing gown.

Roxane was in the pool. She was wearing a plain black costume, rather to Justinia's surprise, considering the richness of even her everyday clothes. She's a good swimmer, thought Justinia, as she watched her doing lengths with an easy, efficient stroke.

"Do you want the pool to yourself?" she called from the side. Roxane paused in her even strokes and waved to her to come in. Blissful, thought Justinia, with the lights and colours of the pool and the statuary rippling around her.

"You make some coffee," said Roxane while they dried themselves down. "I must nip round the back and feed the peacocks."

"There's a delectable young man staying at the Manor," she told Justinia as she came into the kitchen a few minutes later. "I hear it's Zephania Zouche's great-nephew. Tall, good body, very fair, heavenly eyes and an astonishing face. A vision."

"How old is he?" asked Justinia, intrigued by this panegyric.

"Oh a baby, twenty, perhaps, or twenty-one. He's starting at the university in Eyot; he must be going to have the attic flat. Brave man, I wouldn't lodge with Zephania Zouche, she's very careful with the pennies, never heats the house properly."

"Perhaps he has expectations from his great-aunt," said Justinia. "And besides, it's a lovely house, even if you are confined to the attic." She didn't mention how much Digby yearned for the house, had coveted it the minute he set eyes on it, and had been determined to offer for it.

"One old woman living in that house, it's a crime."

"Perhaps she likes the house," she had said. "Maybe it's been in her family for centuries."

"Not a bit of it, I enquired, she bought it about twenty years ago."

"Well, if she doesn't want to sell it, there's nothing you can do about it."

"Even more amazing inside than out," said Roxane. "It has a ballroom and a wonderful music room, and it's stuffed with paintings – good ones, she's a collector, and it seems to be the only thing she doesn't grudge spending money on."

"She must be rich."

"Yes, but no-one knows where the money came from, it's a mystery."

"Is she a recluse?"

"No, you've seen her out and about, haven't you? With two cats, and an easel under her arm. She goes out painting."

Young Piers was well aware of how stingy his great-aunt was, and his anxious mother had been alarmed when he said he'd fixed up for digs with Zephania.

"Piers, you'll freeze. Find somewhere in Eyot, closer to the University. I'm sure you could find a landlady who'll give you a good evening meal and do your washing, and look after you a bit."

"I don't want to be looked after," Piers had said patiently. "I get a whole flat there, and with a few bits and pieces it'll be quite cheerful. Aunt Z has let it out before, she knows you can't freeze lodgers or they'll leave, and that means no rent. She likes music, or so she says, so she won't complain about my practising, and I'll like living in Unthrang, I don't want to live among a bunch of students, I'm past that."

"You're only twenty-one," his mother protested.

"Yes, but there's a big difference between eighteen and twenty-one," he said reasonably.

Piers had spent three years abroad before coming back to England and deciding to take up his place at Eyot University to read music. He was looking forward to a hard-working and peaceful autumn and winter; the last thing he wanted was to indulge in the excesses of student life.

"She's installed a feed-the-meter for heating and cooking, and if she charges too much, I'll make a fuss. After all, family is family."

"And family has never mattered tuppence to Aunt Zephania," said his mother with foreboding.

"You're right," said Justinia later that day when she slowed down in the car to ask Roxane if she needed anything from Eyot. "He is astonishingly beautiful. I saw him leave on his motor-bike. I think he's a musician, he had a music case strapped on his back."

"Bassoonist," said Roxane, who had had several hours to find out more about him. "Lovely, I adore bass instruments. I'll invite him to tea, introduce him to a few select friends. The poor boy will need entertaining if he's only got Auntie Zephania for company."

"He's probably got a girlfriend tucked away," said Justinia.

"We'll see," said Roxane, with a thoughtful look in her eye.

Justinia was passing the bus station in Eyot on her way back home when she saw Sadie standing in the bus queue for Unthrang, several carrier bags at her feet. She screeched to a halt, ignoring a bus which was rumbling alarmingly at her, anxious to pull into its space. She reached over to call out of the passenger window as another car hooted furiously at her because she was blocking its left turn.

"Quick," she said, flinging open her door and rushing round to the other side. "Get in, before they all have fits. Is there anything fragile in these?"

"No," said Sadie, helping her put the bags on to the back seat, and getting into the front.

Justinia leapt into the driving seat, gave the apoplectic car driver a friendly wave and pulled out into the stream of traffic. "There. I wish I'd known you were coming into Eyot, I could have arranged to pick you up somewhere nearer the centre."

"Lucius very kindly drove me in," said Sadie. "But he couldn't fix up to take me back, because he didn't know how long he was going to be, quite late, he thought. He's gone to talk to Simon Praetorius about something."

"Don't you have a car?" said Justinia, thinking that it must be difficult to live out in Unthrang, with its infrequent and unreliable bus service.

"I do, but my daughter borrowed it a while ago, and hasn't brought it back yet."

Justinia was shocked. "Doesn't she realize that you need it? Where does she live?"

"London."

"Then she certainly doesn't need a car."

"She says it makes it easier for her to get around."

Selfish, thought Justinia. "Do you have any other children?"

"A son," said Sadie. "He's at university."

"Is he an undergraduate?"

"No," said Sadie, rather wearily. "He took his degree some time ago; he's doing postgraduate work now."

And I bet she pays for it, thought Justinia.

"Well, tell your daughter to bring your car back, and meanwhile, whenever you want to go into Eyot, just say. I go in and out quite a lot, it's no trouble, and my time's my own at the moment."

"Thank you," said Sadie. "Pauline offered, but she's very busy, and besides . . ."

"I know," said Justinia. "Besides . . . is exactly right."

"I don't usually buy this much," went on Sadie, "but I'm giving a party. You and Digby are invited, of course."

Justinia flashed her a quick smile. "No need to ask us just because you've mentioned it," she said cheerfully. "You hardly know us."

"No, I want you to come, I want as many of my neighbours to come as possible. It's a birthday party, you see, my fiftieth."

"Oh, good," said Justinia. "I love birthday parties."

"It's the day after tomorrow," said Sadie. "So I really had to go in to Eyot and shop today, even though it's a particularly hopeless day for buses."

"Do you want a hand with anything?" asked Justinia, as she drove across the square. "I can do simple kitchen tasks provided I'm told what to do. I have to confess that I'm not a wonderful cook, in fact that was partly why I went into Eyot, to stock up at Marks and Spencer's food department and at Gumble's."

"Lovely to be able to afford to do that," said Sadie. "Best never to learn to cook, if you ask me. I hate it, but I don't mind so much for a party, and Lily's coming over to give me a hand. By which she means, take it all over, for which I shall be extremely grateful. But do come over, any time; even if there's nothing to do, you can have a coffee and a chat, or something stronger if it's later in the day."

"I should like that," said Justinia, helping Sadie to her door with the carriers.

It was much later that Lucius came back from Eyot. He knocked on Sadie's door. "It's late, I know," he said. "I saw your light was on, however; I've just got back, and I was worried that you might have had trouble with buses and so on."

"No, kind Justinia saw me at the bus station, and drove me and my shopping back here. Come in, Sylvester's here, he's smuggled a bottle of brandy out, so we're enjoying ourselves."

"Smuggled?" said Lucius.

"Yes, Lily doesn't allow it, he's strictly rationed, you see, as to calories."

"Poor Sylvester," said Lucius, laughing.

"Oh, he doesn't mind at all," said Sadie. "He adores Lily, and knows she's only thinking of his good. But he does break out now and again, although I'm sure Lily knows exactly where he is and what he's got with him. What about your wife, Merle, wouldn't she like to join us?"

"She's asleep," said Lucius. "She's been writing all day, and she was up late last night, working. Deadlines, you know."

"Of course."

Sadie's sitting room was small, beamed, panelled, bow-windowed and delightful. Lucius expressed his admiration.

"Too small for me," said Sylvester. "Nowhere to put my legs, not to mention the rest of me. How did you get on with Simon?"

Lucius had talked the possible job over with Sylvester. "He says the committee want me."

Sylvester snorted. "I could have told you that."

"How?" said Lucius.

"I'm on the committee," said Sylvester.

"Why didn't you say?"

"You didn't ask. I'm not a key member," he said with untruthful modesty. "They just wanted someone like me to add weight to the proceedings. Because of my international reputation, let me add, nothing to do with my waistline. So what did you say?"

"It's a job I'd love to do," said Lucius. "But there are difficulties, and I don't see any way round them."

"Merle?"

Lucius nodded. "She refuses, point blank, to live in what she calls a provincial backwater. I've said that if we sold our present house, we could afford a house up here and a flat in London for whenever we needed to be there, but she won't hear of it."

Sadie put a substantial brandy in front of him. "Coffee?"

"Yes, please."

"Is that the only problem?"

"No, it's money, the salary is lower than I was being paid before, quite a lot lower. School fees would be difficult – I've got two at boarding school, you see. It's not the end of the world; as Simon pointed out, there are good day schools here. It's Merle again, she says she can't work and look after them, and if I'm very busy, which I can see I would be, then I can't help that much . . . Of course, part of my job would be to find sponsorship, and I think I could do that. If I get enough, my salary can go up, because there'll be more money in the kitty."

"We'll have to persuade Merle, that's all," said Sylvester expansively. "Sadie, stop fussing about, and come and use your excellent sense to help Lucius here to find a way to move up here."

"Hopeless, I would say," was Sadie's discouraging opinion when she'd heard the facts. "Something quite drastic would have to happen to make her change her mind, and I can't see what that could be."

## 5

"Marriage isn't what it used to be," said Sylvester. He took a generous sip of his brandy and gave an appreciative sigh.

"Lovely," said Sadie, raising her glass and admiring the colour. "Charles wouldn't let me drink brandy."

"All you married people are at loggerheads with your spouses." Sylvester shook his head in disapproval. "Gabriel and I never get into these fixes."

"You might if you spent more time together," said Sadie cynically. "Or if you and Gabriel were both crammed into Crag End; you'd get thoroughly on each other's nerves."

"Perhaps," said Sylvester, unconvinced. "But it won't arise. By the time Gabriel comes back from America, Midwinter Hall will be fit for human habitation once more."

"That's it, Midwinter Hall," said Lucius. "I knew I didn't have Unthrang as your address; I'd have recognized the name when the letting agent sent us details of Juniper House. Are you only a temporary here, Sylvester? Why aren't you in Midwinter any more?"

"Pipes, Lucius, pipes. We woke up in total darkness one night not very long ago, to find that everything had fused and there was water slopping about all over the place. Something major had gone wrong with the central heating system. It's a big house, you understand, and there was a lot of damage. A little man came rushing round from the insurance company, you know what they're like, lots of sucking in of breath and clicking of the tongue. Ceilings down, floors ruined, well, you can imagine. Actually, it wasn't that which was worrying him."

"What was it?" said Lucius.

"The heritage people. He shook his head and got very dismal. Said he was afraid there was more behind the walls than we'd bargained for, and of course he was only too right. Within twenty-four hours there was a bevy of them there, bespectacled and earnest young men and women. They descended on me, uttering cries of woe as they looked at the wreck of an original ceiling, and joy when they found hitherto hidden plaster, panelling and I don't know what."

"Is it a listed building?" asked Lucius, helping himself to the tiny bittermints which Sadie had put in front of him.

"Yes, it is, unfortunately," said Sylvester. He stretched out for the plate. "I'll have one or two of those," said Sylvester, "seeing as Lily isn't watching."

"She'll know," warned Sadie.

"I expect she will," said Sylvester, "since I snaffled them from the kitchen drawer. Can't visit friends empty handed at this time of the evening, now can I? Anyhow, by the time they'd found a Jacobean fireplace which looked as though it belonged up at the castle, and traces of a mediaeval wall, and decided that the roof timbers needed attention while the workmen were in, I'd had enough, and I fled. I couldn't work with all those types in; day and night, no doubt; think of the noise. No, no, the best thing was to get away. I rang my friend James. Crag End is his house, but he's away for the winter, and he was delighted to let it out, so here I am, in Unthrang for the duration."

"And enjoying it?"

"Hugely," said Sylvester. "Full of life, this place, never a dull moment, don't know when I'll get any practice done. And now they're predicting a Helm. What excitement!"

Justinia woke with a start; she could hear the telephone ringing downstairs. She opened one eye, Digby wasn't there, he must be up, he would answer it. It would be for him in any case, bound to be. She yawned, shut her eyes and drifted back to sleep.

"Wake up," said Digby. "It's for you, your cousin, she says, I never knew anyone have as many cousins as you seem to. I've switched the phone through." He gave her a hasty kiss as she reluctantly reached out for the phone, seized his jacket from the stand and left.

"Hello?" said Justinia sleepily.

"Justy? Lydia here, lucky you, you were asleep, weren't you? I can tell. Sorry to ring you first thing, but I saw Simon last night, Simon Praetorius, and he said, can you come in this morning, to Eyot, to audition. That's if you want to join the choir."

"Oh," said Justinia, trying to focus her mind. "Does it really have to be today?"

"Yes, it has to be today, he'll explain why when you see him. He's hearing several people, and it's your last chance because he's going away. If you've got anything on, you'll have to postpone it. Get there about half past ten, it's the organist's house in the Close, Number 12. Shall I give him a ring and say you're coming?"

"I suppose so," said Justinia. "But, look, Lydia, I'm out of practice, I haven't prepared anything."

"It'll be a doddle," said Lydia, "you should hear some of the old dinks who sing in that choir, he'll be delighted to have you. Take some music, there must be some piece you know backwards, all musicians have something like that. Come round here afterwards and tell me about it."

For a lazy-seeming woman, Lydia was a great one for getting things done, thought Justinia as she hunted through her wardrobe for clothes. It was another sunny day, but when she had leant out of the window to sniff the morning air and wake herself up, she had noticed that the warmth had gone, there was a chill in the air. A sign, perhaps, that the magical autumn days were coming to an end. A pity, thought Justinia, pulling on a sweatshirt over her jeans. She loved summer, the warmth; the long, light days. She shivered, seeing the dark northern winter lying ahead. Perhaps we can go to Italy, she said to herself. Winter in the south of Italy where her mother lived was never as dark and drear as in England, and there was no comparison with the wild northern winters that would be her lot now she lived in Eyotshire.

Justinia sighed. Digby had been so keen to move up here. Her family, he had said; his office in Eyot, ready to expand; the easy train journey to London, more space, a better quality of life . . .

She watched a faded leaf flutter down to the ground and lie still on a cobblestone. She had enjoyed autumn mornings at the museum, she remembered. She hadn't realized how much she would miss having her own world to go to every day. Don't be absurd, she told herself as she brushed her hair before twisting it up into a clip. Curls escaped, as usual, but she didn't feel like quelling them this morning. I'm already making new friends, there's the Mountjoy clan close at hand . . .

That was another thing she'd noticed recently: despite her family having been put forward as a reason for moving, Digby wasn't in practice very keen for her to see much of them.

The truth was that they had moved because Digby had wanted to. He had made up his mind that that was what they were going to do, and all the arguments he had put forward were simply excuses, bromides to make her think that she had had any say in the decision.

Justinia sighed. Digby wanted a family, of course, and he had been keen for her to give up her job ever since he had started to make a lot of money. Do I want children yet? Justinia asked herself, as she shut the cupboard doors. She thought of Magdalena and her delightful twins, nicknamed Posthuma and Posthumus, because they were born after their father had died, although there were rumours that the late Lord Mountjoy had not in fact been the father.

But Magdalena had had them, her first children, when she was, what, forty-five? Plenty of time, Justinia said to herself, and the thought of babies jogging her memory, she dived back into the bathroom to take her pill. Bother, the packet wasn't in the medicine cupboard. Justinia searched among Digby's potions and lotions; no sign. Odd, she was sure she had left them there.

An unworthy suspicion crossed her mind. Surely he wouldn't . . . Cross with herself for her mistrust, she knelt down and tipped out the contents of the bin.

There, at the bottom was her strip of pills - empty. She was on day seven. There was no way she had finished those pills. She put the empty strip back in the bin and dumped the other things on top. What had he done with them? Flushed them down the loo?

Justinia went slowly downstairs. After a few minutes' search, she found her handbag under the sofa cushions. The paper bag from the chemist was still in it. Justinia felt a sense of relief; at least Digby hadn't yet descended to searching her handbag.

Pensive, she slowly ate a thick slice of toast and butter spread with Marmite, trying to think clearly and logically. Why had Digby done it? Did he think that she would tell herself that she had finished the course, and not bother about them for seven days? Did he really think her that stupid? Perhaps this was what marriage was really about, one personality asserting itself, relentlessly, until the weaker partner gave way and knuckled under.

No, Justinia said to herself. Marriage is a genuine, equal partnership. At least, mine is. I'm not going to accept less. She would ask Digby about it, there would be some sensible reason for the whole business which she simply hadn't thought about, he would be surprised at her not realizing, would make her laugh at herself, as he had so often done.

"Fool," said a voice in her head as she drove to Eyot. "Fool to deceive yourself. Virginia and the rest of them were right, you should never have married him. You should have lived with him, enjoyed the sex . . . and then made a quick getaway as soon as he became assertive."

"No," said Justinia. "You're wrong. I wanted to get married. I wanted the commitment. You can't walk out of people's lives pretending it's only the sex that held you together. It isn't, I and Digby have a lot in common, we get on well. My parents had a good marriage despite all the unbelieving remarks which the family made at the time and I, too, am going to make my marriage work; it's going to last."

"If that's what you really wanted," said the voice, "you should have married a different man."

"I'm not listening," said Justinia, getting cross. "Go away, with your depressing and venomous whispers."

"All right," said the voice. "Remember what I've said, though, and I'll be back."

Justinia roared into a vacant parking place behind the Cathedral, causing the car park attendant to shake his fist at her as she missed the Dean's car by an inch.

The attendant came waddling over to her. "This car park's only for those on Cathedral or school business, and it's not for dangerous drivers."

Justinia got out and locked the car. "I've come to see the Cathedral organist."

"Got an appointment?" he asked, still hostile.

None of your business, thought Justinia.

He gave her an evil smile. "It is my business, that's what I'm paid for, to keep people out of here. You aren't Cathedral staff, you can't stay here for more than an hour."

"Thank you," said Justinia, heading towards the exit sign.

The attendant waited until she had got there and then shouted across to her. "Thought you said you were going to see the organist."

"I am."

"Then you're going the wrong way, you need that gate over there."

He disappeared back into his cabin with a fiendish cackle; none of them could get the better of old George. Nice-looking woman though, Mr High-and-mighty Praetorius wouldn't mind a visit from that one, he'd be bound.

Simon Praetorius didn't. Quite apart from the fact that she looked delectable – and Simon was very susceptible – she had a lovely voice.

"You never thought of having it trained?" he asked, as he swung round on the piano stool and looked at her over the top of his glasses.

"I thought, yes, but I decided better not. It's a risky life, unless you're very, very good."

"How can you know how good you are until you've had the training? I would have thought it would have been worth your while . . ." He shrugged. "What did you do instead? Museum work, wasn't that what Lydia told me?"

Justinia nodded.

"Each to his own," said Simon, losing interest. "Would you like to join the Camerata? It hasn't been going very long, but I need another soprano. Good music, and we're aiming for a professional standard, you'd have to work."

"If I'm up to it," said Justinia, doubtfully.

"Oh, I think so. The voice is there, and you've done quite a lot of singing, haven't you? When you were at Cambridge and then in London. These are good choirs you've sung in. Pity about the training, but there you are, trained singers don't grow on trees in a place like Eyot. Anyone who's good gets the hell out of here as fast as they can, can't say I blame them. Amateurs, that's what we specialize in up here."

He gave a sigh, and then became brisker. "Now, I'm going to be away for some time, that's why I wanted to get these auditions over now, can't expect a stand-in to have to recruit. John Valliaze is taking over while I'm in America – you've heard of him?"

Of course she had, he must be old now and several years retired, but he had been the most famous choral conductor of his time.

"He's getting on, but still got bags of energy, he'll do you all good, keep you on your toes. I like the Camerata members to sing in the Oratorio Choir as well. Nothing like the same standard, predictable repertoire, but it's not too bad as these choirs go. They need good voices, that's why I'd like you to sing in both. Monday nights, Oratorio Choir; Wednesday nights Camerata, both in the school Recital Hall. I'll give your name to the secretary, and you can pay your sub at the first rehearsal, the treasurer will chase you for it. Any questions?"

Justinia smiled at him, pleased. "I don't think so."

"You'll like working with Valliaze." Simon smiled back at Justinia. "Nice to have another Mountjoy in the choir, funny how musical ones keep popping up. Lydia sings alto in the big choir, she isn't good enough for the Camerata, she might be if I could get her to work properly, but she says it isn't worth the effort. She's away quite a lot, too." He was writing her details down on a piece of paper. "Unthrang? Ah, we have some other members from there. Pauline and Nigel Norris, chorister parents, have you come across them yet?"

"Yes," said Justinia.

"Thought you would have. I must leave strict instructions with Valliaze not to let Pauline near the Camerata; she'll be in there like a shot if she gets the chance, and then all my best singers will decamp. And I just had a nice young man in here, at the University, so he'll have to sing in their choir, but he's joining the Camerata, a very good tenor, Piers something."

"I haven't met him, but I know who you mean."

"You'll find it a friendly choir, you'll soon know everyone."

Justinia got up to go as Simon handed her back the piano part of her music.

"Give my regards to Sylvester," he said as she went out. "He's an old friend. Tell him not to get blown away by the Helm, although there's not much chance of that, it would take more than a mighty east wind to lift Sylvester off the ground."

"I'll pass that on," said Justinia with a grin.

"Sylvester won't mind, you should hear the things he says about me."

It was with a much lighter heart that Justinia knocked on the door of Lydia's house.

Lydia opened the front door and ushered Justinia in, leading her through the massive inner door and across the interior courtyard. "Yes, it's Elizabethan," she said, seeing her surprise. "Of course, you've never been to this house before, have you? The Georgian bit is just a front. Alban!"

There were sounds of a piano from a distant part of the house. "He heard me," said Lydia, "and he'll come if he feels like it and can take a break. Well, tell all, how did it go?"

"Fine," said Justinia. "He wants me to sing in the Camerata."

Lydia nodded. "I thought he would, you've always had a terrific voice, and it must be getting better, now you're older. You could have trained when you were at Cambridge, alongside your degree work. You didn't need to tell your parents."

"You know that my mother had strong views about music. She said music was unsuitable as a career for me."

Lydia's surprise showed in her face. "Unsuitable? What a funny word to use."

"It's an uncertain life, that's what she said. Demanding, you have to put everything aside and dedicate yourself to it."

With painful clarity, the gloominess of her mother's room came back to her. How could you live in a huge house, a palazzo, in a country like Italy, and draw such gloom around you? She saw herself as a young girl, unsure of what she was, what she wanted to be. She saw also her mother's face, her soft mouth distressed, her expression saying, how could you upset me like this? She had been so disturbed at the thought of her only daughter taking up music as a profession.

"You aren't good enough," she had said.

Words which echoed in Justinia's head for years to come.

"And there's no security in music, no possibility of taking years off to have a baby and then going back to work. It's an unsettled life, only think how much professional musicians move around. Please, darling, you wouldn't want to upset me, would you? It would make me so unhappy, please don't think of such a thing."

"I believed her, you see. I thought she was right."

"Oh, pooh," said Lydia scornfully. "What does she know about it? I never listen to anything my mother says. Who else? Your singing teacher? Some dreary careers adviser, warning you about how competitive and tough music is as a career?"

Justinia laughed. "No, actually, my singing teacher when I was still at school very much wanted me to sing professionally, but she was Italian, and didn't really know about music in England."

"Well, you were a fool not to give it a go. If you'd carried on having lessons, you could have done a lot of singing at Cambridge. Who's that singer who's made such a name for herself recently, the contralto, Alexia Wryston, wasn't she at Cambridge reading chemistry or something, but singing as well?"

"Yes, I was at the same college as Alexia. She's still a friend, which is surprising, because she used to nag me dreadfully, and was furious with me for not doing something about my voice."

"There you are then. I bet her mother was on at her, get your degree in chemistry dear, then you've always got a secure career, and Alexia said, 'Yes, Mummy,' and went on singing regardless. Bet she never went to work in a laboratory."

"No, she didn't, and she's got a tremendous reputation now, booked up for years ahead. But think about it, Lydia, could you see Digby married to a singer?"

"No, that does strain the credulity rather," said Lydia, giving Justinia a tall glass filled with pink, frothy juice, ice and chunks of fruit.

"This isn't coffee," said Justinia.

"No, it's Alban's vitamin-rich drink; it seems to do him a lot of good, so why not you?"

"Digby's very keen on healthy food and drink," said Justinia.

"His healthy drinks don't taste like this, however. This is heavenly."

"Digby probably wouldn't like it, people who worry about what they eat and drink don't like anything that actually tastes good. Basically, they're Puritans come back to life. No God worth making a fuss and being dismal about any more, so start fretting about what everybody's eating instead. I can see Digby in a black hat and buckled shoes, peering into the windows to see if anyone's eating butter."

Justinia choked into her drink. "That's terribly funny, because actually, he has got this perfect thing about butter."

"Yes, they always have," said Lydia. "Food police."

"I don't think the Puritans really went round peering into people's windows."

"Of course they did. Either to see whether the people inside were celebrating Christmas, which naturally was one of the first things they banned, how they loathed people enjoying themselves and eating and drinking too much; or to make sure Mr and Mrs were making love the right way up."

"Lydia, what fantastical things you do invent!"

"Fact," said Lydia. "Man on top, otherwise it wasn't legal; had to keep a woman in her place, which was underneath, at the bottom, down, lying there at her husband's pleasure."

"I don't see Digby as a Puritan," said Justinia thoughtfully. "He's too much of a dandy, too lively and good-looking."

"Balls," said Alban, who had just come into the room. He swept down on the tray with the glasses. "Lot of dapper Puritans, and I'm afraid your Digby would definitely be among the no-nos."

"Unlike the Mountjoys, who must have been Cavaliers to a man."

"Did they support the king?" said Justinia, trying to steer the conversation away from Digby.

"I doubt it," said Alban, sinking into a sofa and stretching his long legs out in front of him. "Supported themselves, I would guess, same as they always have. Pass those little pastry things, Lydia, I can tell they're from Gumble's, you've been extravagant again. Mmm, I love them, have another one, Justy."

# 6

In Liverpool, Charles was lying stretched out on a bed, hungover and dissolute. He gazed affectionately at the younger man sitting on the bed beside him, who was oiling his legs, stretching first one and then the other under his supple hands, flexing his toes, and then running his hands down inside his thighs.

"Lovely boy, that dancer at the club last night," he said, turning his torso to admire his back muscles in the mirror. "Gorgeous body, amazing technique, well, you can tell he's a trained dancer. Divine make-up, too, wonder who he went home with."

"Not with you," said Charles, stretching out a hand.

His companion pouted. "Not for want of trying, dear, I can tell you. We had quite a chat, though. He's Russian, of course you can see, those Tartar cheekbones and flashing black eyes. He's not dancing regularly at the club, more's the pity; he does dancing telegram work, he was there for a birthday last night. What a shame, because otherwise I'd be there every single night, worshipping."

"Dancing telegram?"

"Yes, you know, he's sent to dance for someone to say happy birthday. A kind of living birthday card; or a present, even, if you got really, really lucky, and he fancied you."

"Dancing telegram, eh?" said Charles, squinting into the light as he rolled over. "Pass me the yellow pages, I've just had a brilliant idea."

In the fells beyond Unthrang, Jack Dickson woke early and stumped out of his grey stone cottage. He cast a knowing eye at the rolling summit of Hell Fell and grunted. Then he stumped back inside.

Annie Dickson was cooking breakfast.

"Helm blowing up," he said.

"Aye, you said it would. We've one due, it's been seven years."

"It has that."

"Helm bar there, then?"

"Shaping up. Going to be a black Helm, I reckon."

"Best be out sharpish then, bring sheep down."

"Aye."

In Eyot, Roxane rose and bestowed a kiss on the bare behind of the man sprawled out beside her in bed. He put out a hand.

"Stay."

"No, and I probably won't see you for longer than usual. The farmers say there's a Helm coming, very soon, and if so, I'll be stuck in Unthrang, I'm not battling through that wind."

He sat up. "Make sure those roses are safe. You need to cut them back, and tie the bush ones down; the Helm will rip them away otherwise."

In Unthrang, Justinia noticed the thin band of purply white cloud building up above Hell Fell. A cloud no bigger than a man's hand.

She lifted the lid of the delicate rose-patterned teapot which sat on the bedroom windowsill, and took out her strip of pills. She hadn't said anything to Digby about the empty packet in the bathroom bin; there hadn't seemed to be a suitable moment to mention it. She hadn't mentioned the choir, either, you had to find the right moment with Digby, and he was very busy at the moment.

She put the lid back on the pot. She was being petty and disloyal, and feeling guilty about it. Look at Digby's generosity to Sadie. When she had told him about bringing Sadie back, laden with shopping, he had been horrified.

"A woman of her age, what can her daughter be thinking of?" he said indignantly. "Tell you what, I'll see if we've a pool car going spare at the office that she can use."

He had been as good as his word, getting a youngster to bring it over the very next evening. The kindness of him, thought Justinia with pride, and he didn't feel he'd done anything very special; he was so thoughtful where other people were concerned.

In Juniper House, Lucius and Merle were having breakfast.

"We've been invited to a party," Lucius told Merle, as she sat glooming into her morning coffee.

She gave him a contemptuous look. "Don't even think of it. I'm not going to some utterly boring local scrum. I expect they all wear smart clothes, get drunk and swap wives."

"Hardly," said Lucius mildly. "I'm going, and I'd like it if you came. It's Sadie's fiftieth birthday. Her husband buzzed off and left her a while back, and this is a gesture of normality and defiance."

"Husbands and wives leave each other all the time. What's new?"

Lucius shrugged. "Nothing, but I like Sadie, she's good company, and she's very perceptive. There are a lot of people going from here. I thought you might like to meet some of them."

"To what purpose? The minute our four miserable weeks here are up, we're going, and I'm certainly never setting foot in this dump again. Therefore, thankfully, I'll never need to get to know any of the town's ghastly inhabitants."

"If you don't take the trouble to meet them, how can you know they're ghastly?"

"Oh, grow up, Lucius. Get this out-of-London fantasy out of your mind. You've had some pretty bad and boring ideas, but I think this one is the worst ever."

Lucius looked out of the window. "My pay-off money won't last very much longer. I need to find work."

"London's the place for jobs, not holes in the country."

"This particular hole has come up with a very interesting job."

"Miserable pay, no status, and completely out of touch with the real world."

"There's nothing come up so far in London."

"That's because you haven't tried. You were a fool to let them push you out, in any case. Other people shut up and get on with the job, I don't see why you had to make such a fuss."

Lucius rarely lost his temper, but he was on the edge of doing so now. He took a deep breath. "The job in Eyot doesn't initially pay much, I admit; nor is the festival a major one. However, I could make it grow into a first division contender, and if I can attract sponsors, which I think I can, then there will be more money for me. We could live comfortably on my salary and your earnings, meanwhile; we've been through all that, although I think we'd have to take the children away from boarding school."

Merle stared at him. "What, and have them at home all the time? Noise, friends all over the house, school runs? And when am I supposed to get any work done?"

"I think they'd like to be at home. Neither of them really likes boarding school, and children should be at home, with their family."

"You aren't any kind of family, working all hours, never at home for ten minutes."

"I know, but with this new job, I would make sure I did have more time at home."

"Besides, it's a really bad idea to take them away from good schools with very high academic standards and put them in the local dump state school. I don't think you would find them very keen on that."

"I went to a state school."

"Yes, how could I forget, moan, moan every term when the school bills come, about how you have to pay for them to have the same education that you had for nothing."

"There are perfectly good schools around here, state and independent. I bumped into the director of music at the Cathedral School yesterday, he's someone I know slightly. He says there might be a chance of music scholarships there."

"Great! What wonderful news!" said Merle sarcastically "A Cathedral School! Paying a fortune to have them stuffed with superstitious Christian propaganda!"

"The schools they go to now are C of E. They go to chapel, have Scripture lessons, what's the difference?"

"I'm not prepared to discuss your half-baked plans any more. Now go away; if you make me any more upset, I won't be able to do any work today, and this proposal has to be in by the end of the week. And we need the money, remember, since you aren't earning anything at the moment."

"Well, discuss it with the children, you might be surprised."

Slam.

"Bugger," said Lucius, kicking the waste-paper basket.

"Don't do that," said Roxane, putting her head round the door. "I might have to charge you for depredations."

Lucius flushed. "Oh, it's you, Roxane. I don't think it's damaged. I lost my temper for a moment."

"Kick on," said Roxane. "But, when you've finished, could you give me a hand? I've got peacocks and various other bits of wildlife to round up and bring in, the Helm is nigh."

"The Helm?"

"Come and help me with the peacocks, and I'll tell you all about it."

Sadie's kitchen was a whirl of activity. Lily was in charge; immaculate, efficient and super-charged with energy. "How can anyone so small and wiry have all that energy?" Sylvester not infrequently asked her.

"An easy conscience and an organized life," said Lily briskly. "And not being an artist. Your energy goes into your music, mine goes into the house and cooking. Each to his own, now leave me alone to get on."

Lily had quickly spotted Justinia's lack of kitchen skills, and had demoted her to counting knives and forks and plates. "Then glasses, and Sadie will tell you who's offered to lend and you can go and collect from them. You'll have to make a list, we don't want a lot of disagreement afterwards about what belongs to who."

Justinia obediently counted and sorted and checked, and was then sent out to Sylvester's house with exact instructions from Lily as to what to bring back. Sylvester greeted her as she pushed open the front door.

"Hello, Justy, what are you doing here?"

"Collecting things. Lily's orders."

"Help yourself," said Sylvester, with a wave of his huge hand. "Tell Sadie and Lily one more tonight, if they can squeeze him in, quite small, so I expect they can. Thomas is coming to stay."

"Thomas?"

"Sharpen your wits, Justy, your cousin Thomas. He's had some treatment for his sinuses, painful things, sinuses, and has to be off school for the rest of the week. Val and Magdalena are going away for a few days, he doesn't want to hang around the sick bay at school, wise boy, catch anything you can think of in those places. Can't go back to the castle because he drives the twins' nanny round the bend, so I said I'd have him. Lily will look after him."

"I'll tell her," said Justinia. "He can stay with us if he's a nuisance to you here."

"No, he can do some serious work on his cello if he's here; bone idle, Thomas, like all boys. Besides, Digby wouldn't thank you, would he? He doesn't trust any of the castle lot."

"True," said Justinia.

Lily was pleased at the news. "Sinuses, indeed! Good food and lots of affection is what that boy needs. He's wandering round like a lost soul these days, no choir duties to keep him occupied, although that's a good thing, thoroughly unwholesome set-up, Cathedral choirs."

Justinia found that very funny. "But why is he a lost soul?"

"Got to go away to boarding school in the south this time next year. One of these posh schools that people with more money than sense pack their children off to."

"Doesn't he want to go?"

"Course not. He's a very sensible boy, is Thomas. His mother spends most of her time in India, so the castle's the only home he's got. If they send him away to school, then he'll feel he's been shut out from there, and has no real home at all. Magdalena isn't happy about it, I can tell you; she knows how much he needs a home. He adores those twins, too. It's Val who's put his foot down, bossy as usual. Says the most important thing is for the boy to get a first-class education, I've no patience with it."

"I hated boarding school," said Justinia. "But Digby loved it."

"Digby would," said Lily into her mixing bowl.

*    *    *

Roxane shut the door on the last of the peacocks, who flung a few discontented shrieks at her before settling down to sit out the storm.

The two cats who lived at the Manor – known to be the only creatures that Zephania Zouche ever showed any affection – made their leisurely way towards the back door of their house, uttering imperious noises when they found it closed. Piers opened the door for them. "Hi, mogs," he said. "Good thing you're back, because old Zephania was about to make me go out and look for you. It's lazing about indoors and the kitty litter tray for you if the old chap is right about this Helm wind. Much you care, as long as you get fed."

He let them into the kitchen and then set off for Sadie's house. He stopped in the centre of the green to look over at Hell Fell. Extraordinary, he said to himself, twisting round to look at it as he crossed the green. He bumped into Roxane on Sadie's doorstep.

"Have you seen that fell over there?" said Piers.

"I have," said Roxane.

"That cloud is the most incredible colour, it's like a bruise. Overpowering."

"It's called the Helm Bar," said Roxane, pushing the door open. "Sadie!"

"In the kitchen."

"This way," said Roxane. "Mind your head."

The chat stopped as the two newcomers joined the crush in the kitchen. "This is Piers," said Roxane. Unnecessarily, because everyone there knew who Piers was.

"Hi," he said, going red.

"Good," said Lily. "We could do with a strong pair of arms, to help with the sand."

"That's what old Zeph sent me over for."

"That's a very disrespectful way to speak of your great-aunt," said Lily reprovingly.

"Oh, she doesn't mind, it's what I call her to her face."

"How are you settling in?" asked Sadie.

"Okay," said Piers cheerfully. "I get along fine with old Zeph, unlike everyone else in the family, because I don't want anything out of her, now or at the hour of her death. To wit, she can leave all her money to a cats' home if she wants to, or better still, spend it all while she's still alive. I want none of it."

Justinia laughed. "Do you tell her that?"

"Yes, no secrets between her and me. She didn't believe me at first, but I pointed out that I've got plans to make my own fortune, so I won't need hers."

"How is a musician going to make a fortune?" asked Roxane, amused.

"Not as a musician, that's for sure. I mean, if you're a Sylvester Tate, okay, name your price; concerts, recordings, the money flows in. But it isn't going to flow for a bassoonist, even a brilliant one, which I'm not. No, once I've got my degree I'm going to go into the music business."

"Pop?" asked Justinia, slightly shocked.

"No, no. That's old hat, done for, no room in that business. No, classical music, it's got a great future. I reckon there's a huge public demand for classical music out there, only no-one's tapping it."

"And you will?"

"Definitely. Now, how about that sand?"

Justinia was mystified. "Sand?"

"I told Crook the builder to leave some bags in my garage," said Sadie. "He didn't have time to take them round house to house, so I said I'd be a collecting point. It's because of the Helm," she added helpfully.

"Does it cause flooding?" said Justinia.

"No," said Roxane. "It's people's stoves. If you've got a solid fuel stove, like Sadie's Rayburn and Zephania's Aga, the Helm wind whips it up into a frenzy, red hot. So you need sand to put on it, damp it down."

"Oh," said Justinia. "Of course. We've got an Aga, but it's oil-fired."

"Should be all right," said Sadie. "If it isn't, just shut it down until the Helm's finished."

"This gives a whole new slant to country living," said Justinia.

"Tell Lucius's wife about it," said Sadie. "That'd give those people who read her twee column something to think about."

\*     \*     \*

When Justinia got back home, the phone was ringing.

"Where have you been?" said Digby. "I've been trying to get you for hours."

"I was helping over at Sadie's," said Justinia.

"Oh, that's all right, then. Listen, if it's Sadie's birthday, what about a present? We can't turn up empty-handed."

"I wondered about that," said Justinia. "But she was quite definite, no presents."

"Nonsense," said Digby. "It's her birthday, she must have a present."

"If you really think so," said Justinia doubtfully.

"Of course. Nobody ever minds being given a present. I'll get out before the shops close, but I don't know what to get her. What do you think?"

"It's difficult to say . . . I know! Something to do with parrots."

"Parrots! Why parrots?"

"She's very keen on parrots. She's got one, very noisy, in a big cage. And she has lots of books on parrots."

"So you think a book on parrots, nice illustrations, coffee table kind of thing?"

"No, no," said Justinia hastily. "I think she's far too expert for that, her books all look very scholarly. I meant, a print, or perhaps an ornamental parrot."

"If you're sure . . ."

"Well, I can't think of anything else."

"Sure she wouldn't like something to wear, cashmere jumper, that kind of thing? She looks as though she could do with some nice clothes."

"That's a bit personal, don't you think?"

"You're probably right, I'll go for the parrots. See you later, darling, put out my clothes for me, would you?"

"Bye," said Justinia as the telephone went dead.

Sadie's parrot hated the wind, and in particular she hated an east wind; she was hanging with one claw on her perch and the other firmly grasping a bar of the cage. She held her head on one side, and looked out with baleful eyes. Sadie advanced towards her with a large black cloth in her hands.

"Bugger off, bugger off," shrieked the parrot.

"Shut up, Jezebel," said Sadie. "It's for your own good."

"Not my bloody fault," said the parrot. "Bugger off."

"It's got a Yorkshire accent," said Piers, who had returned to get another bag of sand for delivery.

"She belonged to an aunt of mine who lived in Yorkshire. Her son taught her to speak, at least to say bugger off, by playing her a continuous loop tape. The rest comes from my aunt's gardener, I think; it sounds just like him."

"Nowt to do wi' me," announced the parrot.

"Oh, be quiet, you ridiculous bird," said Sadie.

"Did your aunt bequeath you the parrot?" asked Piers.

"No, she's still alive, but she flits off all over the place; old age filled her with wanderlust, and she felt the parrot needed a stable home."

"Don't we all," said Piers, dragging another bag of sand across the garage floor.


"Merle, do come and look out of the window," said Lucius, bursting into the sitting room.

"For God's sake," said Merle furiously. "You know how I hate being disturbed when I'm at work."

"Yes, but you wouldn't want to miss this, it's amazing, Roxane was telling me about it, and there's a piece on it in the guidebook."

He brandished the paperback copy of *A Guide to Eyot and Eyotshire*. Merle closed her eyes and sighed. "What is it? Pigs on the green? A muddy peasant dance? Are they sacrificing a sheep?"

"Listen. 'The Helm wind blows down across Hell Fell, and Unthrang and its neighbouring villages are familiar with the roaring and howling sounds which are characteristic of this highly unusual feature of the region's weather. The wind blows in autumn or spring, although several years may pass without a Helm. Locals are quick to notice the first sign of the Helm, which is a cigar-shaped cloud above Hell Fell. This is known as the Helm Bar. If the cloud is particularly dense and dark, it presages a Black Helm, which is a truly terrible wind; inhabitants of Unthrang and the villages retreat indoors when such a wind is blowing and it can last from twenty-four hours to more than three days.

"'A traveller staying in Unthrang in 1830 records that "a most fearsome wind attacks this agreeable town. The Helm, as local people call it, is caused by turbulent currents about the slopes of Hell Fell. It is an east wind of such ferocity that a man can only with difficulty stand upright in the force of it. With my own eyes I saw this morning a horse and carriage blown across the green by this wind".' There."

"So what? You would expect there to be savage winds here, you know how awful the climate is in the north. Primitive people, primitive weather."

"Really, Merle, there you are, writing about country life, and ignoring something dramatic like this."

Exasperated, Merle pushed back her chair and joined Lucius at the window. "Slight wind blowing a few leaves about, strange-coloured clouds hanging over that hill; okay, I've seen it, can I get back to work now?"

Lucius leaned against the casement of the window, watching the astonishing swirl of the dark, billowing clouds. The wind was blowing in small, uneasy gusts, and although the sun was still shining, the light had an unnatural clarity about it.

"The wind bloweth where it listeth," Lucius murmured to himself.

The doorbell rang. "I'll go," he said.

He was back two minutes later. "The postman says they've done an extra delivery now, he doesn't expect to be able to do one tomorrow; there's a letter from London for you, he thought it might be urgent."

"Sheer nosiness," said Merle, taking the long white envelope from him. "No London postman ever looks at the postmark, I expect the postman here tells you what your postcards say, as well. And how convenient, no post tomorrow. I expect this ridiculous wind will blow all the phone lines down, as well."

Lucius knew better than to ask her who her letter was from; he soon found out.

"She can't do this to me. She can't bloody do this. It's your fault, dragging me out of London; the minute my back's turned, they all start plotting against me. Look! Just look!"

## 7

Merle shook the letter in Lucius's face. He caught hold of it and began to read it, but she snatched it back.

"I'm sorry," he began.

"Sorry! You're always sorry, what use it that to me or anyone else?"

"Calm down, you won't let me read the letter, you haven't told me what's in it, how can I make a reasonable response?"

"Reasonable. Oh, yes, you and your goddamned reasonable. I'll tell you what's in the letter, because it means that you're going to have to get off your comfortable backside and find yourself a job – a well-paid job – pretty bloody soon. This letter is from Olivia, right? The editor of *New Living*, in case you've forgotten. My column, in her opinion, is no longer appealing to the readership sufficiently strongly. Listen. 'Readers are living further out of London, and market research shows that they prefer to read about the real country, not the home counties.' Home counties, indeed!"

"People *are* moving further away from London," Lucius said tentatively.

"Don't interrupt," said Merle furiously. "'Therefore, I propose to discontinue the column in its present form, and will return the recent article on country cottages which I feel suffers from the same basic fault of being largely concerned with a countryside which readers will not be interested in, as it is too tame . . .'"

Merle slammed the letter down on a table with such force that the potted plant on it juddered and slid towards the edge. Lucius eyed it, poised for a rescue bid.

"Too tame! What does she know about what the readers want?

Most of them live in London, pretty cottages with lots of antique furniture and dazzling kitchens is what they want, they aren't interested in mud and wind and peasants."

"Perhaps they might be," said Lucius, living dangerously. He had never enjoyed Merle's country column, and although he knew better than to say so, he rather agreed with Olivia.

"They'll be sorry. There are half a dozen mags which will snap up that column, and probably pay me more into the bargain!"

That wasn't true, and Merle and Lucius both knew it. Merle had been finding it harder and harder to place her work. She spent more and more time working on proposals, and less and less time actually writing anything.

"Of course," said Lucius. "Look, stop work for today, go and have a long bath, or, better still, a swim in Roxane's pool. She's said we can use it whenever we want, it's heated, and it's a treat, I can tell you; you've never swum in a rococo swimming pool, have you? Then we'll go to Sadie's party, you can meet Sylvester, and some of the other people; I promise you, you won't find it boring at all."

"Ghastly plonk to drink, no doubt."

"On the contrary, Sylvester has put himself in charge of the drinks, and they will all be excellent. Did you bring your costume?"

Merle had to admit that she had. "After all, it mentioned 'use of pool' in the ad for the house, although I didn't expect to have to share it with half the village."

"I don't suppose half the village uses it, and besides, I should think most of them are indoors right now, battening down the hatches. You'll probably have it all to yourself."

"Such an absurd fuss about a wind."

"No, listen to the rest of what that traveller in the guidebook had to say: 'As the proverb tells us, it is an ill wind that blows no good, and the great Helm wind, while distressing at the time, is renowned for bringing change to people's lives'."

"What rubbish," said Merle.

Even with make-up on for her party and her hair newly done by Mavis at M. Rupert's Hair & Beauty in the square, Sadie looked tired and not altogether happy.

"Can't expect anything else," said Lily. "She *is* tired and unhappy, and a fiftieth birthday isn't going to be the high spot of anyone's life. Forty, well you can tell yourself you're grown up, and you're still full of plans. Sixty, you've come to terms with it all. Seventy or eighty, you're glad still to be on this earth having a birthday at all. But fifty, oh no, that's the one for looking back and wondering what you've done with your life."

Sylvester pulled a face. "Pass me my jacket, Lily, and don't be so depressing."

The sight of himself in his immense figured-velvet jacket cheered him up. It had been made for him at enormous expense by his tailor in Savile Row, who had clucked ominously through his mouthful of pins, shocked that Sylvester wanted anything other than his usual concert outfit.

"Quiet, you old misery," Sylvester had said. "You make a packet out of running up those ghastly affairs the concert-going public insists on us wearing, now pipe down and do as I say, I want evening dress to please me, this time."

"You won't get into it much longer if you carry on slipping out to have little this and that's with your new neighbours," said Lily meanly.

"I'm off the hook for tonight at least," said Sylvester. "Party time. Back to the lettuce leaf and fizzy water tomorrow."

"We'll see."

"Who's the cross-looking woman with dark hair?" Piers whispered to Roxane.

"Merle," Roxane whispered back.

"Shouldn't like to be married to her."

"Mistake to be married to anyone. Look at Justinia, watching herself in case she does or says something that Digby doesn't approve of."

"He's attractive, though, isn't he?" said Piers. "You can see why she married him."

"No, I can't actually," said Roxane. "My tastes are different."

Thomas sidled into the already crowded room with a tray of Lily's cheese nibbles.

"Over here," said Piers. "I'm starving. Who are you?"

"I'm Thomas. I'm staying with Sylvester. Have some of these

little round ones, they're specially good. They melt in your mouth, yummy."

"Where do you live when you aren't staying with Sylvester?"

A reserved look came over Thomas's face. "Um, at Mountjoy Castle, actually."

"Ah, you're one of that lot, are you? Do you know my godmother, Faustina Lennox-Smith? She's very friendly with Magdalena Mountjoy."

Thomas's face lit up. "She's the Bishop's wife. Milo, that's her son, is at my school, lot younger than me, of course, he's only about nine, but he's good fun. Mad, and always in trouble, which worries them, because of being the Bishop's son." A gloomy expression came over his face. "He's really lucky, because he says he's going to stay at the school, his mum doesn't want him to go away."

"Mothers usually don't," said Digby disapprovingly as Thomas offered the tray. "But it's a necessary part of growing up, and I've no doubt at all that the father of this friend of yours will insist that he goes off to a decent school when the time comes."

Thomas gave Digby a not very enthusiastic look.

"My days away at school were truly the happiest of my life," Digby went on. "Where are you heading for?"

"Gryme."

"Top school in the country, always has been. First class academically, that goes without saying, and of course, they take sport very seriously indeed."

"I hate sport," said Thomas.

"No, no, you'll love it when you get there and see the facilities they have. Sport every afternoon, I expect, you'll have the time of your life."

"I imagine quite a lot of the boys won't be very keen on sport, Thomas," said Justinia kindly.

"Yes," said Digby assertively, "but that's where a top school is worth the money; they don't let the boys get away with sloppiness about things like sport."

"Have another drink," said Sadie, coming to the rescue. "Thomas, there's someone at the door."

Pauline, her husband Nigel, and Luther Wroot who was wearing a clerical collar and a face wreathed in smiles, came into a suddenly emptier room. Several people, hearing their arrival, had decamped into the adjoining room.

"Can't think why Sadie asked them," said Roxane, taking an appreciative sip of the glass of champagne which Sylvester had poured out for her, "when you think how Pauline patronizes her."

"Nigel's as bad," said Sylvester, "advising her to settle matters with Charles and look about for a small retirement bungalow for one."

"Aunt Z, who knows about such things, says that she needs a better solicitor," put in Piers. "She thinks a good London firm would put the fear of God into her errant husband in no time at all."

"Zephania's got a lot of sense," said Sylvester approvingly. "But Sadie won't listen, she's in a state of inertia, needs something to jolt her out of it."

"This wind sounds as though it could jolt us all out of everything," said Lucius as he joined them. "Do you mind if I stay in here, because that clergyman in there is more than I can stand. Why does he smirk all the time?"

"Very evangelical, the Rev Wroot," said Roxane. "He believes that the Lord wants us to be happy, so he smiles whenever he remembers; all right, Lucius, smirks, then. He told me I should smile more; made me feel depressed for days."

The coal fire in the small Victorian range was glowing and spluttering, as the wind built up outside. The windows rattled intermittently; somewhere in the house it sounded as though a door was banging.

"It's certainly a strong wind," said Lucius, "but nothing more than you get everywhere. What about this roaring sound it's supposed to make?"

"It's building up to it," said Roxane. "Just wait, you'll be fed up with it by the time it's been blowing for a few hours."

The noise level rose as Sadie's guests grew merrier under the influence of the excellent food and drink. Even Merle, who had spent the earlier part of the evening glowering in a corner, was roused to join in the conversation.

Sylvester opened the piano as Lily came in with a confection topped with a single candle. "I'm not setting the place on fire with fifty candles," she had said. "Besides, there's a lot of work gone into that, and if Sadie had as many candles as that to blow out, she'd send the whole top layer flying. Quite apart from passing out with the effort."

Pauline led the singing of Happy Birthday with a pale, true and uninteresting soprano. Lucius and Piers joined in with Thomas; Justinia, happy and at ease with the wine and the company, stood by the piano, her voice ringing out in the small room. They all subsided into applause and laughter and drank a toast to Sadie, while the wind outside went on with its wild work.

"Superb voice," said Lucius to Justinia. "Simon told me how pleased he was to have you in his Camerata."

"Camerata?" said Pauline sharply. She had ears like a cat, able to pick up the quietest remark which she felt to be within her sphere of interest. Her sphere of interest was very large. "Surely you mean the Oratorio Choir? You have to be invited to sing in the Camerata, and numbers are very limited."

Justinia smiled at her. "Yes, I'm lucky."

"When did Simon hear you sing?"

"I auditioned for him a couple of days ago," said Justinia.

"You didn't tell me," said Digby in a level voice.

Justinia flushed. "I was going to, but I know you aren't very interested in my singing."

"You should be," cried Sylvester. "It's a remarkably good voice for an amateur. Why didn't you train, Justy?"

"Justinia's singing is merely a hobby," said Digby coldly. "It was all right in London, but of course up here, things will be rather different."

Piers, not noticing the sudden tension, had a thought.

"If you're singing in the Camerata, then you could give me a lift in on Wednesday nights, couldn't you?"

"Wednesdays?" said Digby.

"Yes, Wednesday evenings for the Camerata and Mondays for the Oratorio Society," said Justinia.

"What a pity, both evenings when you can't go, Justinia."

Pauline's face brightened. "Oh, you're busy on Wednesday evenings, are you? It's my free afternoon and evening."

Justinia looked at Digby in surprise. "We don't have anything on for Wednesdays, do we?"

Digby smiled at her. "No, nor on Mondays, that's my point. I go to the club on Tuesdays, as you know, and Friday is lodge night, so if you went out on Mondays and Wednesdays, we'd only have Thursdays together. What a pity your choir days don't fit in, or you could have gone."

Merle had been eyeing Digby thoughtfully, and at this last remark, she raised her eyes in amazement. Roxane caught the look and winked at her.

"I know, Digby," Roxane said. "Change your club night to Wednesdays, and the problem is solved."

"I'm afraid not," said Nigel with a wide smile. "Digby and I play squash together on Tuesdays, and I'm afraid I can't change my day. I have choir on Mondays, too; both Pauline and I go, of course, we hardly aspire to the heights that Justinia seems to have reached; we don't sing with the Camerata. Wednesdays, as Pauline says, are her day off, so of course, I like to be at home, too. Then our nanny can have a regular evening out. So important to keep employees happy."

The Rev Wroot beamed at Justinia. "There is a simple solution," he said. "Mrs FitzOdo, or Justinia, as I'm sure I may call you, can join our church choir here. We are a very happy band, and we have many a heart-warming singalong, praising the Lord with music."

Digby approved. "Excellent idea, there you are, Justinia, all the singing you could want, and right on our doorstep."

Speechless, Justinia stared at Digby, and then looked at the Rev Wroot, whose gleaming smile was by now so wide that it had become positively threatening. As she opened her mouth to decline his offer in as polite a way as she could manage, her voice was drowned out by a tremendous roar from outside.

"Is that the Helm?" asked Lucius, awed.

"No," said Piers, who was listening intently. "It's a Harley Davidson, if I'm not mistaken. Now who . . ."

"Simon Praetorius has one," said Sylvester, as the roar subsided into a steady throbbing and then stopped, giving way to the the increasing sound of the wind, steadily growing in fury.

There was a loud ring on the doorbell. "It can't be Simon," said Pauline. "He's in London for a few days before he goes to America."

"Thomas, can you answer the door for me?" said Sadie.

"Are you expecting anyone else?" asked the Rev Wroot, preparing his welcoming smile.

Sadie shook her head as Thomas reappeared, bringing with him a shadowy figure wrapped in a long black leather coat.

"He won't say who he is," said Thomas apologetically.

The stranger was wearing a leather helmet with goggles, like a pilot in an old war film, and had long gauntlets on his hands. He looked round the assembled company before removing the helmet and goggles.

"Sadie?" he enquired in a heavily accented voice.

"That's me," said Sadie.

He swept her a dramatic bow. "Then I am come to bring you greetings for your birthday."

He removed his gauntlets with a flourish, and pulled out of one large pocket a small cassette player, which he handed to Thomas. "Be so good as to plug this in, please. Is this the biggest room?"

He darted through to the other room. "No, this is larger, this is best. In here, please. What is your name?"

"Thomas."

"Good. Then you be my assistant. You clear a space, like this?"

Mesmerized, Thomas pushed the furniture back, leaving a circle of space in the centre of the room, while the man stepped out of his big, black, buckled boots.

Digby was indignant. "Who on earth is this?" he demanded in a loud voice. "Sadie, is this some party game?"

"Quiet," said Sylvester, pulling him back, a wicked look on his face. "I think we're in for some fun."

Nigel was about to say something, but Pauline took her lead from Sylvester, pinned an interested smile on her lips, and hissed at Nigel to shut up.

The stranger stood in the centre of the room and bowed again, his eyes raking the room. He turned to Thomas. "Now," he said. "Press 'Play', please."

A haunting Slav tune filled the room. Slowly, and with cat-like grace, the man unbuttoned his great coat and slid out of it. He handed it to Thomas, who blinked as he saw the brilliant leggings and body-hugging T-shirt which were all the man had on under the coat.

The man took a deep breath, and stood quite still. Then he began a series of languid, sweeping movements. As he came closer to the group of people, they could see his face clearly for the first time.

"Make-up," said Pauline. "His face is thick with make-up."

The Rev Wroot's smile wavered, but he never took his eyes off the man.

Nigel and Digby were beginning to make displeased noises in their throats.

Roxane and Piers were watching with open interest, Lily stood beside them, deeply appreciative. "What a body," she said under her breath.

Sylvester flicked Lucius with a massive elbow. "I think we're going to enjoy this," he whispered.

Lucius looked down at Merle, who had a startled expression on her face.

"Not what you'd expect in Unthrang," she said to Lucius, who took her hand and squeezed it.

The dancer's eyes were outlined with thick kohl, and they looked enormous under the green and purple eye-shadow which stretched up to his black brows. His cheeks were rouged, his lips painted a vivid red, and he wore a single earring.

"Disgusting," breathed the Rev Wroot, unsmiling now, and transfixed.

The beat of the music quickened, and with a fluid movement the man raised his arms and peeled off his T-shirt, revealing a superbly muscled, gleaming torso.

"Wow," said Roxane delightedly. "Sadie, are you watching?"

Sadie, her eyes bright, nodded.

The dance went on. Then, as the music reached a crescendo, the dancer caught the top of his leggings and rolled them expertly off.

There was an audible sigh, echoing the ever louder wind outside, as the dark dancer stood motionless for a moment, now wearing only a posing pouch in glittering golden material.

He danced on, his movements becoming more and more disturbing, more intensely and deliberately erotic. He turned on to his hands and knees and slithered across the floor, his buttock muscles rippling.

Justinia looked anxiously at Thomas, who was watching in total amazement. Lucius, standing beside her, shook his head. "He'll be all right, does them good to be shocked, he's old enough to watch this."

Yes, but am I? thought Justinia, unable to take her eyes off the man's body. And the artistry, what a dancer.

I hope he isn't going to take that pouch off, thought Sadie, anxious for her guests.

I hope he is, thought Roxane ecstatically.

The music slowed back to its melancholy minor key, and the dancer slowed with it, showing off every perfect movement of his muscles. He sank to the floor on his knees, and bent backwards with his arms outstretched in front of Sadie, arching his back until his head touched the floor.

As the dance finished, there was a strange moaning sound. Not from any of Sadie's guests, but from outside, where the wind sighed, died down, and then, just like a train surging into a tunnel, settled into a terrible, howling sound.

"The Helm," said Sylvester, as all the lights went out.

"Nice man, that," said Sylvester.

"Piers?" said Lily, deliberately misunderstanding him.

"I'm talking about Issur, as you very well know," said Sylvester with perfect good humour. "Young Thomas all tucked up?"

"Asleep as soon as he put his head on the pillow," said Lily. "More than enough excitement for a boy his age."

"He enjoyed the power cut."

"Yes, candles are fun for an evening, but he'll find it gloomy indoors here tomorrow, with nothing but candles."

"Oh, they'll get the power back on before then."

"They didn't last time," said Lily, ominously. "Took them the best part of three days, so Sadie told me."

"You'll manage, Lily, you always do. I'll be back in two days, weather permitting."

"If you can get out tomorrow."

"Oh, yes, big car, no problem. I've made it through snow, ice and flood."

"I dare say, but you want to take care just the same."

"Digby says he's going into his office tomorrow morning,

whatever the weather; important meeting. Important chap, Digby, having important meetings all over the place, don't you wish my life was important, Lily?"

"Get off to bed, you need your sleep."

"Yes," said Sylvester with a huge sigh. "Leave me to my dreams, that's all I'm good for at my age. Once . . ."

"Once you were a disgrace, and you still are," said Lily. "And you can give Sadie a few years yet, time to start getting nostalgic when you get to my age. Mind you tell Gabriel all about this young Russian when you telephone, he'll be sorry to have missed all the fun."

## 8

"Outrageous!"

"What's outrageous, Digby?" said Justinia from under the covers, more than half asleep already from the heady effects of the evening.

"I see what it is, no interest in me tonight, I suppose you're thinking how badly I compare with that queer dancer."

"Uh?"

Digby was admiring himself in the mirror. He had a flat, muscled stomach; he pulled his shoulders straight and stood sideways; not bad, not bad at all.

"I wasn't comparing you with anybody," said Justinia. All I want to do is go to sleep, she thought. And what's the point of comparing a crow with a bird of paradise in any case?

That woke her up with a jolt. Crow? What was she thinking of, Digby wasn't a crow. Crows were sleek, malevolent birds of ill omen, ruthless in their aggressively cocky way, not a bit like Digby, who was so kind and whom she loved so much.

Digby was still investigating himself in the mirror. "Too sleepy to be interested in me, is that it? Or is it that you think that I haven't got what that dancer has in the pouch department? Of course, he was padded, you realize that, all those dancers pad themselves up. It's to attract other men, it isn't aimed at you women at all."

He wasn't padded, Justinia said to herself. What was in the pouch was definitely all his. She preferred not to think of Digby in a posing pouch, it wasn't his métier, somehow.

"Of course, it's all pretence. Women aren't interested in male bodies, they aren't turned on by them the way we men respond to naked women."

Much you know about it, thought Justinia, as sleep drifted over her again.

"Well, if that's the way you feel, I'll say good night and blow the candle out."

Digby climbed crossly into bed, gave the covers a firm tug, leaving Justinia with a few meagre inches of quilt, made a discontented and disapproving sound and fell asleep.

Hell, thought Justinia as she lay awake, listening to the wind roaring and battling round the house. In the wrong again. Oh, well, nothing she could do about it now, she'd put it right with Digby tomorrow, she'd never get to sleep with all that wind . . .

Lucius moved closer to Merle.

"Oh, go away," she said in a tired voice.

He moved back to his side of the bed.

"Sorry," she said unexpectedly. "I'm just thinking, I don't feel very physical."

"No, you mostly don't these days," said Lucius.

"Astonishing dancer," said Merle, sitting up and punching her pillow into a more satisfactory shape.

"I hope Sadie's all right."

"What do you mean, all right?"

"Alone in the house with a stranger, he could knock her on the head and ransack the house." Lucius sounded concerned.

"Only if he was very stupid, and he didn't look stupid to me."

"Or molest her."

Merle thought of Sadie's tired and middle-aged looks and shook her head. "I don't think he'd be tempted. Anyway, he's gay."

"Yes, I suppose so," said Lucius.

"And he had to stay somewhere, there's no way he could have ridden his motorbike through this, he'd have been killed."

"He could have stayed here. Or gone to Roxane's, or to the Manor House."

"Sadie wanted him to stay there, she was delighted with him, you could see. And after all, he was her birthday present."

Lucius yawned. "I don't think that's quite the way to put it."

"I'm glad you made me go to her party," said Merle.

Lucius was astonished, but knew better than to say anything.

"I thought it was all going to be the most dreadful bore, but it wasn't at all."

"No," murmured Lucius.

"Did you notice that Pauline didn't offer Issur a bed?"

"Nor did Digby."

"I feel sorry for Justinia."

"Why?" said Lucius, interested. "She's got everything she could want; she's clearly devoted to Digby, although I must say he is rather oppressive; got a nice house; bags of money, you can tell; and no doubt there'll soon be several glossy children."

"Even so, she's not happy, not in her soul. So Roxane says."

And before Lucius could make any response to this very surprising remark, Merle had settled herself down and was fast asleep.

Justinia struggled up from the depths of sleep. What was that terrible noise? The wind. The wind was still roaring and pounding; but above it she could hear someone calling to her; what had happened, why was a voice calling her? If it's you again, you can clear off, she said viciously.

No, it wasn't the nagging voice inside her head. This voice was calling from outside the house. She woke up completely, realizing that, although it was so dark outside, it was actually morning. Digby was still fast asleep, a large hump on the other side of the bed. Justinia slipped out of bed and went across to the window. She looked down, yes, there was somebody in the garden. Somebody large . . . Good heavens, it was Sylvester. What was he doing out there, gesticulating? She mistakenly tried to open the window, barely managing to get it shut again before the wind tore it out of her hand. She gestured to Sylvester and ran along the landing and down the stairs. A slight pressure on the back door and it flew open, admitting Sylvester with a rush.

"Sylvester! Whatever are you doing here?"

"I had no idea the Helm was this strong," said Sylvester, getting his breath back. "Is that Digby of yours up yet?"

"No, he's fast asleep."

"Well, go and wake him, high time he was up and about. I'll

be leaving for Eyot, to catch a train, in about twenty minutes. Digby said he was going to try and get in this morning, I thought it best if we went in convoy. We won't have to drive very far in this bloody wind if we go out of the village in the wrong direction; the great thing is to get out of reach of the Helm, and then we can double back."

"That's very kind of you," said Justinia. "But why didn't you ring?"

"Oh, the telephones aren't working, gone down like everything else. I must say, I was curious about what being in the Helm was like, but now I've experienced it, I would prefer not to have it roaring away. It can't stop too quickly as far as I'm concerned. Tell Digby twenty minutes, no more, or I'll miss my train, and I've got a flight to catch. Of course, it would make better sense if he stayed here, pointless to try and drive through this if you don't have to."

"No," said Justinia quickly. "I'm sure he has something urgent on at the office."

The last thing she wanted was to be shut up in the house in the gloom, with the wild wind wreaking havoc outside and Digby in a mood inside.

"Like that, is it?" said Sylvester intelligently. "All right, then, I'll be back."

Justinia stood anxiously as Digby struggled into his car. She was clutching on to the gatepost to anchor herself from the wind. "Ring me the minute you get into your office," she shouted. Digby, clearly feeling like Biggles setting out on a tough mission, nodded his head vigorously, made a thumbs-up sign, and moved slowly out into the road.

Bother, he can't ring, no phones, she told herself. She measured the distance from her post to the door, and then hesitated for a moment. Could she make it to Sadie's house?

Buffeted into the road and back again, she flung herself into Sadie's porch and rang the bell. She heard voices and heard footsteps approaching; then the door opened, and the wind hurled her into Issur's arms.

He extricated himself and pushed the door with all his weight to shut it, then swept Justinia a fine bow. "Ah, it is the beautiful wife of the disapproving man, good morning. Come this way."

Justinia blinked at the brilliant dressing gown he had on, as she followed him into Sadie's front room. Sadie greeted her with a smile.

"Can I beg a coffee?" she said. "Digby turned the Aga off, and since everything else is electric, I can't heat any water."

Sadie clucked, and made to get up.

"Stay," said Issur. "I will get the coffee." He vanished into the kitchen.

"Thank goodness I'm on bottled gas," said Sadie. "Justy, you should get an emergency camping stove and gas, we're always having power cuts, although they don't usually last as long as this."

"Do you keep candles as well?" asked Justinia, looking at the number illuminating the room with a pleasant, flickering light.

"I have a good supply," said Sadie. "Charles had a thing about candles, he bought them all over the place, at the supermarket, at the cathedral shop, when we went abroad, at Christmas . . . Are you short? Would you like some?"

Justinia shook her head. "No, I should be all right, thank you. I've got several boxes, and there's an oil lamp somewhere, too. It was a wedding present; we've never used it."

Issur swept back into the room, carrying the coffee and two elegant china cups carefully placed on a silver tray.

"Where did you find all that?" said Sadie, surprised.

"I find you have many beautiful things, all hidden away," said Issur. "If you have beautiful things, you must use them. Otherwise it is an insult to the craftsmen and artists who made them. Besides, you need beauty in your life, I can see you have been starved of beauty."

Sadie laughed, and poured the coffee. "What else have you found?"

"I show you, afterwards, and then we clean everything. This is a good task for such a day, such wind and tempest."

Justinia glanced out of the window. "It doesn't seem to be dying down at all."

"No, it won't yet," said Sadie. "It's settled down into its stride now."

"Like a complaining baby," said Issur, stretching his hands out sideways and turning his head first one way and then the other.

"What about you?" asked Sadie. "Don't you want any coffee?"

"Coffee later, thank you," said Issur. "For now, class."

"Class?" said Justinia.

"Yes, although it is late, by now I should already have done a lot of work."

"What work?"

Issur shrugged his shoulders. "Class," he said again. "For a dancer, every day you do class. Of course, it is better that you do it in a proper studio, with other dancers and the maître to make you work properly, but if that is not possible, then you make your own class."

He smiled, and his dramatic solemnity vanished as he looked suddenly puckish. "Do you want to go to the bathroom?" he asked Sadie.

"The bathroom?"

"Yes, because I do my class in the bathroom, you have a mirror and a barre, and so I can work."

"I don't have a barre," said Sadie, puzzled.

"I expect he means the towel rail," said Justinia.

"So," said Issur. "And when I work, then I must not be interrupted."

"I see," said Sadie. "No, I don't need the bathroom, you carry on. I'll finish my coffee and then see if I can find you something to wear."

"Something warm to go on top," suggested Issur. "Otherwise I am fine."

Sadie and Justinia looked at the leggings and T-shirt underneath Issur's open dressing gown, and blinked.

"Not for Unthrang," said Sadie firmly. "Don't worry, I've got some men's clothes."

Issur looked disapprovingly at Sadie's tweed skirt and rather shapeless cardigan.

"What clothes are these?"

"My husband's – my ex-husband's, I should say. That's his dressing gown you've got on."

"So?" said Issur, interested. "I thought it was yours. Is he dead, this husband?"

"No, just living in Liverpool."

"Without you. Are his clothes like yours?"

"No," Sadie reassured him. "Charles was is, rather – particular about his clothes. Very well-dressed, always."

"We see, then," said Issur.

"Come and help me sort out a few things," Sadie said to Justinia. "If you haven't got anything else to do."

"People are always saying that to me now," said Justinia. "And the sad truth is that I don't really have anything else to do these days. And I used to be so busy, the days weren't long enough for all the things I wanted to do. That was when I worked, of course."

Sadie led the way upstairs, holding a large church candle aloft. "You need to find an interest," she told Justinia as she opened the door of the huge mahogany wardrobe in the spare room. "You worked in a museum, didn't you? Are you a scholar? Isn't there a field that particularly fascinates you? I would have gone mad years ago, if I hadn't had my parrots to keep my mind alive."

Jezebel, who had been put in the spare room to spare her the windy chill of the garage, gave a squawk from beneath her black cover.

"Yes, I'm talking about parrots," Sadie told her, jamming the candle into a glass tumbler beside the bed. "But not you, you can come out later."

Sadie heaved a pile of garments out of the wardrobe and laid them on the bed. She and Justinia inspected them in the meagre light afforded by the candle and the dark grey daylight from the window.

"I made a bonfire of all Charles's newest clothes," said Sadie cheerfully. "I enjoyed that immensely. Twenty-three shirts, eight suits, nearly thirty ties . . ."

"Bonfire?"

"Yes, you wouldn't understand, you've never known the kind of rage you feel when, in middle age, your husband ups and offs. I trust you never will. When I realized he wasn't coming back, and that he was starting legal proceedings to try and get my house away from me, something just went Ping! inside me, and I lit the bonfire. Ursula and Colin were frightfully shocked, but since they think I ought to be under the permanent care of a shrink, I took no notice."

"So why didn't you burn these?"

"These are from his younger days, when we were still friends. When we still slept together, and went out together and did the things normal married couples do. When the children were still small, and hadn't started criticizing me, and when the milkman was an old friend in his sixties who left the milk on the doorstep every day . . . When I was still a human being, in fact."

Justinia didn't know what to say.

"Don't say anything. Help me pick out what will fit our delightful young visitor – and what he might agree to wear, because he's obviously very fussy, and remember to enjoy your marriage while you can, and to keep an eye on Digby. Men are never quite what they seem, you know."

"I'm very lucky with Digby," said Justinia. "We talk a lot, we have a very good relationship. Besides . . ."

"Besides, he isn't gay?" said Sadie cheerfully. "I didn't know Charles was until the milkman came along. I thought, how could I be so stupid? After all those years. You can't be sure, after all, your Digby went off to a good boys-only boarding school, didn't he?"

Justinia went pale. "Digby isn't like that, actually he doesn't really approve of gays. And no-one could be more hetero, that I do know."

"Hmm," said Sadie, holding up a pair of bizarre yellow silk trousers, tied in at the ankle.

"Did Charles wear those?" said Justinia.

"Only for fancy dress," said Sadie. "He loved dressing up, and at the time I thought nothing of it. Lots of men like dressing up."

"You mean actors and opera singers? It's their job."

"What about the clergy?"

"I give you the clergy," said Justinia. "I don't think the Rev Wroot dresses up much, though, does he? All very low key and crimplene at St Quivox's."

"I can see Issur in these," said Sadie. "Let's find something to go with them . . . ah, look, perfect, a brocade jacket."

"He'll look like Roxane in her party gear," said Justinia.

"Yes, I saw him eyeing her long brocade coat last night, it's clearly to his taste."

The voice hissed in Justinia's ear as she went down the stairs. "So Digby's perfect, is he? No boyfriends? Ever? No girlfriends, either, since he married you? What a piece of perfection!"

"Go away!" said Justinia aloud.

"What?" Sadie turned round, startled.

"I'm sorry, Sadie, nothing to do with you, I was talking to myself."

"You can try and send me away, but I'll be back whenever I want. You have no control over me at all. If it isn't men, what about other women?"

"Digby is completely faithful to me, I know that for a fact. When he fell in love with me, it was for good."

The voice gave a fiendish cackle. "You spent your teens reading too many trashy magazines," it said maliciously.

"I'm not listening."

"That's all right, then. I'll be back soon."

Sadie looked at her curiously. "Are you all right?"

Justinia forced a smile. "Yes, I'm fine, it's only something I'm trying to sort out in my head, you know how it is."

Sadie nodded. "I do. Take my advice, throw yourself into your music, or a piece of research. Don't idle the days away, waiting for Digby to come home."

"No," said Justinia. "I'd better go. Let me know how Issur likes his clothes. You'll be glad when the wind stops, and he can roar away."

"Maybe," said Sadie, with a serene smile.

Justinia tacked back to her house, and let herself in. The house was shadowy and strangely quiet. No fridge or freezer humming, no subdued ticks from the electric clock in the kitchen, no radio playing.

I must get a clock for my room, thought Justinia. Something ornate, with a soothing tick. She lit a candle and went upstairs to the second spare bedroom, now designated the nursery by Digby, where a lot of her not-yet-unpacked possessions were stacked neatly to one side. He'll make me clear this lot out and throw most of it away when horrible Genevra starts piddling about, thought Justinia crossly, wondering in which box she had packed the oil lamp. She must move her things down to her room; clearly Digby wasn't going to come visiting, so she could leave them packed or unpacked as she chose, and no nags about untidiness. Perhaps she should buy a large chest, then she could bundle it all in there.

Justinia sorted through a box of music and several boxes of books. Shelves, I'm going to need shelves, she thought. Then she came to a box of china; that would need to go down into the dining room. It had been a wedding present from her mother. Digby thought it pretty, Justinia didn't, and rarely used it. They had had one of their first quarrels over that china, she remembered. That was before she learned that it didn't do to argue with Digby. If he didn't win one way, he won another.

There was a box with some paperbacks in it and an envelope. Justinia idly looked inside. A fat notebook. She opened it. Digby's diary, for four years ago. The year they had fallen in love and got married, she remembered with a frisson of nostalgia, putting it aside to go down to Digby's study if he wanted it still.

"Open it and have a look."

The voice was back. Justinia shook her head, as though to dislodge an insect from her ear.

"Can't shake me off," said the voice gleefully. "Go on, have a look. I'll go if you have a look."

Exasperated, Justinia took up the book. "There," she said. "Okay? Now go."

"You haven't looked."

"January 1," Justinia read out. "Resolutions."

"Bye for now," said the voice.

"Double earnings by June," Justinia read. "Finish with Francine and Claudia. Get married. Must be beautiful, sexy, English, biddable. See Notes, page 3."

Biddable! Justinia was amused. But who were Francine and Claudia? She turned to Notes, page 3.

"Possibles:" the entry read in Digby's rather distinguished writing. "Lettice Cox. Emma Frisby. Henrietta Kentigern. Justinia Mountjoy . . ."

Justinia Mountjoy?

Justinia's eye ran on down the four other names on the list.

She turned to page 4, a sinking feeling in her stomach. The names were listed in alphabetical order again, this time with columns and ratings alongside. "Looks. Sex. Parents. Health. Friends." Against each name was a series of ticks and crosses and a number ranging from -2 beside Lettice for sex to 9 for Henrietta beside Health. The right-hand column gave the totals. At the bottom Digby had written: "Results: 1 Henrietta, 2 Emma, 3 Justinia."

Justinia held the candle closer to the page, as though by giving more light, the words on the page would scramble themselves and turn into a shopping list. Lettuce, apples, bananas. Or a Christmas list. Cousin Lettice, a book. Aunt Emma, a scarf.

Only it didn't. Justinia steeled herself and went back to January. She read the neat notes under each week. Followed Digby's pursuit of a wife starting with Henrietta in January, February and into March, when she had blotted her copybook by being found in bed with Digby's best friend, Julian. Digby didn't seem to mind, he simply spent his evenings and weekends and no doubt nights as well with Emma instead.

Emma lasted until May 11th, when she revealed left-wing tendencies and told Digby that her degree had been a higher class than his. That was the end of Emma. And so to choice number three, Justinia Mountjoy. "Terrible family except for mother," he had written. "Minus points: untidiness, takes her work seriously. Okay in bed."

Okay?

"Sex not key to marriage as plenty of other possibilities available in this area," Digby had commented.

What?

With June had come the doubled earnings and the proposal. "All this takes too much time and energy, so will settle for Justinia."

## 9

Settle for?

"Ha ha," said the voice in her ear.

"If you hadn't nagged, I would never have read this," said Justinia unhappily.

"Ah, but you suspected it, didn't you?"

"I did not."

"Did, did, did."

"Didn't . . . oh, shut up."

Justinia got to her feet, shut the notebook, took up the candle, and with a firm tread went downstairs.

"What are you going to do?" said the voice.

"None of your business," said Justinia.

"You aren't going to burn it?" cried the voice in alarm, as Justinia knelt beside the fireplace and laid some kindling on the grate. She methodically tore out the pages and heaped them on top. Then she tilted the candle, and fed the swiftly growing flames with the rest of the notebook.

Silence. There, Justinia said to herself, a kind of peace coming over her. I shouldn't have read Digby's private diary. Now I'm going to forget it. Her reasonable mind told her she wouldn't be able to, but this was a matter of the heart, and in her heart, Justinia felt that however silly and crude Digby had been in choosing a wife – even if it hadn't all been fantasy – when it came to the point, he had fallen in love with her as much as she had with him. What did it matter how and why they had come together, as long as they were together?

Love, said Justinia, to herself, is all that matters.

"Balls," shouted the voice in her ear.

\*     \*     \*

The phone rang.

"Good," said Roxane. "We're back in the world."

"Rather not be," said Piers, who was lying naked with his head in her lap.

"Move," said Roxane. "It could be someone exciting."

Piers helped himself to another grape and listened unashamedly.

"No," Roxane was saying. "Not for the next few days . . . well, it's the wind, the Helm . . . I did explain. It could blow for several days, and we're cut off . . . Yes, trees strewn across the road, very dangerous for cars . . . Yes, I do agree; much better to wait . . . of course, as soon as I can . . . Look after yourself . . . Bye."

"That sounded very affectionate," said Piers suspiciously.

"My charity work," said Roxane, settling back on the sumptuous sofa which fitted so perfectly into the curve between Hermes of the lightning heels and a nymph who appeared to be sleeping off the excesses of a night with Zeus.

"Where did you find this sofa?" asked Piers, rearranging himself to his greater comfort and satisfaction.

"I didn't. My great-grandfather had it made to go in here. For his frolics. He liked threesomes and so on, so he needed plenty of room."

"Disgusting old man," said Piers indignantly.

"He wasn't so old when he frolicked. In his forties."

"Forties!" said Piers with contempt. "He should have known better at that age. When I'm forty I shall be beyond such things."

"Bet you won't," said Roxane, stroking him. "Some parts never wear out."

"Hmm," said Piers appreciatively. "Use it or lose it?"

"Something like that."

Thomas was getting very fed up with the wind. "At least the power's back on, but I wish it didn't just go on and on. There's nothing to do; no, I can't even practise my cello, no-one could with that beastly roaring going on."

Lucius, calling to see that Lily and Thomas were all right, offered to play a game.

"All right," said Thomas ungraciously. "But I don't really feel like it. Can't we go over and see Issur?"

"Is he still here?" Lucius asked Lily, startled.

"Nowhere else for him to be," said Lily comfortably. "That bike of his is stowed away in Sadie's garage, and it won't come out until the Helm dies down. And not even then, maybe," she added under her breath.

"I like Issur," said Thomas. "He showed me some exercises yesterday. Very difficult, you have to stand on one leg. I fell over."

Lucius frowned.

"There's no need to worry," said Lily. "Thomas is fine with Issur, and if he weren't, I'd be the first to know, so stop thinking what you are thinking, and do me a favour by taking this dratted boy out from under my feet."

"You'd know, would you, Lily?" said Lucius, amused now.

"I would. There's nothing in that line that I don't know more about than all the rest of you put together. You take my word for it, and remove young Thomas. Sadie will be glad to see you, she's in a very good mood just now."

Thomas went to borrow a huge coat of Sylvester's which he fancied himself in. Lucius looked at him doubtfully. "It's trailing on the ground."

"Sylvester won't mind," said Thomas. "It's only his country coat." He plunged out into the maelstrom and hung on to Lucius as they made their perilous way to Sadie's house.

Sadie greeted them with a happy smile. "Good, people to talk to," she said. "Although Issur's such good company I hardly feel I've been cooped up here for two days already."

"Is Digby back?" asked Lucius as he took off his coat. He could see a solitary light burning in the room at the end of Justinia's house.

"No, they haven't cleared the road yet. He rings her up, he's staying in a flat the company keeps in Eyot, he's all right."

"I saw her looking out of the window yesterday," Lucius explained. "I thought she looked very desolate. Hello, Issur. Sadie, how do you manage to keep a fire going in this wind?"

"This one is just about all right," said Sadie. "The chimney pot has a kind of conical hat on legs and a grid, and so the wind doesn't affect it quite so much as the others."

"Desolate?" said Issur, doing a quick shadow box with Thomas. "The beautiful Justinia with the husband who isn't here, but who beats her when he is here?"

"Beats her?" said Thomas. "Cousin Justy? Issur, he doesn't."

"I certainly hope not," said Sadie.

"Not physically," said Issur. "Not with a stick or his fists, but with words, yes? And mentally, he torments her. To keep her under control."

Thomas wasn't interested in such finer points of in any case inexplicable adult behaviour.

"Issur, can you show me how to do some more of those exercises? Please?"

"Later," said Issur good-humouredly.

"Yes, we're going to have some tea, Thomas. Go upstairs to Colin's room, I found some old battle games he used to play, I thought they might interest you"

Thomas's face brightened, but he was aware of his dignity. "I'm a bit old for battle games, actually."

"In that case, please go and sort them out and see if any of them are complete, and I can give them to the Rev Wroot for his autumn jumble sale."

"Okay, I'll do that for you," said Thomas as he pottered off towards the stairs.

"We won't see him for hours," said Sadie. "It must be very boring for him, marooned in Unthrang, off school and no-one his own age about. Lucius, where are you going?" Lucius was pulling his coat back on.

"If you don't mind, I thought I'd nip across and make sure Justinia's not too lonely."

"Good idea," said Sadie. "Bring her back with you. Tell her to bring some music, Issur hasn't heard her sing."

Justinia didn't want to come. "Truly, Lucius, I simply don't feel very sociable, and I've got a lot to do about the house."

Lucius looked around at the immaculate room. "Looks all right to me."

"Perhaps you don't have a very noticing eye, but Digby has,

and he'll be furious . . . well, not very pleased . . . if he comes back and everything isn't perfect."

"Can't you get someone in to do?" asked Lucius. "You must be able to afford it."

"Yes, Mrs Toadflax comes in three times a week to do the heavy, as she puts it, but it's the details that worry Digby. And since I'm not working . . . To tell the truth, I thought I would love being domestic and running the house; I was really looking forward to it, particularly when things were so busy in my last few weeks of work. But, do you know, it's incredibly boring. You dust one day, and it's back there grinning at you two days later. All that work and nothing to show for it."

Lucius laughed. "No, you don't strike me as being the domestic type. Come on, get a jacket or something, the wind's still just as bad. Come over and let Issur cheer you up."

I never used to need cheering up, thought Justinia as she zipped herself into her Barbour. Digby had bought her three Barbours when they moved to Unthrang: long, mid-length and short, three colours: brown – well, sludge really – army green and navy. Justinia didn't like them, however sensible they might be. She hated the waxy feel of them, and thought them shapeless. Practical, though. You didn't have to be practical in London, she thought wistfully. And in Italy there was no need for coats like that at all. She sighed and then shook herself back to windy Unthrang.

"Finished dreaming?" enquired Lucius.

Justinia's mind was on another tack. "How is Merle coping with the wind? Can she work?"

"She's hit a bit of a block, writers do, you know."

Justinia was interested. "Journalists, too? I thought it was only novelists and poets. Merle is a journalist, isn't she?"

"Yes, but all writers are much the same, I imagine. I'm not that kind of person, I'm a doer not a maker, so I can't speak from first-hand experience."

Issur pounced on the music which Justinia had wrapped inside her Barbour. "Good, this is the best way to tell the weather to go to hell. There are three ways: to make love, to make music, or to write great sad books, which is what my compatriots do all too often. But we are not gloomy, and so we choose now to make music. Who plays the piano?"

Lucius looked at Sadie, who shook her head. "I'm out of practice," he said, sitting himself down and opening the lid of the piano.

"It is a little out of tune," said Issur at once, listening as Lucius played some chords. "No matter, we performers are used to all adversity. Now, Justinia, you sing."

Justinia had brought some Italian songs with her, which she had found in the box of music upstairs. It was music she had sung in her teens, when she had lived in Italy and learnt with Signora Silvestrini, who had been so angry when Justinia had turned her back on singing.

"You choose the head over the heart, you choose the intellect when you are a musician, you will pay for such a crime!" she had shouted at Justinia. "God has given you such gifts, such a voice as I never heard in an Englishwoman in my life, such musicality, and you throw it all away. Go, there is nothing more I can say to you. Go to your cold Cambridge. I am a travelled woman, I have been to Cambridge; I tell you that there your soul will die and the good Lord will never, never forgive you."

Justinia remembered her teacher's curse as she sang that evening. She was out of practice, she had sung them better once, but she now knew what the songs were about: love and happiness, then shadows of parting and sorrow.

Silence followed. Issur's brooding dark eyes were filled with tears as he leapt from his chair and seized Justinia's hand. He kissed it with a lovely formal gesture. "Of course, all is explained. You are unhappy because your life lacks music."

Justinia laughed. "No, I'm not unhappy at all, no-one could be happier than I am. I'm just a bit down at the moment because I miss Digby."

Issur stared at her. "You, with a soul full of music, miss this busy English husband?" he said incredulously. "No, husbands are unimportant. Art, that is what matters. Where is your teacher, who do you study with?"

"No-one," said Justinia. "Issur, I'm an amateur musician. I had some lessons when I was younger, that's it. I'm not a professional, I'm not an artist."

"Bah!" said Issur with an immense shrug of his shoulders. "Do you suppose I don't know an artist? You are an amateur, yes, but this is nothing to be proud of; indeed, you should be ashamed of yourself. There are reasons for being an amateur, of course, but for you this should not be a choice. You are young, you don't have children to support, old parents starving in a village, uncles in jail . . . Why do you need to be an amateur? You aren't afraid of hard work? No? Then you must put aside this silly business of being amateur and be a professional."

Sadie brought the conversation back to earth. "Don't nag, Issur. Of course Justinia can't just go and become a professional singer. Life isn't like that. Besides, Digby wouldn't like it."

Issur was clearly about to say something very rude about Digby, but Lucius intervened hastily. "Justinia's going to be singing in a very good choir, Issur, plenty of opportunity there."

Issur smouldered, his full mouth drawn in a line of contempt.

Justinia fought back. "You're an artist, Issur, anyone can see that. So why are you a dancing telegram?"

Issur's mouth twitched. "Ah, you fight dirty, and you are right, it is no work for an artist. But I keep my technique, I work, and then in due course I take my place again where I belong."

"Which is where?" said Lucius.

"Leave him alone," said Sadie, quickly.

"One day I tell you my story," said Issur grandly. "Meanwhile, I stay here, in this wind from the devil, I work, I watch my buttocks and we see what happens."

"Watch your buttocks?"

"Yes, my bottom, it's too big," said Issur, suddenly grave. "It can be a problem with dancers who are very strong. It is the way I trained, but you can see." He rose from his chair, turned his back and dropped his trousers. He wasn't wearing anything underneath. Justinia blinked, Sadie looked delighted. Lucius wasn't quite sure where to look.

"Now Justinia, feel." He took her hand and placed it firmly on one muscular cheek. "Feel. Now, when I flex, like this . . . you see? It's too big. Too developed."

Justinia, while admitting to herself that she wasn't averse to feeling Issur's behind, found it impossible to suppress a wild and uncontrolled giggle.

"Oh, oh, I'm sorry, Issur, I'm not laughing at you, but I have so many women friends who are always moaning on about how big their bums are, and here are you, Issur, with the most beautiful body a man could possibly have, and you're worried about your bum, too . . ."

Sadie and Lucius began to laugh as well; apart from anything, Justinia's giggle was very infectious. Issur carefully did up his trousers and watched them, his eyebrows raised.

"Very English," he said drily, "to laugh at bottoms. I tell you, though, bottoms are not a laughing matter!"

That night the wind dropped. Justinia woke at two in the morning, disturbed by the silence. She got up and went to the window. Although the trees were still moving in the wind it was a breeze in comparison to the great east wind which had now blown itself out. The sky was clear, and a huge moon hung above the fells. Justinia padded back to bed and fell into a deep sleep, the first proper sleep she had had for several days.

The morning brought the refugees back to Unthrang. Digby bounced into the house, a huge bunch of flowers in his hand, to smother a still sleepy Justinia with hugs and kisses before bearing her straight back to bed. Pauline and Nigel, who had battled their way out on the first morning of the Helm, "the boys must get to choir, they couldn't manage without them," and had stayed with long-suffering friends in Eyot, who had been strangely glad to hear on the local news that the Helm had finished. They arrived bright and early, hoping to catch the nanny out in some sin of commission or omission. Lily told Thomas that Sylvester was on his way a few minutes before the phone rang and Sylvester himself was telling them that he would be back in about an hour.

"How do you know things like that, Lily?" Thomas asked, awed.

"Trade secret," she said. "Sylvester will have to ring the castle when he's back, fix up about taking you home."

Thomas's face fell. "Do I have to go? It's so boring there, and I am enjoying myself here. Besides, I haven't done any work on my cello, and Sylvester did want me too."

"You can't stay much longer, back to school on Monday."

"No," said Thomas. "It's half-term, and now I'm not a chorister any more, I get a proper half-term."

Lily clicked with her tongue, annoyed with herself. "Of course it's half-term, I was forgetting. We'll see what Sylvester says."

Thomas gave her a forceful hug. "Thank you, Lily."

"And where are you off to?"

"Just going over to Sadie's, to see Issur."

"Don't be long."

Lucius left Merle battling bad-temperedly with yet another piece which she knew before she started that nobody would buy. He slowed down as he saw Thomas running across the green. "When are you going back home, Thomas?" he asked.

"Not yet, I hope," said Thomas.

"Good," said Lucius. "I'm just off to pick up my two from their schools for half-term. Ben must be about your age, he'd be glad of some company." He wound the window back up, as Thomas gave a pleased wriggle and jumped across the stream outside Sadie's house.

Sylvester stopped in the market place to pick up a paper, and found tongues wagging.

"Hardly a stitch on, and a little boy with him."

"That's young Thomas, he's a Mountjoy."

"Up to anything, the Mountjoys."

"That man, he's a foreigner."

"I asked PC Vibbs about it, he said the man was quite respectable, and not offending public decency and the green was open to all . . ."

"Offended me, I can tell you."

"Didn't offend me," said one of the bolder young women who had come in for her woman's mag. "Wish my Jerry had a physique like that, I can tell you."

"Yes, a bit of all right, he is," said her friend. "I went out with a body builder once, but he wasn't a patch on this one."

"I don't expect he's a very masculine man," said Samuel Boot, a pillar of the Rev Wroot's congregation.

"That's hardly a disappointment for you, then," said Flora saucily as she paid for her mag and left the shop.

"I shall ask the Reverend what he thinks," said Samuel. "I think someone has to make sure we keep up the moral standards of this town."

"Who are you talking about?" said Sylvester.

"Sadie's toyboy," said Mrs Duffin behind the counter. "That's what he is, and she should be ashamed of herself at her age. No wonder her man ran away with the milkman."

"Oh, is Issur still here?" said Sylvester. "Good, good."

"He's doing exercises on the green with Thomas," said Piers as he came in to collect his great-aunt's paper and that month's copy of *The Connoisseur*.

"Ah," said Sylvester, getting back into his car.

"Tai Chi, if I'm not mistaken," said Sylvester, handing a bag to Lily and going round to the back of the car to remove his cello. "Mind you, possibly a mistake to do it on the green in his posing pouch."

"Very nice to look at," said Lily. "And if it gives Samuel Boot a heart attack, why, so much the better. Needs livening up, this place. Coffee's ready."

Digby was at work in his study and Justinia pottered happily in the garden. The air felt fresh after the wind, and the temperature had risen several degrees in just a few hours. She looked sadly at the destruction wrought by the Helm, plants flattened, trees stripped of their leaves, and went round the corner of the house to get the wheelbarrow from the garage. A car stopped outside Sylvester's house, and a familiar figure leapt out and strode into the house. "There's Val," thought Justinia, surprised. Of course, he must have come to pick up Thomas, but why was he looking so cross?

"Hello, Val," said Sylvester. "I've been trying to ring you at the castle. Thomas wants to stay on a bit longer."

"Well, he can't," said Valdemar. "You're a busy man, you can't have a boy hanging round your neck. Good morning, Lily."

"Thomas doesn't hang round Sylvester's neck," said Lily firmly. "He knows better than that."

"Then no doubt he hangs round your neck."

"Thomas is no trouble to me, I'm very fond of him. He's still looking a bit peaky, you leave him here with me for a few more days."

"That's what Magdalena says, but I think he should come back to the castle. I don't know why they have these ridiculous half-term holidays, it's most inconvenient. We never had a week off in the middle of term when I was at school."

"If you and Magdalena are busy just at the moment," said Lily, "he'll be better off here rather than mooching round at the castle. Lucius's son will be home today, he's a boy of about Thomas's age, and he needs company."

"Company! That's another thing. What's this I hear about Thomas and some naked man prancing about on the green?"

"News travels fast," said Sylvester. "Do sit down, Val, you make me nervous, prowling up and down. Now, Thomas has not been prancing around on the green with a naked man; do you think Lily would let Thomas get up to anything you'd disapprove of?"

Valdemar gave a shout of laughter. "Of course she would, wouldn't you, Lily?"

"I might and I might not, but there's no harm in Thomas doing Chinese exercises with Issur. Issur may be a dancer, but there's no reason to suppose his tastes run to boys."

"Dancer?" Valdemar's face darkened. "What dancer?"

"Do calm down," said Sylvester. "He's a Russian, perfectly respectable, staying with Sadie."

"Staying with Sadie? Oh, very well, in that case I suppose it's all right. I didn't think Sadie went in for Bohemians, is this man a friend of Charles's?"

"You could say that," said Lily before Sylvester could reply.

"So where's Thomas now?"

"Helping Justinia with her garden," said Sylvester, looking out of the window. No Issur in sight, good.

"I'll just go across and have a word with him," said Valdemar.

## 10

What an attractive man, thought Roxane as she walked back from the shops and caught sight of Valdemar greeting Justinia. One of the Mountjoys, I suppose, wish I had cousins who looked like that.

Justinia wasn't so pleased to see Valdemar. He brushed her cheek with his mouth and she felt the masculinity and appeal of him, as she always did. He reminded her of her father, who had been very like him. Thomas greeted him with a serious face. "Can I stay, Val? Please?"

"I don't think it's fair on Sylvester, but he and Lily seem prepared to put up with you, so . . ."

Thomas was ecstatic. "Great, I mean, Magdalena won't mind my not being there at half-term?"

"Good lord, no," said Valdemar, and Justinia could see that although Thomas badly wanted to stay at Unthrang, he was hurt by Val's casual tone.

"Magdalena will miss you, Thomas," she said quickly. "I was speaking to her on the phone just now, I said I'd keep an eye on you, and if you got too much for Lily, then you could come here. She said it wouldn't be the same at the castle without you, but she does understand that you're having a good time here."

Thomas's face relaxed.

Valdemar's mind had moved on. "Where's your creepy husband, Justy, whatshisname, Digby?"

"You forget yourself, Val," said Justinia furiously.

Valdemar looked surprised. "Why?"

"Oh, never mind. Do you want to see him?"

"God, no. I just wondered where he was, someone told me he'd been drifting round Eyot the last couple of days."

"He couldn't get back to Unthrang because of the Helm, so he stayed in Eyot."

"I see. Magdalena says to bring him over for a meal, well, you've spoken to her yourself. Better come on your own, we enjoyed having you that Sunday. Are you getting bored yet? Time you found yourself something to do, can't spend the rest of your life looking after Digby."

"Why not?"

"Good God, Justy, not you, you'll die of boredom, or get up to some terrible mischief. We've had enough scandal in the family without you adding to it. Come along, Thomas, I'll take you back to Sylvester's house; I don't think you're exactly helping Justy."

Justinia glared at Valdemar's back. Scandal, indeed. He was the one who had piled scandal on scandal, although of course she had heard, indirectly, that her own father in his youth . . . Thank goodness she took after her mother's side of the family: stable and respectable. "And I'm quite happy to make a life out of marriage, thank you," she told an uninterested holly bush.

Digby flung up a window. "Who are you talking to?"

"The holly bush."

"I thought I heard a man's voice."

"No, the bush didn't speak."

"You're being absurd, Justinia," Digby said coldly, and went back to his work.

Thomas and Ben eyed each other.

"Hi," said Thomas.

"Hello," said Ben.

Thomas had the very dark, almost black hair and deep blue eyes of the Mountjoys. Ben was slighter, with his mother's wavy dark brown hair, and brown eyes. They were much of an age and height, as they stood looking warily at each other.

"Do you like battle games?" said Thomas carelessly. "I'm just sorting some out for Sadie over there. I'm too old for them, really, but they're quite interesting."

"What's she got?" said Ben.

"Come and see."

"Okay."

"Race you."

They were gone.

"I hope Sadie doesn't mind her house being invaded," said Lucius, "Ben should ask."

"Oh, Sadie won't mind," said Sylvester. "She's used to boys. Her own son, Colin, wasn't too bad when he was this age. It was only later he became such a prat. Takes after his father."

There was no answer to that.

"Where's your daughter?" asked Sylvester, looking around. "What does she like doing? Will she mind her brother being appropriated by young Thomas?"

"No," said Lucius. "They fight when they're together. She's gone to have a swim."

"How old is she?"

"Ten." He paused. "Difficult age."

Sylvester gave a rumbling laugh. "If she's anything like the girls I know, it's a difficult age from the moment they're born. Pity my young friend Phoebe isn't here; she'd have been company for your girl. She's in America at the moment, her stepfather's wasting his time at an American university. Merle working?" he added unexpectedly.

"Yes," said Lucius. "She always is."

"Come over, then."

"If you aren't too busy."

"Not this evening, although I'll need to get down to some serious work tomorrow. I want to have a talk about your festival."

"Hardly my festival."

"No? Lily tells me you're going to do it. Never wrong, Lily."

They sat in the orchard at the rear of Crag End, near the washing line festooned with Sylvester's and Thomas's clothes.

"Lily's been in a whirl of activity, catching up on things after the Helm," said Sylvester, when he saw Lucius looking at the line. "Doesn't it look ridiculous, my huge shorts, and then Thomas's trousers. Mind you, he'll be as tall as I am one day; after all, his father's a tall man."

"How tall are you?"

"Six foot three and a bit. Don't ask me how much I weigh, that's a state secret. Only Lily knows."

"You look very well on it," said Lucius.

Indeed, Sylvester did look like a man pleased with life.

"Concert go well?" Lucius enquired. "Where was it?"

"Paris," said Sylvester. "Not too bad. Idiotic French conductor, but what do you expect? Now, how do things stand with the festival job?"

Lucius shrugged. "I want to accept, but I can't because of Merle."

"You don't feel inclined to say to hell with Merle, and go your own way?"

"No, because of the children."

Ben and Thomas were discussing serious matters as they planned a mega raid on the Planet Zog.

"Do you like your school?" said Ben.

Thomas pulled a face. "It's okay."

"Are you day or boarding?"

"Boarding. I was a chorister, and it was too much trouble to take me backwards and forwards all the time."

"Same with me, really," said Ben. "Mum's too busy."

"Do you like boarding?"

"No-one in their right mind could like it. I don't like it at home much, though, with Mum and Dad arguing all the time. I hate that. Do your parents argue?"

Thomas made a fine adjustment to a wheel. "Bit difficult for them to argue, my mum's in India mostly. Too far away."

"Have you got a stepmother, then?"

"Sort of."

"So are your parents divorced?"

"Not exactly," said Thomas, wrinkling his nose. "It's all a bit complicated."

"I sometimes think I wish my parents would just get a divorce and get it over with, they're bound to split up in the end."

"Why?"

"They don't agree about anything, and my dad's a bit too kind, and Mum hates that. She throws things at him."

"Like what?" said Thomas, interested.

"Oh, you know, plates and things like that. The trouble is, that although they argue, Dad never loses his temper. That's what Mum can't stand. She's half Hungarian, you see, so she enjoys a good fight."

"Do you really think they'll get a divorce?"

Ben sat back on his heels, making a careful alteration to his spacecraft. "They might. I don't really want them to get divorced, masses of boys at school have got divorced parents; that's why they're there. Children are a nuisance when there's been a divorce. It's just that my parents don't seem to get on."

"What do they argue about?" asked Thomas.

"Everything."

"I'd rather have rowing parents who cared about me than not to be cared about at all."

"Don't your parents care about you?"

"If my mother cared about me, she wouldn't live in India. I think my stepmother does, a bit, but she's got twins of her own now."

"What about your dad?"

"I don't think he cares about anyone."

"Let's start the countdown . . ."

Andrea floated on her back, with only her toes, her face and her little round tummy visible above the surface of the water.

"Who's that?" said Piers, not very pleased to find a child in the pool.

"That's Andrea, Lucius's daughter."

"I didn't know they had children. Where's she suddenly appeared from?"

"School. It's half-term. Leave her be, she isn't very happy."

Piers looked at her in surprise. "How do you know?"

"I can tell."

Andrea opened her eyes, turned over, and swam to the side, where she clung to a large marble foot.

"Do you not want me here any more?" she said directly. "I'll go if you like."

Roxane smiled at her. "No, I like having you in my pool."

Andrea looked at her with angry, dark eyes. "You're just saying that."

"No," said Roxane. "Mind out, I'm coming in." She dived in.

Piers watched them, the tubby little girl and the slim and graceful Roxane. How extraordinary women are, he thought, his hand running over the muscular thigh of a neighbouring triton. Strange bodies, strange minds. There was something reassuring about male flesh that was definitely lacking in a woman, however desirable.

"I'll come this evening," he called to Roxane. She waved lazily at him. Andrea watched him go. "Is he your lover?" she asked Roxane.

"One of them," said Roxane.

"Are you making fun of me?" said Andrea suspiciously.

"No," said Roxane.

"Can you have more than one lover? Isn't it like having two husbands at the same time?"

"It's not illegal, no."

"I suppose some women have a husband and a lover. That makes two at once. Do you have two? Lovers, I mean?"

Roxane lay on her back and paddled the water with her hands. "I don't float as well as you do," she said. "More than two."

"How many, then?"

"Oh, however many I feel like."

"You're making it up."

"Perhaps," said Roxane.

"Do you think if my mother had a lover, she'd be happier, and she'd get on better with my father?"

"You can't take a lover like medicine, to make you better."

Andrea thought about that for a few minutes. "I don't see why not. It's having a new interest, isn't it? Like going to evening classes or taking up quilt-making."

"I hadn't ever looked at it in that light."

Andrea sighed. "I think my mother could have fifty lovers and it wouldn't make any difference. She'd still quarrel with my father every time he came in the room."

"She wouldn't have time with fifty lovers."

"You're laughing at me."

"No," said Roxane.

"You keep on saying, 'No.'"

"Why not?"

"You don't explain yourself."

"Too much effort," said Roxane. She broke into a leisurely backstroke. "Don't fret about your parents. Things have a way of changing, even difficult situations. Often when you least expect it."

"Do you think so?" said Andrea. "It's a change, our being up here. Mum hates being out of London. I like it here. I wish we could stay. I hate London. I hate it nearly as much as I hate school."

"I never liked school," said Roxane. "Such a waste of time, most of it."

"Grown-ups don't say things like that," said Andrea.

"I do."

The Rev Wroot was taking choir practice. There wasn't much to practise, as he favoured easy tunes with a strong beat. Moreover, there wasn't really a choir, since everything was sung by the whole congregation, who needed no lead from anybody. But choir practice was a tradition, and having thrown all the other traditions out shortly after he had been installed, Luther Wroot felt it politic to keep this one. He encouraged all those who felt their singing was a direct way to capture God's attention to come, and his congregation appreciated the chance for a bit of extra praising the Lord with simple chords and tambourine rattling.

The Rev Wroot was relevant, and knew how to appeal to today's youth, as he called them. "Rock your boots for Jesus," he crooned.

"We're rocking our boots for Jesus, yes we are, yes we are!" came the response, as the assembled throng wriggled happily in their chairs. The pews had been removed on the new vicar's orders, to enable space for singing and dancing and playing of musical instruments around a now central altar.

Sylvester rarely set foot in a church except to perform, but he had shaken his head when Sadie had shown him the Rev Wroot's improvements. "Very unwise," he said. "Encourage them along that path, and they'll soon realize you don't need a priest to have a knees-up, and then all those clerics will be out of a job. Good thing, probably, although they'll just be a drain on the taxpayers, who else is going to employ them?"

Sadie had always gone to the village church, ever since she was a girl, but the Rev Wroot was more than she could stomach. "It may be relevant, but I don't see what it has to do with God." Besides, when she had had her trouble with Charles, first the Rev Wroot and then one or two deacons had dropped in, uninvited, to share her pain, and to point out that they welcomed everybody, whatever their marital status.

"No point telling me that," said Sadie crossly. "Let them go and find Charles and welcome him; I wonder if they'd care to bless his relationship with that nasty little milkman."

Digby heard the joyful sounds issuing from the church as he got out of the car. He walked across to the church to look in on them; be neighbourly, he said to himself, not admitting that he was also putting off the moment when he would have to tell Justinia that her mother would shortly be arriving in Unthrang.

He slipped in through the ancient oak door. The Rev Wroot had had plans to sell it, "they fetch a lot, these old doors," he had said. However, the parish council liked its door, and word had got through to the Bishop, who had warned him off. Of course, as the incumbent, he was master in his church, but the Rev Wroot was as wily as he was enthusiastic, and you never knew when you could do with a bishop on your side.

A tall, thin, extremely pale clergyman in dark glasses was standing inside the door, watching the proceedings with a gratified smile. "Welcome," he said to Digby. "Have you come to join in the practice?"

"No, no, not at all," said Digby hastily. "I just heard singing and popped in to see what was happening."

"Raising voices in praise to the Lord," said the clergyman with a satisfied nod of his rather small head.

"Oh, yes, yes," said Digby, wondering if he could make a quick getaway. He didn't mind a nifty Sunday singsong, with easy words and fellowship at the end in the shape of a cup of coffee, but he wasn't in the mood for chatting to strange men in dog collars.

The clergyman followed him out of the church, still smiling, and shut the great door quietly behind him. "Allow me to introduce myself. I'm Hubert Holigost, Succentor at Eyot Cathedral. A humble role, and of course, I have no parish; but I like to take the time to visit some of our nearer churches, especially ones like St Quivox where community worship is so strong. The evangelical voice is making itself so clearly heard here, praise the Lord."

Digby vaguely thought that the evangelical voice must be something to do with the singers. "Oh, yes, angelic voices, yes."

The Rev Holigost wasn't listening. He rarely did. "Our worship in the Cathedral is sadly out of date. The congregation has little chance to participate, and I sometimes think the organist deliberately chooses music which is meaningless to the modern ear."

"Oh, quite," said Digby. "My wife often goes to the services in the Cathedral," he offered. "She's keen on music, and likes to hear the boys sing."

The Rev Holigost's face darkened. "Choral singing of that kind is an anachronism. It should be swept away, there is no place for it in today's church."

"What, do away with the choirboys?" said Digby, startled, as though the Rev Holigost were declaring an anathema on Santa Claus. To Digby, cherubic little boys in red and white were part of his heritage, especially at Christmas, even though he never listened to anything they sang.

"Their gift of music is indeed one to offer up to Jesus, but they should use their voices to praise in a more accessible way. The congregation is excluded, not allowed to sing a note. The service is in old-fashioned language that has nothing to say to us today. All the people can offer is an Amen here and there. Compare that with Luther Wroot's services here, with everyone moved to sing praises and hallelujahs and truly to lift up their voices for Jesus. Well, I am pleased to have met you. Are you a visitor to these parts?"

"No, no, I live here," said Digby.

"Then we may meet again. Goodbye, and go with Jesus." He inclined his head and slid back into the church.

To Digby, a Succentor sounded like a minor official of the Spanish inquisition, and he had a puzzled look on his face as he greeted Justinia. He kissed her and deposited his briefcase in his study before asking her if she knew what a Succentor was. She shook her head.

Thomas appeared in the kitchen door with a grin on his face. "Number two after the Precentor," he told them. "If the Precentor's out of action; properly, I mean, not just sleeping it off, then the Rev Holigost's in charge. It doesn't often happen, which is a good thing, because he's bad news. We call him old Holy Goat. He wears dark glasses all the time because he's practically an Albino." Sensing that Digby wasn't clear about what a Precentor was, either, he added helpfully that the Precentor was in charge of the cathedral music, although Simon Praetorius was really, because the Precentor wasn't always steady on his feet or in his mind.

Digby didn't like a twelve-year-old boy to know something he didn't. He hadn't taken to Thomas from the first, and he didn't think schoolboys should speak disrespectfully of their elders.

"Sorry," said Thomas, flicking a quick look of horror at Justinia. "Thanks for the orange juice, Justy, I'd better be getting back."

Digby frowned. "Why isn't he at school?"

"Half-term," said Justinia, folding up the tapestry she had been working on and tucking it into her work basket.

"He calls you Justy."

"Of course. All the family do."

"Your mother doesn't. I don't. I would have thought the rest of your family would call you whatever those closest to you call you."

"My father called me Justy."

"Your father. Yes." Digby wandered into the kitchen and came back with two glasses of iced mineral water.

"I had a letter from your mother," he began.

"Oh?" said Justinia. "I didn't see anything from her in the post. I thought she was in Italy."

"She's coming to England, and wants to stay with us. Just for a little while."

"Oh," said Justinia. "How long for? Can I see the letter?"

"I left it in the office," said Digby. "It was only a note, she'll be arriving tomorrow, so . . ."

"Tomorrow?" said Justinia. "Oh, lord!"

"Do you mean you aren't pleased that she's coming?"

"Actually, no," said Justinia. "It may have escaped your notice, but my mother and I don't get on very well together when forced to live under one roof. How long is a little while?"

Digby was evasive.

He's written and invited her to come, Justinia realized in a flash of revelation. That's exactly what he's done, and he's told her she can stay for as long as she likes, and she'll be here for weeks. Disapproving of the way I talk to Digby, saying I don't look after him properly, asking why I don't keep proper household accounts – she'll have Digby on her side for that one – when we're going to start a family, why I'm wearing such unsuitable clothes . . . She'll want me to go shopping with her, and spend hours drifting round the kind of shops I loathe, looking at everything; all that time dithering between one thing and another and in the end buying nothing.

"Oh, hell," Justinia told Lydia as she plonked down her bag from Gumble's. "I feel dreadful about it, but you know what mother's like, she lives life in slow motion."

Lydia poured out glasses of wine. "Three, because I hear Alban," she said, as Justinia looked at the glasses on the table.

"You do," said Alban, wrapping an affectionate arm round Lydia's shoulders. "What has happened to upset the beautiful Justy?"

"Bad news," said Justinia. "Mother!"

Alban raised an expressive and bushy eyebrow. "I've met your mother only once, but it was a memorable experience. She even silences Val, does she not?"

Justinia grinned. "Yes, because she treats him like she did my father, and lets him be as bossy as he likes, but pays no attention whatsoever to what he wants. Like a steamroller, my mother. Slow, relentless and unstoppable."

Alban lifted his glass. "Has Lydia told you our good news?" he said with pride.

"No," said Justinia, interested. "What is it?"

"Oh, I'm going to have a baby," said Lydia carelessly.

"Either that or she's turning into a teapot," said Alban. "Haven't you noticed her new, rotund shape?"

"Now you come to mention it," said Justinia. "I thought you'd put on weight, Lydia, but of course, you never do. When is it?"

"February."

"You've kept it a secret all that time!"

"I lost one before," said Lydia. "So I was keeping my fingers crossed and not saying anything this time. It seems to be all right, though."

"You look very well. I am pleased for you." A thought struck her. "Listen, don't tell mother, whatever you do."

"She'll notice if she sees me," said Lydia with certainty. "You know she will."

"You're right," said Justinia gloomily.

"Why shouldn't she?" said Alban, who wanted everyone to know about Lydia's achievement.

"Don't be slow, Alban, she'll nag Justy all the time. When are you going to have a baby? Are there problems, have you seen a good gynaecologist, why don't you and Digby go away for a holiday?"

"Exactly," said Justinia, laughing.

"Good idea, babies," said Alban, looking at Justinia thoughtfully.

"Don't you start, Alban. All in good time."

"Digby the problem? Doesn't he like children?"

"I don't think he does, actually, but he's longing to be a father. I, however, am not longing to be a mother."

"Why not?"

"Alban, don't be so inquisitive. You went for years not wanting to be a father, why shouldn't Justy?"

"The truth is, I don't know," said Justinia. "I hear the prison doors closing, I suppose."

"Trapped in Unthrang with Digby and his brood," said Alban. "Not an inviting scenario, I confess. Why did you marry him, Justy? I've always wanted to know."

## 11

"Alban!" said Lydia. "Take no notice, Justy, you know what he's like."

"It's no secret," said Justy. "I fell in love with him."

Alban looked unconvinced, but a sharp look from Lydia silenced him. "You know best, Justy," he said cheerfully. "I must be off, I'll leave you two to natter in peace."

"Natter!" said Lydia. "Where are you going?"

"Meeting with the Precentor and Simon, last chance before Simon goes."

Alban gave Lydia a warm kiss and told her to look after herself, and then hugged Justinia affectionately. "Don't let them get you down. Flee here whenever you need to, we won't be going anywhere for a bit."

"Alban's been commissioned to write a new work for the cathedral choir," Lydia explained, putting a cushion behind her back and swinging her feet up. "Very exciting; it's going to have its première in the Cathedral here, and then be performed at a Prom next summer in London." She paused, and gave a gentle belch. "I'm always doing that, I can't think why being pregnant has such an effect on one's digestion. Come to think of it, Justy, you'll be involved in this new piece of Alban's. It needs two choirs, so Simon's going to use the Camerata."

Justinia shook her head. "Not me. I can't make the rehearsals, they're at a bad time for Digby."

"Bad time?"

"Wednesdays and Mondays are evenings when he's at home, and he likes me to be there."

Lydia looked at her in astonishment. "What about all the other evenings?"

"He's busy. Work, and his club and so on . . ."

"Really, Justy, you can't let him walk all over you like this. Especially not about your singing, why, you've always sung! And don't tell me that you love him very much, and so you like doing what he wants, I never heard such balls. I adore Alban, but there's no way he'd lay down the law the way your Digby seems to."

"It's the way he is," said Justinia.

"Anyway, if he doesn't like being by himself when he condescends to be at home for the evening, then your mother can keep him company. She may as well make herself useful while she's here."

"Issur's leaving," shouted Thomas, running into the room where Sylvester was practising.

Lily was there in a flash. "Thomas, you know you're never to interrupt Sylvester when he's working!"

"No, no," said Sylvester, sweeping his cello into its case and snapping the locks. "Thomas is quite right . . . Issur leaving? Are you sure, Thomas?"

"Yes, come quickly, look!"

Sure enough, Issur was sitting astride his Harley Davidson outside Sadie's front gate, rakishly attired in his long leather coat, his helmet under his arm. He fastened it on his head and pulled on his leather gloves.

"See?" said Thomas. "And the panniers are packed, he's going!"

Lily took a quick look. "He'll be back," she said, and disappeared into the dark regions of Crag End, where she was waging war against a plague of silverfish.

Sylvester shook his head. "Looks like a departure to me. Can't say Sadie looks too happy."

"What about my exercises?" said Thomas, screeching to a halt beside the bike. "Issur, you can't go."

Issur patted Thomas on the shoulder. Then he kicked his bike into life and roared away, spoiling the effect by stopping at the bus stop where Lucius, Ben and Andrea were standing.

"I'm sorry to see you go," said Lucius.

Issur gave him a quizzical look. "Maybe I still have work to do here, it seems to me that a lot of stirring up of this pot is needed before everything comes right!"

With these cryptic words he launched forward again and disappeared round the corner at high speed, causing PC Vibbs to stop in open-mouthed admiration and Mrs Driffin to mutter darkly about ladies of an age who should know better who got tangled up with men young enough to be their sons.

"I wouldn't mind getting tangled up with that one," said Flora, handing over coins for a stamp. "Lovely man he is, but I wouldn't worry about Sadie, Mrs D. Issur's interested in men, not women, haven't you seen him with old Zeph's nephew?" She departed with a screech of uncouth laughter, to nudge her friend outside the shop and say that she wouldn't mind a threesome with the Russian bloke and Piers from the Manor, only she didn't expect they were going to ask her.

"Flora!" said her friend. "What about Jerry?"

"Jerry isn't dark, handsome and sexy, and he hasn't got a bulge like that Russian's got – have you seen him on the green doing his exercises? Doesn't half give you ideas. And that Piers, well, those fair ones like him are worth it once they get going, you take my word for it. Anyway, he'll be back, that Russian, just wait and see."

"Who says?"

"I do, for one, and Lily for another."

"Wishful thinking."

The bus lumbered up to the bus stop, and Lucius saw Ben and Andrea on to it. "Back on the twelve o'clock bus, remember."

"Okay, Pa," said Andrea, pulling a face. "Look after her, Ben," directed Lucius through the window, as the two children ostentatiously found seats well away from each other.

"Day out?" enquired Sylvester who had strolled across to the bus stop.

"They've taken some money out of their savings accounts; I don't know what they're up to, but they insisted they had to go to Eyot."

"Time you got yourself a job and stopped fretting about the children," said Sylvester.

"Is that what I seem to do?" said Lucius.

"Yes."

Justinia was sorry to hear that Issur had gone, but Digby expressed his delight to Pauline, who came up to greet them as they waited on the pavement for Justinia's mother to come out of the newsagent's.

"Not a good influence, a man like that," pronounced Pauline. "Gavin wanted to go and do those peculiar exercises on the green, but of course I said no. If Sylvester lets Thomas do them, then that's his affair, although I shouldn't think Thomas's family would be very happy to hear about it."

"Valdemar isn't bothered," said Justinia. "Issur's been extremely kind to Thomas; he's looking much better."

"I don't think there's anything wrong with that boy," said Pauline. "All this talk of sinuses, just an excuse to get out of school. He needs to work hard if he's going to pass his Common Entrance, and he has to pass well to get where he's supposed to be going. Gavin gets much better marks in class than Thomas, and he's several months younger. Of course the teachers find Thomas very odd. They all say Gavin is a pleasure to teach, so receptive and keen to work hard. That's what Mr Poughley said at the last parents' evening, 'a perfect pupil,' he called him. 'Exactly the kind of boy who brings credit to the school.'"

How awful to be the star of your school, thought Justinia. No surer sign of heading fast for obscurity, in her view. Mind you, since Gavin was totally lacking in any personality and was so clearly not going to be the star of anything else in life, perhaps it was best for him to win such credit as he could.

Justinia's mother approved of Gavin and his younger brother Peter. "Good, well brought up little boys, not in and out of everything like Thomas. You can see he's going to grow up to be a real problem to someone. He's a handful now, and I find him impertinent."

"I don't think he means to be," said Justinia. "Did you get your *Daily Mail*?"

"Yes, and I've ordered it to be kept for me every day, since I'm going to be here for a while. I live for my copies of the *Mail* in Italy, even though they are so out of date when I get them. I do like to keep in touch with what's going on."

Justinia sighed, feeling like a rebellious child as she walked along behind Celia and Digby, who was working at home today. Her face brightened as she saw Piers on the other side of the road, and she waved to him.

"Oh good, Justinia, I wanted to catch you," he said, loping over towards them. "Good morning," he said politely to Digby, and smiled delightfully at Celia.

"Mother, this is Piers, who is at the university and lives with his great-aunt at the Manor on the green. Piers, my mother, Mrs Mountjoy."

Piers bowed and turned his attention back to Justinia. "About tonight," he began.

Digby smiled a worldly smile and broke in smoothly. "If it's about the choir, my wife and I have decided that it isn't possible at the moment. I'm sure you can make other arrangements for your transport."

"No problem," said Piers promptly. "I can go on my bike. I prefer company, though. It's a shame, Justinia," he went on. "With that marvellous voice of yours, it will be the choir's loss."

Celia's good opinion of this rather beautiful young man started to fade. "I think one should be sure of what one is talking about before one makes such judgements."

Piers gave her an amused smile. "Oh, I do know what I'm talking about, Mrs Mountjoy," he said, not at all abashed. "I'm a musician, you know, and I've done a lot of voice work, spent a year in Spain, studying with Hector Velaz."

"I didn't know that," cried Justinia, delighted. "I thought you were a bassoonist."

"I am, at least, that's my principal study at the university, but I love singing, and since I plan to work with singers, when I start to make my millions, you understand, I need to know as much about it as I can."

"All this is beside the point," said Digby impatiently. "Justinia has other calls on her time on Wednesday evenings. I'm sure the choir will manage very well without her."

Pauline and the boys finished their business in the newsagent's and joined them again. "We're looking forward to seeing you this evening," said Pauline with a gracious smile. "Gavin and Peter want to play their new pieces to you."

"This evening?" said Justinia.

"Yes," said Digby. "Dinner with Pauline and Nigel, for us and your mother."

Justinia's face became blank. "Oh," she said. "I'm sorry, it must have slipped my mind."

"I accepted for us," said Digby cheerfully. "I knew you'd nothing on. We're looking forward to it."

"I am so sorry," said Justinia in a clear, precise voice. She called down the street. "Piers! Piers, wait. I'm coming tonight, I'll pick you up at ten to seven. At the Manor," she added, after a quick look at Digby's face.

Piers turned and raised his hands in a mocking acknowledgement.

"Digby quite forgot that it's my choir evening," said Justinia, turning to Pauline.

Pauline looked put out. "I thought you weren't joining the choir after all. Digby said . . ."

"Oh, but I am," said Justinia. "We're rehearsing that new work by Alban Praetorius – do you know Alban? – and I promised him I would be there."

"Liar," said the voice. "Excellent, Justy, you're coming on. If you carry on like this, you won't need me any more, you do realize that, don't you?"

Merle looked up crossly from her papers as Ben sidled round the door. "Go away," she said brusquely. "You know I'm not to be interrupted when I'm working."

"I know, Mum," said Ben, a trifle nervously. "But Andrea and I have made lunch for you."

"I don't want any lunch. Now go away."

"Please, Mum. We've done it specially for you."

"You shouldn't have bothered; you know I don't stop for lunch when I'm working."

Andrea joined her brother. "All your favourite things, Mum. Smoked salmon, and olives, and that Italian bread . . ."

"And I've made a salad," said Ben proudly. "Three different kinds of lettuce, and those tiny tomatoes you like."

"A sumptuous raspberry pudding," finished Andrea, pleading in her voice.

Merle exploded. "And where did the money for all those things come from? Don't you understand how tight things are, with your father out of work? Lucius," she said in a furious voice as he joined the children, "have you taken leave of your senses?"

"Nothing to do with me," said Lucius. "These two did it all off their own bat. They took their own money out of the building society and went into Eyot to get the food."

"We went to a shop called Gumble's," said Andrea eagerly. "Thomas said that was where we should go. It's wonderful!"

"Please, Mum," said Ben again.

Lucius looked at Merle's angry face and at the despair starting to grow in the children's eyes and surprised himself.

"Yes, Merle, you'd better come," he said, shooing Ben and Andrea out of the room. "Mum's just coming, go and make sure everything is ready."

"It is," said Andrea, resisting.

"Go."

Ben grabbed her and hauled her towards the kitchen. "Idiot," he hissed. "Dad's going to get cross with her."

"Some chance," said Andrea. "He's going to reason with her, and she'll pay no attention, and this is all for nothing." She fought back the tears which were starting to trickle down her cheeks. "It's no good, there just isn't anything we can do, it's hopeless."

Raised voices came from Merle's room. Andrea stuck her fingers in her ears, her face a picture of misery.

"No, listen," said Ben. "It's Dad who's shouting; he's really blasting her."

"She'll kill him, and we'll have to go into an orphanage," shrieked Andrea.

Silence. Then footsteps. The door opened, and Lucius ushered Merle into the kitchen. Her face was white and set as Lucius pulled out a chair for her and told Andrea and Ben to sit down. They slid into their places.

"Have some smoked salmon, Mum," said Ben in a strained voice.

"Thank you, Ben," said Merle in a perfectly controlled voice. "Now, please will someone tell me what this is all about?"

Andrea took a deep breath. "It was my idea, Mum. I wanted to show you that we really can look after ourselves."

"I'm sure you can."

"Not just look after ourselves, but do things for you and Dad. In the house. Food, and so on," said Ben.

"Because if you know that we can look after ourselves, and not be a nuisance, then we won't have to stay at boarding school," said Andrea in a rush. "Please, Mum. I'll keep my room tidy, and do all the shopping, and Ben has bought a cookbook, we can do the cooking. We'll clean the house, and if we go to schools here in Unthrang, then we can walk to school, by ourselves, and it wouldn't be any trouble for you, really it wouldn't. We won't watch TV or make a noise or be any trouble in the evenings and at weekends."

"We promise never to ask friends round, or play loud music or anything that disturbs your work."

"You can go off and leave us as much as you like, we won't mind, honestly we won't."

"We'll do all our homework without you having to nag."

"And our music practice."

"Please."

Lucius sank his head into his hands. Then he looked up. "Do you really dislike being away at school, or is this just a half-term scene to make your mother feel uncomfortable?"

Andrea got up and went round to her father. She hung over him, leaning her head on his back. "Dad, you don't know how awful it is. You're never by yourself, and you have to share a room with people you really hate, and you have to be with them all the time. You have to do what everyone else wants, even if it's something you loathe."

"Mostly," said Ben, trying to sound dispassionate, "I hate being tired, which I am all the time at school. Also, some of the older boys . . . well, you know, Dad. It's bad enough at day school, but when you board, you can't get away from people."

"The staff don't care about you at all," said Andrea. "They tell you to stand on your own two feet, and how you must learn to get on with other children, but all they mean is, don't bother me, I don't want to know about it."

Lucius could feel his daughter's tears wetting his shirt.

"And every term you send us back, and say it won't be so bad, and every term it gets worse and worse."

Andrea was making heroic efforts to pull herself together; she knew her mother hated tears.

"I'm sorry, Mum, I try not to cry, and I'm getting better. I hardly cry at home in the holidays at all. But I do every night at school, and it's difficult to stop." She fumbled in her shorts pocket for a handkerchief.

Merle said nothing.

"And we'd like to live here, if it's cheaper and we're short of money."

"We'd like to live anywhere if we can be at home all the time."

"We'd rather be here, because this is the best place we've ever been, but we know London is best for you."

Ben looked at his mother's face and shook his head at Andrea. "It's no good," he said. "She doesn't want us to be at home."

Lucius gently put his hands up and unwound Andrea's arms from round his neck. He stood up. "I didn't know you felt this strongly about it."

"You should have done, but you wouldn't listen, because you didn't want to upset Mum."

Lucius winced. "You know how good your present schools are?"

"Good for turning out neurotics," said Ben.

"You need a good education, it's desperately important."

"You had a good education, and now you're out of work."

Lucius bit his lip. "You'll have to go to local schools. You may find it very different."

"I don't care," said Andrea. "I'd like to go to the primary school here. I know Helen and Genetta and Caroline, they all go to the school here, and they'd be my friends."

"I could go to school in Eyot, couldn't I?" said Ben hopefully. "A lot of the kids from here do that. They go in on the bus. If I work really hard, could I try for a scholarship to Thomas's school? He'd like to stay if he could, he says. As a day boy; he says it's not too bad as long as you don't have to board."

Lucius looked at Merle. Her face was now tense with rage. He took a deep breath. "Right. I have come to a decision. I will ring up the Festival board in Eyot this afternoon and accept the post of director."

"Dad!" shouted Ben. "Well done."

He felt Andrea's hand clutching his. "And can we stay at home?"

"Money is going to be tight, and I think we would be unable to find the fees for both of you where you are."

Ben's face broke into a smile. "Oh, great, Dad," he said happily. "I hate the rows you and Mum have, but I hate going away to school even more."

"You must finish this term there."

"I don't mind that," said Ben.

"No," said Andrea. "I won't. It's no good, I'm not going back, you can't make me. If you drag me there, I'll just wait until you've gone, and then I'll run away."

Ben nodded at his father. "She will, you know. She's been planning to, she could get into serious trouble."

Merle got up, and faced her family. Before she could open her mouth, Lucius took her by the arm. "No, you are not to shout and scream at me. Or, if you must, you're going to do it in private, Ben and Andrea have had more than they can take of our arguing. If you want to go back to London, that's fine by me. I'm staying, I'm taking the job here, and there's nothing further to say." He turned to Ben and Andrea. "Eat what you like, then pop the rest in the fridge, your mother and I will have something later."

Sylvester was surprised to find his kitchen full of children.

"Lucius left these two here, he's had to go into Eyot," Lily explained.

"I don't mind," said Sylvester in his amiable way. "They aren't disturbing me. Your mother working?" he asked Ben and Andrea.

"No," said Andrea. "She's locked herself into the bedroom and won't come out."

"Dad's going to be director of that festival in Eyot," said Ben with satisfaction.

"Ah, excellent," said Sylvester, beaming. He thought for a moment and then frowned. "So I take it your mother isn't entirely pleased about this?"

"She's just a bit upset, she's had a lot of work," said Andrea loyally.

Lily and Sylvester exchanged looks over the children's heads.

"Understandable," said Sylvester. "I wonder . . ."

"No," said Lily. "You leave well alone."

"I wouldn't have thought . . ."

"Never mind what you'd think."

"We told them," said Andrea happily. "It was an ultimatum. Issur told us that was what we had to give them. He said you have to ask, but in such a way that they have to say yes."

"Subversive," remarked Sylvester.

Ben looked solemn. "No, he wasn't turning us against Mum and Dad, he said we had to make them understand how we felt. He says children shouldn't be in cages. He thinks our schools are like cages."

"Issur is a sensible man," said Lily. "Now, out of my kitchen, Sylvester, there's certainly no room in here for you with this lot."

Thomas, who had been absorbed in a mechanical puzzle, grinned at Sylvester. "Lily's very rude to you," he said.

"Not at all," said Sylvester. "Put that away, young Thomas, I feel a teaching mood coming upon me. No pulling faces, let's hear how those scales of yours are going."

Merle hadn't been to the stable block where Roxane lived before. She knocked on the door; someone was at home, because a light was streaming out of a ground floor window, and she could hear a radio.

A strange man put his head out of an upstairs window. "Hello?" he said.

Merle looked up to see a tousled mop of hair and a lively face with dark, slanting eyebrows looking down at her.

"I'm sorry," she began.

"No need to be sorry. Do you want Roxane? She'll be down in a sec."

A few minutes later the main door opened, and Roxane, dressed in her long brocade coat, opened the door.

"I don't think this is a good time," said Merle. "You have a friend here . . ."

"Ah, Ned. He's my horticultural adviser. An expert on roses, have you seen my rose garden? Come in."

Roxane cleared a pile of papers off one of the chairs at the table and pulled it out for Merle, her eyes taking in the dark circles under Merle's eyes and the signs of strain around her mouth.

"I've come to ask if we can extend the rental of Juniper House," said Merle.

"Of course," said Roxane. "You can stay as long as you like."

"Lucius has decided to take this job up here," said Merle.

"You don't have to explain," said Roxane.

Ned, now dressed, came into the room. "Ned, a drink for Merle. Merle, this is Ned."

"We met," said Ned. He had a slanting smile which matched his eyebrows and gave his whole face a slightly satanic expression.

"Merle is a writer," said Roxane, sitting on the corner of the table. "Her husband, Lucius, is a what, Merle? Musician? Administrator? Something useful in the arts, in any case. Ned is an opera freak," she said to Merle. "Are you musical?"

Merle shook her head. "Not these days, I don't have time."

"Are the children enjoying their holiday? I like having them around, they're good company."

Merle's face twitched. "I'm glad you like them. Because they're staying. Andrea isn't going back to school, and Ben is finishing at his school at the end of this term."

"Too expensive?" said Roxane laconically. "Don't fret yourself over it, from what Andrea says, they aren't exactly happy at school."

"So I gather," said Merle. "You found that out very quickly. I, on the other hand, have been sending them back to somewhere they hate, and pretending I didn't know how unhappy they were."

"Tricky one, that," said Ned, filling her glass. "I wouldn't worry about it. My parents never listened to me when I told them how miserable I was at school. In the end I gave up trying and just hung on until the bitter end. At least yours have escaped."

"You're a good Englishman, and possibly the worst thing that happens to an Englishman is his public school. But my mother was Hungarian. She was Jewish, but lucky Jewish, because the Nazis didn't kill her. But they put her family into camps, and she herself ended up in a camp – for displaced persons. That's where

I was born, she met and fell in love with an Englishman who was working in the camp."

"Yes, I can see that boarding schools pale in comparison," said Ned.

Merle turned a stricken face to him. "No," she said. "On the contrary, that was why I owed it to my children to make their lives as happy as possible. And I haven't done it."

"It sounds as though they're happy now," said Roxane. "They were delirious when they came out into the garden, before Lucius bore them away."

"Yes," said Merle. "He didn't trust me with them, so he took them over to Sylvester's."

"Nonsense," said Roxane. "He knew you were having a fit of the heebie jeebies and wanted to leave you in peace to enjoy them properly."

"I make Lucius very unhappy," said Merle darkly.

"I think Lucius could be very pompous and boring if he wasn't married to someone like you," said Roxane. "Have another glass of wine, and let's think about finding you a lover."

"A lover?"

"Roxane, really," said Ned, laughing.

"No, I'm serious. That would make Lucius sit up, and it would give Merle something to think about instead of how bad a mother she is."

"I don't have time for a lover," said Merle, feeling very strange from the effects of three glasses of fizzy wine imbibed at speed.

"I always have time for a lover," said Roxane. "It's my cure for everything."

By the weekend, Justinia felt that her mother had been staying for weeks and weeks. Celia had thrown herself with delight into Digby's plans for the house, and they sat together every evening, looking at Genevra's sketches and samples. Celia was longing to meet Genevra, and had plans, after expert discussions, for making sorties on all the antique shops in the area.

"And sales, country sales are excellent for finding good pieces. Justinia and I will find some marvellous things, just you wait and see, Digby."

Digby was delighted to have Celia on his side; so pleased that he had almost forgiven Justinia for her act of rebellion in going to the choir. Celia had soothed him with practised ease. "Digby, you mustn't be so dominant all the time, of course Justinia must feel that she can have her own interests. Give her plenty of scope, and you'll find she'll gradually come round to your way of thinking, it's much more effective than being forceful, which so often leads to a quarrel."

Digby's mouth set in a firm line. "We don't quarrel, Celia, because I won't let Justinia argue with me."

"Quite right," said Celia approvingly. "A few disagreements, however, add spice to a marriage. As long as you've made it up by the end of the day, I'm a great believer in never letting the sun go down without making up."

Celia's husband had learned this the hard way: viz, you did what Celia wanted, or she fell into a melancholy, and drooped around the house in the most dismal fashion. Moreover, when in these moods, there was no getting near her in bed. His original solution to this had been the typical Mountjoy one of immediately finding someone else to go to bed with, but Celia had foiled these pursuits by removing him to the remote Italian countryside, where dalliance was all too obvious and could be dangerous. She subdued him with an iron will, which was buried deep in her soft-seeming personality, and succeeded in turning him from a rake into an ideal husband. Other women would have been bored by this, but to Celia he was just one of the many works of art which adorned her dark Italian home, and she remained very fond of him.

"Of course," she confided to Digby, "he was a strong man, and very strict with Justinia always; he loved her, naturally, but he made sure she was kept under control. When she was a child she had quite a wild streak, you know, but he never let her get the better of him. That's why she fell in love with you, she naturally responds to a strong man."

"Yes," said Digby, feeling particularly strong as Celia fixed him with her sad brown eyes, and he thought of Justinia as he liked her best. In bed, and under control. That was the key to a successful marriage.

## 12

To Thomas's delight, Magdalena said she would come over to pick him up. "I'll drop in on Justy," she told Sylvester on the phone, "and then take Thomas away, I do hope he hasn't been a nuisance."

"Don't talk like that about him," said Sylvester. "Of course he's not a nuisance, and even if he were, why shouldn't he be? He's not in this world on approval, as far as I know. He's welcome to come whenever he likes; he's a charming boy, and he's made several friends here."

"Has his nose dripped all the time?"

"What a revolting thing to say, Magdalena, why on earth should his nose drip . . . oh, I see, sinuses. Not that I've noticed. There's nothing wrong with Thomas except that he feels he doesn't belong anywhere, and that's something you and Val will have to sort out, since his mother's never here. No, I do not think he'll be happier when he goes to his new school next year . . . that's one of Val's worse ideas; he's only insisting on it because his father sent him away. Yes, I don't doubt that it may make him more grown up and independent, but why should he be grown up? He's got the rest of his life to be that, God help him."

Justinia had made sure that her mother and Digby would be out when Magdalena came. Magdalena and Celia had never got on, and Digby was always rather stiff with Magdalena, since he found it hard to restrain his disapproval of Valdemar, who was down as a Bad Man in his books. Justinia hadn't told the other two that Magdalena was coming, and had declined an invitation to accompany them on an expedition to Eyot to look at some particularly dire silks for the sitting-room curtains. To Justinia, the sample which they had cooed over looked as though it had started life at the bottom of a pond; she could see yards of it draped around the sitting room to most depressing effect.

"No, you go, you know I have no taste in these things, and anyway" – with a swift and not very loving look at Digby – "it's nothing to do with me, Genevra's in charge."

"Digby and you have to approve of what she's doing," pointed out Celia. "You're paying her, so you must be satisfied with what she's planning. I have to say, I think it was a stroke of genius on Digby's part to bring her up from London, such an excellent eye. I'm almost tempted to invite her out to Italy, there are several rooms I'm not completely happy with."

"You go ahead," said Justinia. "I'll make lunch for when you come back."

Celia gave Justinia a warm and approving smile. She was determined to remedy Justinia's utter lack of interest in cooking. "You like food," she would say. "So you should be at your happiest in the kitchen, preparing it."

Justinia liked eating food, but loathed cooking it; she knew better than to say so to her mother, who never in any case paid much attention to what her daughter said or wanted. Justinia waved goodbye to them and closed the front door. Her mother had left the new cookery book she had brought as a present on the kitchen table, and Justinia swiftly consigned it to the darkest corner of the bookshelf.

"No Digby or Celia?" said Magdalena.

"I thought you'd rather not."

"Oh dear, is it that obvious?"

"Only to me," said Justinia, laughing at Magdalena's expression. "Anyhow, much as I love Digby, I have to say that he is a bit difficult when mother's here."

"I can imagine. Did you tell Digby I was dropping in?"

"No, I said I'd make lunch, and that sent them off in a good mood, because they both love me to be domestic."

Magdalena looked enquiringly towards the kitchen.

"And are you making lunch?"

"Of course not. I bought everything at Gumble's yesterday,

and hid it. It won't take a minute to get it ready, and they'll be so greedy when they see all the luscious goodies on the table that they won't say a word. Especially not after a morning spent looking at dingy things for the house."

Magdalena looked around, startled. "Why do they want dingy things? These old houses need as much light as possible, they never have big windows, and besides, it's so often grey outside."

"You know what mother's like," said Justinia, tucking her feet up under her on the sofa. "Maximum gloom."

"Yes, but Digby?"

"Has fallen under the influence of a smart little number from London called Genevra. She's an interior designer, and Digby thinks she's wonderful. She arrives on Monday to do us over."

Magdalena frowned. "The whole house? Justy, you'll hate that."

Justinia felt a prickling in her eyes; she couldn't cope with sympathy, and she told Magdalena so. "I'm putting it out of my mind, it's only a house, and if it makes Digby happy . . ."

"It's your house as much as his."

"It doesn't feel like it." Justinia managed a wry smile. "I'm keeping one room out of Genevra's clutches, so I'll have a retreat in time of need."

"Coward," sang the voice in her ear. "You can see how Magdalena thinks the less of you for letting Digby trample all over you, so why don't you assert yourself?"

"Go away. You don't know anything about it."

"I know everything about it, because I haven't got a mind covered with bolts and locks, unlike you. Go on, ask Magdalena what she really thinks of Digby."

"I don't care what anybody else thinks of Digby. The only person who matters is me, and I'm prepared to do a lot to please him, because . . ."

"You love him," jeered the voice.

"Justy?" Magdalena was saying anxiously. "Are you all right? You seemed to be in a trance."

"I'm sorry," said Justinia. "I had a sudden thought; it was rude of me, what were you saying?"

"I was saying that it might be good for you to get away for

a few days, go to London, see some friends, perhaps. If Celia's here, Digby will have company, I know you've told me that he hates to be in the house by himself."

I could, thought Justinia longingly. Go and see how the department is doing, although that could be a mistake . . . go to the opera . . . What bliss!

Sylvester found Sadie in her garden. This was at the rear of her house, and sloped up quite sharply. Sadie was red in the face with her exertions.

"What are you doing?" said Sylvester, eyeing a large stone which Sadie had placed in a wheelbarrow.

"Hello, Sylvester. I'll take this one up, and then I'll call a halt and we can have a cup of tea . . ."

"At this time?" said Sylvester doubtfully.

"What time is it?" called Sadie as she heaved the wheelbarrow and its load up the steps at the foot of the path.

"Half past six."

"I had no idea. Missed tea, then, time for something stronger."

"Good idea," said Sylvester. "Oh, do be careful."

Sadie was having a fight with the wheelbarrow, which was leaning at an alarming angle and clearly had no intention of bearing the stone to the spot Sadie was aiming for. Sadie wrenched at the handles, and the wheelbarrow sulkily swung further over in the wrong direction.

"Hold on," said Sylvester, climbing up the path and reaching out for the handles. He gave them a tug, and the wheelbarrow, realizing it was no match for Sylvester's bulk and sinews, trundled obediently on to the little clearing where a heap of rocks were already stacked.

"Thank you," said Sadie. "Are you all right?"

"I may be large," said Sylvester, "but I am not about to drop dead from a heart attack. Playing the cello keeps me in good form, let me tell you. Now, where's that drink?"

Sadie found a bottle and left Sylvester to cope while she went to clean up. When she came down, she had changed out of her gardening clothes and was wearing a large and vivid robe. Sylvester blinked.

Sadie looked at herself in the little ormolu mirror which hung above the fireplace. "It isn't right, is it?" she said sadly. "I've been trying to smarten myself up a bit, looking through my cupboards. They're full of things I'd forgotten about, but when I get them out and try them on, I do see why I'd forgotten about them. It's shopping on my own, fatal, I always buy hopelessly inappropriate clothes, which mostly don't fit very well. So I fall back on my tweed skirts for winter and cotton frocks for summer . . ."

Sylvester didn't want to be unkind, but he quite saw what she meant. He was famous himself for the exuberance and vividness of his off-duty clothes, but then he was a man. And he hoped he didn't looked depressed and faded the way Sadie did.

"Drink up," he said. "Tell me what you're building up in your garden. A funeral pyre in case Charles comes to call?"

"Charles!" said Sadie with venom. "No, I'm building a folly, for Jezebel. She needs more fresh air."

Sylvester was silent for a moment, trying to remember if Jezebel was Sadie's daughter; the name didn't seem quite right somehow . . .

"Jezebel's the parrot," said Sadie helpfully. "My daughter is Ursula."

"Yes, the parrot," said Sylvester gratefully. "Of course. Why a folly?"

"Displacement activity, I expect," said Sadie, who suffered from few illusions.

"Missing Issur?" asked Sylvester.

"Terribly. I know it's silly; he was only here for a few days, but . . ."

"I know those buts," said Sylvester. "No word from him, no address, no plans?"

Sadie shook her head and looked sadly into her drink. "No, he just upped and offed. Bored, no doubt. Other jobs waiting, he must have lost money while he was here."

"An unusual man."

"Quite unlike anyone I've ever met." She paused and looked quizzically at Sylvester. "How old do you think he is?"

Sylvester pondered. "Mid-twenties? Thirty? Difficult to say."

"Isn't it? He wouldn't tell me, but he is young, you can see he is. But in some ways he's so old." She sniffed. "I'm sorry.

Sylvester, I'm embarrassing you, I don't mean to cry. I do miss him, though."

"Doesn't embarrass me," said Sylvester in his kindly way. "Very little embarrasses me. Or shocks me, if it comes to that. Now, dry your eyes, finish up your drink, and come back with me for dinner."

"Sylvester, I couldn't."

"Lily says . . ."

Sadie managed a smile. "If Lily says I'm to come, then there's no point in resisting, is there?"

"None at all."

After dinner, Sadie, feeling better for having a proper meal inside her, sat beside Sylvester's ample fire. Sylvester drew the curtains, and they sat in companionable ease together, Sadie dreaming, Sylvester humming through some music.

A ring at the door.

"A visitor," said Sylvester. "Perhaps it's Lucius, I haven't seen him around recently, too busy, I suppose. Shall I go, Lily?" he called out, but Lily was already there.

"It's the vicar," she said unenthusiastically as she showed the Rev Wroot in.

"An unexpected pleasure," Sylvester said politely. Sadie just glowered.

"I wondered if I might have a word," said the vicar, glancing uncertainly at Sadie. "I thought that perhaps you, Mr Tate, being so much more a man of the world than I am, with going abroad, and knowing artistic people . . . and Sadie, too, I would value your opinion."

He seemed very on edge, not like the confident and sleek clergyman they knew all too well.

"Anything we can do," said Sylvester courteously, ushering the vicar to a chair. "A glass of something?"

The Rev Wroot looked nervously at Sylvester's brandy, whisky and other strong-looking drinks, taken out of the cupboard by Lily since Sylvester had a guest. "I don't normally touch spirits, you understand, but perhaps . . . well, a very small glass. That's very kind of you."

I wonder why he became a clergyman, thought Sadie. Why not

a social worker, if he wants to help people? Or a folk singer if he wants to play his beastly guitar? All this Jesus, Jesus, as though he was recommending a toothpaste or a happy pill. Don't suppose he's ever read the Book of Job. Don't suppose he believes in Satan, well nobody does, very unfashionable, Satan. Don't suppose he believes in anything except people being nice to each other, and having a good weekly singsong to give them appetite for Sunday lunch. And since people aren't nice to each other, he's living in cloud-cuckoo land, full of pink souls. Don't suppose he believes in the soul, either. She took an extra large gulp from her glass, and glared at the Rev Wroot, who was looking startled to see Sadie with a large glass full of what was clearly an alcoholic drink.

Sadie wronged him. The Rev Wroot's soul, against all expectations, had sat up and bitten him.

"It was our visitor, Issur," he began. "While he was here, I invited him into our church; of course, our Lord tells us to welcome strangers. He came. He sat at the back, and I have to say, he made me feel very nervous. As a priest, administering the sacrament, I never feel nervous, I am doing the Lord's work, but on this occasion I have to confess that I actually dropped the chalice. It's those dark eyes, somehow they seem to look straight into you, did you notice that?"

"Powerful eyes, yes," said Sadie. I mustn't laugh, she said to herself. I mustn't catch Sylvester's eye.

Sylvester sat very still, his gaze on the ceiling; massive and impressive, he looked very reassuring to the Rev Wroot, who had no idea that Sylvester held very strong views on the clergy, mostly critical.

"Issur didn't take communion, nor did he join in any of our songs of praise. Nor did he come for fellowship after the service. He just stood there, brooding, his arms crossed. He wouldn't speak to any of our congregation, and of course they all wanted to offer the stranger in our midst a sign of peace."

The Rev Wroot took a tentative sip of his drink, and then another. "Normally, I don't touch any alcohol," he said. "We see that sadly, so many people nowadays, including priests, even quite senior ones . . . but I stray.

"The congregation had left, there were only the three of us in the church, myself, in the vestry with Samuel Boot, who was tidying up the tambourines, and Issur. He seemed to have grown in size, somehow, so he seemed rather menacing. I have to say I felt some alarm as he came down the nave towards us, he appeared to be so angry. Samuel . . . Well, I have to say, Samuel is not altogether at his best with young men of a certain type, and he gave what I can only call a giggle at Issur.

"Issur looked at him for a moment, then he picked him up, literally picked him up, and carried him out of the church. I rushed after them, fearing that Issur was planning to do some harm to Samuel, because he did look, as I said, very angry, and also somehow wild. But he put Samuel down on the grass without hurting him in any way. Then he came back into the church and shut the door. I don't think even Samuel would have dared to venture back in, so he needn't have . . . Anyway, he took me by the arm, very courteously, and led me back towards the altar.

"He waved his hand at the altar, and at our happy banners, which as you know help to make our place of worship welcome and cheerful."

That wasn't how Sadie would have described the banners, with their simplistic evangelical messages conveyed in garish colours. She didn't mention this, though, being too fascinated by the Rev Wroot's story. "Go on," she said. "What did Issur do next?"

The Rev Wroot looked at Sadie with perplexed eyes. "He didn't *do* anything. He asked me why I had made a tawdry shell of a holy place – well, of course I objected very strongly to that. Then he said that I as a priest had no right to cut my people off from God. I protested, my whole life is dedicated to bringing our Lord into the lives of my parishioners. Then he said there were many people in the town who didn't want a happy little God, and needed to be able to worship their own darker and more powerful God in their own church.

"Then I knew that I was dealing with a deranged person, and I knew at once what he was talking about . . ."

The Rev Wroot lowered his voice and leant forward confidentially. "The Black Mass."

"No," said Sadie, stifling a laugh. "What horror."

"Horror indeed."

"Did you make the sign of the cross?" asked Sylvester with interest.

"I did. And he laughed. Laughed! He told me not to be ridiculous. Now I felt I had to be firm. I said he must leave."

"Did he?"

"No. He said that he wanted to look around, and he took my arm; he is very strong, I find. He led me, or took me, I should say, to the vestry, and started opening cupboards and chests. You know that my predecessor in the parish was hardly modern in his outlook, and I have never cleared out the relics of his incumbency as I should have done. Issur found all kinds of things I hadn't known were there. Incense and incense burners, and candles and vestments . . . All so wrong for our modern worship. Issur was pleased with everything he found, especially a set of black funeral robes. Velvet. With gold tassels!" The Rev Wroot shuddered. "Then Issur said, 'You see. Everything is here, for proper worship.'"

"Of course, I tried to explain to him that there is simply no place in today's world for the ancient rituals and ceremonies for which these things were once used."

"And what did Issur say to that?" enquired Sylvester, who was enjoying himself hugely.

The Rev Wroot shook his head sorrowfully. "He said some very pungent things, which I wouldn't care to repeat. Then he said to me, 'Beware, Mr Wroot. God will come, whether you want him or not; not all your happy little songs and dances can protect you.' Then he told me that the second of November was a very important day. Of course, it is, it's All Souls, naturally, I know that; but it isn't an occasion we celebrate in our friendly church. It's too gloomy."

The Rev Wroot fell silent, and looked solemn. "Issur laughed, but not in a happy way at all. 'I shall come here on November the second,' he told me. 'And so I expect, will many others, to honour the dead and to say prayers for their souls.'"

"Of course, I told him that he would do no such thing, and if that was what he wanted, they always have a sung Requiem in the Cathedral on that date, although I know for a fact that many of the clergy there, such as my good friend Hubert Holigost, would like to see an end to it. It is very unwholesome, and there is far too much emphasis on the music, which of course is sung by the choir, with no participation by the worshippers."

"So did that satisfy him?" asked Sadie.

"He laughed again. I regret to say it was not a happy, joyful laugh, but a dark and wicked laugh. He said, 'Who lives will see,' and left. Banging the door behind him, although I can't say whether that was intentional, or whether the wind caught it as he was going through."

"Been talking to Lily," said Sylvester thoughtfully.

"I beg your pardon?"

"That's one of Lily's favourite expressions: who lives will see." Sylvester got up, and beamed at the vicar. "Very harrowing, I can see that. When did all this happen."

"Several days ago," said the Rev Wroot miserably. "Before Issur left."

"Yes, well it had to be before he left."

"You would say so," the vicar went on gloomily. "But this is not entirely the case, because I'm not entirely sure he's gone."

Sadie sat up. "What? Of course he's gone. We all saw him leave. Besides, if he hadn't gone, where would he be?"

"I fear that although he may not be with us in the flesh, he is in spirit."

"What, you think he's dead?"

The Rev Wroot pursed his thick lips and nodded his head up and down. "I am afraid so. I am very much afraid that this may be the case."

"Pooh, nonsense," said Sylvester in his robust way. "Why should he be dead?"

The Rev Wroot fixed his sincere gaze on Sylvester. "I have had these . . . I hardly know what to call them. Apparitions? Visitations? At night, I hear his voice, laughing. I can only describe it as wild laughter. And in my mind's eye, I see him."

"Who, Issur? What's he doing?" asked Sylvester sceptically.

The vicar sighed. "Dancing. Dancing, not in a gross manner, but it is nonetheless disturbing. I feel he is leading people that I can't see, in some greater dance . . ." His voice trailed off. "It is most distressing, and I can only feel that it is an omen, an omen of some mischief to come. Who knows what may not be planned for All Souls? Something is amiss, or why should I be . . . I can only say, haunted, by this man. I ask you, what do you think is going to happen?"

## 13

"Nightmares," said Sylvester. "You've been having nightmares, that's your problem. Have a hot drink before you go to bed."

The Rev Wroot shook his head. "No, this is all too real, it has none of the quality of a nightmare, and besides, I am often wide awake when it happens; these are not only nightly visitations. I have spent much time in prayer over the last few days, as you can imagine. Even then, I have to confess that I am unable to get him out of my mind. I hear him, mocking me."

"Don't pray, then," suggested Sadie, ever practical. "Then perhaps you won't think about him."

"A priest must pray, I have to ask for guidance. And when I go about my daily duties, I still hear that wild laughter."

He made a gesture of appeal. "Does it not seem to you that he came and talked about a Requiem because he foresaw that some accident was going to happen to him?"

"Not at all," said Sylvester firmly. He could see that, although Sadie had little time for the vicar and his visions, she was nonetheless worried at the idea that Issur might have had an accident. "If anything had happened to Issur, we would have heard about it, or seen it in the papers. No, no, Wroot. It's probably your own conscience troubling you, because you think Issur may have had a point. I myself know several people who don't care to come to your church any more."

The Rev Wroot was on firm ground here. "My congregation has grown continually since I changed the method of worship to something more relevant and more meaningful to today's young people. Under my predecessor, there were often barely a dozen in the congregation at Eucharist."

"True," said Sadie. "But then your predecessor had other problems."

"Why not both wings?" said Sylvester flippantly. "Some services for those who want to hop about and bang tambourines, and some for those who prefer poetry and music in their services – and I mean proper music, before you say anything, not that rumpty-tum stuff you favour."

"It is what people prefer," said the Rev Wroot huffily.

"Course it is. It's the same with kids and a diet of coke, hamburgers and nasty little crunchy snacks. If they like it, why worry about them eating fruit and veg and other more demanding food? And I'll tell you why worry, because otherwise their teeth will all fall out and they'll all pop off early from degenerative diseases. You can't thrive on pap, you know. Not in food, not in music, not in education, not in religion."

"I understand that as a musician . . ."

"Exactly," said Sylvester, who didn't think there was anything to be gained from further conversation with the Rev Wroot. "Go and ask your bishop," he added. "Do him good to have a solid problem to wrestle with, idle lot, bishops."

The Rev Wroot bristled. "Bishop Jack is a very hard-working man," he began.

Sylvester gave a hoot of laughter. "Bishop Jack? Bishop *Jack*!"

"That is what he wants to be called," said the vicar stiffly. "He is a man of the people."

"Not with a mitre on his head and a crook in his hand, he isn't," said Sylvester. "Besides, as far as I know, Lennox-Smith is still the bishop, isn't he? Take it from me, it's all humbug. Besides, don't you see that if bishops are just like us, then we don't need them? Which we don't, now I come to think of it."

The Rev Wroot was following his own train of thought. "I have been to talk this over with the Bishop. I am afraid to say he took rather the view you have. He felt that if I was so worried, then I should have a Requiem mass. He offered to send his chaplain to assist, apparently he's very well up in that kind of thing."

"There you are then," said Sylvester, who was beginning to be bored by the Rev Wroot. "Problem solved."

"No, I fear not," said the clergyman sadly. "I feel sure that such a service is doomed to failure, I feel I am being warned that disruption threatens."

Sadie could see Sylvester getting visibly restless. "Don't worry about it. I'm sure the Lord will guide you," she said, trying to sound helpful. "And after all, there's no sign of Issur, I doubt if he has any intention of being in Unthrang on All Souls. More's the pity," she added under her breath.

Lily, who had considerable powers of telepathy, surged through the door, knowing that Sadie and Sylvester had had enough of their visitor. "Going?" she said to the vicar, relieving him of his glass and handing him his coat in one swift movement.

She hustled him out of the house and out of the door, and faint goodbyes and thanks could be heard as he made his way across the green.

"I bet that's taken your mind off your folly," said Sylvester to Sadie.

"Sylvester, it was so funny, and one couldn't laugh."

"No, but one can now. Let me fill your glass."

Digby was deeply asleep, emitting gentle but controlled snores. Justinia sighed, and turned over for the tenth time. She reached out for the clock. Twenty-five past three. Last time she looked, it had been ten to three.

"Trouble sleeping?" asked the voice.

"Oh, go away," said Justinia. "Why can't you leave me alone?"

"Because you won't listen."

"I have nothing to say to you."

"You don't need to have anything to say to me, you only have to listen to what I have to say."

"I want to get to sleep."

"You can't get to sleep. You've been awake for more than an hour. Why don't you get up and go downstairs and do something? That's the way to get back to sleep, you won't get to sleep lying here thinking about how grim it is to be awake at three in the morning."

Justinia pulled the covers over her head.

"That won't do any good. Go on, go downstairs."

"I don't happen to want to go downstairs."

"Afraid of the dark?"

"I am not afraid of the dark."

"You were afraid of the dark when you were little. You were almost as afraid of the dark as you were of your father."

"I was not afraid of my father. I loved my father."

"You love Digby, but he's fast asleep. He never wakes up in the early hours, does he? Of course, you could wake him up, make love with him, that would make everything all right, wouldn't it?"

"Digby hates being woken up."

"And you mustn't do anything that Digby hates, must you?"

"I wish you would shut up. I wish you would take yourself off."

"All right," said the voice with a rumbling laugh. "I will."

Thank God, thought Justinia. Perhaps it's something I'm eating. If I go to the doctor and say I'm being harassed by this voice . . . Justinia could imagine exactly what the doctor would say. Not, 'Oh, you've got a voice, too, have you? I used to have one as well, but I got rid of it by . . .'

No. The doctor would purse her or his lips, depending on which surgery she ended up in, and ask about whether she planned to start a family. Anything wrong with you must be due to being female. Puberty, then having babies or not having babies, then the menopause. After that, you were just a saggy, boring old coot, who needed to be hustled out of the surgery as quickly as possible.

Justinia turned over again. The curtain had blown open, and Justinia could see the inky darkness outside. Owls. Some animal screeching in the distance. Scuttlings. Perhaps she should turn the light on, read. But the light might wake Digby up, and then he would be angry, or reproachful; in any case, not very pleased.

She could go downstairs. That would be best. She got out of bed, quietly; she mustn't disturb Digby. She felt for her dressing gown in the darkness and wrapped it round herself. Once she got to the end of the passage and turned the corner, she could put the lights on . . .

The air in the passage felt strangely warm, the sounds from the open window were those of a hot, unEnglish climate . . . insects, an animal calling. Underfoot, her bare feet were on warm stone, not polished floors. Justinia remembered those stone floors. She was back in the Italian house, terrified after a bad dream, looking for her mother to comfort her. In a moment, there would be lights, people running and calling. And instead of her mother's arms, her angry, towering father, shouting at her, rebuking her, sending her back to bed, alone, a light forbidden.

"Not a happy memory," said the voice in her ear.

Justinia was almost glad to hear the voice; she hadn't had a voice when she was little, perhaps she could have done with one.

"Memories are funny things," the voice went on in a thoughtful way. "Here you are, a grown woman, unable to go downstairs when you're sleepless at night, all because of a shadowy memory of childhood."

The owl hooted outside. A door opened and light streamed out.

"Who is it? What's the matter?"

It was Celia. She saw Justinia, shivering, and rushed forward, in a swish of silk, to draw her into the room. "Darling, whatever's the matter? "She brushed the hair back from Justinia's forehead. "You don't still have those terrible nightmares, do you?"

"No." said Justinia, slightly surprised that her mother knew about them.

"That's one comfort, then, it used to worry your poor father and me so much."

"It didn't worry him," Justinia said. "He was angry with me. I was just remembering when I came to find you and he wouldn't let me, he sent me back to bed, alone, in the dark." Her voice tailed off in a sob.

Celia's face showed her surprise. "Justinia, what are you talking about? Your father was firm with you about ordinary, everyday things, but he would never have done a thing like that."

"I remember it, quite clearly,"

"Then it must be one of your nightmares you're remembering. It never happened. Now, let's go downstairs, and I'll make you a hot drink. Is Digby awake?"

Justinia shook her head.

"Good, he needs his sleep, he works so hard, and he'd only

worry if he thought you weren't sleeping very well. I shan't mention it to him, I'm sure it won't happen again."

"So much for your memories," said the voice.

"Whatever she says, I remember it happening."

"What about all the other days and nights? Three hundred and sixty-five days a year, say some dozen years of childhood . . . how many of them do you remember?"

"You remember what's memorable."

"Or do you make your memories up? Remember what you want to remember, an incident here mixed with what someone said there, and, hey presto, a memory to last all your life."

"I don't know what you're talking about."

"Myth-making. Let's talk about your father. Strict, wasn't he. Unkind to you, it would seem."

"I don't remember him being unkind. I never remembered what happened that night until now. Go on, suggest he was a tyrant, lamming into me, abusing me, too, no doubt. It's all very boring, and I want to go back to bed."

"I can believe he never laid a hand on you. How about with his tongue, with his disapproval? Did you have to earn his love and affection by being good, by doing what you were told." The voice paused, then moved in for the kill. "Just like you do with Digby."

I'm not going to rise to that, Justinia told herself firmly, as she took a deep breath. "That's how all children grow up into civilized human beings instead of ending up as savages." There; a cool, sensible response.

"No, it isn't. There are ways and ways of getting other people to do what you want."

"It wasn't what he wanted, it was what was right."

"Right. He was a right man, was he? Very tiring."

"Tiring is what you are," said Justinia furiously.

"There you are, dear," said Celia approvingly. "Nodding off, you're nearly asleep. Back to bed now, and I'll tell Digby to let you sleep in tomorrow."

Justinia yawned. "I'm sorry I woke you up," she said.

"You didn't, I was already awake. I often read and listen to the radio at night; no, it isn't insomnia, I don't need as much sleep as I used to. Off you go, good night, darling."

\*     \*     \*

Sadie watched Digby set off for work, after bidding an affectionate farewell to his mother-in-law. He should have married her instead of Justy, she thought uncharitably. He would have had the wonderfully feminine creature he thinks he likes, and she would have had him exactly where she wanted him. And there they are, mother and husband, busily turning the screw on Justy . . .

"She may escape," said Sylvester, coming across the green, snuffing the misty morning air.

"Pigs have wings," said Sadie.

"It's the good thing about you, Sadie, the interest you take in everyone else. I even believe you take a kindly interest in Pauline and Nigel's lives."

"Not really, nobody could, because their lives run on such smooth tracks, with never a moment of self-doubt or disillusion. Actually, I don't feel at all kindly towards Nigel this morning."

"More trouble with Charles?"

"Yes, and Nigel is such a wimp, or maybe he's secretly on Charles's side. I'm sure he thinks it would be best all round if I simply handed over the keys to the cottage and became quietly homeless. "Couldn't you live with Ursula?" he says. I ask you. Ursula would have me in a home in a flash."

"Home?"

"For disturbed and deranged females."

"Sadie, I don't think there are such places."

"Ursula would find one," said Sadie with conviction. "It's the principle of the thing, Sylvester. I am not going to give up my house without a struggle; in fact, I'm not going to give it up at all, full stop."

"That's the spirit. I must say, I'm surprised at Nigel, though. Not like a lawyer to advise a client to settle, where's the money for him in that?"

"I suppose he doesn't think he'll make much out of me whatever happens, so he's better off getting it settled, and then he can take on more lucrative work, lots of billing hours or whatever it is that solicitors do with their time."

"Find a new lawyer," suggested Sylvester. "A good one, this time."

Sadie sighed. "It would be the answer. But where? And I might end up with one even worse than Nigel. At least propinquity makes him more careful, he knows how news rattles through Unthrang, so he has to be a bit careful. If I go to another firm with a partner who doesn't live locally, he wouldn't give a damn."

"Find a woman who specializes in protecting women from their acquisitive husbands."

Sadie laughed. "Should I advertise, do you think? Anyway, I won't let myself be depressed, it's a lovely day, so I'm going to work in the garden."

"How's the folly coming along?"

"Very well; it's going to be such a des. res. that I'll be able to put visitors up in it."

"With the parrot."

"It's far too good for Jezebel."

"Offer it to Charles, then."

Piers sat up in bed, looking out of his attic window at the fells. Purple, this morning, he thought. I could go for a walk. Take my mind off Roxane. I don't feel like going into university, no tutorials or rehearsals today, one seminar, which I can cut . . . Perfect day for a walk. With Roxane; intoxicating interludes on the way on the warm grass.

He might as well get up, sitting in bed wasn't doing him any good at all. Maybe Roxane would be back sooner than she had said, what could take her so long in Eyot?

"I need to buy food," she had told him.

"There are food shops in Unthrang."

"Not Gumble's."

"Gumble's? How can you afford to buy food at Gumble's?"

"It pays to buy the best," said Roxane with a serious face. Then she gave him a wicked look out of her drooping eyes . . .

Oh, hell, thought Piers How can I concentrate on my work when I keep on thinking about her? A couple of hours solid practice, that'd do the trick.

It couldn't take all day to buy food at Gumble's. She had her charity work, she had said. What exactly was her charity work? Why was she so cagey about something she clearly took very seriously?

And what about the pool engineer? Piers felt a surge of rage. Nobody needed a pool engineer who was that beautiful. Tall, black and breathtakingly goodlooking. Was he really a pool engineer at all?

"Of course," said Roxane lazily. She had invited Piers to nip over and watch him at work if he wanted. "He loves my pool and knows all its little ways." She turned her dancing eyes on him. "Pool maintenance is crucial, you wouldn't be happy about swimming in there if all the chemicals and filters weren't exactly right, would you?"

Why did the pool engineer have to stay the night? That's what Piers wanted to know. He could hear Roxane's laughing voice.

"Piers, angel, he comes all the way from Manchester, the least I can do is put him up for the night. Then he can get in a full day's work on the pool."

And just how often did this astonishing man come to tend the pool. Twice a year might be reasonable, in Piers' opinion.

"Not nearly enough," said Roxane firmly. "Once every three weeks or so, I do assure you, it's absolutely necessary, such a lot of upkeep on a pool like mine."

And what about the rose grower, Ned? Surely Roxane couldn't need that much advice on her roses?

"It isn't only the roses, of course roses are his special thing, but he has green fingers, quite magical, and I do have a lot of garden to cope with, what with my house and Juniper House as well. I have to keep that in good order, otherwise no customers to rent it, and then where would I be?"

Piers padded downstairs to the kitchen to fix himself some breakfast. Aunt Z was nowhere to be seen, she must have gone out painting. Piers admired her for her energy; his mother had said she must be in her seventies, but Piers reckoned that eighty-something was nearer the mark.

There was a large notice on the fridge, written in his great-aunt's elegant, flowing italic script. "First one down, feed the cats. Second one down, don't feed the cats; they are liars."

Piers grinned. "You've been getting double rations," he told the two cats who were weaving themselves round his legs with insincere protestations of affection. "You've had your breakfasts, and that's it until tonight." He opened the back door, shooed one cat out and took the other out by main force. Then he rushed back in and quickly shut the door, leaving them issuing grumbles and threats on the other side. "Go and catch some mice, crunchy, chewy addition to your diet; just don't leave the tails about, very messy habit," he advised, before returning to the kitchen and seeing what food he had left in the fridge. Not much, and funds were low. Perhaps Roxane would offer him a meal of Gumble's delicacies this evening. Probably out doing more bloody charity work, he said gloomily to himself.

In Eyot, Lucius bumped into Roxane as she was walking down Leofric Street.

"Hello, Lucius, come and have lunch. I know a good pub round the corner."

Lucius was pleased. "I will, although I can't be long."

"Busy?" enquired Roxane, as they squeezed themselves round a tiny table in the courtyard, having judged it warm enough to sit outside.

"Yes. The minute I said I'd do the job, they ushered me into an office, lugged in an immense heap of paperwork and left me to it."

"Do you have a good secretary?"

Lucius was draining his glass of cold beer, which he put down with a grateful sigh. "I enjoyed that, thirsty work, sorting things out. No, I only rate part of a secretary, and my share doesn't seem to include any of the thinking or doing bits of her. I don't really want a secretary of the traditional kind, not someone who takes dictation and keeps my diary. I can write my own letters, and keep my own diary."

Roxane raised her eyebrows. "Enlightened."

"No, it's easier and quicker that way. What I need is a helper and assistant, who doesn't actually assist, but who could take on some of the things that have to be done, and get on with them. However, people like that come expensive, and I've got a very limited budget for a few hours of extra help . . . it isn't going to go far."

Roxane tucked into a plate of steaming fish pie. "Maybe Justinia would give you a hand, she's very competent."

Lucius looked thoughtful. "Does she want to work?"

"She's not exactly enjoying the idle life, it would get her out of the house, turn her thoughts away from Digby and on to something rather more useful and rational, and she'd enjoy the pocket money, no doubt."

"Isn't she an archaeologist of some kind?"

"Not at all, she worked at the British Museum, true, but exhibitions and PR and general organizing is what she mostly did. Her special field at Cambridge was Greek pots, but she realizes that there's not a lot of scope for working with Greek pots, especially not in Eyot. Besides, I think she found she enjoyed the other side of her work more. She told me she didn't have a scholar's mind. Pass the mustard, please . . ."

Lucius obediently handed over the mustard, intrigued by Roxane's suggestion.

"I could ask her, I suppose." He thought of having Justinia working in close proximity. Delightful, but would it be wise?

"There is that," agreed Roxane. "Otherwise, what about Merle?"

"Merle!" Lucius dropped his fork, and bent down to retrieve it.

"You'll need a new one," said Roxane helpfully.

Lucius returned from the food bar with a clean fork and a thoughtful expression. "Roxane," he said, "you're a shit-stirrer."

## 14

"True," said Roxane unrepentantly. "It was a good tease, though."

"Yes, I can see that." Lucius dug into his lasagne. "It's nice, this; full of spinach," he said with relish. "I love spinach, but Merle loathes it, can't even bear the smell of it cooking, so we never have it at home."

"Is Merle reconciled to the idea of living up here?"

"I wouldn't say reconciled exactly," said Lucius carefully. Merle had, in fact been in an unrelievedly bad temper ever since he had started work in Eyot. "It's a bit difficult for Andrea, but she's used to her mother's moods, so she's coping quite well."

"She shouldn't have to," said Roxane definitely. "How old is she, ten? Merle ought to snap out of it, she doesn't have to become a doting mother, but she owes the child some normal motherly interest. How's school?"

"Andrea says she's enjoying it," said Lucius, feeling he should defend Merle's very tiresome behaviour, but quite unable to do so.

"You can't defend the indefensible," Roxane pointed out. "I haven't seen Andrea at the pool recently, tell her to come over."

"I told her not to, you don't want to be bothered with a little girl."

"She isn't a bother. If she were, I wouldn't invite her. I was once ten, so I know what it's like; not a good time. I didn't have a mother at all, because mine died when I was born, so, in a way, I can sympathize with her. In any case I like her. Tough little thing, your Andrea, and plenty of brain."

Lucius was always pleased to hear his children praised, but his face darkened again as he thought of Merle shut away in her room day after day, emerging only to take long walks in the fells.

"I can't see that they do her any good; physical exercise is supposed to be an antidote to depression, but she comes back just as gloomy, if not more so."

"How's her writing going? Doesn't she write out her depression? I thought that was what writers did."

"Her writing isn't going very well at the moment," said Lucius evasively, thinking of Merle's endless diatribe against her agent and *New Living*, and all the other publications who had rejected her work.

"Touch of writer's block, perhaps," said Roxane.

"Something like that," agreed Lucius. He finished his lasagne and drank a glass of water.

"Coffee?" said Roxane.

"No, thank you, I want to get back and tackle the piles of work before they reach the ceiling. Can I get you one?"

Roxane stood up and stretched. "No, thank you. I'll have one later on. I have some things to do. Art shop, food . . . you know."

Lucius escorted Roxane as far as his office overlooking the river and bid her a cheerful goodbye.

That's one very nice man, thought Roxane, as she strolled along the bank. Why do nice men so often marry appalling women? Is it nature redressing the balance? They marry drains, who suck the life blood out of them and leave a dull husk . . . Poor Lucius.

She looked at her watch. Quarter past two. She was meeting Roddy Gumble at the shop at half past. Time for a swift reconnaissance round the shelves, then back to his flat.

Merle wasn't the only person in Unthrang who had retreated into her room. It was Genevra day at Digby's house, and she had arrived early, builders and decorators in tow. She was put out to find that Digby had changed his mind about the window in the bedroom, and was clearly disinclined to believe Justinia's explanation. The builders, who were from Eyot, soon put her right. "Nobbut a gummock'd put window there, not in Unthrang, not in t'Helm."

Genevra's expression at this advice, imparted to the accompaniment of much head nodding and grunts of assent from the other men, made Justinia want to laugh. It was clear that Genevra hadn't understood a word; Celia hastened to reassure her that it was indeed Digby's decision.

"There's an unpleasant wind that blows from the east," she explained. "Hurricane force sometimes; Digby told me all about it."

"Oh, very well, then," said Genevra, displeased. She swept on her round, Celia in approving attendance, Justinia trailing along behind. Occasionally Genevra would turn round to demand that she remove something or see to something else. Justinia said nothing, after all, Celia was hanging on Genevra's every word; it would all be related to Digby – in tedious detail, no doubt – over dinner that evening.

Genevra reached Justinia's room. It was empty except for her piano, moved with expertise by the men from Calimpal & Klimper, and her dragon table. Genevra surveyed it with disapproval.

"Are you planning to leave this room as it is? No wallcoverings? Nothing to sit on? And the floor is very rough."

Justinia stood in the doorway. "Don't worry about this room, I'm going to do it myself, and there are one or two other things of mine which I'll bring in here. I'm going to buy a rug for the floor, so you see, I shall be very comfortable."

"Rug?" said Genevra, clearly suspecting that Justinia was about to hot-foot it down to the Co-op to buy some viscose number with tasteful flowers on it.

"I might," said Justinia. "They've got some good rugs at the Co-op, I had one when I was a student."

Thankful that she was working to Digby's orders and not to those of his wife, Genevra retreated to the safety of her wall-coverings and swags. Celia lingered for a moment, worried about her daughter.

"I hope you aren't going to be difficult about this room, Justinia darling," she said. "Nothing too fanciful, too eccentric. Digby has a right to live in the kind of house he wants."

"It's my house too."

"Yes, but men like to have the last word, you must remember

that. And Digby is after all the breadwinner; whatever you choose to put in here, the money to pay for it will come from Digby, won't it? I know you put all the money you got from your father into buying this house, and I don't suppose you've got anything put by from when you were working, have you? You never were very good at saving; even as a child you always spent your pocket money as soon as you got it."

Stung, Justinia was about to round on her mother when she realized the justice of what she was saying. "When I was working, I contributed a lot to housekeeping and living expenses," she said defensively.

Yes, she thought. When I was working. Now I'm not, and whatever I want to spend has to come from Digby. Exactly like pocket money. Will he dock it for any misdemeanours like my father used to? Tell me to try harder next week, so that I can have the full amount? And remember to say thank you, pocket money is a privilege, not a right . . .

"I'm sure we can find you some pretty things for your room," her mother said in consoling tones. "Digby won't grudge the money, he's doing very well, he tells me. Now come along, we must catch up with Genevra, marvellous designer, such original ideas."

"I've got a few things to do," lied Justinia. "You carry on."

"I don't like to see you sulking, Justinia, not at your age. Digby's quite right to want the house done properly. After all, when the time comes to sell, it must present the right appearance to attract a good buyer."

"Sell? We've only just moved here. I don't want to sell it!"

"Not immediately, of course, but Digby was telling me that if all goes according to plan with his business, he'll be able to afford a bigger house in a year or so."

The nerve, Justinia said to herself as she stood silently waiting for her mother to take herself off. They had bought this house together, planning, so she had thought, to live in it for years and years. She had never seen it simply as a stepping stone to higher things. If you liked a house, the way she liked this one, then why feel you had to move?

"Aha," the voice crooned irritatingly in her ear. "Are you really surprised? Isn't that a little naive of you? You noticed how Digby drooled over the Manor when you first came to Unthrang, didn't you? He won't be content until he has a house like that."

"Houses are joint. You both decide. Digby's not like that. He won't make me move if I like it here."

"Oh no? Who lives will see, that's what Lily would say. Digby will do what suits him, and then persuade you that it's all for your benefit. Did you decide to move north? Did you want to give up work? Of course not, but that's what happened."

Justinia didn't even have the energy to tell the voice to go away. It came and went as it pleased; she would have to see somebody about it, she couldn't go on like this.

"If you want to be left in peace, just do what I say," said the voice cheerfully.

"And what do you say?"

"Go to London, after the next choir rehearsal. Lydia's got a flat in London, hasn't she? Ask if you can go there for a few days. Get away, find a new perspective, look at life outside the bars before you come flapping back to your perch inside your elegantly decorated cage . . ."

"Oh, bugger off," shouted Justinia.

"Justinia!"

Her mother was back. "Justinia, not that kind of language, if you please. With the builders in the house, whatever will they think?"

"I don't give a . . . What do you want, mother?"

"Genevra has a question about the drawing room. If you'd come and look, we can discuss it."

"Sorry, I've got to go out, you talk it over with her, I'm sure Digby will be delighted with whatever you decide. Or ring him up, his number's by the phone."

Justinia fled.

Piers waved to her as she ran across the green. "Hey, Justy! Come over, we need help."

Startled, Justinia slowed to a halt and looked around; who was calling her? Then she saw Piers' fair head leaning out of an upper window. She waved back to him. "Why?"

"Come to the back door," shouted Piers.

Justinia set a new course towards the Manor and went round to the back.

Piers came downstairs to let her in. "Hi," he said. "We need some expert advice." He led her through the small modern kitchen into the vast, original kitchen, with its stone-flagged floor and stone-arched windows.

Justinia hadn't been inside the Manor before, and she blinked at the size of the fireplace. "You could roast a bison in there," she observed.

"They probably did," said Piers. "One of the locals told me that the previous owner actually used this kitchen, and she used to light the fire by putting logs on it, pouring paraffin over them, and then standing back to throw lighted matches at the fire until it burst into flames."

"With a huge whoosh, I should think," said Justinia, impressed. "Who did your great-aunt buy the house from? Had they lived here long?"

"The biddy who lived here, the flame-thrower, was the last of her line; her family had been here for generations. Ancient enemies of the Mountjoys, one gathers. When she died, she left everything to some animal charity, and the house came on the market when Aunt Zeph was looking for somewhere big enough to house her collection of pics."

Piers dragged open the heavy oak door that led from the kitchen to the rest of the house, and stood back to let Justinia through. He gave the door a push to close it, and it swung to with a heavy groan.

"She was the youngest of several brothers and sisters, none of whom married. They were keen on animals, hence the charity, although I think they were choosy about which animals were to to be fed and watered and looked after, like dogs and horses, and which had been put on this earth for them to shoot or drag about on the end of a fishing line. One gets the impression that a day not spent in pursuit of some creature was a day wasted."

"They must have been very rich," said Justinia. Various of her Mountjoy relations had the same viewpoint of creation, and she knew how single-minded such people were, and how there was no time in such a busy life of slaughter to do anything so prosaic as earning a living.

"Hugely so, although I expect the war watered it all down a bit. They certainly let the house go to rack and ruin, Aunt Z did a lot to it when she came here. Not your interior designer approach, I hasten to add; more stonework and gutters and getting the light right for her works of art."

"Where did her money come from?" said Justinia curiously, as they made their way along a wide passage, hung with some fine pencil sketches.

"I'm not sure," said Piers. "She's my dad's aunt, but he's dead, and I never got round to asking him. My mum is a bit vague, says she made it abroad, or married a rich foreigner. She says she thinks Aunt Z was on the stage; perhaps it all came from rich admirers."

Justinia stopped in front of a particularly pleasing sketch of a river with wooded banks rising steeply from a rocky base, with a castle perched near the top. "Isn't this the Rhine?" she asked.

Piers had a closer look. "Could be," he agreed. "I'll ask her, if you like."

"These aren't done by her, are they?"

"Good lord, no," said Piers. "Hers are happy splodges, attractive, but hardly great art. I don't belittle her, they aren't at all bad, and how many great-aunts are out relishing life enough to paint the way she does? Hope I'm like that when I get to her age."

"You'll be incredibly rich by then, remember."

"Mock not, I shall be incredibly rich long before I get within sight of my dotage. Make it while you can enjoy it, that's my aim."

They had arrived at a set of double doors of a dark and richly polished wood. Piers turned one of the large brass handles. "In here," he said.

Justinia stood at the threshold of a fine-sized room, which had obviously been built as a ballroom. Floor length windows with deep casements and folded back shutters ran along one side of the room; on the other side, where delicate chairs must once have been placed beneath candle sconces for weary dancers, the walls were now covered with paintings.

There were two people in the room. The girl, who looked about fourteen but who must, Justinia realized, be a university friend of Piers's and therefore at least eighteen or so, gave Justinia a beaming smile. "Hello," she said. "I'm Pansy, I sing in Simon's choir, I saw you there last week."

"Of course," said Justinia, smiling back.

"This is Marius," said Pansy. "Smile, Marius."

Marius cast a glowering glance in Justinia's direction. "Pay no attention to him," said Pansy brightly. "He mostly smoulders, but he's quite good company really, aren't you my precious?"

My precious turned intense and glowing eyes on Pansy, who took it all as her due. "Did Piers tell you we need your help?" she asked Justinia.

Justinia had been looking at the pictures, and came to with a start.

"Sorry?" she said.

"Takes a little time to adjust, doesn't it?" said Piers. "Impressionists by the yard. Lesser known artists, but still quite something. I have to say, before you condemn Auntie Zeph as a foul capitalist, that she did acquire most of these a long time ago, when they weren't at all fashionable. She collected them, so she tells me, because she liked them."

"Who wouldn't?" said Justinia, walking slowly along the wall of pictures, awed. "Piers, are they safe here?"

"Probably not," said Piers cheerfully. "I think that's why she let me come and lodge, because she's not a sociable person. A tough young man on the prems makes her feel safer, although I don't think I'd be much use against a gang of burglars. It's not so bad, though; Unthrang is a very nosy place, as you may have noticed, and anyone arriving, day or night, with a large van to carry away her pics would be immediately noticed. She has alarms, too."

"Think of the insurance," said Marius unexpectedly.

"She isn't insured," said Piers. "Not worth it, she told me, because money wouldn't buy the pictures back if she lost them, and each picture has memories which you can't put a value on. Besides, she thinks insurance companies all have direct lines to professional burglars."

"She could be right," said Marius, becoming quite human. "My dad's in the police, and he reckons some of these insurance firms are real leaky buckets."

"Marius," cried Pansy, impressed. "I never knew your dad was in the police."

"It isn't the sort of thing you go on about," said Marius, reverting to his glowering mode.

"No, it doesn't go with the brooding poet look, does it?" said Piers.

"Are you a poet?" said Justinia.

Pansy squealed with laughter. "No, he isn't. He's a chemist, aren't you, precious? He plays the horn as well; he's in the university orchestra, that's how we met."

"What do you play?" Justinia asked her.

"The clarinet and the piano." Piers took control of the proceedings. "That's why we wanted you, Justy, we need another pair of ears. Pansy's done a pianotuning course, and there's this piano in here, untuned, which we need to use. Only Pansy's forgotten her tuning fork, and of course, we need an A."

Justinia laughed. "Sylvester must have a tuning fork."

Piers shook his head. "Out," he said succinctly. "Lily, too. Just when you need them here, very thoughtless."

"What about Pauline?"

"No way," said Piers with feeling. "She'd be over here, telling us she knows an A by instinct."

"Has she got perfect pitch?" asked Pansy.

"I don't know; I doubt it, but I don't want her here in any case, and I don't think Aunt Z would like it much, either. She and nauseating Nigel have been angling to get asked here ever since they moved to Unthrang, so old Zeph says; she doesn't fancy them, and I quite agree."

"I don't have perfect pitch," said Justinia. "And I'm not a musician, either, so I don't think I can be much use to you."

"You've got a magical voice," said Pansy. "You should be a musician, it's a terrible shame to let it go to waste. I mean, a choir in Eyot is all very well, and Simon's good, and of course working with Valliaze is going to be heaven, but you should be in London, abroad; recitals, recording . . ."

"Opera," put in Piers. "You're embarrassing her, Pansy, shut up. What I suggest is, we form a committee to decide on an A. Then Pansy can tune the piano to that."

This seemed a doubtful enterprise to Justinia, but the merry enthusiasm of others was infectious. They hummed and tried all kinds of variants, arguing and criticizing each other's opinions, until they finally took a unanimous vote on the most promising note.

"A," sang Piers, as Pansy got to work.

"We were quite wrong," he told Justinia later. "We were creeping up towards a B flat, hopelessly out. It was because we were going for a bright sound, fatal, because you're bound to end up sharp. Marius had a terrible time with his horn, and not much sound work got done; however, a good time was had by all, so who am I to complain? I've given in and had it properly tuned now. Pansy will probably never forgive me, and Marius will challenge me to a duel, but never mind."

I wish I were eighteen again, Justinia thought, as she walked moodily along the bank of the Eyot. The beck which ran through Unthrang debouched into the Eyot, and it was a favourite walk of Justinia's to follow the beck to the Eyot and then to walk along the shady banks of the wide and presently sluggish river. The Eyot meandered from there towards the city, and Justinia loved the moment when you came round a gentle bend in the river and could see the distant spires of the Cathedral.

I'd like a boat, she thought idly, watching the water swirling round a fallen branch. It wouldn't cost a lot. Then she pulled herself up short. More than I can afford, she reminded herself. Everything I want, I have to ask Digby for; what a dreadful thought.

As Justinia walked, her feet rustling up the brown leaves strewn across the river path, she remembered walking as a child in Italy, the warmth in the air, the dark green of the cypresses against the reds and browns of the autumn landscapes. The warm chatter as she walked along streets; people relaxed and lively, how different from English northerners. She could see the door that led to her singing teacher's apartment. It was a tall, ancient door, with a mouldering coat of arms in stone above the lintel. It was never locked; one push and you were into the courtyard, with a fountain plashing idly in the centre. Then scrunch, crunch on the gravel and up the stairs to Number 5.

Justinia could hear her teacher's voice. "Breathing. It's all in the breath. Breath is life, and when you draw breath, you draw in life. Then you breathe that life into the music, it isn't just a technical matter of having enough breath to float a note, to sustain a phrase, it's more than that. It's the spirit of the music you have to convey, you have to understand the soul of the music. Then the audience can understand it, too; then you have given the composer his due and communicated. Now, with the diaphragm, again . . ."

I was so happy then, thought Justinia. I could truly have said then, if anyone had asked me, that there was nowhere I would rather be, nothing in the whole world I would rather be doing, than singing. I enjoyed Cambridge, I found it all interesting, but there was never a single second when I was lifted out of myself the way I used to be in my singing lessons.

Back in the here-and-now of the English countryside, an evil mist was beginning to creep up from the surface of the river, a dank chill stealing the warmth from the day. What have I done? thought Justinia. I've lost that, I won't ever feel like that again. Tears wetted her cheeks; self-pity, she thought irritably, brushing them off. You got yourself here. You chose, you made all the decisions. I listened to my mother, it's very difficult not to listen to your mother. Lots of people take advice from their mothers and are glad they did, because in the long run it works out all right.

"Perhaps those mothers have their daughters' best interests at heart."

"Oh, you again," said Justinia dispiritedly. "I wondered why you weren't bending my ear."

"You were doing very well on your own," said the voice in a kindly tone. "I think you should find out why your mother didn't want you to be a singer. She was very vehement about it, wasn't she? Very set against it. Why did it worry her so much? She always supposed you'd get married, and that would be your career, she didn't really imagine you'd have to earn a living for yourself all your life."

This hadn't occurred to Justinia before, but now it had, it was strange. The way her mother had spoken, you would have thought that she was a son with a wife and children to support, who had been planning to throw up a sound career to do something really feckless . . . which was hardly the case. People who studied music didn't, by and large, end up homeless and penniless; why the panic?

\*　　\*　　\*

Sylvester watched Justinia as she walked slowly down the cobbled street from the market place and across the green to her house. He shook his head.

"I don't like to see Justy looking like this," he said to Lily, who was tidying the room.

She seized a cushion, pummelled it, gave the tassels a good shake and put it back on the sofa. "She's losing weight," she observed. "She isn't happy."

"I hadn't realized how oppressive Celia was," said Sylvester, as Lily briskly shooed him to the other side of the room. "I don't understand at all why Hugo was so devoted to her; I can't imagine a more unsuitable wife for a Mountjoy."

"She's a witch," said Lily darkly. "Look how she has Digby eating out of her hand."

"I don't know anything about her," went on Sylvester. "She doesn't look English, not with those eyes and her languor, although of course that's totally deceptive, she's a very power-ful woman. None of the Mountjoys know much about her either. I bumped into Virginia in London, we had a drink, I asked her about Celia. Says her parents were very dull, correct people. Very middle class, and boot-faced, she can't think where Celia got her looks from. Must be a throw-back, she says, because Celia was stunning when she was younger."

"Goes without saying," Lily said disapprovingly. "The Mountjoys always go for exceptionally attractive women. And men."

"She reminds me of someone," said Sylvester. "Can't place it; not anyone I know, it's a photo I've seen, or a painting . . . from the 1920s. Unlikely; Virginia says her parents were unknown and unmemorable – and not very happy about their daughter marrying Hugo, because of his reputation . . . Celia wouldn't have it, said he would reform, and the fact that his brother had a title carried the day."

"Italian," said Lily in a decisive voice. "Celia has Italian blood, you can tell from the colouring, the eyes, hair . . . And that's why she likes living in Italy."

"You could very well be right," said Sylvester. "Think about Justy's voice; it could easily have come from an Italian ancestor.

Interesting." He plucked his cello case out of Lily's way. "Unfortunately, we'll never find out, because Celia never talks about her family."

"How do you know?"

"Justy told me. Digby's often tried to find out, you know how inquisitive he is about people, but Celia simply says that her parents are dead and changes the subject. Justy doesn't remember them at all, so it's no good asking her."

"Asking who?" said Sadie, popping her head round the door. "Oh, sorry, Lily," she said, as Lily advanced with duster in hand.

"Take Sylvester away," said Lily. "I can't be doing with him in here when I'm trying to get things straight."

"Come on, Sadie," said Sylvester. "I'll take you to the Cow and Prisoner for a change."

"Low-calorie beer," Lily called after him.

## 15

"Camel's piss, that low-calorie beer," said Sylvester a few minutes later as he ordered himself a pint of his favourite brew. He handed Sadie her drink and looked around with a pleased expression. "I miss the Midwinter Arms, but I have to admit it's more comfortable here."

"There's Lucius," said Sadie as they moved away from the bar.

"And young Andrea," said Sylvester. "Good, more the merrier. May we join you, Lucius? How are the arts? Hello, Andrea, why aren't you tucked up in bed?"

Andrea liked Sylvester. "Don't be silly, it isn't my bedtime for ages yet. I was cooking supper, but I burnt it, so Dad's buying me supper here. We're taking some back for Mum. She didn't want to come, she never does."

"What are you having?" said Sylvester, looking at her plate.

"Macaroni cheese," said Andrea. "It's got bacon bits in it, and it's very cheesy."

"Smells good," said Sylvester. "Eat up, you need your victuals, you're a growing girl. Lucius, can I get you a drink?"

Sadie helped herself to peanuts. "What are you having to eat tonight?" enquired Sylvester, as he loomed over them with Lucius's drink in his hand.

"I hadn't thought," admitted Sadie. "I'll find something, I'm not very hungry these days."

"Do you like macaroni cheese?"

"Yes, but . . ."

Sylvester headed back to the bar.

"They'll bring it over," he said, easing himself on to a bench seat. "You must look after yourself, Sadie, can't let yourself go, fatal when you get to our age."

Sadie laughed. "That's generous of you, Sylvester, you won't hit fifty for a while yet."

"That's not the point. Any news from Issur?"

"No."

"When's he coming back?" asked Andrea, looking up from her supper. "We liked him, Ben and me."

"He isn't coming back," said Sadie sadly. "He has to work, you see."

"Oh, but he is," said Andrea. "He told me he was."

The three adults stared at her.

"When?" said Sylvester, taking on the role of chief interrogator. "When did he tell you he was coming back?"

"Oh, before he left," said Andrea vaguely. "He said he had to go away for a bit, but he'd be back. He's going to teach me how to do proper back arches; I can't do them, I always collapse."

"Hmm," said Sylvester. "Lucius, is Andrea . . .?"

"Truthful?" supplied Lucius. "Generally, yes. Andrea, you aren't inventing this, are you?"

"Why should I? If you don't believe me, ask Ben when he rings up at the weekend. I don't know why you shouldn't believe me, though," she went on, becoming aggrieved, "it's very rude not to believe people, you don't go round not believing what *you* say to each other, do you?"

Sylvester assured her that they weren't doubting her. "It's just that perhaps you didn't get what he was saying right."

"I'm not that stupid." Andrea's voice was scornful. "He'll be back by All Souls, that's what he said. 'In time for All Souls' were his actual words, if you want to know. He said he'd be needed."

"How strange," said Sylvester. "Sadie . . ."

"Yes, I'm thinking what you're thinking," said Sadie. "The Rev Wroot and his obsession with Issur and All Souls."

"This is becoming interesting," said Sylvester with enthusiasm. "I wonder what he's up to. Why should we need him?"

Sadie's food arrived, and was placed in front of her. She smiled at Sylvester. "Thank you. I don't know why, but I'm suddenly very hungry."

\*    \*    .\*

Digby was in top form as he ate the delicious meal Celia had cooked; it was a mystery to him why Justinia had never been interested in cooking; she could have learned so much from Celia. Still, she had time on her hands now; there must be courses in Eyot.

Digby had arrived home too late to catch Genevra, rather to his disappointment. She had left early to get back to London, would be in constant touch with all the workmen, would come up at least twice a week.

"She could stay here," he said, his mouth full of chicken in a fragrant lemon and rosemary sauce.

"No," said Justinia, who was pushing her food around her plate. It wasn't that she didn't like it, it was only that she didn't feel very hungry, she told her mother when Celia demanded to know why she wasn't eating properly.

Digby and Celia both looked at Justinia with interest.

"No," she said. "I'm not pregnant, I'm simply not hungry, finish, end of story. And no, Genevra's not staying here. I have to put up with her during the day, with her silly laugh and strange vowels and fatuous ideas; twenty-four hours a day is more than I could stand."

"That's a very selfish attitude," said Digby, frowning.

"She'll have included huge expenses in her fee for staying overnight in Eyot if she needs to, plus lots more for catching early trains and so forth, and that won't be taken off if you put her up here; she can jolly well fend for herself," said Justinia.

Celia caught Digby's eye, and he shrugged his shoulders and helped himself to more chicken. Celia would make Justinia see reason, why was she being so difficult and argumentative all the time?

With practised ease, Celia turned the conversation to Digby, a favourite subject of his. Yes, things were going very well with the business, nice for someone to take an interest – this with a hurt look at Justinia – the culture side was doing particularly well.

"Of course, they don't spend per capita the way businessmen do, but they're large groups; good numbers in orchestras and choirs. Fills the hotels up, you see, they take the beds. Then I get a good reduction for the individual business travellers I send to those same hotels, so we make an excellent extra profit there. Symbiosis, I call it. Another five years of this, then I shall float the company, and Justinia and I can take off for wherever we want."

"I'm happy here, thank you," said Justinia untruthfully. She wasn't happy here at all, but she wasn't stupid enough to think she'd be happier on a Caribbean island or wherever Digby thought would be a good spot to spend large amounts of money.

"Besides, you'd be bored without work to do," she told him. "You might take a few months off, but after that you'd get restless and start looking round for something else to do."

Digby laughed, and reached across the table to take Justinia's hand. "You're quite right, how well you know me." He released her hand, giving it an affectionate pat, and leant back in his chair. "In fact, I'm looking into the possibility of developing another side to the business, sponsorship, you know. Of musical tours. There could be a niche there for you, Justinia, after all, you know about music."

Not your sort of music, I don't, thought Justinia.

Charming, thought Celia, thinking yet again what a good husband Digby was for Justinia. If only she would settle down, start a family, become more absorbed in the daily round of life. Celia had seen a look in Justinia's eyes once or twice recently which had alarmed her. It was a withdrawn, self-sufficient look which belonged to her younger days. It boded plotting and planning, and a wild, fiery temper pitted against those who knew better, and only had her best interests at heart. Her parents when she was younger. Her husband now.

"You should have a five-year plan," she told her daughter. "A life-plan. There was a piece about life-plans in the *Mail* this morning."

Digby was scornful. "Her life-plan would be the same as mine, Celia."

Justinia pushed her chair back from the table and rose to carry the plates across to the sink.

"Not unless your life-plan includes a good deal of singing," she said casually, saving scraps and bones on a plate for the Manor cats.

"Singing?" said Digby. "A life-plan isn't about hobbies, Justinia. It's goal-setting, not indulging whims."

"Singing would be a whim for you," Justinia agreed, setting a frothy creation of chocolate and cream on the table. "It isn't a whim for me."

Celia took Justinia to task as they loaded the plates into the dishwasher and made coffee.

"You mustn't think too much about your singing, Justinia darling, that's all behind you now. You made your decision, and it was the right one. You're qualified, in a good profession, and you've a good marriage, with everything to look forward to. Don't spoil it by taking yourself too seriously. I've heard you practising a lot, and you're doing those breathing exercises again, aren't you?"

Justinia gave the glasses a quick swirl under the tap before tucking them in on the rack.

"Won't you think again about this choir? You'll be off again tomorrow evening, not back until late, and Digby hates it so. He's miserable when you aren't here."

Justinia shut the dishwasher door with a defiant thud. "He's not back until late on at least three evenings a week. I have just one evening out, I don't go to the Monday choir rehearsals, although Simon Praetorius asked me to."

"But that's exactly why you should be here on Wednesdays, if you're out, that makes four evenings a week which you don't spend together. Darling, you must see that that isn't fair on Digby."

"Don't nag," said Justinia, pressing the switch on the coffee grinder to fill the kitchen with an angry roar. "If Digby doesn't like us not being together for four evenings a week, then he can give up his squash or those ridiculous masons."

"These things are important to a man," said Celia. "You don't have to stay in every evening, no-one would expect that. You could join a class on one of the evenings when Digby isn't here, have you considered that? Cooking, for example."

In the early hours of the morning, the dark silence of Unthrang was broken by the roar of a motorbike. It drew up outside

Sadie's house, throbbing loudly. All over the green, lights went on; windows were thrown up; heads appeared.

"I hear a lean, mean machine," said Sylvester, resplendent in an enormous silk dressing gown, as he made his way downstairs. Lily stood at the top of the stairs, a small, trim figure, full of energy even at two in the morning.

"No need to go putting your nose out into the cold," she said with scorn. "We all know who that is."

In the vicarage, the Rev Wroot, who slept in a room away from the green, stirred in his sleep. The noise broke into his dream as the wrath of God, chastising His servant Luther Wroot for straying from the paths of righteousness. He whimpered and turned over, foolishly imagining that if he lay on his other side, the wrath of God would pass him by.

Merle was woken from a deep sleep by the roars and splutters from the bike, although if questioned, she would have said she was awake in any case. She suffered, so she claimed, from perpetual insomnia. Lucius and Andrea, both tired after their respective busy days, slept on undisturbed.

Piers uncurled himself from Roxane's naked and sleeping form, dragged the bedcover off the bed to wrap round himself and set off down the lane towards the green. He couldn't risk missing anything exciting; in his view, every lively moment at Unthrang had to be treasured, since they were few and far between.

Digby disapproved deeply. "It's that dancer, what an exhibitionist the man is," he said, getting back into bed beside Justinia.

"What?" said Justinia, sleepily reaching out for Digby. "Oh, good, Sadie will be pleased." Digby rolled away from her, drew the covers back over himself and returned to the serene slumbers of a man who knows he is on the right track.

Village louts, Celia said to herself, yawning and retrieving her novel, which had fallen to the floor an hour or so earlier.

"Issur!" cried Sadie, opening the door to him. His eyes swept up and down her rather bedraggled dressing gown, and he made a tch-tch noise as he looked at her untidy and uneven grey hair.

"Here are my things," he said, darting back to his bike, which had bulging panniers as well as further bumpy bags piled up behind the seat. Issur deftly pulled at straps, and carried an armful into the hall. He was unloaded in what seemed like seconds to Sadie; then he was off, to put his Harley Davidson into the garage. "Otherwise peasants might come to look, and spoil my chrome," he explained, shutting the front door behind him. "Back to bed, Sadie, you need to sleep, we are going to have to do something about you."

"Do you want something to eat? Or drink? Where have you been? Why have you arrived so suddenly? Why didn't you let us know where you were?"

Issur ignored all her questions, merely sweeping one of his elegant bows, and then he was off upstairs to his old room. Five minutes later, after a swift visit to the bathroom, clatter, clink, as he arranged his things on the shelf, a watchful Sadie saw the light in his room go out.

"He's come back," she said to herself, awed. And, with a feeling of intense relief and happiness, she turned her own light out, and once again the green returned to to its normal tranquillity, only the owl in Justinia's garden breaking the night's stillness.

"Andrea!"

Lucius opened the door to the kitchen, no-one there. He went back to the hall, and called her again, not too loudly, as he didn't want to wake Merle. The front door burst open, and Andrea came in, her eyes bright and her cheeks pink.

"Where have you been?" began Lucius.

"Issur's back," panted Andrea. "He's on the green, doing his exercises." She gave a pleased wriggle as Lucius handed her a jacket.

"Is he?" he said. "When did he get here? It must have been late."

"Two in the morning," said Andrea, eyes round. "Whoosh, on his motorbike. Peter's just told me. I didn't wake up, which is a pity."

"Nor did I," said Lucius. "Come on, or you'll be late and so will I."

Lucius liked to walk the few hundred yards with Andrea to her school. One morning when he had been later leaving than usual, he had watched her going off, carefully letting herself out, no-one to say goodbye to, and he had felt a surge of surprising fury against Merle, depressed and late-sleeping upstairs. He had remonstrated with her, only to be told coldly that he had known she wouldn't have much time for the children, and if he was that worried about Andrea, then why didn't he go with her to school?

"I will," he had retorted, and he had kept his word. It meant he arrived at his office in Eyot later than he would have liked, but it was worth it to be hugged by Andrea before she ran into the playground to join her friends.

"How about a swim this evening?" he suggested, as he said goodbye at the school gates.

"In Roxane's pool?"

"Yes, she asked me why you hadn't been for a while."

"You said I wasn't to make myself a nuisance," Andrea pointed out, pleased that Roxane had asked. "With you? Will you come too?"

"I'm not much of a swimmer, as you know . . . all right, yes, we'll both go."

As he drove to Eyot he wondered for the umpteenth time what he could do to help Merle. Her agent wouldn't speak to her any more, she could only get through to the switchboard at the agency, to be told, day after day, that Gail Ugton was in a meeting, or out of the office, yes, she would make sure she got a message, and she would ring back later . . . only she never did. Olivia at *New Living* made no pretence; her secretary told Merle straight out that she couldn't speak to Olivia, not today, tomorrow or any other day.

Merle thrashed around all day, starting pieces, binning them, sending letters to old contacts, reworking old pieces that might have a new market. The few acceptances she had had for short pieces were no compensation for the work that had been rejected, and she suspected that they had only been taken because friends felt they owed her. That wouldn't last, and Merle hadn't given enough favours in her time to have many to call in.

Lucius felt profoundly sorry for her, because he understood how hard it was for a successful person suddenly to have the centre of her life taken away from her, and he was well aware that a loyal husband and two rather nice children were no compensation, in her view, for the lost work. He had suggested that she strike out in a new direction, try her hand at biography, perhaps, which she had always said she would like to do, or do some research in a new field. He got his head well and truly bitten off for his pains, and had retreated hastily to the safety of his own work, which was daily becoming more demanding and interesting.

"I'm sorry," he had said to Andrea. "It's hard on you, Mummy not feeling too good."

Andrea looked at him with the clear eyes of childhood. "She gets herself into a state, and then she doesn't know how to get out of it," she said gravely. "A friend of mine, her mum's depressed, and she takes pills to make her happy again, but I don't think pills would work for Mummy."

"No, I don't think they would," Lucius agreed sadly. "Never mind, we'll manage."

They did, although Lucius found it hard to have to come home in time to be able to give Andrea a hand with her homework, and perhaps to have a game before she went to bed. He was well aware that Andrea came home by herself; Merle never fetched her. She let herself in, made herself something to eat, or perhaps went out again to see a friend. Lucius didn't like not knowing where she was. Unthrang was as safe as anywhere was these days, but even so . . .

Pauline had offered to look after her, but that would have meant Andrea spending hours in the car every day, going in to fetch the boys from the Cathedral, very boring for her, Lucius thought.

With her usual tact, Pauline had given Lucius the name of a very good man, a psychiatrist. "Expensive, of course, because he only sees patients privately, but he's worth it."

Merle doesn't need a psychiatrist, Lucius said to himself, as he slid into the car park near the station. She isn't ill, only disoriented, she'll get going again soon.

Issur resumed his normal routine. He did his morning class in the bathroom and took a vigorous shower. Then he bounded down the stairs and into the kitchen, where Sadie was eating a bowl of cereal. "No," he cried, whipping it away from her. "This is not suitable food for you. There must be some changes here, and we start by throwing this pig food away."

He flung the contents of the bowl into the bin and opened the fridge. "There is practically nothing here, we must go shopping."

"I was going to go along to the shops this morning," said Sadie weakly. "Why did you take my muesli away? It's very wholesome."

"No, all this heavy starch is not at all good for you. You should eat fruit at breakfast, with a little yoghurt, which we will make ourselves, look, you have a yoghurt-maker."

"That's Ursula's. My daughter," she added, seeing Issur's blank expression.

"As long as it works, it is no matter to whom it belongs. It must be clean, of course, everything must be clean. And we can't do proper shopping here in the village, we need more than we can buy here."

"Town."

"Town?"

"Unthrang is a town, not a village."

"Small town, village, what's the difference? Now, clothes, these clothes will not do. I can't be seen with someone wearing such clothes. Quick, upstairs, we look in the cupboards."

Sadie protested in vain; she was borne inexorably upstairs, where Issur attacked drawers and wardrobes with enthusiasm. He flung armfuls of clothes over the banisters. "What a horrible colour; what is this for? And this? Is this to clothe an elephant in the circus, perhaps? Away with it!"

"Issur," said Sadie, hanging over the landing rail and looking at the heap of clothes beneath. "It'll take me hours to put all these back!"

"Put them back?" said Issur, amazed. "You do not put them back, that would be silly, they are out, they go to the rubbish. At once, immediately."

"The bin men don't come until next week now . . . Issur, one can't just throw clothes away, some of them have hardly been worn at all."

"And I can see why they have hardly been worn, it would make you ill to wear such things."

"You may have a point," conceded Sadie, looking at a strange grey and pink number she vaguely remembered buying for a foreign holiday. "I did try to have a clear-out a few days ago, actually, I thought I ought to smarten myself up a bit."

Issur paused and looked at her. Then he shook his head. "This is smartened up?"

"I did try. It got a bit depressing after a while, so I mostly just put things back."

"And now we have to remove them all again, this is not efficient," said Issur severely. "Also, I do not think smarten up is what you have done."

"What's the point of trying to be smart when there's no-one to appreciate it?" said Sadie.

"Yes, well, now there is someone to appreciate it, but I cannot do much appreciating when you look like this." He dived into a pile he had put to one side. "Among these I think we find something, yes . . ."

"These are Charles's things," said Sadie, shocked.

"So? Did he have a disease which you will catch from his clothes? No? Then put them on, please."

Issur bundled Sadie into her room, and stood guard until she came out, looking, she had to admit, much better dressed in a shirt of Charles's, with one of his scarves and a pair of her own long-forgotten trousers.

Issur regarded her critically. "This will do, for the moment. But never tie a scarf like that." He untied it, and with a quick twist and flick, transformed it into something altogether more dashing.

"I'll be cold like this," said Sadie doubtfully.

"Wear a jacket, then."

"I've got a cardi."

Issur stared at the shapeless woollen cardigan which she dragged on over her shirt.

"Cardi? This is truly horrible. Take it off, and you are never to wear such a thing again. A big jersey, this one, yes, if you must wear something."

"Where are we going?" asked Sadie.

"I told you, to the nearest big town."

"Eyot, then. Oh, but we can't go anywhere," said Sadie,

suddenly remembering that she was carless. "Digby very kindly leant me a car, but it's had to go in for a service."

Issur made an expressive gesture with his hands. "So?" he said. "I wasn't thinking to go in your car. We go on my bike, I much prefer to go by bike. I have a spare helmet, and we get there very quickly."

If at all, thought Sadie, hanging grimly on to Issur's leather back as he played bending races with the cars on the road. She shut her eyes and hoped her children would at least give her a decent funeral.

"Here we are," said Issur with pride. "In no time, just as I said. This is Eyot? Very well, where is the smartest part of the town?"

"City."

"City?"

"It's a city. A big town with a cathedral."

"City, then. If there is a cathedral, that is good, because after we have done everything, we go and I light a candle. For my dead father, you understand."

"Issur, why have we come to Eyot?"

Issur gave a laugh, deep in his throat; it was an infectious laugh, but not a safe one. "We come for a transformation scene, like in a pantomime. Off we go."

Pointless, Justinia said to herself. Nobody could practise with this noise going on.

The workmen's bangings and sawings provided a thorough-bass to the whistling which accompanied a stream of happy tunes emerging from a dilapidated but surprisingly powerful little radio, set up on democratic principles on a window sill to spread the sound to all quarters of the house.

Sylvester, who normally wouldn't stop his morning practice for anyone, bent his rules when he saw Justinia coming across the green.

"Noisy?" said Lily, relieving her of a large mac.

"Ghastly," said Justinia. "And all to no purpose, as far as I'm concerned."

"You'll have to move while it's going on, like I have; only thing to do," said Sylvester. "Come in here, sit down . . ."

"No, you're working," said Justinia. "I'll park myself in the kitchen and talk to Lily, as long as you've got some genuine, caffeine-stuffed coffee, because we've none at all at home."

Sylvester's brows rose. "Run out of coffee? Dreadful; Lily, we must have lots to spare."

"It isn't exactly that we've run out, rather that *I've* run out, because Digby doesn't approve of coffee, and he makes us all drink decaf."

"I'd forgotten, how depressing for you."

"I'll bring the coffee in here," said Lily, giving Justinia a gentle push into Sylvester's room.

"How long are the workmen in for?" asked Sylvester, joining Justinia as she stood by the window.

"Weeks," said Justinia gloomily. "It's the whole house, top to bottom, except for my room, although I'm sure that when he's done all the rest, Digby won't be able to keep his hands off it."

"You can't have that, must have a place of your own," said Sylvester. With a husband like Digby, you'd go mad otherwise, he just restrained himself from adding.

"Digby's decided to re-do the kitchen, so that'll give me a reprieve. After that it'll have to be a huge sign saying 'non plus ultra' and the barricades up to keep Genevra and her hordes out."

Lily brought the coffee in. "Black for you," she said severely to Sylvester. "And the Danish pastry is for Justinia, she needs feeding up."

"I couldn't sit in front of Sylvester and eat a Danish pastry all by myself," said Justinia, laughing at the dark and lugubrious expression on Sylvester's face.

"And it's no good looking like that," Lily told Sylvester. "You ate an enormous breakfast, you couldn't fit anything more in, even if I let you, which I won't. I don't suppose you've had anything at all to eat today, have you?" she went on, turning to Justinia. "No, I thought not, and you won't be eating it by yourself, because I'm going to have one as well."

Sylvester gave in with a good grace, and sat down with a large black coffee. Justinia nibbled at her pastry until she saw Lily's sharp eyes watching her, whereupon she settled down to eat it properly.

"Issur's back," she said, suddenly remembering.

"Yes," said Sylvester. "Nice for Sadie, looks to me as though he's taken up residence there."

"Do you think he'll stay this time?" said Justinia.

"Looks like it," said Lily.

"I must go over and say hello."

"They aren't there at the moment," said Lily. "They went out."

"You never told me," said Sylvester reprovingly.

"You were practising."

"Out for a walk?"

"No, they were on Issur's bike; I would have thought you'd have heard them."

"Sadie?" said Justinia, awed. "On Issur's bike? In a helmet?"

Lily snorted with laughter. "Yes, and very silly she looked, too, perched up behind Issur in his leathers, but never mind, time she got off her bum and started living again."

"I wonder where they've gone," said Justinia.

"Time will tell," said Lily. "Now, finish your coffee, Justy, and then pop back home to get your music. The piano is in the other room, so you can work in there while Sylvester's practising."

Justinia's face brightened. "Can I? I was thinking of asking Piers if I could go over there, but it's a bit difficult for him, after all, it isn't his house."

"Better here," said Sylvester. "Noses to the grindstone, and then you can stay to lunch."

"I'd like to," said Justinia. "But I don't think my mother would approve, she likes a friendly sit-down with Genevra, and she won't be pleased at my coming over here to practise, she thinks it all quite unnecessary. I'm supposed to concentrate on domestic duties."

Sylvester was getting his cello out once more, and his mind was on music. "If you still want to please your mother rather than yourself at your age, then there's no hope for you," he said.

Which is true, thought Justinia, as she slipped in through the back door and made her way stealthily to her room. A vain effort; her mother stood in the doorway, directing two burly men who were carrying a big chest of drawers. Other pieces of furniture stood in the passage outside.

"What's this?" demanded Justinia.

"Darling, I couldn't find you. We need to put these things somewhere, and since this is the only room which isn't being done at present . . ."

"And what am I supposed to do while my room is being used as a furniture depository? I can't get to my piano, and who's pushed it over against the wall?"

"That's to make more space, Justinia, and please don't raise your voice like that."

"Is something wrong?" said Genevra, sliding round the corner, a smile pinned to her face.

"Yes," said Justinia. "Please ask these men of yours to take this lot out of here."

"Oh, I'm afraid I can't do that, they have to go somewhere, you do understand, I'm sure."

"Fine, but they can go somewhere else. You aren't doing the sitting room yet, are you? They can go in there."

"Darling, Digby would hate that, you know how he likes everything to be just so. And he needs somewhere civilized to sit in the evenings," said Celia.

"Your husband gave specific instructions for these items to be stored in this room," said Genevra with a triumphant little laugh. "And since Digby's paying the piper, he calls the tune, wouldn't you agree?"

Pauline saw Justinia slam out of her house, wrapping her long mac round her; clearly, something was up. Pauline grabbed her Barbour, half strangled the dog into its collar and lead, and shot out on to the green. "Hello, Justinia, where are you off to?"

Pauline was taken aback at the look of black fury in Justinia's eyes, but nothing daunted, she launched into helpful chat. "Goodness, aren't we in a temper, you haven't been arguing with your delightful mother, have you? We did enjoy her company at dinner last week, and isn't Digby charming to her? It's a pleasure to see a man getting on so well with his mother-in-law."

Justinia said nothing, but walked on. Pauline fell into step beside her. "Off to the shops? I see you've got some music with you, are you making a photocopy? You have to be careful about that, you know."

Justinia looked at the music in her hand. She didn't want to tell Pauline she was going across to Sylvester's to practise. "A couple of pages need repairing," she said inventively. "I'm out of Sellotape."

"Oh, I see. I'm just taking Pericles for his walkies, but I'll go that far with you. Then we'll cut across by the beck and up on to the fells that way, won't we, Pericles? We are looking forward to seeing your house when it's finished," she went on relentlessly. "Digby was telling us all about it, and I can see what a lot's being done, it looks as though your interior designer has a very hard-working team. How can you tear yourself away? I'd want to be there every minute, although of course with the busy life I lead, that would be quite impossible."

If your life is so busy, thought Justinia angrily, why aren't you somewhere else leading it?

"You're very silent today," said Pauline. "Are you feeling all right?"

"I'm feeling fine," said Justinia, untruthfully. They had reached the newsagent's, she could escape.

"Is this where you're heading for?" asked Pauline, disappointed. "I thought you'd want the proper stationers, in the High Street. I know you don't need a newspaper, because I saw yours being delivered this morning. Almost as many as we have on a Wednesday, that's when the boys' science magazines come, they're so disappointed if the newspaper delivery is late and they have to leave for school before the papers come. We are lucky that our boys are so intelligent, it does make a difference. How's your cousin Tom, by the way? I hear he's got some problems at school. A pity that his voice broke early, because the choristers work so hard, they don't have time to get up to any mischief. Of course people say it's a pity for the choir, too, because Tom had such a good voice, but I don't think it was that good, really. A bit boomy, if you know what I mean, and pitch is so important. I have to say, Gavin and Peter never sing a wrong note."

"Then they must keep their mouths shut all the time, I never heard of a singer who didn't sing wrong notes sometimes. Bye, Pauline, I must dash, lot to do, see you around."

Justinia dived desperately into the shop, and by great good luck Mrs Toadflax came along on the other side of the road with her large bearded collie, an amiable dog which had, however, taken an immediate and inexplicable dislike to Pauline's Pericles. By the time Pauline had unwound herself and the dog's lead from the lamppost and Mrs Toadflax had muttered some cross words about people who didn't keep their dogs under control, Justinia had managed to make good her escape. She hurtled round the corner and bumped into Piers.

"Can't stop, Pauline," she hissed.

Piers immediately grasped the situation and cheered her on her way, shouting after her that he'd be round at seven if that was all right, had she remembered it was choir night?

Justinia skidded to a halt and called back to him that she would come over to the Manor, and then, seeing Pauline alarmingly in control again, she made herself scarce. Piers, who wasn't keen on dogs, stopped to admire Pauline's rather oppressed-looking one; let Justinia make good her escape, he thought altruistically, as Pauline started to tell him about how musical her boys were.

"Don't encourage them," he told her earnestly. "Accountancy, that's the ticket for your boys, take it from me. Or taxidermy, that's the coming profession, I understand."

Pauline gave him a look which clearly indicated what she thought of him, and headed for the fells.

Poor dog, Piers said to himself as he went into the newsagent's. Poor kids.

Baulked of her prey, Pauline set off up the fell path at a brisk pace. She hadn't really intended to walk the dog at all, but since she was here, a walk would do him good. Her eyes scanned the landscape as she climbed steadily upwards, exuding energy and fitness. She rounded a patch of bracken and saw a gloomy figure walking slowly along the path in front of her.

It was Merle, her head down, her hands thrust into the pockets of the long grey coat she wore. She didn't hear Pauline tracking her, and gave a start as Pericles woofed at her feet.

"Don't worry about him," said Pauline. "He's quite harmless, aren't you, Pericles?" She gave a savage jab at its lead; the dog gulped and subsided in an obedient heap.

"I don't like dogs," said Merle, seeing no reason why she should placate Pauline.

Pauline gave her an appraising look. "I always think it's a sign of mental health to like animals," she said.

"I do like animals," said Merle. "Tigers, ferrets, pythons . . . all favourite creatures of mine."

Pauline laughed her bracing laugh. "We mustn't get carried away, although I know how easy it is to do so when one is depressed. I was discussing your problems with your husband only the other day."

Merle rounded on her. "You were what?"

Pauline drew her breath in. Really, people were being difficult today, you would think they didn't want to be helped.

"I have to say, he was very unforthcoming, I recommended a psychiatrist for you, but he didn't take the name, I think he was in rather a rush. Had he had more time, I was going to tell him about the excellent work they are doing with depressives at the Dell Clinic. It's only about ten miles from here, you have your own room, it's all very pleasant. I'm on the board of trustees, so you see . . ."

"I'm not depressed," said Merle flatly.

Pauline was on safe ground here. "Oh, but you are. I can recognize it, you see, and it's often the case that people who are depressed are the last to acknowledge it. It's such a relief for them when they can admit it and ask for help."

"I'm glad for them," said Merle. "However, I'm not depressed. I am simply taking a solitary walk, which I find clears the mind and helps me sort out ideas for my work."

"That's exactly my point," cried Pauline. "Once you accept that you're depressed, and it's nothing to be ashamed of, I can assure you of that, then you can stop pretending that work is the problem and start finding out what really is the matter with you."

"I am *not* depressed," said Merle. "My work isn't going particularly well at the moment, I don't like living up here, and I'm bad-tempered with my family as a result. That's it, if you really want to know, which you obviously do, although I can't see why, since it's absolutely none of your business. Please don't try to discuss me with my husband, he's very loyal, and you'll only upset him. Now, if you'll excuse me, I'm going this way."

"I'll walk with you."

"No thank you," said Merle. "I am planning to walk along extremely narrow paths, sheep tracks, in fact, and there is definitely not room for two people, especially not when one of them is accompanied by a large dog. A dog, moreover, that looks to me as though he's the one I saw worrying sheep the other day; if I were you, I'd keep him off the fells for a while. I hear that the farmers are getting fairly fed up."

"Well," said Pauline, gazing disbelievingly at Merle's back as she set off up a narrow, rocky path. "Some people have no sense of gratitude. After all, Pericles, I'm only trying to help!"

"Telepathy."

"What do you mean, Lydia, telepathy?"

"It's telepathy, your ringing me to ask, can you use the flat in

London. I decided this very morning that I have to go to London. I need some large clothes."

Lydia put her hand over the receiver. "It's Justy," she told Alban. "She wants to go to London, so she'll be able to stay in the flat with me." She turned her attention back to the phone. "Listen, Justy, it couldn't be better, because Alban can't come, there's some terrific row brewing at the Cathedral, about music, and he was worried about me going up by myself. I said, how ridiculous, after all, you read in the paper every day about some pregnant woman crossing the Sahara . . . No, Justy, I do not think the Sahara is safer than London . . . More peaceful, yes, but think how energetic, camels and so on, far too exhausting for anyone in my condition . . . I can shop for hours without a trace of weariness, you know I can, that's quite different, no effort at all. After choir rehearsal tonight, then . . . Lovely. See you."

"Perfect," she said as she put the phone down. "You can stop fretting, Alban, Justy wants to spend several days in London, so I'll have company, and you can feel that Justy's looking after me, not that I need looking after at all."

"Better safe than sorry," said Alban darkly. "Why does Justy want to go to London? Is that foul husband of hers being beastly?"

"I gather there has been something in the nature of a tiff; to do with the house, I think, this peculiar woman Digby's called in to do them over. Also, I suspect she can't take much more of her mother."

"Understandable," said Alban.

Celia, in her gentle way, was persuading Justinia that she didn't really want to go to choir rehearsal, and that she most certainly didn't want to go to London. If she did, she shouldn't.

Gentle like a waterfall thought Justinia resentfully. Frothy and plashing and charming to look at, and all the time inexorably wearing away the solid stone. I won't give in, Justinia told herself. It's only a choir rehearsal; she's reacting as though I wanted to set off every Wednesday to attend a terrorist meeting.

"Don't worry about it," advised the voice in her ear. "Don't argue, you never win any argument with your mother. Just go. Go to choir rehearsal, you're on strong ground there, it's absurd for Digby and your mother to object to the choir. Go to

London, too, what harm can that possibly do? A shopping trip to the capital, how seemly, how regular, how safe, how entirely unthreatening."

"Digby's afraid I'm going to take up with some of my old friends, that's why he doesn't want me to go. Also, he hates me being away, which is really very sweet."

"Pathetic. And since Digby spends a lot of his spare time with his old friends, he can hardly object to you doing the same."

"The cases are different. But I'm going. I've told Lydia I'll go with her, and that's an end to it."

Celia showed her disapproval. "If you want to keep your husband, then the first rule is to be there for him. Even if you don't find it convenient, it's more important than anything else you have to do."

"We aren't living in the dark ages here, you know," said Justinia. "If that's what I have to do to keep Digby happy, then let him be unhappy, and if it makes him run off with someone else who is willing always to be there at his convenience, then let him run."

What am I saying? she thought, horrified. "I didn't mean that, of course I don't want Digby to run off with someone else, but it doesn't arise. He understands, we're both adults, we have our own lives to lead as well as our life together."

"Darling, I'm not criticizing you, and of course, what you say is true – for some men. It isn't true of a man like Digby, who is so home-loving and also a little possessive of his wife, which is so nice for you, admit it."

Justinia wasn't admitting anything, but in the event Digby behaved beautifully. He came home unexpectedly at lunchtime. "I was due to have a round of golf with Eddie Sackbutt; he can't make it, put his back out, poor chap. So I thought I'd come and have a word with Genevra, and then we can go for a walk, Justinia, pity to miss being out on such a lovely afternoon."

It was indeed a lovely afternoon. The fells were bathed in the warm sunlight of an Indian summer, and it was hot enough for Justinia to feel comfortable in a T-shirt. She was happy to be with Digby, good idea to get away from Celia for a bit, he said as they walked along hand in hand. Digby was in terrific form, and Justinia felt that what had seemed to be ever-growing problems were no more than irritations. It was petty to be so resentful, especially when Digby was showing such an interest in her choir.

"You see, I've got a deal brewing up with a chap, Kevin Wursthorn, you don't know him, but he's a very able fellow. An impresario, I suppose you'd call him. Concert management, you know the kind of thing. He's in the field I was telling you about, musical tours and so on. He wants to get together with us to promote choirs, groups ensembles, right across the range, anything that will attract an audience. Nothing too highbrow of course, but it's got to be quality, people want class these days."

"How do you come into this?" said Justinia.

"Ah, we provide the other half of the package, we make all the travel arrangements in this country and abroad. We want to choose a few likely groups to start with, make a big noise about it, good PR and so on, so that more people get to hear of what we have to offer. It's the way forward, link up with someone whose business meshes with yours and expand together, plenty of growth there."

"What kind of choir are you thinking of?"

Digby became evasive. "Nothing firmed up yet, it's early days. We certainly want an Eyot-based group on our books, very important to have a strong local profile, you know. Maybe we can get something going with Lucius and his festival, as long as it isn't all too deadly serious. You've got to give people what they like, there's no money in all this esoteric stuff. Religious music could be a winner, modern, of course, something with a bit of a tune to it, none of your Latin chanting."

Digby wrapped an arm round Justinia's waist. "I know you like all that kind of music, the old stuff, I mean, but that isn't where the money is. You go along and enjoy your choir; maybe you can get them to sing something a bit more jolly than those pieces you used to perform in London. But you appreciate that I have to focus on music with appeal, otherwise there's no profit, and then where would we be? No nice house, no money to spare, you wouldn't like that at all."

Digby didn't see the remote look on Justinia's face as he darted off on a new track, "I think we ought to buy a dog. It would be company for you now that you're at home all day, and it would get us out of the house and up here more often. A big dog, one that needs a bit of exercise."

"It would leave hairs on all your new covers," Justinia pointed out.

"True. But it's good for children to have a dog, and it's best to get one settled in before you start a family."

Yes, that's the next item on the agenda, thought Justinia glumly. All her pleasure in the beauty of the afternoon and in Digby's company had evaporated. What a prospect, she thought. Super house, super dog, super children. Super wife. Hard-working, fit and successful husband.

Ghastly.

## 17

"I know you'll enjoy yourself in London," Digby was saying. "Go out, take Lydia to a show, enjoy yourself. Do some serious shopping, lots of clothes, you don't want to let yourself get dowdy now we've moved out of London. Have a word with Genevra, bet she knows all the smartest shops. Bang up-to-date, you can see that."

They walked back towards Unthrang in silence, Digby planning ever more successful schemes and coups, Justinia trying to blot everything out of her mind except for the beauty of the high fells and the languid grace of the Eyot threading its way far below. Digby came down the steep paths with swift expertise, all those years of skiing and squash showed. Justinia moved more slowly, not anxious to be with him; I never used to feel like this, she thought. I must pull myself together, take an interest in what he's doing. I wonder what unfortunate choir he and this friend are going to take up and promote, thank goodness that Simon's choir will never sing the kind of music that Digby likes.

She grew depressed at the thought of good tunes pervading the land; at least, she told herself, there are still the music societies and of course the cathedral choirs, rooted in their ancient traditions, a bastion of excellence in a world of quick-and-easy and give-them-what-they-like.

Merle floated on the surface, her tired mind a blank, her senses lulled by the water and the rippling patterns of light falling across her eyes from the high windows. Roxane had persuaded her to have a swim. "You've hardly been at all, and I do say in the details for Juniper House that there is a pool available."

Merle was still seething from her conversation with Pauline. Roxane had nodded wisely when Merle told her of her hillside encounter.

"Poisonous woman," she said. "Into everything, always right, always knows best. Her husband's as bad, and those poor children are going to grow up to be just the same."

Merle turned over and trod water in a seal-like fashion, looking up at Roxane who was balanced on the edge of the pool. "Do you think that all children grow up to be like their parents?" she said.

"In *re* Pauline and her brood?" enquired Roxane. "Or generally?"

"You said you thought Pauline's children would be just like Pauline and Nigel, which is a dreadful thought, I have to say. It set me thinking, I shouldn't like Ben and Andrea to turn out like me."

Roxane shrugged an elegant shoulder. She was wearing a costume that looked as though it was made of crushed velvet, in deep autumnal browns and reds, with an astonishing turban of crimson silk wrapped round her head.

"If you don't want your two to turn out like you, change your ways," she advised. "It's partly genes, of course, but children do acquire their parents' attitudes in a rather depressing way. Cheer up, though, look how nice and well-liked Lucius is, apart from no doubt being very clever and good at his job."

"Ben rang last night, I still want him to stay at that school, you know, it's much the best place for him, and I was telling him how important it is to get a good education." She paused.

"And?" said Roxane, tracing a pattern on the water with a trailing foot.

"He said that all our education hadn't done me and Lucius much good, so he wasn't that bothered about it."

"Very wise, your Ben."

"Hasn't your education helped you?" demanded Merle.

Roxane looked around her. "It gave me a well-stocked mind, but I can truthfully say that it has never helped me to earn a living. It hasn't paid for all this."

"You mean that you inherited the house and everything from your father, and the money to keep it all going, and that would have happened with or without an education."

"No, that isn't quite what I mean," said Roxane. "I still use my own particular skills to keep myself in food and clothes and to keep a roof over my head, and a garden in good order and to have a pool fit to swim in. They just aren't skills that I acquired at school or college."

"Your illustrations, of course. I wouldn't have thought illustration was very well-paid."

"One manages," said Roxane, sliding gracefully into the water. "Are you managing? Lucius tells us that you have writer's block, is it unblocked?"

"Like a drain?" said Merle. "No, I don't have writer's block. I can write, but nobody wants what I write."

"Then you have a problem," said Roxane directly. "Better change what you write, quick, or you'll end up depending on your husband for every penny, like poor Justinia; soul-destroying."

"Very true," said Merle, depressed.

The green was surprisingly busy. Digby had the car parked in front of the house and was attacking the interior with a mini vacuum cleaner. Justinia was doing some savage weeding in their front garden. Sylvester was on his way back from the post office, and had stopped to talk to one of the Manor cats. Lily was pruning a fruit tree in the front garden of Crag End, Piers was on his way to have tea with Roxane, but had paused to chat to Sylvester, Pauline was officiously pinning notices about what people shouldn't do on the green on to convenient posts. Merle, her hair still damp from her swim, came out of Juniper House with Roxane, who needed to buy some tea to give to Piers, although tea was not what Piers had in mind.

Issur's Harley Davidson shot neatly and noisily across the cobbles on to the road which ran alongside the green, and juddered to a dramatic halt outside Sadie's house. The passenger dismounted from the pillion and took off her helmet.

"Where's Sadie?" said Sylvester, surprised.

"Who's that with Issur?" asked Digby disapprovingly.

Justinia blinked and looked hard. Merle came up to her. "Do you see what I see?"

"I don't believe it," said Roxane.

The pillion passenger eyed them self-consciously.

"Good God, it's Sadie," boomed Sylvester across the green, as he realized who it was. "Sadie, what have you done to yourself?"

"Had a decent haircut, by the looks of it," said Lily, "and very nice, too."

"It is Sadie," said Justinia. "It does suit you, Sadie."

"Much better now," said Issur with satisfaction.

Sadie's hair had not only been beautifully cut, it had also been coloured and she was now a natural-looking blonde. A facial and make-up had followed; Sadie looked ten years younger.

Sylvester eyed her with approval. "That's an improvement, Sadie," he said.

"You look lovely," said Justinia. "Goodness, what a difference."

"You've been to Reggie's," said Roxane with an expert eye. "I'd recognize his cutting anywhere. Bet he liked having you there, Issur."

Issur raised an innocent eyebrow and winked at Roxane. "All very good," he said. "But this is only the beginning. Next comes much exercise, to trim the body, and good food, to give vitality and tone. Hard work, but it will be worth it."

He took Sadie by the elbow, and with a cheerful wave to the assembled crowd, propelled Sadie into her house.

"Well," said Pauline, in a voice rich with scandalized indignation. "Well."

The Rev Wroot shook his head. "I fear worldly thoughts are to the forefront of her mind, whereas at her age she should be cultivating wisdom."

Roxane gave him a scornful look. "Wisdom! Might as well cultivate tomatoes for all the fun there is in that. No, Issur's going to give Sadie a new lease of life, and not a moment too soon."

"Almost a peripeteia," said Piers dreamily, as he devoured Roxane with his eyes. "A reversal of fortune and circumstance, a dramatic change in a person's life where everything is changed into its opposite."

Roxane was struck by this. "You mean Pauline developing a kindly tongue and leaving off thinking that her children are geniuses?"

"Something like that."

"And Merle cheering up and writing a bestseller, and Justinia giving Digby the kick in the bum he so richly deserves, and the Rev Wroot converting to Catholicism?"

"Could be."

"And me, Piers? What of me?"

"Ah, you become a virgin again. You see, it's all a fairytale. Come here and enjoy your present circumstances; live for the moment, that's all we can do."

"I know about that. I, too, have read the classical authors. Tomorrow do thy worst, for I have lived today."

"Precisely."

"I won't be able to give you a lift back, Piers," said Justinia, as she picked him up outside the Manor that evening. "I'm staying in Eyot tonight with friends, and then going up to London first thing tomorrow."

"No problem," said Piers. "Lucius is coming to sing with us, now he's settled up here he can start joining things, and he'll drive me back."

"What about Andrea?" said Justinia. "He usually likes to be home in the evenings with her, Merle not being very forthcoming just at present."

"Lily's picking Andrea up from school, which she's very excited about, and she and Sylvester are going to look after her until Lucius gets back. No pub for us, though, which is a pity, because I love the post-choir jar, that's when you pick up all the gossip."

"You'll have to ask a friend to take notes for you. I can't offer, because I shall have to rush off, my friends will be waiting to eat, and Lydia is always hungry in the evening."

"Lydia," said Piers thoughtfully. "Ah, Alban Praetorius's wife, tall, indolent, beautiful and expecting, if I'm not mistaken."

"You aren't," said Justinia, amused. "Do you know her?"

"She came to a university do the other day with the great man, who I gather is involved in some terrific hoo-ha with the Cathedral powers-that-be, some commission that's turned sour, I hasten to add, he's not indulging in theological disputes. I must say, I wouldn't care to cross that man myself, even if I were protected by the dignity of canonical robes."

"I haven't heard anything, perhaps he'll tell me about it tonight."

"Yes, ask, and then you can fill me in; I do like to know what's going on."

As usual, all Justinia's cares and concerns were forgotten while she was singing, and she was still glowing with the pleasure of it when she arrived at Lydia's house. To her surprise, Thomas opened the door.

"Hello, Thomas," she said. "What are you doing here?"

"Ask no questions," said Thomas mysteriously.

Lydia greeted Justinia warmly. "Thank goodness, now we can eat, although I don't see that Thomas will be able to manage a meal, he's been eating non-stop ever since he arrived."

"So have you," said Thomas with a grin. "And I've got masses of room, I'm really quite empty. I'll tell Alban that Justy's here."

"Why is he here?" said Justinia, putting down her bag, and gratefully accepting the glass which Lydia held out for her.

"Bit of a scam, really, anything to get away from school, poor boy. He has composition lessons with Alban, and Alban lays down the law about when he can teach him, which happens usually to be fairly late in the day. So he has special permission to stay with us overnight, as long as he's back in good time for school in the morning."

"It's all right with the school because Lydia's a cousin, you see," explained Thomas, sliding back into the room. "Alban's on his way. And old Puffy, that's my headmaster, thinks that composition lessons with Alban Praetorius on my report for Gryme are going to look awfully impressive. He's dying for someone from the school to get a scholarship there, no-one has yet."

"A scholarship there would be a feather in your cap," pointed out Justinia.

"I suppose so," said Thomas doubtfully. "I don't want to go at all, but Val says I have to, and old Puffy wets himself every time he thinks of "Gryme" written up on the scholarship board. Still, now there's talk of Gavin trying for a music scholarship there, and that might take the pressure off me a bit. Old Puffy worships Gavin, and he's making a real meal of it, insisting he be head chorister because it'll impress Gryme, special concerts laid on for him to play the fiddle, captain of this and that . . . Ugh!"

"Does Gavin want to go there?"

"Gavin does what he's told; he doesn't mind as long as he thinks it will bring him universal admiration," said Thomas with great good humour. "However, if I have to go there, I'd prefer he didn't because he's so boring he makes you yawn just thinking about him. He's a real drip, and none of us can stand him, because he's so full of himself. It doesn't bother him, because he knows he's wonderful, and his parents know he's wonderful and old Puffy thinks he's wonderful . . . Is supper ready, yet, Lydia? I don't think I can hold on much longer."

He gave a realistic groan and reeled across the room, landing up on Alban's feet as he came through the door.

"Get off, you great boy," said Alban. "And you've been sitting in here talking to Lydia when you should have been doing that work I set you. You are an idle boy, and will come to no good."

Thomas gave him a sideways look. "Were you hard-working long ago, when you were my age?"

"Don't be impertinent. But since you ask, I was; work, work, all day long, first to put my hand up in class, hours of prep every day . . ."

"Were you head boy? Captain of rugger? Did you win lots of prizes? All that kind of thing?"

"Naturally."

"Pay no attention, Thomas," said Lydia, yawning. "Oh, I'm sorry, I get so sleepy by the end of the day. Alban's making it all up, his mother told me that he never did a stroke of work that he didn't have to, and he loathed games, and his school said that although he had some potential, it would never be fulfilled until he learned to apply himself."

Thomas grinned. "Of course the secret of getting on at school is simply to concentrate entirely on pleasing the teachers and all the other adults around. If you're prepared to flatter them by showing how eager you are to please, you can't go wrong."

"Reality breaks in at some time," said Justinia, laughing at Thomas's mobile face as he acted out a too-good-to-be-true schoolboy. "I think you've got a future on the stage, Thomas. Shall I sit here, Lydia?"

She was amused to see how solicitous Alban was about Lydia, fussing around her to make sure her back was comfortable, frowning when she had a second glass of wine, urging her to eat some fruit.

"Bed, Thomas," said Lydia as they rose from the table.

"Just a few more minutes," pleaded Thomas. "It's very bad for you to go to sleep on a full stomach; I might walk in my sleep and give you a fright, and that would be very bad for you, wouldn't it, Alban?"

"Well, you can stay up a little longer," said Lydia.

"I'm not tired at all," said Thomas. "I'm never tired, and think how little I've got to do now that I'm out of the choir, hours every day to myself, no effort required."

Alban made coffee and brought it into the sitting room. "Alban's become very domesticated," said Lydia with a lazy smile.

"You've got to look after yourself, not get too tired," said Alban, thumping down into his special chair and stretching his legs out in front of him. "Have a brandy, Justy, I'm going to, I've had a bloody awful day. Thomas, get the brandy, you know where it is."

Thomas gravely poured out two glasses and handed them to Alban and Justinia. He then poured a tiny one for himself, and retreated to a corner of the room where he hoped to escape notice.

"I know what you're up to, Thomas," said Alban. "Don't skulk, you may have some if it's only a finger, and as long as you add some water. Country's going to rack and ruin, boys of your age at the brandy."

"Why have you had such an awful day?" asked Justinia.

Lydia, who was lying on a chaise longue with her feet up, opened one eye. "Don't ask him," she advised. "Or he'll tell you."

"Everyone ought to know," said Alban furiously. "It's an act of wanton destruction, criminal, and nobody gives a bugger about it."

"About what?" said Justinia patiently.

"It's the cathedral choir and that bloody man who's suddenly in charge."

Thomas, interested, drew his chair further in. "Do you mean the Succentor?"

"Succubus would be more like it," said Alban. "How they ever let him anywhere near the place, I can't imagine. Apart from his horrible ideas, just looking at him is enough to give anyone the creeps."

"Who are you talking about?" asked Justinia.

"I think he means Canon Holigost," said Thomas helpfully. "He's taken over from the Precentor, who's had a nervous breakdown, and he's doing things to the choir; he says he wants to make it relevant. He does look a bit strange, because of the paleness, and under those dark glasses his eyes are sort of pinky blue. We reckon he goes in for devil worship, actually."

"Nervous breakdown!" said Alban with scorn. "I'll give the Precentor nervous breakdown, nothing to do with his nerves, they've had to cart him off to dry him out. Couldn't manage to stand up for the psalms last week, getting far too noticeable, so off he goes. Meanwhile this hell-hound is let loose on the choir, and by the time he's finished, it'll be past saving."

Justinia was puzzled. "What has this Holigost got to do with it? I mean, he's clergy, isn't he? Surely the organist makes the decisions about the choir?"

"Right, but Simon's away, bloody idiot, trust him to piss off to America just when he's needed here. The assistant organist is some dim creature who's only been here for a few weeks, and it turns out that he rather agrees with Holigost. There's no need for an assistant organist to have any views on anything, he should stay up in his organ loft where he belongs and not go meddling with what he doesn't understand."

Justinia was concerned. "Is the music they sing changing, then?"

Thomas nodded. "They're singing some fairly nasty numbers, I must say. He's dug up really funny settings, like Throb in C. Actually, he'd like to do away with the Mag. and Nunc altogether, I heard him telling another canon about it. He won't let the choir sing any Byrd or Tallis or Bach, because it's highbrow and out of touch with today's spirit. Modern worshippers can't relate to old music, it isn't in their idiom, Canon Holigost says. Everything has to have a good tune, and he's bringing in all kinds of peculiar prayers."

"Tunes!" said Alban. "The trouble is, this man is a complete musical idiot. He knows nothing about it, but insists on wading in, full of opinions and demands."

"Alban's right," agreed Thomas. "He sings very loudly in the hymns, but completely out of tune and pretty bad timing too. He sounds like a parrot booming out from the stalls there."

"It'll all blow over," said Lydia. "They're always having crises in the choir."

"Yes, I dare say," said Alban. "However, they've gone too far this time, and they're going to have a fight on their hands. The latest thing is that this specimen from the nether regions wants to cancel my commission."

Justinia stared at Alban. "They can't do that!"

"You go and tell Holigost that. He wants to make a token payment and call the whole thing off. Never mind the whole bloody thing's finished and scheduled for performance. Damn it, they've already started rehearsals for it."

"We were working on it this evening," said Justinia. "Valliaze, who I must say is wonderful, thinks very highly of it."

"Yes, well, Holigost doesn't. He thinks it won't speak to the ordinary person, and therefore is to be replaced by a festival of folk and a youth-music rave in the Cathedral. Whatever youth-music is."

"Wow," said Thomas, awed. "It's never got as bad as this before."

Justinia couldn't believe how good it was to be back in London. "Red buses," she said happily. "Proper taxis. People who look as though they've got a purpose in life."

Lydia had a purpose in life, too. "We'll just leave our things, and then set off for some serious shopping. Clothes for me, gigantic sizes, because I'm larger round the middle every day. Presents for Alban, and for Thomas, I do like that boy."

"What about things for the baby?" asked Justinia.

"Like what?" said Lydia.

"Little garments. Things for the cot. Bottles. Toys. You know."

"Oh, plenty of time for that later," said Lydia, who couldn't imagine what having a baby was going to be like, and certainly couldn't see herself buying clothes or toys for someone she had never met. "And I've got a package to deliver to Alban's publishers, better do that first, because otherwise I might forget, and he would be peeved."

"Peeved?" said Justinia, thinking of Alban's powerful personality.

"No, he'd actually be furious," said Lydia frankly, "but he wouldn't dare show it, because of my condition."

Justinia enjoyed shopping with Lydia. Lydia adored clothes, and had some imaginative ideas about what a tall, pregnant woman should wear. "Not dungarees," she said with a shudder, as the assistant offered her a snappy pair of striped ones. "I'd look like something out of the circus in those; no-one over the age of ten should wear anything with a bib."

She bought herself men's trousers with big waists, several voluminous and vivid kaftan affairs – the bright colours distract attention from the bump, she told Justinia – and a huge and very expensive wrap around coat which looked more like Dracula's cloak than anything else. "Just the job," said Lydia enthusiastically. "I've long coveted the Dean's cloak, and now I have a vastly superior one of my own."

"No-one will see you in the dark," said Justinia, in fits of laughter.

Lydia considered the point. "I'll put some of Thomas's glow stars on it," she suggested.

"How does the Dean survive, crossing the road in his invisible cloak?" said Justinia. "Perhaps he ought to go to an ecclesiastical supplier where they make luminous crosses to go on his back, you know, like cyclists wear, but suitably ecclesiastical for a senior member of the clergy."

Justinia bought an *Evening Standard* to look at during one of their frequent pitstops. "I can't go for long without having a little something," explained Lydia, "or I feel sick, and then I get vile indigestion. Also," she said, lowering her voice to a theatrical whisper, "there are the belches."

"A concert tonight?" suggested Justinia.

Lydia shook her head. "No, I want to go to the theatre, there's never anything decent on in Eyot. We'll be musical tomorrow. Theatre tonight, and supper afterwards."

"Won't you be tired?" said Justinia doubtfully.

"No, because I can sleep late in the morning. You sound like Alban; don't, I need to get away from all that for a few days. Is there anything choral on tomorrow, or a song recital? That's what you'd like, isn't it?"

It was, but Justinia enjoyed every minute of the American play that Lydia chose, and she realized, when she finally turned the light out in her room at well past midnight, just how much fun the evening had been. Not only the play, but the good food and wine and ripples of laughter; Lydia had been in a very amusing mood. "It's so gorgeous to get away from one's husband, isn't it?" she said. "I love Alban dearly, you understand, but it's wonderful when he's not here, I'm sure you feel just the same about Digby. Of course I do miss Alban, but I think we ought to do this more often."

Justinia wasn't missing Digby at all, and what's more, she wasn't feeling guilty about not missing him. She sank into a happy if slightly tipsy sleep, glad to be in London with the hum of traffic in the background; no owls hooting, no sheep baaing, no unknown animals screeching.

The next morning, Justinia left a sleepy Lydia pottering around the flat and set off for the British Museum. She hung about for a few minutes in the department, attracting admiring looks from visitors who found her much more worthy of attention than the shelves of Greek vases; they should study the paintings more closely, thought Justinia, that would give them a shock. Then an ex-colleague came past and greeted her with joyful cries, sweeping her off to say hello to the others.

Why was I dreading coming here? thought Justinia later as she drifted past the endless display cases.

"Because you liked working here," said a familar voice in her ear. "Independence, it's called. You're missing it, and coming here is like biting on a sore tooth."

"Oh, you're back, are you?" said Justinia. "I thought you'd stayed up north."

"You wish you were still working here, don't you?"

"In fact, no," said Justinia, surprising herself. "I would like to work again, and I was pleased when the head of the department said she'd love to have me back, even on a part-time basis. Flattering, but I'd rather do some work connected with music."

"Like being a singer?"

Justinia laughed. "That isn't possible."

A man in a brown leather jacket eyed her uneasily as he hurried past; he thinks I'm mad, talking to myself, thought Justinia.

"Not mad, just getting a few things clear," said the relentless voice.

Justinia felt suddenly tired. "Do leave me in peace, just for a few days. Couldn't you do that?"

"No, that wouldn't be wise at the moment. I'll go now, though, you need something to eat."

Reluctant though she was to do anything which the voice suggested, Justinia had to admit that she was hungry, and she headed for the self-service restaurant. She was standing looking at a dish of bean and fig salad when someone spoke at her shoulder.

"I wouldn't, Justy, beans and figs, fucking disastrous, unless you're planning an evening alone."

## 18

Justinia whirled round. "Alexia!"

"Hello, Justy. What are you doing here? I heard you'd left your museum eyrie to head for the northern wastes. How's your husband?"

"You can't remember his name," said Justinia accusingly.

"No, that's perfectly true."

Alexia was shorter than Justinia, with square shoulders and dark, shoulder-length hair framing a heart-shaped face. She had a perpetual lift to her mouth, as of one who found life good. "This is Toby," she said, gesturing to a dazzling black man who was standing behind her. "Toby, grab a table for us, what would you like, pasta?"

Alexia piled this and that on to two plates, talking all the time and telling Justinia what she should have to eat. "You'll love this one, and you must try this, it's my absolute favourite."

Justinia had forgotten Alexia's energy and capacity for bossiness. She hadn't changed at all. Toby gave her an amused smile as Alexia arranged the table to her satisfaction. "You go there, Toby, because I want you to be able to look at Justy, she's so fucking beautiful, it isn't fair. Now, be quiet, Toby," she added, although Toby hadn't said a word. "I want to hear all Justy's news. What are you doing?"

"Visiting London for a few days," said Justinia. "I've dropped in here to see friends at the department where I used to work."

"And?"

"And not very much. I live with Digby in our house in a small town in the north called Unthrang. My mother is over from Italy and staying with us, the decorators are in, and I'm not pregnant, nor am I planning to be . . ."

"None of that is at all interesting," said Alexia, taking a large forkful of radiccio lettuce, which she ate with gusto. "Singing. Music. What are you *doing*?"

Justinia felt uncomfortable under Alexia's acute gaze. "I sing in a choir in Eyot. A good one. Valliaze is conducting us."

Alexia's eyes narrowed. "Not too bad, although he must be about a hundred. What else? Who are you working with? Someone in Leeds?"

"No-one, actually. I don't have lessons at the moment, although . . ."

"You," said Alexia, "are shirking." She turned to Toby. "Listen, this woman here has the most fucking fantastic voice, she's the one I've told you about, and she won't bloody use it, never would, always thinking about her mother's advice. I wish your mother had popped off years ago, Justy; no, don't make polite protesting noises, it would be the most generous and maternal thing she could ever have done for you. She'd be quite happy down among the wraiths and spirits in the underworld, turning those extraordinary eyes of hers on to Hades and taking him away from that dreary Persephone, and she wouldn't have been able to get at you and stop you doing the one thing you should be doing, what you were bloody born for."

Alexia's powerful voice and rich language meant that everyone in the restaurant's attention was riveted on their table. Toby seemed quite unperturbed. "Eat your salad, Alexia, and quieten down. It's a mystery to me that you have any friends at all, what with your extremely uncouth language and your loud comments on matters which should be approached with sensitivity."

"Sensitivity," spat out Alexia, together with a shower of crumbs. "Sod sensitivity. What I'm talking about is art, and not crummy amateur Sunday papers art, but professional, ancient and essential art. The only thing that matters. It matters more than anything, Justy, to people like you."

She took a deep and appreciative drink of iced orange juice and put the glass down on the table with a defiant thump. "Sex, family life, the social whirl, fit them in when you can. If you live for those things, and I can see that's exactly what you're sodding well doing, then you're going to end up a nervous wreck. Fact. I've seen it happen time and time again. If that husband of yours doesn't like you singing, of course he doesn't, you only have to exchange two words with him to know what he'd think about singing, then tell him to go screw himself, and you get off your arse and get going."

Justinia fought back; you had to, with Alexia, or you were overwhelmed. "Listen, Alexia; no, listen! I'm doing what I want to do, okay? I love my husband, I'm happy as I am. I like the life I'm leading, I don't need anything more."

"Liar," said the voice in her ear.

"Ah," said Alexia triumphantly. "You're lying. I can tell, I've always known when you were lying."

Toby raised his elegant eyebrows at Justinia and gave her an encouraging smile. "She means no harm, you know. She's told me about you, she admires your voice so very much, it really hurts her to think that you aren't using it."

"Please, Justy," said Alexia, leaning forward and grasping Justinia's scarf. "It's not too late. If you haven't got a job any more, then you've got time to work at your singing. Let someone hear you, someone really, really good. If they say, 'Oh, yes, a nice voice, but nothing special,' then go back to your choir in wherever it is. But I bet my fucking boots that anyone who knows anything is going to say, train, you should train, it's all there." Alexia put an arm round Justinia's shoulders and gave her a hefty squeeze. "Please, please, Justy, do that. Valliaze will tell you who to go to, you couldn't have better advice."

It was a somewhat dispirited Justinia who left the British Museum. Alexia had come too near the bone, and as Toby had politely changed the subject and Alexia had told Justinia about the work she was doing: booked up three years ahead, opera in America, recitals in Japan, classes in Vienna, recordings in Germany, Justinia came the closest she had ever been to envy, and despised herself for it.

In mediaeval times, she reminded herself, they used to represent envy with a pair of huge metal teeth that bit into you and hung on; you can't grudge Alexia her success – because that's what envy is, grudging – when you shut the door on any chance of that kind of life by making the choices you did.

I played safe, she thought bitterly. I listened to my mother, I did the sensible thing. And now I regret it. Words her father had spoken when he was dying floated into her mind, "You never regret what you've done," he had told her, "only what you haven't done."

The life bloody unlived, she told herself viciously, as she jumped off the bus at the end of the street where Lydia's flat was.

Lydia was making lists. There was a lot of furniture stored in the flat, and one room was completely full of books and several large and unwieldy pieces of furniture.

"These are mine," said Lydia. "I brought them from home when my mother had a clear-out, actually most of it is my father's, but he doesn't want it, said for me to take the lot. There are a few pieces which are going up to Eyot, the men are coming tomorrow, but the rest will have to be sold, goodness, what an effort."

Justinia peered over a huge black sideboard made of bog oak, and looked at the furniture which was piled up almost to the ceiling. "And I suppose the ones you want to send to Eyot are all at the bottom of the heap," she said.

"Of course," said Lydia.

"Are you taking that enormous sofa?"

"No," said Lydia regretfully. "I'd love to, because it's so comfortable, I can't tell you the hours I've spent lounging on it; however, we simply don't have room for it."

"I'll buy it from you," said Justinia. "It's exactly what I'd like to have in my room, my room downstairs, I mean, not the bedroom. The room which *isn't* being done up by that artful Genevra."

"No, I won't sell it to you," said Lydia, pleased. "I'll give it to you, then I can come and visit and lounge to my heart's content."

She swept away Justinia's protests. "Shut up about paying for it, Justy, it isn't as though we needed the money. If you buy it, I expect you'll have to ask Digby to hand over the loot, and then it won't feel yours in the same way that it will if I give it to you."

It's the day for my friends to put the boot in, thought Justinia, as she dissuaded Lydia from lifting a large table. "Not in your condition, Lydia, no. Quite apart from how you'd feel if you lost the baby, I'd never be able to face Alban again, and I like Alban."

"He likes you, too," said Lydia. "Says you're wasting your life away, though, he and Simon were discussing your voice . . ."

"Don't you start," said Justinia with a sigh. "I met a friend this morning who's a singer, and she had a go at me. Let's talk about something else."

Lydia thought for a moment. "Virginia," she said triumphantly.

"That is something else," agreed Justinia, "but not quite what I had in mind. Virginia scares me, I try not to think about her."

"She rang up, she's heard from Val that we were in London for a few days; that man is a terrific gossip, had you noticed? So we're summoned to dine with her and Ralph tomorrow evening."

"Oh, no," said Justinia.

"Ralph's a very good cook."

"It isn't that. Lydia, did you accept for me?"

Lydia looked at her with scorn. "Listen, duckie, we're talking about Virginia. She asks you, you go. If you don't want to, you can ring her up and tell her yourself."

"Um," said Justinia.

"There you are. You're a coward, same as me."

"Oh, hell. Well, there's always this evening, what shall we do?"

"Justy, would you hate it if we just stayed in and watched the telly? It's very boring of me, but there's an old film on I've been dying to see, and I went out this morning and got rather tired . . ."

"And we were up and out late last night, no, of course I don't mind," said Justinia. "I'll see if there's a concert or anything I really can't miss on tonight, pass me the paper. Otherwise I'll join you for a takeaway and a peaceful evening."

"Lovely for me, but boring for you," said Lydia perceptively. "You have far too many peaceful evenings at home, don't you? Why don't you go to the opera, what's on at Covent Garden?"

Justinia looked. "Oh, heaven, *Rosenkavalier*, but I don't suppose there's a chance of a ticket."

There wasn't, although the man who answered the phone in the box office suggested in his high, smooth voice that Justinia could always turn up on the off-chance, "and it is an off-chance, I have to be honest with you," that there were some returns. "They're snapped up, simply snapped up, because it's a divine production, really marvellous, it makes me go all goosefleshy whenever I slip into the auditorium."

Knowing that there were unlikely to be any tickets made Justinia want to go even more. "Why didn't I book up when the tickets first came on sale?" she moaned to Lydia. "Why do I feel I'm in hibernation now that I live in Unthrang? I could so easily come to London, I've got masses of friends I could stay with."

"You could stay here," said Lydia calmly. "Any time."

"Then why don't I do it?"

Lydia yawned; she really was feeling very sleepy. "Oh, because the masses of friends are probably people Digby isn't keen on, and he wouldn't be very happy about you coming here too often, would he? Family favours, and he doesn't like your family."

"True," said Justinia, prowling up and down. "I'll make some coffee," she said abruptly.

"I don't want coffee," said Lydia. "I want a peaceful evening. For heaven's sake, go and see if there's a return."

"You just want to get me out of the house."

"Too right," said Lydia. "It's very unsettling, you padding about the place like a stripy number at the zoo, I had no idea you were such a restless person."

Justinia flung herself down on a sofa. "I'm not, I don't know why I'm on edge like this."

"Go and see if there are any tickets," said Lydia soothingly. "If nothing else, a nice little trip on the tube will calm you down."

"All right, I will," said Justinia. "I'd better get changed, can't go looking like this."

She put on a black dress which could be studenty and subdued if she was up in the gods, or elegant enough if she ended up in the stalls. That would be extravagant, with prices the way they were, but she hadn't bought much, despite Digby's lavish plans for her to do so; in any case, there probably wouldn't be a ticket at any price.

"You'll need a mac," Lydia said, opening one eye as Justinia headed for the door. "Rain."

Lydia was right, it was raining, a soft, London rain. Justinia dived down into the underground, enjoying the familiar hot, stale smell, the people, the advertisements. Just like the old days, she thought rather wistfully. She pulled her mac more closely around her as she emerged at Covent Garden station; the rain had become more determined, and passing cars sent shafts of water up from the gutters.

As she approached the opera house, she could see that there was a long queue snaking along the pavement, and her heart sank. "Is this for returns?" she asked a friendly-looking woman in a yellow mac.

"I'm afraid so," she said. "And not much luck tonight, by the look of it. I've already seen the production twice, it's worth trying for, I can tell you."

Justinia hesitated for a moment; she could see it was hopeless to join the queue. Perhaps she could ask if there were any tickets left for later performances, persuade Digby that he didn't mind her coming down to London for the opera. Buy two tickets, and bring him? Justinia could picture Digby in her mind's eye: cross, disapproving and tense with indignation at having to sit through such a farrago of nonsense.

"A woman dressed as a man pretending to be a woman, oh, it's preposterous, Justinia!" His reaction when she had taken him to a Wagner production, and he had realized that the eighteen-stone tenor who looked like a frog was supposed to be a Nordic hero, had been unforgettable.

Justinia turned round and began to walk slowly back the way she had come. Perhaps she would find a café open somewhere, she didn't want to spend the evening in Lydia's flat. She heard hurried steps behind her, and moved aside to let the person past.

"Excuse me," said an unfamiliar man's voice as a dark figure drew level with her.

Justinia stopped, a wary expression on her face.

"I'm sorry, I didn't mean to startle you, it's very rude to accost you like this, but I couldn't help overhearing you back there. At the opera house. I have a spare ticket, I was going to hand it in, and then I saw you. You looked so disappointed, you see, and I wanted you to have it."

Justinia looked at him appraisingly for a moment or two. Was this a sophisticated pick-up, or a disinterested gesture of kindness? A friend of her mother's had advised her once to always assume the best of people; you might be disappointed, but you'd often be pleasantly surprised. Besides, she desperately wanted to see the opera, and he was hardly going to abduct her in mid-chorus.

He was a tallish man in his late thirties or early forties, with a humorous mouth, and a lively, intelligent face.

Justinia looked at him for a moment. "Thank you," she said. "That is kind of you. She stood, waiting, while he found the ticket and held it out to her. It was a good seat. "I must pay you," she said. "I can write a cheque inside . . ."

He hesitated for a moment, longing to say no, it would be a privilege to offer a seat to this utterly delightful-looking woman; that, he told himself, would be a mistake.

Justinia found a flat surface on a ledge inside on which to write a cheque. "Who do I make it out to?" she asked.

"Gervase Drummond. Thank you," he said, adding, "Mrs FitzOdo," as he glanced at the name on the cheque before putting it away.

"Justinia FitzOdo," she said. She felt the familiar lifting of her spirits as she put away her cheque book and looked around the lobby. She gave a deep sigh. Heaven.

She bought herself a programme, refusing to let her companion do so. "It was kind of you to sell me the ticket, but there's no reason why you should buy my programme."

He stayed by her side, noticing how many men paused to have another look at Justinia, who seemed quite unaware of the admiring glances as they made their way upstairs to the Dress Circle. Extremely good seats, thought Justinia. He must have booked them a long time ago.

"I'm lucky enough to have a good deal to do with opera," he explained, "so it isn't very difficult for me to get tickets, even for something as successful as this. I get freebies for most productions, but this was one I wanted to see again. Do you go to the opera often?"

"No, I live a long way from London," she said uninformatively. "And my husband isn't very keen, so I don't go as much as I'd like to."

"Do you sing yourself?" he asked.

Justinia looked at him in surprise. "Why do you ask?"

"Your voice, it sounds to me as though you were a singer."

"Strictly amateur, choirs, that's all," said Justinia. And then the lights dimmed, the orchestra finished its tuning up, and the applause began for the conductor.

Justinia relaxed into her seat as the familiar music of the overture filled the house. The curtain rose on the Marschallin's bedroom; Gervase gave a quick look sideways as Justinia sat up expectantly.

How very distracting, he thought, trying to focus his attention on the stage and not on the still figure beside him. Who is she? Why does she have a husband? Naturally she has a husband, but why doesn't he come with her to the opera, what kind of a man leaves his wife hanging round the opera house hoping for a return?

Justinia came back to earth an hour and a half later. She gave herself a little shake; back to reality from a world of magic. "Thank you so much," she said to Gervase as they rose from their seats. "I tend to forget how much I love all this."

"I should thank you," he said. "I could have found myself sitting next to someone who fidgeted and coughed throughout, having realized after the first ten minutes that it wasn't quite what they had in mind."

"Surely not," said Justinia, laughing. "I'm sure all those people hoping for returns were keen fans. I feel guilty at jumping the queue."

"Do you?"

"No, not really. They're probably Londoners, they can come another day; I don't know when I'll be here again."

"May I buy you a drink?" he said, getting up from his seat.

"Thank you," said Justinia.

The bar was, as always, thick with people, but Gervase was back in no time at all with two foaming glasses.

"Fizz goes with Strauss, don't you think?" he said. He had a merry look in his eye, and Justinia felt herself warming towards him.

"I'm sorry that the person you were coming with couldn't come, but you must thank whoever it is."

"I don't suppose I'll be seeing her again," he said. He didn't seem very upset about it, Justinia thought.

He told her a little about himself; he was a lawyer who advised the board of the opera house and several other music organizations.

"I have a passion for music, you see."

Justinia found him a witty and amusing man. Digby never makes me laugh, she thought for a fleeting and disloyal second, and then stamped on the thought savagely. He has other virtues, she told herself, and very lovable ones; in any case, why am I comparing them? Digby's my husband, this man is a total stranger whom I'll never see again.

The bell rang for the second act.

I must find out who she is, Gervase thought as they returned to their seats. Mrs FitzOdo, who lives a long way from London, that's all I know. She gives nothing away, and in two hours' time, she'll go, and I'll never see her again. I could ask her to dinner, but she won't come, and she wouldn't appreciate the invitation . . .

What an attractive man, thought Justinia. Just think of all the crashing bores you could have ended up next to instead of him. And he's keeping his distance, thank goodness. I do hope he's not going to embarrass me by asking me out to dinner. I'll get a taxi as quickly as I can afterwards, he'll probably have a car, offer me a lift; well, tough.

## 19

FitzOdo, he said to himself as he drove away afterwards. An unusual name. He felt slightly put out that she had so adamantly refused to be taken home; clearly, she didn't have any intention of pursuing the friendship.

Did she dislike me? he thought, going cold. Could you find a woman so attractive and she have no sense of rapport at all with you? Of course, she was married, happily so, no doubt, because her husband was a lucky man and probably knew it, but married women made new friends; not her, it seemed, at least, not with him. Why should she? A total stranger, she knew nothing about him; but damn it, she didn't have to be that wary.

He decided to call in at his club where he'd left some papers; he could see if anyone was about, he found it lonely at home without Sonia, although he was genuinely relieved to see the back of her. That wasn't an interlude of which he was proud. He felt suddenly depressed, was his life now going to be a series of Sonias? If only his marriage hadn't gone so badly wrong. He asked himself yet again whether he shouldn't have done what Grace wanted, and given up the house in London – and his work, don't forget, that was the unspoken agenda – and move to Hereford to breed shire horses.

Well, Grace now had her house in the country and several extremely large horses, together with an equally large, new husband who owned an indecent number of acres, never went to London and hated music almost as much as Grace did.

He remembered one of their interminable rows. "You never said you loathed music, you came to concerts, you came to the opera, you knew a lot about it, you never said you considered the whole thing a waste of time. I thought we had at least that in common."

"You do that when you're in love with someone," she had replied, cruelly. "You're fascinated by everything they like, want to share it, haven't you noticed? But you can't keep it up for ever. Music and fishing, I hate them both. Of course, I wouldn't mind you going out to the occasional concert or opera, but it's nearly every bloody night!"

"I love it, and it's also part of my job."

"Then change your job. Do something more worthwhile, more down to earth, why aren't you out there helping people?"

Grace, with her crazy idealism. She still lived in an aura of organic principles; how long before she appreciated exactly what Geoffrey did with his acres to allow her the huge sums of money she spent on her entirely natural garden and utterly natural, thunder-footed horses?

He paused in the lobby. FitzOdo was an unusual name. She didn't live in London, but any FitzOdos in the phonebook might well be related to her husband, would know her, know where she lived. "Pass me that phonebook, would you?" he said to the porter. "Thanks."

He ran a finger down the Fitzs . . . Fitzackerley, FitzGeorge, murmuring the names aloud as he went.

"What are you doing, Gervase?" said a man who had just come through the doors of the club.

"Looking for a name, FitzOdo, nothing listed." He handed the book back across the desk. "Thanks, Nigel."

"FitzOdo?" said the man thoughtfully. "Unusual name, my wife's cousin married a FitzOdo, Digby FitzOdo, that's it. Could he be the fellow you're looking for? I wouldn't have thought it likely that you knew the man; not your sort of person. I can't say I took to him myself, and I know Virginia was furious when Justinia said she was going to marry him."

Gervase looked at Ralph in astonishment, unable to believe what he'd heard. "You know Justinia?" he said, his face lighting up. "Ralph, let me buy you a drink, what astonishing luck!" Come on, tell me all about her."

"We're all very fond of Justy," said Ralph, sitting himself comfortably in a vast leather armchair. Gervase sat across from him, on the edge of his leather chair, taking in every word Ralph said. "She's in London at the moment, actually, coming to dine with us tomorrow. How come you know her?"

Piers woke first, feeling hot and slightly sticky. He stared for a moment at the silk brocade bedcover; where was his duvet with Mickey Mouses on it? Then he remembered, and stretched out a hand, unsure what he was going to find. Warm flesh, but whose? Too muscular for the slender Roxane, must be Issur. He broke into a smile at the thought of Issur's wonderful body, just as wonderful as Roxane's in its own way.

Issur was awake now, looking at Piers with those strange eyes. Piers remembered his Welsh granny telling him about the Old Ones. "You can always tell an Old One, from the moment they first open their eyes. You can see it at once, they have an ancient, knowing look."

Issur, Piers decided, would definitely be classified as an Old One by Granny Megwynn. "Won't Sadie be wondering where you are?" he asked Issur.

"No," said Issur, sliding himself past Roxane's still sleeping body and out of the huge bed. "She is very tired, she hasn't had such a lot of sleep these last few nights, she won't have missed me."

"Are you going back there now?" whispered Piers.

"Not yet," said Issur. "First, I go to the pool, take a shower and have a swim. It's still early."

"I'll come, too," said Piers, admiring Issur's naked body as he moved easily across the room to pick up his clothes. He didn't bother to put them on, but simply slung a towel across one shoulder before making his way downstairs.

They swam in silence, the pool lit in the early morning dimness by underwater lights. The statues were shadowy; it was very quiet and dark.

"Have you always liked both men and women?" asked Piers.

Issur rolled on to his back and looked at Piers. "All things to all people," he said. "To be both a man and a woman can be important for an artist."

"An artist in what?" said Piers, suddenly feeling that Issur wasn't only talking about dance.

"An artist in life," said Issur, with a smile as though he was laughing at some inner joke.

"Are you going to stay in Unthrang?"

"For ever? Of course not. I have some things to do while I am here, some people to see on their way, and then I go back to where I've come from."

"Liverpool?"

"Possibly," said Issur, with another smile.

"I think I'm falling in love with Roxane," Piers confided.

"Really?" said Issur mockingly. "Who would have guessed?"

"I think she has other interests."

"I think you are right."

"I don't want her to have other interests."

"She has a nice style of life, you know."

"What's that got to do with it?"

"A lot, perhaps."

"She seems to have men round all the time. There's Ned, and the man who does the pool, I couldn't stand him, and then she has long talks on the phone with Roddy Gumble, who I suppose must be something to do with the shop. And there's someone else, who owns that place where people with incredible amounts of money buy things for their houses – and for themselves."

"Such as exotic clothes, and silk bedcovers."

"Yes," said Piers. "I can't think where Roxane gets the money from. I don't think she can make much with her illustrations, I know it's not very well paid, that kind of work."

"You think Roxane is in love with these men?"

"Of course not." Piers was cross at the suggestion. "Of course not, how could she be in love with all of them? It's just strange, and she has this charity work . . . well, what charity work is it? Old people? Children? Animals? Birds, even; she won't talk about it."

Issur pulled himself out of the pool. "People are not always what they seem," he said. "Now I run back to Sadie's house, very fit, such good exercise, and so starts another day."

"What are you going to do today?" asked Piers curiously.

"I think today I will call on my friend the priest."

"Luther Wroot? What on earth for? That man's a pest."

"Ah, no, he changes, you wait and see."

\*　　\*　　\*

It was a subdued Rev Wroot who greeted Issur. Almost a gloomy one; for a moment, he was forgetting to smile with joy in the Lord. He introduced Issur to a fellow clergyman, a little, round, gingery, freckled man with a pursed little mouth but a very friendly expression. He wore a black soutane, in marked contrast to Luther Wroot's jeans and sweatshirt.

"This is Father Hamish," said the Rev Wroot, without any great enthusiasm. "He was sent by the Bishop's chaplain, he's dropped in to advise me about a service." Luther Wroot gazed angrily at Issur.

"A Requiem service, for All Souls," said Father Hamish merrily. "Excellent idea, pull the parish together, too many Christians feel alienated these days, worthy worship of course, very jolly, but not everyone's way, we have to reach out to all corners of the parish, isn't that so, Luther?"

The Rev Wroot managed an uncertain smile, and went on gazing intently at Issur.

"I have contacts in Unthrang, so we'll be able to find some experienced servers and so on. You'll need a crucifer, Luther, and a thurifer, and a boat boy."

The Rev Wroot shuddered. Issur smiled at him, a smile, the Rev Wroot felt, which was rich with incense and black velvet.

"Of course it's a pity we can't manage a sung Requiem," Father Hamish went on. "They always used to sing a Requiem here for All Souls."

Issur was listening attentively. "No music?" he said.

"Well, hymns, but it'll have to be a said Mass. I don't think the present congregation could do much in the Requiem line, you need an organ or a small orchestra as well as a choir, and the settings aren't so easy, not when when you're used to Mission Praise and so forth."

Issur exploded. "No music? Of course we must have music. There can be no worship without music. Music is essential." He flung out his arms in a dramatic gesture, and out of the corner of his eye caught sight of a burly figure on the other side of the green. "Sylvester," he called. "Sylvester, come, there is a problem, there is no music."

Sylvester came across at full steam, his face alight with curiosity. "Ha, it's Father Hamish," he said.

"You know Father Hamish?" said the Rev Wroot weakly.

"Yes, yes, Hamish here helps us out with the Midwinter Festival, don't you?"

"Mmm, yes, indeed, how are you, Sylvester?"

"I'm well, Hamish, I'm always well. Now, what's all this about music? What's going on? What are you all plotting? I can tell you're up to something; planning to burn an effigy of the Bishop on bonfire night, are you?"

"Now, now, Sylvester, I can't allow that kind of talk," said Father Hamish.

"Can't stop me," said Sylvester with satisfaction. "You can't make remarks about the Bishop, of course not, that would be most unseemly. I, however, can say what I like."

"It's a Requiem Mass, Sylvester," explained Issur.

"Oh, good, good, all those dreams you've been having, hey, Luther?"

The Rev Wroot looked even more unhappy.

"Excellent, Sadie will be pleased," said Sylvester. "So what's the problem?"

"No music," said Issur.

"No music? Don't be silly, can't have a sung Requiem without music."

"Yes, but Sylvester, who is to sing it?" said Father Hamish. "There is no longer a choir, certainly not a choir which could tackle a proper setting; I would suggest a plainsong setting, but of course that's even more difficult."

"Away with your chanting. Hamish is a Gregorian freak," he explained to Issur. "Great expert, but I expect all your cronies are booked up for November the second, aren't they, Hamish?"

"That is indeed the case."

"Say we could rustle up a choir, is the organ working?"

"No," said the Rev Wroot, with some relief. "No, Mrs Crumhorn, who used to be organist here, asked me recently if she could slip in while the church wasn't in use, just to run her fingers over the keys. As you know, I entirely disapprove of the organ for religious services, it is an outmoded instrument, but it would be unchristian not to let her play when no-one is around. However, she informed me that repairs were needed, the organ has fallen into disrepair with lack of use. So there can be no question of organ music."

Sylvester was thinking hard. He let out a bellow to Piers, who was walking back to the Manor House with the papers. "Piers! Come and join the cabal."

"Cabal," said the Rev Wroot, squirming. "Please, can we have no irreligious words, we are on church land."

Sylvester looked at him in some surprise. "What did you learn at that theological college? Wasn't English, was it? Piers, we're going to have a sung Requiem here, on Thursday next."

"Oh, good," said Piers. "Which one?"

"We need advice. Let me say at once, there is no organ."

"And no choir," added Father Hamish.

"But we must have a Requiem, and one with music," said Issur firmly. "This I owe to those of my family who are dead."

"Let's have a decko," said Piers, ducking into the church.

"Good acoustic," said Sylvester, following him in. "I've played here once or twice. Well, what do you think?"

"Duruflé," said Piers. "My favourite Requiem. I can gather a few voices, twelve, fourteen, I'm sure there'd be volunteers from the Camerata, and I'll round up a few more at the university."

"There's Justinia," said Sylvester. "And we'll get young Thomas over, he can sing alto. Now, orchestra, we need another cello."

"You mean you'll play?" said Piers, surprised.

"Naturally, you don't think I'd miss this, do you? After all, it is my local church, even if only temporarily."

"I thought you weren't very church-minded."

"Nonsense, I love churches, play in them all the time. It's the incumbents who get up my nose, but I think we can keep the Rev Wroot in order."

"Yes, what's got into him?" said Piers, lowering his voice. "Conversion?"

"Of a kind," said Sylvester with a rumbling laugh. "We shall see, we shall see. We need violins, what a pity Gabriel is away. Never mind, I can twist a few arms. Lydia can bring her double bass, if she can reach the strings with her tummy the way it is. She'll enjoy herself. Piers, if you can provide the singers, I'll see to the instrumentalists. Who's going to conduct?"

"I wonder if Valliaze might."

"Valliaze! Of course, I'll invite him to dinner afterwards, he can never resist Lily's cooking. Well, that's all settled."

Father Hamish made a little moue with his mouth at Sylvester as he emerged from the church. "I take it we shall have a musical offering, then?" he enquired, his little round eyes full of amusement.

"Yes. Who will take the service?"

Father Hamish's little smile grew more pronounced. "My colleague here has asked me to officiate, and he will assist. I shall bring one or two fellow clergy over with me, put on a good show. Now, I will say goodbye, because I'm just going to slip over to ask Josiah if he will serve."

"The undertaker?" said Sylvester. "Very suitable for a Requiem service. Oh, I'm going to enjoy this. You'd best be off, too, Wroot, spreading the good word about the parish and telling your regulars to stay at home on that night, lest they be polluted."

He walked back across the green with Issur and Piers. "Well done, Issur," he said. "You've set the cat among the pigeons there."

"How's Justinia?" Celia asked as Digby put the phone down and wandered into the kitchen.

"Hard to say," said Digby disconsolately. "Said she didn't have time to talk, going out to dinner with that cousin of hers, Virginia. Said she had to rush, couldn't be late."

"I can't think why she wants to go to Virginia's," said Celia. "Never mind, you can talk to her tomorrow."

"Why doesn't she ring me?"

"It isn't her flat," said Celia. "Although I wouldn't think Lydia would mind."

"She never asked how I was. And I've no idea what's she's been up to. She said she hadn't done much shopping, so why doesn't she come back? It's a bit thick, if you ask me."

"Let me get you something to drink," said Celia soothingly. "Iced orange juice?"

"Thank you," said Digby absently. "I mean, there was no real need for her to rush off to London like that if she didn't want to shop. It's petty to moan about Genevra putting one or two bits and pieces in her room, out of the way. She quite upset Genevra, it was very rude of her."

"Everyone enjoys a trip to London. After all, you go quite often, don't you?"

"That's different. That's business."

"You see old friends, too, don't you?"

Digby's eyes narrowed. "Do you think she's been seeing old friends?"

"I don't know, Digby, but it's what people do when they go to London, isn't it? Hairdresser, lunch with friends, theatre, shopping, a dinner party or two. It's all very harmless."

"I'd just like to know exactly where she is, and who she's with."

"Well, you know where she is tonight; she's with Virginia, and although I've never really got on with her, I don't have much in common with these overpowering women, she is family, and I think a quiet evening with her cousins is hardly anything to get worked up about."

"They're Mountjoys," pointed out Digby.

"Respectable ones."

"No Mountjoy is respectable," said Digby crossly.

It looked a seemly gathering; Digby could hardly have disapproved. However, within a short time of her guests arriving, Virginia could sense undercurrents. This she hated; undercurrents were fine, could add to the pleasure of an evening – provided she knew what was going on. Which she didn't. And where was Ralph's friend, had he got the time wrong? She hadn't been too keen when Ralph suggested they ask him.

"Rather at the last minute, don't you think?" she had said, frowning.

"It's a last minute affair," said Ralph. "Couldn't be otherwise, not knowing that Lydia and Justy were in town."

"It would help with the balance," said Virginia. She didn't give a hoot for even numbers, but she felt unrelieved family was always dull. "I might give Selina a ring, see if she and her husband might like to come."

"Whatever for?" said Ralph. "She's very attractive, I'm always glad to see her, but hen-witted, heavy going for a whole evening, don't you think? And isn't her husband a crushing bore? Foreign Office?"

"He is a bit grim," agreed Virginia. "But he's a contemporary of Lydia's, in fact they may have been up at Oxford at the same time, and I promised Selina's mother I'd ask her to dine, so it will be duty done."

Ralph raised an unbelieving eyebrow at her. "This doesn't sound at all like you, Virginia."

"It does," said Virginia laconically. "Her father's Lumley's Bank, expanding overseas."

"Ah," said Ralph.

Virginia then decided to commandeer a young employee from her office, good to have another young man. "He's musical," she said. "It'll be a treat for him to meet Lydia, he'll know all about her famous musical husband. And he can talk to Justy about singing."

Lydia and Justinia arrived on the doorstep at the same time as Selina and husband.

"Oh, yes," said Lydia, unsmiling. "Angus and I were at Oxford together," she told Virginia. "And Selina, how lovely to see you again."

Angus was suave, although underneath his rather rigid exterior he was disturbed. Selina would remember that he and Lydia had been together for most of their time at Oxford, she couldn't mind, nobody did these days, but you could never be sure with Selina.

Selina was patronizing Lydia, while Lydia sat back and wondered how she had ever wanted to spend so much time with Angus.

"You've put on weight since we last met," Selina told Lydia. "It suits you."

Lydia stared at her.

"It was at a Commem Ball, wasn't it?"

"I don't remember, I'm afraid," said Lydia.

Virginia appeared with a cushion. "Put this behind your back, Lydia, you'll be more comfortable."

"Yes, you must look after yourself," agreed Ralph. "Otherwise that ferocious husband of yours will be beside himself."

"Oh, you're pregnant, are you?" said Selina artlessly. "And you're married."

Justinia glanced at Virginia, who shrugged her shoulders.

"And do you live in London?" Selina went on.

"No," said Lydia. "Eyot."

Selina gave an affected little scream. "Oh, I couldn't, I couldn't live in a provincial northern city like that. However do you manage?"

"I found the woad a bit tricky at first, but I've got the hang of it now."

Virginia's young man provided a welcome pause in the proceedings. He had beautiful manners and was also well-informed, he knew exactly who Lydia was. "What a treat," he said. "Goodness, this is something to tell my friends about. I can bring them up to date almost from the horse's mouth. How is your husband's new work going? I read about it in the paper, it sounds terrifically exciting, I and some friends are planning a weekend in Eyot to catch the première."

Lydia smiled, he was a very appealing young man, full of musical talk. "Better ask Justy," she said. "She knows far more about matters musical than I do."

But Justinia had been annexed by Selina. "Is Lydia a friend of yours?" she asked with a bright smile.

"Cousin," she said.

"Oh. And how do you come to know Virginia, she's such a pet, isn't she?"

If you keep piranhas for pets, thought Justinia. "She's a cousin, too."

"What a lot of cousins. What's Lydia's married name?"

"Praetorius."

"That's unusual."

The young man heard and looked at her with scorn. "Alban Praetorius. She's married to Alban Praetorius. The composer," he added in a reverent voice.

"Is he famous?" enquired Selina.

"Very."

"I've never heard of him."

The young man looked politely disbelieving.

"You've brought a musical groupie home," Ralph whispered

231 •

to Virginia as he extricated himself from an extremely dull conversation with Angus and headed for the kitchen.

"It seems so," said Virginia. "What a fool Selina is. She'll have to do better than this when that husband is posted abroad."

"Sooner the better," said Ralph. "Too many bores in this country, that'll be one the less. And Lydia clearly knew him rather well at Oxford, and Selina doesn't like that."

"Yes, it's all rather tense in there," said Virginia. "Where's your friend?"

"Gervase? He'll be here any minute, I expect," said Ralph.

"That'll loosen things up," she said. "He won't know anyone."

"Only Justy," said Ralph.

## 20

"What an exhausting evening," said Virginia as she removed her earrings. "Excellent food, Ralph, thank you."

Ralph lay on his back, his arms crossed behind his head, looking up at the ceiling.

"Trouble ahead for young Justy, wouldn't you say?"

"Gervase is obviously very taken with her, but when is he going to be able to see her again? She'll be off back to Unthrang tomorrow; it could be months before she's back in London. Besides, Justy's still so attached to her husband, I never thought it would last, that marriage. How long is it now? Four years?"

"Lydia was in very good looks, it suits her to be pregnant."

"Lydia is always in good looks," said Virginia approvingly.

"Unfortunate, that Angus is obviously an ex-lover of hers."

"I would have thought she would have had better taste."

"He probably wasn't so bad when he was younger."

"And Selina's people being so friendly with Gervase's wife's family."

"Ex-wife."

"Can't imagine why she left him, lucky to get him, men like him hardly grow on trees."

Ralph was following his own train of thought. "Pity your young man isn't an ex-lover of Selina's, that would round things off nicely."

"Couldn't be. He's gay, got a very nice boyfriend who's in Sweden this week."

"I don't know what the world's coming to," said Ralph, beckoning to Virginia to come to bed.

\*     \*     \*

Gervase had extracted the address from Lydia, and he was at the flat at twelve o'clock the next morning, much to Lydia's amusement.

"Justy's gone," she said, as she let him into the flat.

He stopped on the threshold, obviously disappointed. "Gone? Out? When will she be back? I had hoped she would have lunch with me."

"To Eyot," said Lydia. "Don't stand there, I don't like having conversations on the doorstep."

Gervase obediently followed her into the flat. "Eyot."

"Where she lives," said Lydia.

"It's a long way away," said Gervase.

"About two hundred miles," agreed Lydia.

"Back to her husband."

"Back to Digby, yes."

"What's he like, this Digby?"

"I can't stand him," said Lydia frankly. "Nor can Virginia, nor can any of her Mountjoy relations. Her mother adores him, and so, unfortunately, does Justy. Or did."

"Did?" His voice was casual, only his eyes betrayed his interest.

Lydia chose her words carefully. "I suspect, and it is only a suspicion, Justy is very loyal, you know, that Justy hasn't been too happy with Digby since they moved northwards. He's a bit, how shall I put it, over-assertive, likes to have his own way . . ." She paused. "No, expects to have his own way. As of right, you know the kind of person. He's always been like that, but I don't suppose Justy found it so oppressive when they were living in London and she was working."

"Tell me about her," said Gervase, sitting down. "Oh, I brought some flowers."

"For Justy," said Lydia.

"No, for both of you," said Gervase courteously. "Please, I want to know all about her."

Justinia was lost in thought as she gazed out of the window. Little houses, big houses, neat gardens with pools and washing lines went flashing past. Fields, hedges, a river, a scrapyard.

"Can I join you?" said Lucius.

"Hello," said Justinia, warmly.

"I hadn't expected to meet you on the train," said Lucius, sliding into the seat opposite Justinia. "Digby said you wouldn't be back yet."

"No, I decided to come back sooner."

"Weren't you having a good time?"

"Yes, but . . ."

She could hardly tell Lucius, ". . . but I met a man at the opera who was . . . Let's say, I might have been interested in him if I weren't happily married, and instead of him going one way and me the other, we met again the following evening at Virginia's, which was the most extraordinary coincidence . . . and I realized that being, as I thought, happily married, is no protection against finding a man so attractive in a very worrying way . . . and beginning to wonder exactly how happy my marriage is."

Justinia changed the subject. "What were you doing in London? Work, the festival?"

"Yes," said Lucius. "I had a meeting in London yesterday, and then I thought I might as well stay on, to sort out a few things to do with the house."

"What about Andrea?"

The whole of Unthrang knows that Merle doesn't look after Andrea, thought Lucius glumly.

"She was staying overnight with a friend," he said. "She's made a lot of friends."

"Are you selling your house in London?" asked Justinia. "Now that you're working in Eyot. Or is Merle going to stay in London and come up for weekends?"

"I'm not sure," said Lucius. "She hasn't made up her mind . . . it depends how her work goes, and to be frank, it isn't going at all at the moment. Very depressing. But while I was in London, I arranged for a couple of agents to come and look the place over, then we'll know where we are if we decide to rent it out or sell it."

"Tell me about your work," said Justinia. "How's it all going?"

"I incur odium daily, for steering the festival away from a loss-making series of people's events and workshops towards professional performances."

"No supporters?"

"More than I had thought there would be. They're starting to creep out from under the stones where they've sensibly been hiding while the yooha elements screamed with rage at anything approaching professional competence. To be properly trained, to do a job well, if it happens to be in the arts, is to be an elitist; to the dungeons with the professionals, is the cry."

"You're very vehement."

"I feel very strongly about it."

"How are you getting back to Unthrang?" asked Lucius as they made their way over the bridge towards the exit. "Have you got your car here?"

"No," said Justinia. "I could ring Digby, only he isn't expecting me, and he'd normally stay on in Eyot until later, it's lodge night. I was going to stay in London for a couple more days, you see."

"I can give you a lift," said Lucius.

Justinia turned and smiled at him. "Thank you," and then, as she spotted a sturdy figure in a dark coat and a wide-brimmed hat among the throng below. "Oh, look, isn't that Valliaze?"

It was, and he waved to them, and waited at the foot of the stairs as they came down. He removed his hat to Justinia, and gave a bow.

"I'm here to buy a ticket, remarkably good value, because now I'm a pensioner, I have a card and get all kinds of wonderful reductions. I could have done with these prices when I was younger and travelled so much for work. Have you been away together?" he added, with a sly look at Justinia.

She laughed, and said she and Lucius had both been in London, but not together. "And Lucius was there on serious business, work and personal, while I was simply being frivolous."

"I know, with Lydia Praetorius, who's your cousin," said Valliaze.

"How did you know that?" said Justinia, surprised.

"Ah, because I've been talking to Alban, an old friend of mine; he's in a state of rage over this appalling cathedral business, and beside himself without his Lydia. I hope she comes back soon, she's the only one who can control him. Otherwise, there may be a case of clergicide."

"Clergicide?" said Lucius, amused.

"Yes, Alban will undoubtedly end up murdering this tune-loving clergyman at the Cathedral, who lays down the law on matters about which he knows absolutely nothing, namely music. He's destroying the cathedral choir, which should really have a preservation order on it; he wouldn't be allowed to vandalize the fabric of the cathedral, why should get he away with vandalizing the choir? On top of that, he's likely to cause one of our most distinguished composers to have a heart attack if he isn't stopped."

They passed under the big arches into the station forecourt. "Where are you going?" Lucius asked Valliaze. "Can I drive you anywhere?"

"No, I'm only going home; it's a short walk, and I have to walk, my doctor says so."

"Go on," said the voice to Justinia. "Ask him."

"No."

"Yes. Now."

"No."

"Are you all right?" Valliaze asked. "You're looking strange, as though you're hearing distant voices."

"Not at all," said Justinia. This voice was getting out of hand and becoming noticeable.

"Do as I say, and I'll be off," it buzzed in her ear.

Justinia gave in. "Could I ask a favour?" she said to Valliaze quickly; he was just about to set off across the road.

"Of course," he said, coming back on to the pavement and giving her a foxy smile. "I love to do favours for beautiful young women, although, sadly, I rarely get the chance these days. Tell me what it is you want."

Justinia took a deep breath. "I wondered . . . well, I'd like to go to someone, for someone to hear . . . to sing to someone who could give me advice about my voice. Lessons, and so on . . ."

Her voice tailed away; Lucius and Valliaze's eyes were fixed on her.

"Good for you," said Lucius.

"This is excellent news," said Valliaze, cheerfully. "I think, if you have time, we could adjourn to the Mountjoy Arms to talk about this matter. Lucius?"

Lucius looked at his watch.

"It's difficult for you now," said Justinia. "Another time . . ."

"No," said Lucius. "Being inquisitive, I'd like to know what Valliaze thinks, all in my line of business, after all. There'll be a phone in this pub, won't there?"

"Of course," said Valliaze. "If not a public one, then the landlord will let you ring, he's an old friend of mine."

"Then I can ring home and check that Andrea is all right."

"Your wife?" said Valliaze, as he plunged into the traffic. "Is she ill?"

"Daughter," said Lucius, making a leap for the pavement as a bus thundered past them. "She's fine, it's just to see that she got home from school okay and so on."

Valliaze dived down a small street. "Here we are," he said, holding the door open for Justinia. Lucius paused outside to look at the sign, and went into the pub laughing.

"Have you seen the inn sign?" he asked Justinia, as he caught up with them.

"No, it's the family crest, I suppose. Very boring."

"Not a bit of it," said Lucius. "Someone with a sense of humour painted it, it shows a naked woman languishing in a pair of strong arms."

Justinia laughed and laughed. "The Mountjoy reputation," she said.

"It's an old sign," Valliaze said as he guided them to a table near a welcome log fire. "Are the Mountjoys still like that today?"

"Some of them," said Justinia.

"It adds interest to life," said Valliaze, remembering his own well-lived youth and middle years. "We'll sit here, and enjoy the fire while we can. They say, the weather experts, that more freak weather is on the way, because warm winds are going to blow. So there'll be no need for fires, and we shall all be out in our shirtsleeves."

He settled himself comfortably at the table. "Now, you go and make your phone call, Lucius, and then we get down to serious business, hey?"

*     *     *

"Andrea? Everything all right?"

"Hello, Dad. Yes, of course. Are you in London?"

"No, I'm in Eyot, I'll be home quite soon. How's your mother?"

Andrea sounded buoyant. "She's in a good mood, she's in the kitchen with Issur."

"Issur?" said Lucius, surprised.

"Yes, and do you know what? Mum came and met me from school, with Issur, and then Issur came back here with us. He and Mum are sitting at the kitchen table, drinking funny tea with lemon in it, and talking like mad."

"Oh," said Lucius. "What are you doing?"

"I've just re-arranged my room. Issur said I should, because the bed was under the window. He said I shouldn't have a bed under the window in the winter."

"He's probably right," said Lucius. "And what are you doing now?"

"Learning some spellings."

"Difficult ones?"

"No, easy-peasy," said Andrea scornfully. "Then I'm going to make supper. Will you be back for supper?"

"Of course."

"Good."

"Tell your mother I rang."

"Okay," said Andrea. "Bye."

Lucius put the receiver down and made his way slowly back down the passage towards the bar. Issur. What was Issur doing at Juniper House? How unexpected, him sitting at the kitchen table, talking to Merle. For a moment his hackles rose, in an ancient and uncontrollable reaction, then he laughed at himself. Issur's interests clearly lay with his own sex. It was good for Merle to have someone to talk to, and if Issur had got her to meet Andrea, it was more than he had managed to do.

Still puzzled, he sat down at the table with Justinia and Valliaze again.

"Everything all right?" said Justinia.

"Yes," said Lucius.

"To the matter in hand," said Valliaze, finishing his drink.

Lucius rose swiftly to get him another; he slid back into his seat.

"Lucius, have you heard of Stephanie Lucchesi?"

"Singer," said Lucius at once. "You can't be thinking of her, Valliaze, if she's alive she must be, what, in her eighties?"

Valliaze nodded. "Alive, in her eighties. And I think she should hear Justinia sing."

"Why her?"

"If you had ever heard her sing, or listened to her recordings, you would understand at once. It's the voice, you see. Let me tell you about her."

Valliaze sat back against the plush velvet buttoning and began his story.

"Stephanie Lucchesi was the daughter of an Italian father and an English mother. They were solid bourgeois people, he was a merchant, she was the daughter of a merchant. Stephanie was a very musical child, and she began singing when she was quite little.

"Her voice was very, very good. She was well taught, and she began to sing minor parts in the local opera when she was in her late teens. She went to Milan, to study, and to bigger parts. Then she had the chance to go and sing in Germany, and she leapt at it, although her parents were completely against the idea. She was strong-minded and passionate about her music; nothing was going to stand in the way of her music.

"Fortunately for her worried parents, she soon met a very respectable young man, a German engineer, and fell in love with him. She made it quite clear that she was still going to follow her career and be a professional singer, and he didn't object; he was too much in love with her to deny her anything.

"Then he had to go to China on business. They had a young son by this time, and Stephanie stayed behind in Europe to look after the child and continue with her career."

Valliaze rearranged himself more comfortably on his seat, looked at his audience to make sure they were attending, took several sips of his drink, and went on with his narrative.

"You've heard of Hans Schütz, of course. Now, at this time, he was a rising young star in the conducting world. Very dynamic, very intense about his music – and very handsome. Stephanie worked with him, and they fell in love. Everybody in the opera world knew that they were having a wild and passionate affair; but not, of course Stephanie's parents, and not her husband. He returned from China after a year away to find that his wife was pregnant.

"It didn't take him long to find out who the father was. He was so incensed that he marched into the opera house during a rehearsal, accused Hans Schütz of seducing his wife, and challenged him to a duel. When he refused, he struck him across the face with his cane.

"Of course, the story spread everywhere. Stephanie's parents were furious, and took her husband's side. They said she must give up singing for good, settle down as a housewife and mother, and try to live down the shame. The husband, from duty rather than affection, said that he would acknowledge the child, and everyone said what a wonderful fellow he was."

"Poor Stephanie," said Justinia with feeling.

"I've heard bits and pieces of this, but never the whole story," said Lucius, fascinated. "Go on. What happened next?"

"Stephanie did her best. She had the baby, which was a girl, gave up her singing, and tried to be a good wife and mother. No good. By falling in love with Hans Schütz, she had fallen completely out of love with her husband. He was cold and unloving towards the little girl, and that upset her. There was no help from Hans Schütz, because the opera house had sacked him – on account of the scandal – and he'd gone back to Germany. He wouldn't answer Stephanie's letters or see her; he was afraid it might harm his career.

"Finally, Stephanie couldn't stand it any longer. She went back to Milan, where they were more than glad to employ her. Her husband then dropped a bombshell: she could do a modest amount of singing, provided she accepted that she was first and foremost his wife, provided she only sang roles he approved of for her, and with the conductors he chose. And provided the little girl, who was by now three, was adopted, Stephanie wasn't to know who by, and she was never to make any attempt to see her."

"The shit," said Justinia furiously.

"Otherwise, he would divorce her, gain custody of their son and make sure that she never saw him. Stephanie was desperate by this time, and her parents put a lot of pressure on her to give up the girl. Her mother said she would find a good English family for the child; she felt in any case that the child was growing up to be too like Stephanie, and could only be saved from a wicked life by going to a family where she would be more strictly brought up.

"Stephanie agreed, and I don't think she ever forgave herself for letting the child go. It was about this time that I first got to know her; she was awesome to work with, a consummate artist, a superb musician . . ."

Lucius had been doing some sums. "Her career must have gone on until I was old enough to be interested in opera, why didn't I ever hear her sing?"

"Stephanie didn't stay with her husband, as anyone with an ounce of sense could have foreseen. She came to England at the beginning of the war, because she wasn't a Mussolini fan, and she couldn't have gone on singing during the war in Italy. She had numerous lovers, made a lot of money, was at the top of her profession. Then her son, who was in the Italian army, was killed. She was devastated, and about that time she caught a throat infection. It was nothing serious, but it was badly treated, and did some damage to her throat. She had an operation which seemed to have been successful – but her voice wasn't the same. She had lost a lot of weight, that might have had something to do with it. It was perhaps ninety or even ninety-five per cent as good, but that wasn't good enough for Stephanie. She retired at once, and never sang in public again."

"What a waste," said Lucius.

"What did she do?"

"She married again and went to live in America, and she taught at a not very well-known college there, and produced some fine singers. Then her husband died, and she came to live in England. She'd come to this part of the country on holiday, and liked it; it held no memories for her, so she bought a house and settled down."

"Do you mean to say she lives in Eyotshire?" said Justinia.

"Indeed she does, in Unthrang."

"Unthrang!" said Justinia, astounded.

"Nobody knows who she is, she's fairly reclusive, she uses her married name, which is Zouche; she changed her first name to Zephania when she married, wiping out the past, I suppose."

"Zephania Zouche," Lucius and Justinia exclaimed together.

"Piers' aunt," said Justinia.

"The woman who lives in the Manor," said Lucius. "Well, I'll be damned."

## 21

"I wonder if Piers knows about his aunt," said Justinia, as they drove through the dark lanes to Unthrang.

"No," said Lucius definitely. "He would have said."

"Should we tell him?"

"She would have told him if she'd wanted him to know."

"Perhaps it never came up. It may not have occurred to her that he would be interested."

"But he would be."

"Oh, yes."

"I wonder when Valliaze is going to get in touch with her," said Justinia.

"He said he would right away. I'm going to see if I can dig up any old recordings, I'm intrigued and want to hear what she was like, and why Valliaze is so sure that she's the one to give an opinion on your voice. After all, there must be dozens of teachers he could recommend, in London or Manchester."

Lucius slowed down to let a poacher cross the road. The man lumbered across, the pockets of his disreputable old jacket bulging, and held up a grubby hand in acknowledgment.

"Mountjoy pheasants," said Justinia in an absent-minded voice. "I suppose I should tell Val."

"But you won't, will you?"

"No, I'm afraid I'm not very country-minded when it comes to preserving game. I don't like the thought of breeding up birds for the fun of taking a pot-shot at them."

"Do you like eating pheasant?"

"Yes, very much," confessed Justinia, laughing at herself. "As long as someone else has plucked and drawn and cooked them, I'm all for it."

Lucius laughed too. "I shall be very interested to hear what Zephania says about you. If she says you should train, would you take her advice?"

"I don't know," said Justinia thoughtfully. "I think I just want to know. Otherwise I'll go through life thinking, if only . . ."

"How would Digby feel about your training?"

"He wouldn't see the point. He's so ignorant about music. He doesn't understand that it isn't enough to have a good voice and to make a reasonable sound in a choir. In fact, he doesn't even understand that I couldn't sing in the choirs I do unless I had been trained a little when I was younger, and had done quite a lot of practice. If he was told that I had a really good voice, then the next step in his mind would be appearing top of the bill at Covent Garden. He doesn't know that however good you are, you need technique. I don't suppose he knows the meaning of the word, let alone how long it takes to acquire it."

She sighed. "Classical music is so bloody difficult. You don't achieve anything without hard work, and an awful lot of it. You know all about that. So does Piers. But Digby? If you can belt out a number with a good tune, then you can sing. He doesn't know the difference between trained and untrained, and he never will."

"Just like the Succentor," said Lucius.

"Awful man," said Justinia, closing her eyes. "He and Digby should get together and share horrible ideas about music."

Lucius was wondering how on earth Justinia had come to marry Digby. Women seemed to find him attractive, although he couldn't see why, but surely warning bells must have rung in Justinia's ear.

"Warning bells did ring, didn't they," said the voice, startling Justinia. "Only you didn't pay any attention, thought you knew best."

"Oh, bugger off," said Justinia wearily.

Lucius looked at her in astonishment. "I'm sorry, what have I done? Or are you swearing at an insect?"

"No, no," said Justinia. "It's nothing to do with you, Lucius, I am sorry, I didn't mean to say it out loud. It's just that I hear a voice in my head, a floating voice which comes and goes, and nags away at me, as though it's speaking in my ear. It's very irritating, and I wish it would go away. I think I must be over-tired; I don't know. Anyway, I hate it."

"I'm not surprised," said Lucius, slowing down as they approached Unthrang. Funny, he thought as he dropped Justinia outside her house. Justinia seems so in control, but she shouldn't be hearing voices. Clearly, all is not well in the FitzOdo household. He shook his head as he swung the car into the drive beside Juniper House, swerved violently to avoid one of Roxane's peacocks and scrunched to a stop. Home, he thought. It really feels like home, this place, far more than the house in London does – or ever did. I wish Merle liked it here, I wish she liked anything at all.

Sadie had decided to have a sort out. Not of clothes this time, but of papers. The departure of most of her and Charles's clothes to Oxfam, the jumble sale or the dustbin had left her with a lot of space. Time, she thought, to go through her own books and papers, which were mostly in cardboard boxes in the garage, and give them a home inside.

Sadie wasn't exactly expert at do-it-yourself, but, she told herself, anyone can take cupboards down. She stood and surveyed the wall of tasteful bedroom fittings which Charles had had installed, and which she had always disliked. She was advancing on the first door with a hammer and a determined expression when the doorbell rang.

Thwarted, she went downstairs, hammer in hand, to open the door. Sylvester eyed the hammer suspiciously.

"What are you up to now, Sadie?"

"Oh, it's you, Sylvester," said Sadie. "Come in. I'm just about to demolish those horrible fitted cupboards in the bedroom."

"You should have wondered about Charles when he ordered those," observed Sylvester as he followed her into the house. "All those curly bits and the gold trimmings, a dead giveaway if I may say so."

"Easy to be wise after the event," said Sadie. "I thought it was a rush of bad taste to the head, Charles never did have very good taste."

"Do you know anything about taking down cupboards?" asked

Sylvester. "That seems a very small hammer for the job. What other tools have you got? What's your plan?"

"To thump and bang at it until it's loose, and then to drag it down to the garden and burn it."

"Don't you think you could do with some professional help?"

"Can't afford it," said Sadie cheerfully. "If I want anything done, I've got to do it myself."

"Wouldn't Issur help you?"

"He might, but he's out, and I want to do it now. Then I can put up some shelves, which I bought by mail order. They were delivered this morning." She pointed to the long cardboard boxes which were stacked up against the wall. "Easy-fix, they're supposed to be, so I should be able to manage them."

"Stay there," said Sylvester, heading for the front door. He could move with surprising speed when he chose. "I'll be back in two minutes . . ."

He was, with Lily in tow. Lily gave Sadie and the hammer one swift and scornful look, and then demanded to be taken upstairs.

"You can't just bang away at those," she said definitely. "You'll bring half the wall with them if you aren't careful."

Sadie was crestfallen; she would have argued with Sylvester about it, or with almost anyone else, but she wasn't going to argue with Lily. Lily was always right about that kind of thing.

"But if I don't take the cupboards out, then there's nowhere else I can put the shelves."

Lily thought for a moment, her eyes narrowed. "Josiah Smile," she said, triumphantly.

"No, no, these cupboards are far too flimsy to make into coffins," said Sylvester. "You aren't being very helpful this morning, Lily."

Lily took no notice. "Josiah's daughter, Mordred, is getting married, and she wants Joseph to put fitted cupboards in for her. He was grumbling about it, all that fancy work she wants isn't really in his line of business, he told me. He can make a good, straightforward piece of furniture . . ."

"Especially if it's got brass handles," put in Sylvester.

". . . such as a plain cupboard, or in a kitchen. Mordred wants lots of twiddly bits, as he describes it. It seems to me that twiddly bits is what you've got here, Sadie. Tell him he can have your cupboards if he'll take them away, and in return he'll get one of his lads to put your shelves up for you."

Sadie thought this was a brilliant solution, especially since she had opened up the instructions for the Easy-fix shelves and found them unintelligible.

"I think you've got that diagram upside down," Sylvester said helpfully.

"It makes no difference at all," Sadie told him. "The pictures make no sense, and I think the written instructions are translated from the Hungarian by someone who isn't entirely at home with the English language."

"What are you going to put on these shelves?" asked Lily.

Sadie explained. "I've got a lot more books on parrots, and journals, papers, all that kind of thing. Charles thought it was all a waste of time, so he would only let me have a few in the house. I've been meaning to go and get everything out, now that it's clear he's gone for good. Mind you, he'll probably sue if he finds out I've thrown his precious cupboards out. Claim he should have been given custody of them, I wouldn't be surprised."

"He'll put Nigel on to you, I dare say," said Lily. "Time you woke up and got yourself a proper lawyer, before you find yourself without a roof over your head."

Sadie sighed. "Don't depress me, Lily, I keep on trying not to think about it. Ursula's threatening to visit, to talk it over with me, I think Charles has been getting at her."

"Well, if you need support, you know where I am," said Sylvester. "Now, put that hammer away, and we'll pop across to the Smiles' establishment and put Lily's proposition to him. Then you can come back with us for lunch. Or is Issur expecting to be fed?"

"No," said Sadie. "He's gone into Eyot, he won't be back until later. I'd like that, Sylvester, if it's no trouble, but I won't be able to linger. I have to do my hundred lengths in Roxane's pool before Issur gets back, or he'll be annoyed."

"A hundred lengths?" said Sylvester incredulously. "Sadie, is this wise?"

"Oh, yes, I'm feeling much better for the exercise, and I'm into a size smaller clothes already. Issur's very determined, it's much easier just to go along with what he tells you."

Lily snorted and went back to Crag End, while Sylvester and Sadie set off in the opposite direction towards Josiah Smile and Sons, Trust Us for Kitchens and Funerals.

Lucius woke up with a hangover, unusual for him. But then, he had passed a most unusual evening, drinking vodka with Issur until the small hours and discussing fate, Greek drama and football.

"It isn't even as if I knew anything about football," Lucius said to his distinctly blurred mirror image as he tried to shave. There was a perfunctory knock on the door, and Andrea sidled into the bathroom.

"Mummy said to bring you this," she said, looking at him with interest. "She said you've got a bad head. Have you hurt it, or was it drink?"

Lucius didn't feel like lively conversation just at that moment; he took the glass from her and waved at her to go. Then a thought struck him. He looked at the glass. "Mummy said? Is she up?"

"Oh, yes," said Andrea. "She's been up for hours, working. She's going to take me to school, she says."

She vanished and Lucius gazed at his very perplexed-looking reflection. Was he still asleep? Was he dreaming? No, nobody could dream about feeling this awful, it had to be real.

"What was in that drink?" he asked when he finally made it downstairs. Merle was busy in the kitchen, a surprising sight, but not one he felt inclined to query.

"It was a prairie oyster," she said. "Good for your stomach. If you drink a lot of water," and she plonked a bottle of fizzy mineral water on the table in front of him, "your head will clear, too. Dehydration, that's the problem. Have some orange juice, too, that'll help, and honey."

Lucius did as he was told, watching Merle out of the corner of his eye.

"What are you doing?" he asked, once the fizzy water, orange juice and honey had been despatched as per instructions.

"Preparing a stew so that it can simmer all day on the Rayburn. For supper," she added, seeing his puzzled expression.

"But you don't . . ." he began.

"I haven't been cooking recently, no, I am aware of that. However, I'm cooking now, I want Andrea to have a proper meal in the evenings; it's not very nourishing, a packed lunch and then whatever she can manage to cook in the evenings."

"I've done my best," said Lucius. "I'm not a very good cook, at least, she doesn't like eating what I make. I've taken her to the pub sometimes."

"Pub food," said Merle. "Hopeless. I've made you some toast, have that and some fruit, that'll keep you going. And make sure you go out and have something to eat at lunchtime, not a sandwich in the office, or you'll suffer all afternoon."

"Remind me not to drink vodka again for a very long time."

"It did you good, you can't be tight-arsed if you're full of vodka."

"Tight-arsed?" said Lucius indignantly. "Tight-arsed? I'm not . . ."

But Merle had gone.

Where was she? he wondered, as he went to find his briefcase.

Working. In the study, working. Working at speed, too, by the sound of it. He stood by the door, listening. And Andrea had said she'd been up early working. What at? What had come over her?

Best not to ask, he told himself as he went out of the house into the strangely warm autumn morning. He stood still for a moment or two, looked up at the clear blue sky, and went back inside to hang his coat up on the hatstand, there was no way he was going to need it.

"Lovely day," Roxane called to him as he opened the door of his car. She was leaning out of an upstairs window, apparently wearing a strip of silk and nothing else. "Indian summer," she went on. "Warm winds blowing up from the Azores, set to stay, wonderful, and amazing at this time of year."

Lucius waved back at her from the car window as he drove away, thinking, as he slowed down for the Manor House cats, how much weather there seemed to be in Unthrang.

"Requiem tomorrow," said Sylvester, surging through Justinia's kitchen door. "We're rehearsing this evening, six o'clock prompt, in the church. Voices, that is, we'll have a full rehearsal with the orchestra tomorrow before the actual service. Black, please."

"What?" Justinia stared at him. "Sylvester, what Requiem, who for?"

"Of course, you've been away, and Digby's been up to his own musical mischief in Eyot, he wouldn't have told you about what the Rev Wroot's been up to."

"Digby?" said Justinia? "Mischief? What mischief?"

"Oh, he wants to sponsor the cathedral choir, tremendous hoo-ha about it, but I dare say he'll get his way. Money talks, you know, and it talks very loudly within the precincts of the C of E."

"You're joking," said Justinia. "Sylvester, what an absurd idea. Digby's never even heard the cathedral choir."

"He has now. He went with the Succentor, they're as thick as thieves, those two. The whole deal will be in the bag any day now."

Justinia sat down at the kitchen table and propped her head in her hand. "Sylvester, have you been tippling?"

Sylvester was affronted. "I have not," he said, with immense dignity. "I never drink during the day, wipes you out if taken before six, and I couldn't waste all that time. Lost practice, and think of all the goings-on you might miss."

"I seem to have missed out on some goings-on while completely sober," said Justinia. "Digby, the choir ... And Digby hardly knows the Succentor. No, it's absurd."

Sylvester shook his head. "Unfortunately not; I think it could all blow up into something quite serious. Alban's up in arms because the Succentor has persuaded the Cathedral to cancel his commission. It's not the financial loss, because he'll find someone else to take it on; no problem, he was doing it for the Cathedral for much less than his usual rate, in any case. It's the principle of the thing, you see. Inaccessible music, too difficult, out of touch with today's ... blah, blah, you know the rest. Alban's making waves, it's been on the news, letters to *The Times*, oh dear!"

"I know about Alban's commission, but I don't see what that's got to do with Digby and the choir."

"Same thing. Give the choir a new look, get them to sing folksy music, rumpty-tum happy tunes for the singalong brigade, pretty boys with sweet voices. Forget the training, forget the musicianship, they've just got to look good and belt out the numbers."

"But why?"

"I told you, money. The choir costs a packet to run, and Digby and his Wursthorn chum are providing a pile of loot. They get their business promoted, flashy medals round the boys' necks, logos on choir folders, special appearances, you know. The Succentor's pushing it all through, because if he brings home the bacon, he can do what he likes. Rumour is, Evensong's going to be cut down to two evenings a week, and then probably to one. The other evenings it's going to be Sung Worship, so that the people can be more involved."

"I don't believe you," said Justinia flatly. "There'd be such an outcry. Surely the Dean . . ."

"The Dean's put his foot in it, because a young reporter asked him about whether he thought music brought people closer to God, and the Dean, a busy man as you know, snapped back that he didn't have time to think about God, he had a cathedral to run."

"Oh, hell," said Justinia.

"That's what the Dean said when he saw the papers. Haven't you seen any of this, Justy?"

"No, Digby didn't say a word about it, well, he wouldn't . . . and I haven't looked at a paper, or seen the news. My mind's been on other things."

"Have a word with Digby, see if you can persuade him to lay off the choir. The Succentor won't get his way if the money is no longer on offer."

"I'll try," said Justinia doubtfully, remembering other Digby enthusiasms; nothing would deflect him if he had a scheme which was both dear to his heart and likely to make him substantial sums of money.

Sylvester patted Justinia's shoulder as he left. "Cheer up. After all, the Rev Wroot has seen the light, perhaps a thunderbolt will strike the Succentor before he wipes out eight hundred years of musical tradition . . ." He paused. "The Requiem's Duruflé, by the way. Don't be late."

\*      \*      \*

Pansy walked across the green with a light and happy step, while Marius strode alongside her in what appeared to be a dark and profoundly thoughtful mood. In fact, he was wondering what time the Requiem rehearsal would finish. Well before closing time, he hoped; he liked the look of the Cow and Prisoner.

Piers was inside the church, talking to Valliaze and Justinia. A cluster of other singers were arranging themselves in the choir stalls; in the body of the church sat some members of the Rev Wroot's regular congregation, who had stayed on after Evening Worship to see for themselves the forces of darkness polluting their church.

Sylvester arrived, looking very jovial, gave Valliaze a clap on the back which made the conductor totter, and greeted the assembled singers.

"What about them?" he asked Piers as his eye was caught by the gloomy faces lined up in a row.

Piers explained, and Sylvester looked at them disapprovingly. "Vegetarians," he said dismissively.

Pansy's eyes sparkled. "How do you know they're vegetarians?" she whispered to Sylvester.

"Because they look so dreary."

"I know some very bouncy vegetarians."

"Real vegetarianism is a state of mind," said Sylvester firmly. "It hasn't got much to do with being or not being a carnivore, but it's got a lot to do with hating what's enjoyable. If you like eating lettuce, chew away, but if you eat it because it's good for you, beware!"

Pansy gave a gurgling laugh.

"Now, tell me your name," said Sylvester. "Piers gave me a list, and I like to know who's who."

"I'm Pansy, and this is Marius."

Marius turned a brooding countenance on Sylvester and said hello.

"He's your young man, is he?" said Sylvester. "Good, good. Now, I think we're all here . . . no, we aren't, where's Lucius? I told him not to be late."

"I'm here, Sylvester," said Lucius, coming through the door at that moment. "Sorry I'm late, it was Merle."

"More trouble?" asked Sylvester sympathetically.

"No, no, not at all," said Lucius, looking very cheerful. "Quite the opposite, I'll tell you later, I presume we're heading for the pub afterwards?"

"Naturally."

Sylvester sat himself at the piano, ran his fingers over the keys, made a face, and nodded at Valliaze. The singers flipped open their music, and the rehearsal began. Only Piers noticed Great-Aunt Zeph slipping into the back of the church and sitting herself down in the shadows. He wondered why she was there, then Valliaze called him to attention, and he turned back to the music.

Valliaze pointed his baton at Justinia. "Sing from letter H, he commanded. "Sylvester, can I have a G, please."

Justinia, surprised, sang. He stopped her, made some comments, then told her to do it again. "And fill the church, please." He nodded, pleased. "Now, all the sopranos, there are five of you, fill the church five times over."

They did, the clutch of glum women winced, Sylvester gave a satisfied grunt, and the rehearsal continued.

Valliaze kept them at it for about an hour. "Not bad," he said. "Now a short break, and then we go on, we'll work on the Kyrie next."

Some of the singers wandered outside. Although it was already dark, the air was still warm. "Astonishing weather," observed one of them.

The Rev Wroot came out of the church with his little throng, looking very perturbed. They weren't at all happy about this, that was clear, but what was he to do? He had wrestled with his conscience, he knew those dreams came from the Lord, he was being led, it wasn't the warped decision of a proud mind.

The women grumbled off into the darkness, and he watched the singers, Pansy in the centre of them, full of mirth, Marius looming protectively over her. The Rev Wroot had watched them sing, had listened to them with his eyes shut, and against his will, he had the horrible feeling that perhaps there was something to this kind of music. Perhaps, just perhaps, the guitar and the tambourine weren't after all on a direct line to the Almighty, whereas he could well imagine the Lord listening to this music.

He shook his head, as if to shake these revolutionary thoughts out of it. He was allowing this backward-looking celebration of All Souls as a gesture to the lost souls of his parish who lacked an enlightened view of the modern way of church music; once over, the church would revert to its proper forms of worship. And he, the Rev Wroot, might stop having these strange dreams, stop being haunted by the body and voice of Issur, and be restored to his normal and certain strain of Christianity.

Valliaze, who had eyes in the back of his head, had in fact noticed Zephania Zouche's arrival, and he greeted her with enthusiasm. "Now," he said, steering Justinia towards her. "This is the one I told you about."

Piers watched the little group, wondering at the tension in his Great-Aunt. She was looking at Justinia as though she had seen a ghost. She said nothing, simply searched Justinia's face with expressionless eyes. The silence stretched, began to be uncomfortable. Then Zephania gave a sigh.

"I am sorry, how rude of me to stare, you must forgive a very old woman . . . but this voice comes like a ghost from the past, a reminder of another world, another time."

Her voice became brisker, and she laid a surprisingly strong hand on Valliaze's arm. "You don't need to ask my opinion, you're a better judge than I am."

Valliaze smiled, and patted her hand. "Of course I am, but this voice is unusual. It has a quality and a character that is distinctive; you had such a voice, and so, I wanted you to hear her."

"I'm glad I did," said Zephania, looking again at Justinia, her eyes bright although the face surrounding them had the faded wrinkles of age. "Yes, I'm glad." She spoke directly to Justinia. "Valliaze says you wonder if you should take you singing seriously, train, become a professional."

Justinia felt awkward. "Yes, well, I wanted to know if it would be possible, worthwhile . . . although at present, I don't see how . . . My husband, you see . . ."

Zephania interrupted her with an impatient gesture. "Husband," she said in a voice full of scorn. "Husband! What have husbands to do with singing?"

## 22

Silence. Valliaze looked at Zephania, Zephania looked at Justinia, Justinia looked out through the church door to the darkness beyond.

Zephania put out a hand towards Justinia. She touched her gently under the chin, making Justinia look at her. "It would be a crime not to train," she said. "A crime to your voice, and to the music you should be singing."

She became brisker. "Very well, now you must go to London, to Yseult Drury. I will telephone her, to say you're coming. She will tell you what anyone would tell you. She will say that if you work hard, extremely hard, then in three years, you will be able to sing anywhere in England, you will already start to make a name. In five years, you will sing internationally, you will have a career. If you work. If you work and work and work."

She paused, and gave Justinia another hawkish look. "What she won't tell you is that this will cost you your marriage, it will make your family angry with you, your friends will say, why do such a crazy thing? Why give up so much for a dream, when it may all come to nothing?"

Valliaze nodded approvingly.

"So, in the end, it's all up to you. There is no point in this asking, am I good enough, is it a voice worth training? You should know this for yourself, you're a grown-up woman, why do you need to ask? If the hunger isn't there, then settle down in this little town, and live a contented life." She gave a dramatic shrug, "How you could be contented when you not only have such a voice, but also a great love of music, this is a mystery to me. English, it's because you're English."

Justinia said nothing, her head was ringing with the voice, triumphant and insistent, crowing, "Told you so, told you so."

Zephania beckoned Piers with an imperious finger. "Piers," she said, "we're going to give a dinner party. Find someone to cook, I'm too old, and you can only cook baked beans. On All Souls, yes, that's appropriate. You, child," she said to Justinia. "With your husband, and your mother."

She smiled as Justinia looked startled. "In Unthrang, my dear, everyone knows everything. With your mother. Now Piers, you can give me your arm and take me home, I feel very tired. Then you will come back to finish the rehearsal."

Piers leapt to attention, raised his eyebrows dramatically at Justinia, gave her a large wink, and led his great-aunt towards the door.

Justinia hadn't meant to join the others at the pub after the rehearsal. She felt she ought to get home to Celia and Digby, but she found herself swept along in the rush. Piers peeled off to fetch Roxane: "I like to keep an eye on her," he explained. The others were talking about Zephania Zouche; word had spread about who she was, her legendary voice, her career, her love affairs.

"Fancy her being Piers' great-aunt and him never knowing," said Pansy as she wound herself round Marius. "It's all very exciting. Justy, aren't you thrilled? Simply to get through Yseult Drury's front door is more than any of us would ever dream of; goodness, it's all happening for you!"

Lucius helped Sylvester with the drinks, although Sylvester, in a particularly expansive mood, refused to let him contribute. "No, no," he said, with a dramatic wave of his hand. "I've arranged it all, most of these youngsters are students, they haven't got two pennies to rub together, they deserve a drink, all the work they've been doing. Mrs Herb is laying on a bit of food as well, young people are always hungry. Now Lucius, while we're away from the crowd, tell me your news, quick."

"News? Oh, Merle. Yes, the most amazing change. It's Issur's doing, you know. When he was there the other evening, the day I got back from London, he sat and talked to Merle for hours. I don't know what he said, but whatever it was, she's woken up, thrown out all those stale and tedious pieces she was writing and has sat down to write about Unthrang, the country as it is, the people, the weather, the lot. She won't show me what she's written, but I can tell she's pleased with it. She's bypassing her agent, says the woman's a shit, and she'll handle it herself, and she despatched a thick envelope to some editor this evening. Of course, I don't know whether anything will come of it, or whether she'll just get another rejection slip; it doesn't matter. I haven't seen her lit up like this for . . . oh, years! Andrea can't believe it, either, but she takes a gloomy view, she's afraid it won't last."

"And you?" said Sylvester.

"If it doesn't, I shall ask Issur over again," said Lucius firmly. "There's something about that man."

"Mmm," said Sylvester. "This the lot?" he said to the landlord.

"Yes, and Mrs Herb'll bring the food directly. She's just upstairs, getting a room ready, someone coming up for a few days fishing."

"Let's hope he catches a big fish," said Sylvester. "Good for business, a successful catch. He'll tell all his friends, and before you know where you are, you'll be booked solid."

Pansy was proposing herself as cook. "Yes, I do know how to cook, Piers," she said, smiling her dimpled smile. "I cook in the vacs, proper cooking, we're not talking hamburgers here. You supply the dosh and give me a hand with the shopping, and I'll produce a feast."

Marius nodded. "She is a terrific cook," he confirmed.

"Do you want to let her out of your sight, though?" said Piers.

"Don't tease him," said Pansy reprovingly. "The poor precious has to work that night, after the service."

"Work?" said Sylvester as he joined them. "Studying? All night?"

Marius shook his head gloomily. "Money," he said tersely.

Pansy explained. "It's his night job. Three nights a week, at Bilberry's, you know, the place where they make those dramatically expensive bags. He's night watchman."

"Don't you sleep all through your lectures the next day?" asked Lucius.

Marius gave a rare smile. "No," he said. "I borrow a goose."

"A goose?"

Pansy let out a peal of rippling laughter as she saw their astonished expressions. "Geese make excellent guards," she told them. "And this goose especially. Marius takes it along in a cat basket and lets her out. She stalks up and down the factory all night, inspecting the property. Any disturbance, such as intruders, and she'd raise the roof, hissing and cackling and flapping her wings. So Marius just curls up in his sleeping bag and goes to sleep, while Griselda – that's the goose's name – does the rounds."

Sylvester was fascinated. "Where does Griselda come from?" he demanded.

"A friend who keeps several geese. Griselda's a pet, so she doesn't get eaten come Christmas. She seems to enjoy her outings," said Marius.

Sylvester beamed approval. "Hang on to this young man," he advised Pansy. "He'll go far!"

Justinia was in disgrace when she finally got home, a little tipsy, but filled with a radiant happiness and with a look of determination on her face that made even Digby hesitate to ask her what she'd been up to. She ignored their disapproving noises, dropped a kiss on each of their heads, announced she was going to bed, and vanished.

Digby showed how displeased he was the following morning, by setting off early and noisily for work without saying a word to Justinia, who rose late, and, feeling hungrier than she had for a long time, wandered down to the kitchen.

Celia, who had been up and about for hours, was folding linen in the bathroom when she heard a large vehicle draw up outside the house. She looked out of the window to see what was going on, and went down to open the door.

"Justinia," she said, as she came into the kitchen. "There's a furniture van here, they say they have something for us, has Digby bought any furniture? He didn't mention it to me." Her face was looking particularly distressed. "I'm sure it's a mistake, they say it's a sofa, a very big sofa."

Justinia leapt up from the table where she was sitting with a cup of coffee and the *Unthrang Chronicle*, "The Best of the News from Your Town".

"That was quick," she said. "It's mine, from London."

Celia was shocked. "Justinia, it must have been very expensive, you shouldn't buy furniture like that without consulting Digby, and I don't feel it's the kind of thing he'll like."

"He doesn't have to like it," said Justinia. "It's going in my room, and it didn't cost a penny; Lydia wanted a home for it."

"Darling, it's hardly practical. There's so much in your room just now, and . . ."

"Still?" said Justinia austerely. "Then it'll have to go, I'm sure these nice men will help me shift it."

The van men beamed at the offer of coffee and cake, and willingly agreed to accept twenty pounds for moving things out of Justinia's room.

"You could live on this sofa," said Justinia as she took a flying leap into its depths and stretched herself out luxuriously. "Wonderful!"

"Excessive," said Celia, and Justinia didn't bother to ask whether she was referring to the sofa or to Justinia's enthusiasm.

Digby had gone to Eyot early not only because he was in a huff with Justinia, but also because he had a meeting with the Rev Holigost. He parked behind the Cathedral, incurring the early morning wrath of George, and knocked in his brisk way on the Canon's door. He was at his best when on business; alert, competent and with energy evident in every step he took.

The Succentor, looking particularly pale and Machiavellian this morning, greeted Digby with enthusiasm. His plans were going well: the Dean, who could have made difficulties, had been neutralised, the other Canons had been silenced by various means. The way was clear to a new, purer regime in the Cathedral. Life, felt the Rev Holigost, was going his way, as of course it should. The sun, he knew, shone on the righteous.

It shone on everyone that morning; the spell of unseasonably warm weather showed no sign of breaking. The cafés in St Wulfstan's Square, which spilled out on to the pavements during the summer, had got out their tables and chairs once more, and already some tourists were sitting outside with maps and guides, planning their day.

"We're going to the school," said Holigost. "I want you to listen to a new boy; a remarkable voice, and also a born leader, so keen on singing, just what we need."

The headmaster of the Junior Department, the round and ubiquitous Mr Poughley, met them at the school gates, his uninspiring face wreathed in the smiles he reserved for rich and important people. A man who was going to come up with large sums of money to sponsor the choir was clearly both rich and important.

Mr Poughley was definitely on the Succentor's side. He knew that what was happening would infuriate Simon Praetorius, perhaps even drive him to resign, but since he and Simon had co-existed in a state of armed neutrality for several years, he wasn't particularly bothered by this. That his old friend the Precentor would also be horrified by what was going on didn't bother him either for more than a few seconds. Facts were facts, and money was money, Mr Poughley told himself.

He greeted Digby with flattering attention, at his most charming and affable, although his natural mood at this time of the morning was one of bad temper. His eyes gleamed at the prospect of all the publicity which the Succentor's plans and Digby's money would bring to the choir and to the school, and therefore to him. Mr Poughley loved to be in the limelight.

The boy was waiting in the school hall. "This is Darren, a newcomer to the choir," said Mr Poughley. "Darren, Mr FitzOdo, who is going to be involved with the choir, would like to hear you sing."

"Yes, sir," said Darren, nodding and showing off his mop of golden curls.

The headmaster ushered him towards the piano. "I asked Mr Rowley, one of the piano teachers here, if . . . ah, here he is."

Mr Rowley, a long, lugubrious individual, gave Darren a look of loathing and settled himself on the piano stool.

"Darren, where's your music?" said Mr Poughley, seeing that the boy's hands were empty.

"I know it by heart, sir," said Darren with a winning smile.

"Clever boy," said the Rev Holigost approvingly.

"Can't read a note of music, learns it from a tape," observed Mr Rowley to no-one in particular. Then he crashed into the opening bars of the hit song from a particularly soupy religious musical that was pulling the crowds into theatres all over the world.

Darren took on a soulful, alert mode and went into action. His voice was indeed remarkable, and Digby and the Succentor were radiant with delight. Mr Rowley watched them cynically as he played. With a different character, early training and any real musicality, Darren could have been a good singer. Given what he was, Mr Rowley reckoned he was heading for fame and stardom without a doubt.

"Perfect," breathed Digby, as Darren held firmly on to his final high note. In his mind's eye he could see that appealing, boyish face on recordings, programmes, posters.

The Succentor had the same vision, but in his mind's eye he also saw people streaming into the Cathedral as it opened its doors on a new world, liberated from centuries of exclusive and dreary tradition. The choir would be a beacon, would lead the way to an entirely new era of cathedral music, one in which everyone would participate, and in which the wonderful talents of boys like Darren would be used to provide music that everyone could understand and enjoy.

"Back to your friends now," said Mr Poughley.

Darren smiled his thanks at the assembled adults, and left the hall. Outside, his face returned to its habitual expression of watchful self-satisfaction. He aimed a nasty kick at a small boy hurrying by, pushed his way disagreeably through a group of girls who were waiting to go into the art room, pulled himself together as a master went past, and headed for the cloakroom to crow over his fellow choristers with the news that he was going to be the star of the choir, and they had better watch out or he'd have a word with the Succentor about them.

Thomas, beyond his reach as an ex-chorister, was the only one to take him on. "Shut up, you smug little tick," he told him. "Otherwise, I'll wire your balls to the national grid, and you'll be singing treble for ever."

\*　　\*　　\*

Sadie woke up with a sense of pleased anticipation. Miraculously, Josiah Smile had swept in with his son and two minions the previous day, and by elevenses, the cupboards in her bedroom had been expertly removed. By five o'clock in the afternoon, she had ceiling-to-floor shelving.

"I'll send a lad round tomorrow to put the undercoat on," promised Josiah.

Sadie was firm. "No, no, I love painting. I'll do them. Very soothing, painting; very therapeutic."

Josiah was doubtful, and he gave her detailed instructions about primers and rubbing down and top coats. Sadie smiled obligingly, and, the minute the front door shut behind the little band, she was upstairs with a box, unpacking the contents and loading them on the first shelf.

Issur disapproved. "This is a job half-done," he said. "These shelves need to be properly finished, otherwise they will never look good."

"I don't want them to look good," said Sadie. "I want them to hold all my books and files."

"I do not think I want to wake in the middle of the night and see these crude shelves."

"Keep your eyes shut, then," Sadie advised. "Concentrate on other things."

"Other things are important, yes, and most enjoyable, but even so, you should try not to have much around you that offends the eye."

Sadie looked at Issur fondly. "When you're there, I don't notice shelves, I wouldn't notice if the side of the house fell off and there were the stars."

"All very well and poetic, but not practical," said Issur severely.

Issur was hard at work at the barre, and Sadie set to with a will as soon as she had gulped down a cup of coffee. She was supposed to start the day with the set of exercises prescribed by Issur, but after all, carrying boxes upstairs was very good exercise. Then she had this evening's service to look forward to, a sung service in her own church, bliss; she hated having to go miles for the kind of service that she felt comfortable with, in the Cathedral or in other parish churches where she hardly knew anyone.

Sadie was modern in her outlook, but not tacky, and she considered the kind of service offered by the Rev Wroot was the essence of tackiness. "And I simply don't believe that tackiness can bring you any kind of spiritual benefit," she told Jezebel, who sat in her cage and said several very interesting-sounding Russian words.

Sadie had brought the parrot upstairs for company, and she wondered, not for the first time, exactly what Issur had taught the parrot to say, and why, after never learning anything beyond her Yorkshire comments, she had decided to widen her scope.

There was a ring at the doorbell. "Bother," said Sadie, climbing carefully down the stepladder she had set up in order to reach the top shelves. "Who's that? Can't be the milkman at this time of day. Can't be the postman, he's been. Can't be the electric, it isn't due. Can't be a friend, because they'd know the door wasn't locked."

By this time she had reached the front door. She opened it with a politely welcoming smile on her face, which changed to a look of horror when she saw who it was.

"Hello, mother,"

"Ursula," said Sadie weakly. "What are you doing here?"

"I thought I'd have a run up, see how you are."

"My car," said Sadie, looking past Ursula.

"Yes, but I haven't brought it to leave it here, after all, you don't really need a car, and I can't do without it. Colin says it's a good idea for me to have it, he says I look after it better than you do."

Sadie opened her mouth to say what she thought of her son's opinion, and then thought better of it. You couldn't argue with Ursula or Colin, alike as two shrivelled up peas in a pod, she thought resentfully; however had she managed to produce two such children?

Of course, in the eyes of the world they were a success. Degrees, friends, no drugs, or not more than the university usual, respectable slightly left-of-centre views; they felt just as they ought on all subjects.

Boring, thought Sadie. No sense of humour, and if they bored their mother, what must they do to everyone else? Only it didn't matter, because they chose their friends carefully; other people just like themselves.

Sadie silently handed Ursula the key to the garage and retreated inside. Ursula made her way round to the back door, dragging a large bag behind her.

"Are you planning a long stay?" enquired Sadie.

"A week or so," said Ursula.

A day would be too long, Sadie said to herself, thinking longingly of the empty, inviting shelves upstairs.

Ursula darted in and out of the downstairs rooms like a demented spider, her eyes flickering around.

I'm not going to say anything, thought Sadie wearily. She's going to discover it all for herself, she's going to lecture me until my ears drop off, she'll ring her father. Oh, shit.

"Would you like some coffee?" she said, moving over to the the kettle.

"Only if you've got decaf, Mum, and I hope you don't use tapwater."

"I do," said Sadie equably.

"You mustn't," said Ursula earnestly. "You must buy a filter jug. It's poison, what comes out of the tap, pure poison."

And so are you, Sadie said to herself. Any moment now, she thought, Issur will finish his exercises, and come bounding downstairs. The bathroom door opened and shut, and the sounds of a stirring chorus from Rimsky Korsakov wafted down the stairs.

Ursula's eyes narrowed, but she said nothing.

She knows, Sadie said to herself, watching her. Somebody has told her about Issur, and that's why she's here.

"Ah, Issur," she said brightly, as he flung open the kitchen door. He stared at Ursula.

"Who are you?" he said.

Ursula bristled. "I could ask the same about you," she said indignantly. "What are you doing here, coming into my mother's kitchen like that?"

Issur's brilliant dark eyes flashed over Ursula. "Aha, that's who you are," he said. "The daughter. More beautiful mother of a not-beautiful daughter, I think." He gave Sadie a wonderful smile. "How is it possible," he asked in a pleasant conversational tone, "for you to have such a tight-arsed daughter?"

"Really," said Ursula, going a dull brick red colour.

Sadie was laughing. "Issur, you shouldn't say that."

"Why not? I didn't know this phrase, but Merle told me, I like it, it is very descriptive. Not only of men who don't want to go to bed with you, but also of women like this one, who look as though they have zips on all orifices."

Ursula was getting cross. "I don't know who you are, and I don't know why my own mother is standing here letting you insult me, but . . ."

"Oh, shut up, Ursula," said Sadie. "You were very rude to Issur, so he retaliated. I wouldn't bother, you won't get the better of him."

"So what I heard is true," said Ursula, with some satisfaction. "This is the toyboy who's wormed his way into your affections. What's he after? Doesn't he realize that you haven't got any money? That you don't even own the house?"

Issur's dark brows snapped together. "It is not suitable, I think, for you to speak to your mother so," he said, very quietly.

"I shall say what I like in my house," cried Ursula.

"It's not your house," said Sadie crossly. "It's my house. Now, stop it, both of you."

Ursula took no notice. "I suppose you think he's here because he likes you, how could you be so stupid, mother? It's your age, but that's really no excuse. I think any doctor would agree with me now that you need to go away for treatment."

"I am here," said Issur grandly, "because I wish to be, and because I have work here in Unthrang. I don't care this," and he snapped his fingers dramatically in Ursula's face, "for your mother's money, or no money, or her house. I am here because I like to go to bed very much with your mother, and we do many things that I think would make your hair stand up like so, and I tell you that I would rather go to bed with your mother than have fuck with you, which would be like going to bed with a bath sponge."

# 23 ∫

Issur lolled against the larder cupboard, looking impossibly handsome and grand. Ursula, true to form, burst into tears.

"Now you cry, you become silly little girl, you make Mummy comfort you, how old are you?"

Ursula wailed more loudly, and Sadie looked helplessly at Issur.

"She wants to make you feel guilt," he observed. "If she can do this, then she has won. Me, I do not think you need to feel guilt. You like what we have done, heh? In bed, and out together, and now you look very nice, with hair and clothes, like a beautiful woman."

Ursula raised her by now very blotchy face and bared her teeth at Issur.

"You've made her look horrible, and artificial, you've stolen her affection, you've turned her against her own children."

"If you came here," said Issur calmly, "or telephoned her, or wrote letters, then I would believe in this affection. But since you do none of these things, but come up here, in the car you have stolen from her, in order to criticize and say everything bad about her, your own mother, then I do not believe in these affections."

Ursula wailed again. "You don't love me any more, I'm not wanted here, I'm excluded from my own home, rejected by my own mother. I shall go, I've come all this way, and . . ."

Sadie seized her chance. "Much the best thing, dear. And, you know, I've just realized, I don't think I've loved you for years. You're too like your father, both you and Colin."

Ursula looked at her with narrowed eyes. "You'll regret this," she said. "Just you wait until I tell Daddy about what you're up to."

Issur gave a contemptuous snort. "I have met your Daddy, and I think Sadie has nothing to fear from such a man. There is a bus coming in five minutes, I will carry your bag to this bus for you, and then we say goodbye."

"I'm not going on the bus," said Ursula, rising. "I shall drive myself back."

"No," said Issur. "That is not your car. You may stay, of course, you can have my room, because naturally, I share with your mother, because otherwise how could I make love to her? Or you can go – on the bus."

Ursula did go, but, needless to say, she didn't go straight back to London, as Sadie soon discovered.

Nigel buttonholed her on his way to St Quivox. "Pauline and I couldn't make the first practice, but of course we're experienced enough not to need much rehearsing."

Sadie was unimpressed. "I thought you were regulars at the Rev Wroot's Sunday knees-up, isn't this rather high for you?"

Nigel gave her a cold look. "During term time, we worship in the Cathedral. We attend the services here in the holidays, we believe it is important to support our local parish church. Naturally we're helping Sylvester out with this Requiem, we like to be good neighbours."

"Fine," said Sadie. "Is this a neighbourly visit as well?"

"Not exactly. I wanted to have a quick word with you; Ursula called in to my office in Eyot this morning, very distressed, with a disturbing report about you and . . ." He hesitated. Sadie, usually a pushover, was looking rather militant.

"I'm not interested in anything Ursula may have said to you," she said. "What I do is none of her business."

"But Sadie, as your daughter, she has your best interests at heart, just as I do."

"Ursula cares about nothing except her own interests. And I'm not sure about your interests, but I'm fairly certain they aren't mine. I'm thinking things over, Nigel, and I'll ring you at your office later this week. Now, if you'll excuse me, I've got one or two things to do before I go across for the service."

Nigel opened his mouth to argue, looked at Sadie's resolute expression and thought better of it.

"Menopausal," he said, as he caught up with Pauline. "I'd better give Charles a ring, I think Sadie needs to see a doctor; she isn't capable of thinking clearly just at the moment."

"Issur," said Pauline in a voice rich with disapproval. "At her age!"

"At any age," said Nigel, equally disapproving.

A vivid memory of Issur dancing on the night of the Helm flashed into Pauline's head, together with a stab of envy at the thought that Sadie and Issur might . . . Of course it was all pretence, Issur was a man's man, he had never so much as glanced in her, Pauline's, direction, and she didn't need to look in the mirror to know that there was no comparison between her and Sadie.

Like her children, Pauline had an ineradicable belief in her own perfection. Since she neither recognized nor appreciated such qualities as a sense of humour or a lively personality, she had never noticed that she, her husband and her brood were distinctly lacking on that side of the scales. Life was very straightforward when you were always right.

Thomas lingered behind the church wall when he saw Pauline and Nigel coming, but they spotted him. "Why are you here, Tom?" said Pauline. "Shouldn't you be at school? Are you ill again?"

"No, I've come to sing," said Thomas, holding out a well-thumbed copy of the music by way of explanation.

"Oh?" said Pauline, in a not very approving way. "Whose idea was that?"

Thomas shifted uncomfortably from one large foot to the other. "Er, Sylvester asked me. He needed an alto, he said, and Mr Poughley said I could come."

Pauline was affronted. "He never suggested that Gavin and Peter should sing. I am sure the Dean would have given permission, it is their local church after all, whereas it's hardly yours."

Sylvester swept up the path, much to Thomas's relief. Pauline gave him a mirthless smile. "Good evening, Sylvester. We were just wondering why Thomas is joining us."

"Excellent alto, knows the piece, does him good to get away from school for a few hours, doesn't it, Thomas?"

Thomas nodded in agreement, and ran ahead into the church, leaving Pauline and Nigel to mutter to themselves. Sylvester smiled wickedly, he knew quite well what Nigel and Pauline were mumbling about. He was too polite to tell them that Peter was hopeless and that Gavin got right up his nose; he was far too kind a man.

"There's Lydia," he said, as a large and shabby car drew up. Lydia eased herself out of the passenger seat, and Alban went round to heave her double bass out of the back.

Sylvester greeted them both with enthusiasm. "Good, good," he said. "I knew we could rely on you, Lydia, we're just going to have a quick final rehearsal, shall I take the stool? Are you staying, Alban?"

"I expect he's going to decamp to the pub," said Lydia cheerfully. "He's rather off churches and clergymen just at present."

"I'm not surprised," said Sylvester. "Come and dine with us afterwards, Valliaze is invited and Lily is cooking something wonderful."

Lydia protested that there wouldn't be enough, but Sylvester roared with laughter and said that Lily was catering for several more than just the three of them. "She knows I like to ask people for a meal."

"Excellent," said Alban. "You'll have to put up with Thomas as well, though, because he's staying overnight with us."

He turned to Lydia. "I'll take this in for you, and don't let yourself get tired, Lydia, you must be careful."

Lydia gave him a seraphic smile and winked at Sylvester. "I feel fine," she confided in him as they walked together into the church. "Alban does love to fuss."

"Quite right, too," said Sylvester. "It will do the Praetorius-to-be a lot of good to hear you playing the double bass, though. I would imagine it comes over as a soothing rumble."

"Soothing is what your Vicar is going to need, from what I hear," said Lydia, casting an expert eye over the Rev Wroot. "If that's the man, he looks in a terrible state."

"Hamish will calm him down," said Sylvester, waving a huge

and friendly hand at the group of clergy. Certainly, the Rev Wroot looked to be in agony.

"It needn't be spiritual agony," he pointed out to Lydia as he helped her adjust her music stand. "He could just have indigestion."

"Hello, Piers," said Roxane as she wafted up the aisle to greet him, dramatically dressed as always, with a vivid silk scarf of many colours wrapped around her head. "Are you all in good voice? I'm looking forward to this."

"A Requiem Mass isn't meant to be a jolly affair," said Piers without a smile. Damn her, he thought. She's so beautiful, and all I can think is, where has she been this afternoon, who's she been with.

"Coming to the pub afterwards?" Roxane went on.

"No," said Piers, rather shortly. "My great-aunt's taken it into her head to invite Justy and her family to dinner. I'm buttling."

"Come over later, then," said Roxane with an inviting smile. "To my house. For a nightcap."

"I'm sure you have plenty of other friends you could ask," said Piers, moving away.

Roxane stared after him, her eyebrows raised. "What have I said?" she asked Sylvester, who was passing by with an armful of music.

He stopped, and looked at Roxane. "It's your charity work, I dare say," he said. "I don't think Piers is the charitable sort."

"Ah," said Roxane, thoughtfully.

The service was duly ceremonious and dignified. The clergy processed down the aisle in their black and gold robes. Hamish looked serene and spiritual, which was quite an achievement, thought Sylvester, when you were both rubicund and round. Josiah Smile's cadaverous expression lent tremendous gravitas to the proceedings, the boat boy looked a poppet with his thatch of red hair and lace fringed surplice, the crucifer and thurifer carried out their duties with skill and enthusiasm, and even Alban, slipping in towards the end of the service to make sure Lydia was all right, had to admit that the music was surprisingly well-played and sung.

Several of the Rev Wroot's happies had decided to attend,

probably on the principle of knowing your enemy before you overcame him. Mrs Toadflax, a stalwart of the tambourine, was seen to sob quietly into an enormous handkerchief during the Dona eis pacem. "It made me think of my mum and dad, and little Cyril, you shouldn't feel sad like that in church, it's quite wrong."

"It must have reminded you of your Bert, too," said her neighbour sympathetically.

Mrs Toadflax stiffened. "No, it did not," she said. "I don't want him to be granted peace, wherever he is; he never gave me any!"

Alban's mouth twitched, and then another comment from one of the ladies drew his attention to the Rev Wroot, and he looked with satisfaction at the tortured expression on the Vicar's face.

"I like to see the clergy suffer," he explained to Issur, who had retreated to the rear of the church after communion, to get a better view of it all.

"This clergyman certainly suffers," said Issur, gesturing at the Rev Wroot. "But from the suffering comes a reward; now he will find himself happier, he will worship in a proper way, with everything as it should be. How can you have religion with bang-bang music, and no incense, no liturgy?"

"This is only a one-off, isn't it?" asked Alban, interested despite himself, as he slipped into the pew beside Issur. "I think it'll be happy worship as before, won't it, once this is over?"

Issur shook his head, and it looked to Alban as though he were laughing at a very good, private joke.

"No," he said. "Nothing here will be as it was before."

"Hmm," said Alban, giving Issur a more appraising look. "Have I met you somewhere?"

"You are the composer, I can see this. Oh, yes, you will know me, you will have known me a long time, I think." Again, the secret smile and brimming amusement. Unusual man, thought Alban; since he moved in a world which was stuffed with unusual people, it didn't bother him in the least.

It had taken some persuasion to get Celia to accept the invitation to dinner at the Manor House. Her eyes grew sombre. "I feel that I shouldn't go, my instinct tells me not to," she said dramatically.

Justinia had grown up with her mother's instinctive moods and feelings, which usually went with a simple disinclination to do whatever was on offer. Digby, less familiar with her ways, tried to soothe her fears and rationalize her unease away. He became authoritative, and Celia, who had her own way of dealing with authoritative men, was settling down to a battle of wills which she knew from the start she would win, when she remembered that she was trying to teach Justinia to be more submissive to Digby. She must set a good example, she would give in to Digby with a good grace, and go.

Digby was wild to go, at last he would be able to see the inside of the house. "Do you think she'll let us look round it?" he asked Justinia.

Justinia hadn't told him that she had already been inside it, and she hoped he wouldn't demand to be shown over it, like some prospective purchaser, which was, of course, exactly what Digby felt he was.

As a result of all this, Justinia came down to earth with a bang at the end of the Duruflé, as she saw Digby waiting for her, his face and body alert at the prospect of the evening ahead. Her stomach gave a lurch, and she had to concentrate to attend to Thomas, who was hurling himself about the vestry.

"High, after the performance," observed Sylvester, who was thanking the musicians, and handing them little envelopes which were received with polite murmurs of surprise and thanks. "I thought we were doing this for free," said Pansy, smiling enchantingly at Sylvester.

"No, no," said Sylvester. "Musicians are worthy of their hire, can't let the profession down. I'll make the church council reimburse me for some of it, in any case, can't let them get away with everything."

"What about your fee?" said Thomas wickedly. "Isn't that simply enormous, Sylvester? Won't it bankrupt the church?"

"Quiet, boy," said Sylvester good-humouredly. "Justy, you look tired, surely this little affair hasn't worn you out?"

Justinia reassure Sylvester. "No, of course not, it's the prospect of dinner with Zephania Zouche and Digby . . . and mother."

Piers appeared at her elbow. "Pansy and I are just going across," he said. "Only the final touches needed, Pansy's a whiz at cooking, you've no idea. And don't worry about the Great-Aunt letting the cat out of the bag, I've explained that your voice is a no-go area while hubbie and mama are around. She didn't seem surprised; in fact, she's in a very abstracted mood, she may not take much part in the conversation at all."

"Mind you come and report it all to me tomorrow," Sylvester called after Justinia.

Digby took Justinia's arm in a possessive way. "I don't see why Sylvester needs to know about a dinner party to which he hasn't been invited," he said in reproving tones.

Justinia removed her arm under pretence of looking for something in her bag. "He was invited actually," she said. "But he has people dining with him tonight, so he couldn't go."

"Oh," said Digby.

Pansy stayed in the kitchen, she was too busy to join the others. Piers had put on his dinner jacket in order to be butler, and Pansy had added a Parisian touch by wrapping a wide white apron around his waist. He looked very dashing as he moved between kitchen and dining room. "Keeps you fit, all these passages," he said.

"Are they enjoying the food?" said Pansy, turning her becomingly flushed face with interest in the direction of the voices coming in a murmur from the dining room.

"I think so," said Piers. "Very strange, Auntie Zeph can't take her eyes off Celia, and is cross-examining her about her life story; I like Justy, but her mother seems a slightly depressing type, I can't see why old Zeph is so interested."

"Good manners?" suggested Pansy, piping fragile patterns of spun sugar around an array of exquisite, tiny cakes held together with whipped cream. "There's a fruit salad, too, very light and sweet, I thought this might be rather rich for your great aunt."

"As far as I know, she's got the digestion of an ostrich," said Piers. "She must have, because she often lets me cook for her. That looks wonderful, I hope you've saved some for in here."

"Of course, and some for Marius, I know your aunt won't mind."

"I'll take it in, hear the next thrilling instalment of Celia's early life in suburbia, for that's what it seems to have been,"

"Funny," said Pansy. "She's very exotic-looking, I would have said she had grown up in the warm south rather than the suburbs."

As Piers slipped into his chair to join the party for dessert, his great-aunt had turned her attention to Digby. She was asking him about his work, and Digby was holding forth on the glorious deal he was making with the cathedral authorities for the sponsorship of the choir.

"Those boys are worth a fortune," he told Zephania. "They're wasted, completely wasted, stuck away in the gloom, chanting out-of-date music. This will bring them into the real world with a bang, they'll sing all over the place, do ads on telly, lots of cross-over work, it's going to be great."

He turned to Piers. "This is what you want to get in on, Piers. Classical music is a has-been, it's too serious and dull for most people. You've got to liven all that old music up if you want to get it across. Give people something they can listen to without bending their ears off."

Zephania's face gave nothing away, but Justinia felt disapproval of Digby's plans stirring beneath the polite mask of the very old. "Do you support your husband in this?" Zephania asked Justinia.

Justinia glanced at Digby. "No," she said, taking another fig from the bowl of fruit.

Digby looked sulky, as he rebuked Justinia. "Justinia doesn't really understand how things work," he said with a little laugh. "You can't live in the past, everything has to move on. Like the boys' voices, it's a waste of time spending years teaching them to sing those psalms, when you can teach a quick boy a catchy number in an afternoon, if he's got a good voice."

Justinia looked down at the table and crumbled a piece of bread on her side plate.

"Crunch time," said the voice in her ear. "This is what you've married, this is what you're stuck with for years and years and years."

Justinia started, and Piers, who had been watching her, wondered what was wrong. Apart from having such an ass for a husband, and she must have got used to that by now. His mind drifted to thoughts of Roxane, the name alone filled him with desperate longing. Had Justinia felt like that about Digby? She must have done, and look where she had ended up, that's what happened when you fell in love, all reason and sense and balance deserted you.

A trap, that's what it was. You deceived yourself into thinking it was all pleasures of the flesh, all wholesome, enjoyable sex; warmth and friendship, too, a pleasant and essential part of life. Nobody told you that ordinary, everyday urges could become passion, and then, when you were already punch-drunk, that a rather greater god would move in for the kill, and that you didn't have a hope of escaping in one piece.

Bugger the Greeks, thought Piers disconsolately. They were right, and we're wrong. So much for twentieth-century progress. There was Justinia caught up in the gluey maze of her marriage to Digby, and here he was, obsessed with Roxane, who somehow seemed to be able to manage to keep her emotions in order.

"I'm going to become a monk," he told Pansy as he clanked the delicate little coffee cups and saucers down on a silver tray.

"Not until you've done the washing up," said Pansy.

It was a warm and heavy night, with only a mild breeze ruffling the air. The curtains at the open window fluttered slightly as Justinia turned over yet again in her search for ease and the comfort of sleep.

Lust for the Manor, which had risen to fever-pitch now that Digby had set foot in it, spilled over in more fleshly lust, and he had pounced on Justinia the minute their bedroom door shut. Justinia heard the plaintive goodnights from her mother as she drifted down the passage to her room, then all other sounds were muffled out by Digby's urgent attentions.

Despite everything, I do love him, thought Justinia as she abandoned herself to familiar and delicious sensations. Digby was as vigorous and stimulating a lover as always, and it was only some days later that Justinia wondered just where he had acquired some new and different approaches, which had seemed so pleasing at the time.

Digby padded back from the bathroom to roll himself into a cocoon of happy slumbers, while Justinia, the tension flooding back, lay and looked into the half-darkness of the room lit by the nearly full moon.

She pushed back the covers and went to look out of the window. She could hear sheep baaing from the fells; closer to, the owl kept up its melancholy hootings. Things scurried and stirred in the bushes, the air was fragrant with warm, autumnal smells. Lights were on in one or two of the neighbouring houses. Alban and Lydia's big car was gone, Justinia noticed idly; earlier that evening, when they had come back from the Manor, the cars had still been grouped around Crag End.

Theirs is a later and a merrier party, Justinia thought as they passed Sylvester's House earlier in the evening. She and Digby and Celia hadn't lingered long after coffee, when Zephania had become quiet and withdrawn.

"Old people need their rest," Celia whispered to Digby, who, realizing that he wasn't going to get to see the rest of the house, took a dignified and courteous farewell of their hostess.

That didn't stop him creeping round the outside of the house, standing on tiptoe to try and peer into the great drawing-room windows, estimating the size of the rooms.

"Fantastic, incredible," he kept saying. "Needs a lot of work, of course, look, all this should be repointed. I wonder if there's damp, I don't suppose she's had any damp-proofing done."

"Digby, someone will think you're a thief and call the police," Justinia hissed at him.

"A good garden designer would soon sort this lot out," said Digby. "Where's Celia, she knows a lot about this kind of thing?"

"She's gone home," said Justinia crossly. "Digby, do stop making plans for someone else's garden and come away."

Digby emerged, pink in the face, dusting his hands and knees down. "Amazing," he said. "I must have it, really, there's so much that needs doing. I can just see us living here, terrific."

Justinia didn't bother to point out that the present occupant was still very much alive, if aged, would probably survive for several years yet, and would then will the house to some distant relative who would promptly move in.

"It's meant, I'm meant to have this house," Digby asserted. "I am glad we came to Unthrang, if you didn't live here you wouldn't know what a marvellous house it was."

A thought stirred in Justinia's head as she looked out of the window towards Crag End. Alban. Digby's remarks at dinner about the cathedral choir. The appalling arrangments and changes he and the Succentor were planning, worse than anything anyone had imagined.

"All fixed up bar the shouting," Digby had announced, very pleased with himself.

Decision time.

Justinia crept out of their room and down the back stairs to the kitchen. She stealthily took the phone off the receiver, and waited for a second, afraid that her mother or even the sleeping Digby would have heard a faint click on one of the extensions and was even now listening in.

"Don't be stupid," said the voice. "Get on with it."

# 24 ∫

"Don't you ever sleep?" said Justinia, dialling.

"No, not even when you do; I haunt your dreams, hadn't you noticed?"

"I don't remember my dreams when I wake up, perhaps I don't have any," retorted Justinia. "No, sorry, is that Alban? No, I was just talking to . . ." Her voice tailed off.

"Pull yourself together," came the command in her ear.

"I'm sorry to ring you up in the middle of the night. Did I wake you up?"

"It's Justy," said Alban, sounding faintly puzzled. "Are you drunk? Who are you with?"

"No-one, I was thinking aloud, and I'm not drunk. Were you asleep?"

"No, but Lydia is."

"Oh, I hope I haven't woken her."

"No, I switch off the phone in the bedroom. I'm in the studio, trying to work."

"I'm sorry to disturb you. Listen, do you know where Simon is, your brother?"

"He's in America," said Alban.

"Yes, but can you get hold of him? Tell him about the choir, what's happening, and about your commission."

"Ah," said Alban. "Digby's been spilling more beans, has he? Plans worse than anything we could have imagined, is that the one?"

"Yes," said Justinia, feeling very treacherous.

"You think I should contact Simon?" He was silent for a moment. "I think he's gone to ground, he's dumped Evie and the children with her cousins in Cincinnati – where is Cincinnati, do you know? – and taken off to commune with nature. Probably gone to Los Angeles to find himself a girl or two, if the truth be known."

"I think you should get hold of him and make him come back," said Justinia. "Quickly."

"That bad?"

"That bad."

"And urgent, you say."

"Very. No time to lose. Digby is a swift mover once he's made up his mind that a project is go, as he puts it."

Silence.

"Alban? Are you still there?"

"Yes, of course I am. I'm thinking. It's no good ringing Simon. He never listens properly on the phone, and I won't be able to persuade him to come back."

"He's the only person who can stop Digby and Holigost."

There was another silence. "We need him here, in Eyot. I'll have to fly over and bring him back."

"It's a long way," said Justinia, feeling guilty.

"That doesn't bother me, I hop across all the time. I think it's necessary." Alban said finally. "However, it's difficult. I don't think I can leave Lydia alone here. Not now."

"Could she go to her mother?" said Justinia. "Or her grand-mother? I'm sure Lady Wray would have her to stay."

"Mmm," said Alban. "I feel fairly sure, however, that nothing would induce Lydia to stay even for one night with her grandmother."

"You go and stay with her," said the voice in her ear. "Give you a break, do you good, you can sneak off to London for a day without Digby knowing. He's got Celia to look after him. He'll be all right."

"Oh, yes?" said Justinia. "And how do I explain what I'm doing? Oh, by the way, Digby, Alban's hopping off to the States to bring Simon back so that he can put a stop to your plans."

The voice was contemptuous. "Digby will be full of admiration for a world-famous composer who has to go to New York to deal with a recording of his latest work . . . or to judge a competition . . . or to discuss the performance of one of his operas at the

Met. Digby may be a Philistine, but he knows important when he hears about it. Make something up, you silly woman."

"Shut up," said Justinia, wrapping her rather flimsy nightgown round herself.

"What?" said Alban, affronted.

"Nothing, nothing relevant, Alban," said Justinia wearily.

"You have got someone there," said Alban suspiciously.

"No I haven't." Justinia made up her mind. "I'll come tomorrow. Then you can go off straight away. If Digby doesn't like it, tough."

"Attagirl," said Alban approvingly.

Issur took advantage of the warmth to resume his Tai Chi on the green, and the tall figure standing on one leg was the first person Gervase saw as he drove slowly into Unthrang. He blinked, and raised his eyebrows. Biddies walked along beside the green, pushing their shopping trolleys; a young mother with a pushchair and a toddler beside her went past; the postman; a dark stocky man who was clearly a pillar of the community . . . They didn't seem to think there was anything extraordinary about the ripplingly muscled man with the remarkably striking face and the exiguous posing pouch.

True, more than one appreciative glance was sent in Issur's direction, but they were glances of familiarity and lasciviousness, not of shock or surprise.

"Oh, well," Gervase said to himself as he drove the car through the arch into the cobbled yard of the Cow and Prisoner. "Local, is he?" he enquired of Mrs Herb, who welcomed him with pleased northern greetings.

Mrs Herb didn't stop to look out on the green, she knew who Gervase was talking about. "Aye, he's staying with Sadie, fine figure of a man, that one. Foreign, but there's nowt wrong with him otherwise."

Gervase followed Mrs Herb up to the low-ceilinged, dark-beamed bedroom, with an uneven polished wooden floor. He looked around with real pleasure, admiring the thick white cover on the bed, the white linen towels hanging by the basin, the china bowls and jugs on the old polished chests and low cupboards. A gleaming copper warming pan hung on the wall together with an assortment of prints and dark, small paintings of fish.

"A lovely room," he said to Mrs Herb.

"Aye," she said. "Folk generally like it. Will you be stopping in for dinner? Residents eat at 7.00, if that's all right by you."

Gervase just stopped himself from saying aye, thanked Mrs Herb, and swung his bag on to the little canvas trestle at the foot of the bed. "Oh," he said, as Mrs Herb reached the door. "Do you know the FitzOdos?"

"Aye," said Mrs Herb. She gave Gervase a shrewd look. "It's Mrs FitzOdo you'll be wanting to see. She's gone t'Eyot, won't be back for a day or so."

"Oh," said Gervase, sitting down rather abruptly on the bed.

Mrs Herb thought for a moment. "Sadie'll know the address, or Mr Sylvester. They live t'other side of green. Crag End for Mr Sylvester, Yellow Cottage for Sadie."

"Oh, thank you," Gervase said. "But I can hardly just go and knock on the door and ask for Mrs FitzOdo's address, a stranger . . ."

Mrs Herb gave him another look. "Nowt to worry about," she said. "You'll be the lawyer Mrs FitzOdo met in London, Lily told me you'd be up. Well, best be going, nowt gets done by itself."

Gervase stared at the door as it closed behind Mrs Herb. A sense of unreality crept over him. Unthrang, clearly, had more to it than you could possibly guess from the stark information in the AA handbook. Pop. 3,300 was all very well – but 3,300 what? Witches, he decided, and, taking a towel, he went in search of the bathroom.

Gervase was taken aback when the door of Yellow Cottage was opened by Issur. The Russian's slanting black brows snapped together as he looked Gervase up and down. "So," he said.

"I'm sorry to bother you," began Gervase. "Is . . . er, Sadie in?"

A smaller, plumper figure appeared beside Issur. A pretty woman, thought Gervase, although not young. This must be Sadie.

"Come in, come in," she said. "A friend of Justy's? Yes, of course I know where she is, she's staying with Lydia."

"Lydia? Lydia Praetorius?" Gervase face lifted.

"You know her?"

"Yes, I met her in London. With Justinia."

Sadie led the way into her little sitting room. "This is Issur," she said. Issur bowed.

"I'm Gervase Drummond."

"Sit down," said Sadie. "Why are you in Unthrang?"

"To see Justy," said Issur, his face alight with mischief. "This is clear."

"I've come for a bit of fishing," said Gervase. "I wanted a few days away from London."

"You're staying at the Cow and Prisoner? You'll be very comfortable there."

"Yes," said Gervase. "Could you let me have Lydia's address? I'd like to look her up while I'm here."

"And Justy," said Issur.

"And Justinia, too," said Gervase. He accepted the glass that Sadie had poured out for him, and he looked round the room. His eye fell on an untidy pile of papers, which looked very familiar to him.

"Of course," he said. "Sadie. The errant husband, the house ownership."

Sadie looked startled.

"I'm sorry," said Gervase. "Very rude of me, but Justinia was telling me, when we had dinner at Virginia Luthier's house – do you know her? – about her friend, and she asked me if I could recommend a really tough lawyer."

Issur nodded approvingly. "So. This is what Sadie needs, not this tight-arsed man here, with strange wife and strangulated sons."

"Strangulated . . .?"

Sadie laughed. "Not literally, but I know what Issur means. My solicitor, Nigel, and his wife, who is very upright and full of good deeds, have two sons, who are ruthlessly oppressed and controlled by them."

"Ah," said Gervase. "Is he a good solicitor?"

"Hopeless," said Sadie. "I pay him, but really he seems to be working for my husband. I realized the other day that the two of them were at the same school. I expect they slept together then, and so now Nigel's on his side. Not on mine."

"It happens," said Gervase.

"My husband ran off with the milkman," Sadie explained. "He wants the house."

"Is it in joint names?" asked Gervase.

"Nigel says not," said Sadie. "I'm not so sure, because if it were clear-cut, he wouldn't keep on trying to get me to sign bits of paper."

"May I?" said Gervase, getting up and going to the table where the papers lay. "I don't wish to interfere, but I am a lawyer, although in rather a different field. Justinia was very concerned about you; perhaps if I could familiarise myself with the matter, perhaps make some preliminary enquiries . . . then I could find you a good solicitor from Eyot. I know a very good woman who specializes in these kind of cases."

Sadie's face lit up. "That would be amazingly kind," she said. "But it's hardly fair, when you're here for a holiday."

"Have some more to drink," said Issur. "And then we will talk about Justy. And then tomorrow you will go and see her, in Eyot. Forget the fish, I think."

"I will go to Eyot tomorrow," said Gervase, trying to regain lost ground. "To make a few enquiries on Sadie's behalf."

"Of course," said Sadie, gravely.

"And to see Justy," added Issur wickedly.

"Gervase!" said Lydia, surprised and pleased. And then, "You've come to see Justy, and she isn't here."

Gervase blinked. "Ah," he said slowly. "I gathered . . . That is, Sadie told me . . . I understood she was staying with you, here, in Eyot. I'm visiting Unthrang, you see. For the fishing."

"For the fishing," repeated Lydia. "Yes, of course. And you thought you'd look Justinia up."

"Er, yes."

Her mouth twitched. "What balls," she said, unexpectedly. "You've come up after Justy, and she's gone to London for the day."

"For the day?" said Gervase. "Or is she staying up there?"

"She'll be back this afternoon. She went by train. You can go and meet her."

"I'll do that," said Gervase.

"What are you going to do meanwhile?" asked Lydia.

"Explore Eyot, I suppose," said Gervase. "And I promised to look up one or two things for Sadie."

"Come in," said Lydia. "You can't stand on the doorstep all morning, the neighbours will start talking, and then when Alban gets back from America, he'll turn into a jealous and enraged husband."

"Talking about jealous husbands," said Gervase, after he had duly exclaimed over Lydia's extraordinary house, "tell me more about Justinia's husband."

"Come back when you've done your good deeds and have some lunch," said Lydia after a few moment's thought. "It's only me and the cats. That is, if you don't mind the belches."

"Belches?"

"I tend to burp," said Lydia, thinking how horrified her very formal grandmother would be if she could hear her say that, let alone if she could hear the belches. "The infant, it digs its feet or fists into my stomach."

"Very uncomfortable," said Gervase.

"Makes me laugh," said Lydia.

When Gervase had left, Lydia sat for a while with her feet up on the chaise longue which Alban had bought her. She didn't feel tired, that stage of her pregnancy had passed, and, despite Alban's fussing, she felt perfectly well and fit, if a trifle puffy here and there. But Lydia liked sitting down, or better still, lying down, preferably with an apple and a good book, or failing that, with just her thoughts. Divine idleness, Alban called it; her grandmother labelled it wicked laziness, and her mother worried that she hadn't had enough vitamins when she was growing.

"After all," Lydia told the cat as she got back on to her feet, "I did do quite a lot of growing. Now, you come with me." She heaved the large cat over one shoulder. "You can help me dust Alban's room."

Lydia wasn't much given to dusting, not being of a domestic disposition, and she mostly left the cleaning to the gossipy daily.

Alban's studio was different. It was sacrosanct; he would have died rather than let Mrs Gridlock and her trug across the threshold. On the other hand, he never had any inclination to get busy with a duster or cloth himself.

Lydia had noticed him sneezing a lot recently, and as she drifted into his studio, she could see why. "Look, Madrigal," she said to the cat. "I bought this yesterday." As she spoke, she was opening a box with Dustbug written on it in large, gaudy letters. "You see? A mini-hoover, no cord, charges itself up. Just the thing for Alban's room, no effort involved."

Madrigal leapt off the piano when the Dustbug growled into life, and hid, spitting, under Alban's chair. Lydia took no notice. "It's all a hum, Madrigal," she said. "I know you aren't really scared, but if you want to stay under the chair, you carry on. Mind you," she continued, swooping along the top of the grand piano and making swirly patterns in the thick dust, "mind you, you do look pretty silly hunched up down there."

The Dustbug growled and sucked its way round the room for about ten minutes before it dwindled into a dull drone and stopped.

"Oh," said Lydia, looking at it in surprise. "I wonder why it's done that?" She read the box. "Good," she said. "It only lasts for ten minutes of use, and then it has to be recharged. Ten minutes is just about right for a spell of cleaning, clever, these people."

She put the Dustbug back on its base and plugged it in. Then she sank into Alban's huge armchair. Madrigal jumped on her lap and settled down comfortably. He was very fond of Lydia, she was handy with the can-opener, and very restful to have around.

"What do you think about Justy, Madrigal?" said Lydia, stroking the thick fur. "I think Gervase has fallen for her in a big way. I like Gervase. He reminds me of Alban, but he's more balanced and probably a lot less selfish. Gervase has got that same crackling energy, though. So has Digby, of course, that was why Justy fell for him, I suppose. Gervase isn't another Digby, though. He's more worldly, for one thing, and a lot more civilized. Digby is all business and the latest fashion in houses or cars or whatever; I should find it very tiring. Justy's very loyal, she doesn't complain about Digby. It would be better if she did, if she complained to her friends about his little ways, it would mean that she didn't really mind them."

Madrigal yawned and stretched his paws out. "But, do you know, cat," Lydia went on, "I think that if Justy gets going with her singing, which she possibly might this time, then I suspect she isn't going to have any time for Digby or for Gervase or for anything but her music. In which case, is it fair to encourage Gervase? Although if it is a *coup de foudre*, which I've heard about but never actually seen, then there's no point in encouraging or not encouraging Gervase, it won't make the slightest difference."

The phone rang. Madrigal leapt up, affronted, and Lydia picked up the receiver. It was Valdemar, wanting to know where Alban was.

"Best thing," said Valdemar, when he heard where Alban had gone. "Complete balls-up, this whole business. Those clergymen aren't fit to run a school chapel, never mind a cathedral. They should laicize the whole administration, get some people in who know what's what."

"The Dean does," said Lydia.

"Oh no he doesn't," said Valdemar. "That's why I was ringing Alban up, I thought he ought to know. The Dean had a heart attack late last night."

"Oh," said Lydia. "Is he all right?"

"Dead," said Valdemar. "Expired in the arms of his French mistress, if you want the details."

"No!" said Lydia. "Alban will be beside himself. French? Who was she?"

"Madame La Plage, owns that chain of shops, lingerie, you know."

"Of course," said Lydia, intrigued. "Frou-frou Fanny. Good Lord, how exciting."

"Not for her," said Valdemar laconically.

"I suppose not, in the circs," said Lydia. A thought occurred to her. "Will this change anything at the Cathedral? I mean all this trouble about the music? The choir, and Alban's new work . . ."

"God knows," said Valdemar. "However, I think Simon Praetorius needs to be here just at the present time."

"He will be," promised Lydia. "Alban's being met at the airport by some friends. I'll get on to them right away, tell him the news. If Simon's being difficult, this ought to bring him to heel."

"Tiresome man," said Valdemar unsympathetically. "By the way, someone told me Justy's left her husband, run away to London. Any truth in the story?"

"No, of course not," said Lydia. "Justy's staying with me for a few days, because Alban wouldn't leave me by myself, and I didn't want to go to grandmama's."

"Can't say I blame you," said Valdemar. "Is Justy there with you?"

"Not at this moment, no," said Lydia. "In fact, she's gone to London, she should be seeing Yseult Drury, who is a singing teacher, even now."

"I know who Yseult Drury is," said Valdemar annoyingly. "Good thing too, about bloody time Justy put her house in order and found herself a life. Tell her to give me a ring when she's back, Lydia, Magdalena wants to talk to her."

"I'll do that," said Lydia. "And please don't mention about Justy going to London. Digby doesn't know."

"Secrets from her husband?" said Valdemar. "The beginning of the end for that marriage, if you want my opinion. Virginia thinks so, too."

"You are a gossip, Val," said Lydia.

"Not at all," said Valdemar. "I like Justy, and I think she made a dreadful mistake when she married that man. Much better to go and sing, you can't live life to please other people."

Valdemar's words were at that moment being echoed in London by Alexia, who had met Justinia on Yseult's doorstep. She greeted her with coarse cries of joy, which increased in volume when she learned why Justinia was there.

"Hang on one sec, while I push this lot through the letterbox, it's some music she wanted. No, I don't want to see her, she scares me witless."

Alexia hurtled along the pavement, Justinia in her wake, and bundled her into a café. "Jesus," she cried. "Coffee, strong, for two, and some of those cheesy things." Seeing Justinia's startled expression, she explained that Jesus was the Spanish waiter and an old friend. "Fucking marvellous tenor," she went on. "Keeps himself going with waiting jobs while he's studying over here. Now, tell."

The voice was there, chanting, "Hooray, hooray, told you so, told you so."

"Do you ever hear voices?" Justinia asked.

"All the time," said Alexia. "You do when you're a singer."

"No, not those kind of voices. Voices in your head."

Alexia looked thoughtful. "No, I don't actually, but I've got a chum who does. He says they start up when he's taken a wrong turning; not in his car you understand, we're talking Life here. They nag on, until he changes his ways. That kind of voice?"

Justinia nodded.

"There you are, then," said Alexia. "Told you you were meant for a singer. Come on, sick it up, what does that cow Yseult say."

"I liked her," said Justinia.

"Then she was complimentary. She thinks you should train, become a professional, yes?"

"Yes."

"A sodding miracle," said Alexia, her face alight with pleasure. "Who does she want you to go to?"

"She says she wants to teach me."

"What, herself?" Alexia looked at Justinia in amazement. "But she bloody well doesn't, not these days, only established singers, they come from all over the world to work with her. You mean, it's up the stairs once a week, sixty minutes of Drury time?"

"That's what she said."

"Well, fuck me up a gum tree," exclaimed Alexia.

Justinia blinked.

"I had an Australian boyfriend," said Alexia. "Not very refined in his speech, I'm afraid, but very rewarding in other ways."

"Talking of refinement," began Justinia.

Alexia let out a peal of laughter. "Same old Justy," she squealed. "You sound exactly as you did in Cambridge, lecturing me on my foul mouth. That's the great thing about growing up, don't you think, Justy? You can be precisely what you want to be, and if you offend people, well, that's their sodding problem. Right, now, fizz, this really is something to celebrate."

"Hold on a minute," said Justinia. "She says I must live in London. To go to the opera as much as I can, and there's a workshop on Saturdays, and she thinks I need to see an Alexander practitioner."

"So?"

"So, I live two hundred and fifty miles away. With a husband who likes me at home when he is."

"Oh, bugger that," said Alexia scornfully. "You can't let him stand in your way. I hear all kinds of rumours flying down from Eyot about massacres in the cathedral choir. I know one or two of the lay clerks, isn't your Digby at the bottom of that?"

"Not single-handed," said Justinia. "There is a clergyman egging him on."

"God save us from the clergy," said Alexia. "Well, you can't live with a man like that, Justy. Throw him over."

"Alexia, it isn't that easy. He hasn't done anything to hurt me, well, not intentionally. I love him. I believe, strange as it may sound, that married means you stay together. He isn't unfaithful . . ."

"How do you know?"

Justinia ignored the remark, "He's open and truthful with me, we have a shared life."

"A shared house, too, I hope," said Alexia. "That's important, because you're going to need money. Lots of money, because Yseult doesn't come cheap, and then you've got to live. Tell you what, you can have a room in my flat, minimal rent, good piano, just the job."

Justinia gave up, and laughed. "Lay off, Alexia. I've got to talk it over with Digby, but I don't think that it's going to work. Not at present."

"Coward," shrieked the voice. "Cowardy, cowardy custard. What is it, your duty to Digby, or are you afraid that even with what Zephania and Yseult have said, you still might not make the grade?"

"Oh, go to hell," said Justinia, exasperated.

## 25

Piers stood ashen-faced at Sylvester's door. Lily had come running to answer the urgent peal on the bell; she took one look at Piers, and hauled him inside.

"Sit down," she commanded, pushing him into a chair. She heard Sylvester coming into the room behind them to see what was going on, and briskly told him to pour Piers a stiff brandy.

"Your great-aunt?" she said.

Piers nodded, still looking numb about the mouth.

"Dead?"

"I think so," said Piers.

"Good heavens, if you aren't sure we'd better get over there," cried Sylvester in alarm. "Quick, Lily, call the doctor."

"I have," Piers said. "He's there. He went upstairs. I just came over, because . . ."

"Because you've had a shock," said Lily. "Quite right, too."

Piers was anxious to talk. "The cats hadn't been fed, and I was down late. That was unusual, because the old girl's usually up by eight, and she feeds them if she's first down. She did, I mean. The whole house was somehow quieter than usual, it sounds silly, I know, since Great-Aunt Zeph doesn't – didn't – exactly racket about the place. Anyhow, I felt something was wrong, so I went upstairs, and knocked on her door. There was no answer, and I opened the door, just a little, and looked in. She was lying in bed. I thought she was asleep, at first. Then I saw her hand was hanging down, and she looked, well, cream-coloured. Not alive-looking. And she seemed much younger."

Lily nodded. "Died in her sleep. I thought she was winding down. Don't you take on, Piers, best way to go, would you want her dragged off to hospital, tubes, resuscitation? No, she deserved a peaceful and dignified end. Now, you'd better go back, the doctor will want to see you. Sylvester will go with you, and then he'll bring you back here. The doctor will give Josiah Smile a ring for you, I dare say, don't you worry."

The town was agog at the news, which had swiftly flown round the green. Roxane came running across to Crag End from the Manor House, "PC Vibbs is there, he told me you were with Sylvester, Piers, oh, you poor man." She sank down beside him and took his hand. "Oh, Piers."

He looked at her with troubled eyes. "It was dreadful, Roxane," and then he buried his fair head in her lap and wept.

"Best thing," said Lily. "Leave them alone, Sylvester, they'll sort themselves out."

Celia came over later on to see if there was anything she could do, as she put it, but really to find out what Lily knew. Her face was grave and her eyes dark with sympathy. "It's a shock for a young man," she said to Lily. "Zephania hasn't got any children?"

"Yes, she has, but I don't suppose they'll be much use," said Lily, cryptically. "Piers' mum is coming up."

"What a to-do," said Celia.

"Yes, what a to-do," said Lily with a silent laugh. "Does Justinia know?"

"I telephoned Lydia and left a message," said Celia. "Justinia was out, shopping, I suppose." She took a sip of her coffee. "This is very good, Lily. I do get rather tired of Digby's wholesome brand, it has very little taste. Lydia said that Justinia would be very upset when she heard about Zephania, I don't see why, when she hardly knew her."

"Oh, there are reasons," said Lily darkly.

"There are several policemen over at the Manor House," said Celia. "I hope they don't think the old lady's death was suspicious in any way."

"No, it's the pictures," said Lily. "She had a very valuable collection of paintings. Her solicitor is coming over this afternoon to arrange what to do with them, they don't want them left in the house."

"I don't see what difference it can make," said Celia. "They've been there all this time, with only Piers and Zephania to guard them. Piers is staying on, isn't he?"

"Yes, he is."

"He'll be lonely, in that great house."

"No," said Lily. "Some friends are coming over."

Merle and Andrea stood and watched the heavy van manoeuvring its way out of the Manor House gates.

"It's Zephania's pictures," Merle told Andrea. "They're very valuable, so they've been taken away to be locked up somewhere safe."

"Are they nice pictures?" asked Andrea.

"I don't know," said Merle. "I expect so. Impressionists, minor ones, but still good, so Piers told me."

"It's a pity if no-one's seen them all these years," said Andrea. "What's going to happen to them?"

"It depends on her will," said Merle.

"And will Piers go on living in the house?"

"I don't know, perhaps. It may be sold."

"Then Digby would buy it," said Andrea, shrewd beyond her years.

"It would be nice to have people we know there," said Merle. "Whoever it is will be our neighbours."

"Not if we go back to London," said Andrea gloomily.

"You don't want to go back, do you?"

"No," said Andrea.

"That's good, because I think that Daddy and I are going to look for a house up here."

Andrea's face was radiant. "Really, Mummy? You aren't just saying that? You won't change your mind? Are you going to sell the house in London?"

"We've had an offer for it," said Merle. "We'll see if we can find a house in Unthrang, but there aren't many on the market."

"I want to stay in Juniper House," said Andrea in a definite voice. "So does Ben. He wrote and said so."

"Yes, but Juniper House isn't for sale. We might be able to go on renting it, but I think we'd prefer to buy a house of our own."

"There's Roxane," said Andrea, waving furiously. "Hello,

Roxane, why are you carrying a big bag like that? Are you going away?"

Roxane smiled at Andrea. "No, but I thought Piers might be lonely in the Manor all by himself, so I'm going to keep him company. Marius and Pansy are coming over, too, do you know them?"

"Yes, Marius is the very dramatic one, and Pansy's always laughing. I like her. So does Piers, because he told me so."

"Oh," said Roxane.

Justinia was surprised when she saw Gervase standing on the platform as her train drew into the station at Eyot.

"Hello," she said. "What are you doing here? Are you catching this train?"

"No," said Gervase, relieving her of her music case. "I'm here to meet you. Lydia told me you would be coming back from London by train this afternoon."

"How did you know which train?" asked Justinia.

"I guessed," said Gervase, untruthfully, since this was the third train from London he'd met; in fact he'd spent two hours waiting at the station. He hadn't minded. The trains took him back to his childhood and his electric train layout with its signals and stations. He remembered his passionate boy's greed for track and a devastating quarrel with his best friend, who took some special points without asking, and who had been banned from the house for several weeks in consequence.

"So what are you doing in Eyot?" asked Justinia as they left the forecourt.

"I'm actually staying in Unthrang," said Gervase. "Fishing."

"Fishing," said Justinia, her thoughts elsewhere. "I'm staying in Eyot at present, with Lydia."

"I know," said Gervase. "I'll escort you back there, if I may."

"I don't see why not," said Justinia. "We may as well walk; you didn't come by car, did you?"

"No, Lydia said it was easier on foot, and it's a pleasant walk over all those bridges."

They walked on together in silence, Justinia absorbed in her own thoughts, reliving her day in London, hardly aware of Gervase's presence, while Gervase was realizing that she was even more attractive than he remembered. Had he noticed before how lovely she looked from the side, with the clear line of the jaw and her graceful head with that rich-coloured hair piled up on top? Her mouth curled up at the ends, she smiles a lot, thought Gervase, although she isn't smiling now.

"Was it successful?" he asked. "Your trip to London? Lydia said you were going to consult an expert about your voice. It wasn't a doctor, I hope," he said as the thought suddenly occurred to him.

Justinia forced her attention away from Yseult's flat and into the present, here and now in Eyot, with this nice man who was trying so hard to make conversation.

"No, no, I went to see someone who teaches singing."

"Anyone I know?"

Justinia stopped and stared at him. "I don't see why . . . Oh, I forgot, of course, you have a lot to do with opera, don't you?"

"Yes," he said, cold inside; she barely remembered him. He had come all this way, her image burning in his mind, driven by a desperate need to see her again, hear her voice. And he was a stranger to her, she couldn't even remember what he did.

"Yes," he said again.

"Yseult Drury," said Justinia, her face lighting up.

His eyebrows rose. "The top, then," he said. "Did you go for a lesson?"

"Not exactly," said Justinia.

"Brilliant teacher," Gervase went on, his eyes on her face. "Brilliant."

Justinia looked suddenly sad. "That's what everyone says." She hesitated, and then turned towards Gervase, laying her hand on his arm in an urgent gesture. "If she said she'd teach someone, and they weren't sure . . ."

"Then they'd be throwing away the chance of a lifetime, apart from wronging themselves in an unforgivable way," said Gervase firmly. "She only takes on the best, she says herself that she never teaches a singer she feels doubtful about." He looked down at Justinia. That's what's setting her on fire, he thought, as though seeing her from an unimaginable distance. That's what she really cares about.

He chose his words carefully. "If she has said she'll teach you, then you have to forget everything else and go to her. You'd never forgive yourself if you didn't."

"That's what Alexia says," said Justinia. "Art comes first."

"I think perhaps, for you, it does," said Gervase.

Lydia pottered about the kitchen, talking through the arch which led into the informal sitting room. "Have you remembered it's choir rehearsal night tonight, Justy?" she said with a straight face.

"Oh, I completely forgot!" cried Justinia, leaping up. "Help! What time is it?"

"Calm down," said Lydia. "I was teasing you; it's been cancelled."

"Cancelled?" said Justinia, sitting down again with relief. "Why? There's nothing wrong with Valliaze, is there?"

"No, but the Dean died last night, and the whole cathedral world is in turmoil, not least because he wasn't alone when it happened."

"Where was he?" asked Justinia.

"In bed," said Lydia.

"Of course, he was a widower," said Justinia. "He wasn't with a man, surely. Or, horror, a boy!"

"No, his companion was female, which is one good thing; a Frenchwoman, you wouldn't know her. Anyhow, they're trying to keep the lid on the scandal, hopeless, of course, the place is teeming with reporters."

Lydia flashed a quick look at Justinia. "And, rather sadder news for you, Justy. Zephania has died as well. Very peacefully, in her sleep."

"Oh, no," said Justinia.

"So Piers couldn't come, and Marius and Pansy are out in Unthrang with him, and Lucius decided he'd better see if he can give a hand. Then with you in London, and no-one sure that you would be back in time, and all the fuss about the Dean, Valliaze cancelled. I think he's rather upset about Zephania himself. He's been ringing up all sorts of people to tell them, and he's writing an obit for one of the London papers."

"A lively place, Eyotshire," observed Gervase. "I'm sorry about this friend of yours, Justy. Did you say Zephania? That wouldn't be Zephania Zouche, would it?"

Justinia nodded.

"Do you know, I thought she was already dead. She must have been, let me think . . . oh, well past eighty."

"She didn't look it," said Justinia.

"I thought you might like to go out to Unthrang," said Lydia. Justinia looked at her. "No, I can't leave you."

"I'm perfectly all right," said Lydia, "but I know you promised Alban, so I've asked Faustina to come round this evening. She's more than happy to, says the Bishop won't be in till late, not with this Dean business going on. Milo, her son, has gone to stay with a friend, so she says she'll stay here until you get back."

"I won't be late," Justinia promised. "I'd just like to see Piers, and find out exactly what happened. How did you hear about it?"

"Your mother rang," said Lydia. "No, I did not say you'd gone to London, of course I didn't, you goose, do you think I'm stupid? And, by the way, Digby won't be there, Celia says he's gone to Manchester on business and is staying overnight."

Justinia was relieved, she didn't want to see Digby just yet. "What about you?" she said to Gervase. "Are you staying in Eyot?"

"No," said Gervase. "If you like the idea, I'll drive you to Unthrang, and then I'll take you out somewhere for dinner, and bring you back in good time to relieve Faustina."

"Oh, you don't have to take me out to eat," said Justinia. "I can forage at home."

"I told the inn I would be dining out," said Gervase, politely, hiding his sense of hurt at Justinia's apparent indifference. "I would be glad of company."

"No, Justy, I don't think Gervase wants to eat a sandwich with you and your mother," Lydia said firmly as she saw Justinia open her mouth to speak. "If I know Celia, she'll be in a full-blown sepulchral mood, reminiscing about funerals and wakes and I don't know what gloomy doings. You can't inflict that on Gervase."

Gervase saw Justinia hesitate. "Perhaps Sadie would join us," he suggested. "I met her yesterday, and I think I can give her some useful advice."

"Justy, stop procrastinating," said Lydia. "Go out and have a good time, take that delicious Issur with you as well, and for heaven's sake, don't hurry back on my account. Faustina's going to borrow several highly unsuitable videos to bring with her, and we're going to settle down to enjoy ourselves."

"Such goings-on," murmured Gervase. "And with the Dean hardly cold in his bed."

"He died happy, one supposes," said Lydia cheerfully. "And I love watching videos when Alban isn't here, because when he is, he wanders in and out, making rude comments about the film and the actors until I want to scream."

Sadie put her head round the door. "Are you practising?" she asked.

"Just finished," said Sylvester, holding his cello and bow in one strong hand while he reached out for his cello case. "I got up extremely early this morning, to practise; I had a feeling it was going to be a busy day. Come in, come in. What's the news?"

"Let me tell you that this lawyer Justy picked up in London is a real charmer, and, I think, terrifically clever. He's obviously head over heels with Justy, and she hasn't noticed; I can't think what's the matter with her. I know she's married, but you'd think you would at least notice it when a man looks at you like that."

"I think Justy has enough on her plate at the moment," said Sylvester. "I don't think she can take any more, not until she's sorted herself out."

"Well, she's got more sorting out to do than she thought," said Sadie. "It must be worrying for her, but when Gervase, that's the lawyer, was looking up a few details on Yellow Cottage, he found out that Justy and Digby's house is only in Digby's name."

Sylvester let out a low whistle. "Has he told Justy?"

"He mentioned it, and she seemed, oh puzzled. Not upset, or furious . . . almost as though he was talking about someone else, not her and Digby. She was a bit strange altogether, I hope she isn't heading for a breakdown or something."

"I wonder what Yseult said to her," mused Sylvester.

"If that's the woman she went to see in London, she wants to teach Justy."

"Does she, now?" Sylvester looked thoughtful. "Mind you, I'm not surprised. But what about you?"

Sadie shifted in her chair. "It's all very well making the most of oneself, and I like having a good hairdo and so on, but I can't say these clothes are as comfortable as my old ones, and it does take a lot of time to keep oneself looking good. I seem to remember Charles wasting a lot of time on his appearance. Is it worth it, I ask myself?"

Sadie could sense Sylvester's impatience, and she laughed. "All right, all right, I'm saving the best bit until last. Gervase doesn't think Charles has a hope of getting his hands on the house, or on my savings. He reckons Nigel has been up to some pretty underhand work, delaying tactics would be a very polite way of describing it. There now!"

Sylvester was delighted. "So you're going to be able to settle down without any worries, build a few more follies and cultivate your garden."

Sadie sighed. "You know, Sylvester, when you put it like that, it doesn't sound quite as inviting as I once thought it would be."

"Ah, Needs and Meta-needs," said Sylvester wisely. He was standing by the window, keeping a watchful eye on the green. "Here come Lily and Lucius, now why isn't Lucius at work?"

"Ask him," said Sadie.

Lily deposited Lucius in the sitting room, said hello to Sadie, told Sylvester she would make coffee, and departed.

"Sylvester wants to know why you aren't at work," said Sadie.

"I've taken a day or two off," said Lucius. "The solicitor and the police are fussing because there isn't a proper inventory of everything in Zephania's house. They've taken the pictures away for safekeeping, as you know, but Piers keeps on finding other bits and pieces which might be valuable. He's alarmed by it all, so I said I'd go through the house room by room with him, and we'd make a list."

"Good thinking," said Sylvester. "That'll stop any grubby solicitor or policeman suspecting him of stealing the spoons."

"They might suspect me," said Lucius.

"No, you're far too respectable," said Sylvester. "How's Merle?"

Lucius's face took on a pleased expression. "She's had some very good news; she sent some pieces off, country living as seen daily in Unthrang, and they've snapped them up. And they want to commission a whole series."

"Excellent, excellent," said Sylvester, genuinely pleased.

"Andrea tells me you might be going to settle in Unthrang," said Sadie.

Lucius grinned. "Other people know your business before you do in Unthrang."

"That's its charm," said Sylvester. "Is it true?"

"Yes," said Lucius. "It's just a question of finding a suitable house. We'd love one on the green, of course, but they don't come up very often."

"I can't sell you Yellow Cottage, even if I wanted to," said Sadie. "It wouldn't be big enough."

"There's always the Manor," said Sylvester.

"Rather above our price level, something tells me," said Lucius.

"Ah, but Digby will be wetting himself at the thought of buying it," said Sadie. "If he did, then his house would be on the market."

"It's a big if, though," said Lucius. "Does anyone know who's inherited the house yet?"

"Not if Piers doesn't," said Sylvester. "He'd be the first to know, I should think."

"The pictures are going to a gallery in Manchester," said Sadie. "Zephania told Piers about that some time ago."

Lily brought their coffee in and lingered to chat. "Lydia rang," she told Sylvester. "I didn't interrupt you, seeing that you were working. Alban's found Simon, and they're on their way back. Steam coming out of Simon's ears, she said."

"About time, too," said Sylvester. "He's got to put a stop to that ridiculous Succentor and his sordid little schemes."

"Will he be able to?" asked Lucius.

"He can try," said Sylvester. "I expect Holigost will take the opportunity to try and slide a few more horrors through while everything is topsy-turvy because of the Dean. Just the time when men like that put the boot in; Simon will have to jump on him hard."

"It's funny, isn't it?" said Sadie. "The Rev Wroot, who was

an arch ally of Holigost's, has now moved firmly over to the opposition."

"Has he?" said Sylvester, sitting up with interest and nearly sending his coffee cup flying. "I hadn't heard about this."

Lily tsk-tsked at his clumsiness. "Sadie's right," she said. "They're talking about it at the shops. He's throwing out all those banners and slogans, and he and Father Hamish are thick as thieves, looking at catalogues of monstrances and incense and I don't know what."

Sylvester gave a deep sigh of satisfaction. "How glad I am to be here in Unthrang in such interesting times," he said. "Midwinter is a mere nothing in comparison."

"Go and buy some frilly knickers," said Lydia. "Nothing like frippery undies in time of crisis, restores the spirits wonderfully, I find."

Justinia cupped her hands round the big bowl of coffee which Lydia had poured out for her the moment she saw how tired and drawn her cousin looked.

"Didn't you have a good time last night?" she asked.

"Yes and no," said Justinia, yawning. "Except that, for some reason, Gervase was telling me about our house, that it's Digby's and not mine. I didn't really . . ."

"What?" said Lydia, suddenly alert. "You bought that house jointly."

"Of course we did," said Justinia wearily. "That's why it doesn't matter what it says on the deeds. If I paid for half of it, it's half mine. Not that it matters who owns it, that's the point of marriage, you share everything."

"What's mine is mine and what's yours is open to discussion," murmured Lydia, ruffling Madrigal's fur as he sat complacently on her lap. "I think I'm going to have a squashed child, cat, and it will all be your fault."

Justinia got up and carried her empty cup and saucer to the sink.

"Are you going to get in touch with Yseult Drury?" Lydia asked directly.

Justinia turned the tap on. "Who knows?" she said. "I doubt it."

Lydia was worried that Justinia intended to push it all to the back of her mind, not think about it, pretend it had never happened, and carry on with life as before.

"I wish I could," said Justinia. "It's hardly possible, however, with this voice dinning in my ears; nag, nag, nag."

"Go to Fanny's," said Lydia. "It's only five minutes away. Look at some pretties, forget about everything. Then I'll take you out to lunch, and this afternoon we'll go to the cinema."

"I'd like that," said Justinia.

"Unless, of course, Gervase arrives and wants to take you somewhere."

Justinia sighed. "I hope he's up to his armpits in muddy water, fish leaping all around him, no thoughts of an expedition to Eyot."

"You're going to find it very difficult to keep that one at arm's length," observed Lydia.

"I don't know what he thinks he's up to," said Justinia. "I wear a wedding ring, and an engagement ring, I'm happily married, I live with my husband; if he goes after fish on the same principle, he'll have a lot of empty hooks."

Justinia walked slowly along, lost in thought. She had made her decision, there was no way she could go to London. To do so would be a betrayal. Maybe Digby had no right to want her to be at home, but that was the way he was, that was the man she had married, she wasn't going to run off whinging the first time things got tough.

It isn't his fault that all this has happened, she argued with herself. I chose, years ago, not to do music. That's nothing to do with Digby. It isn't fair to him, to marry one woman and find that she's changed overnight into someone quite different, with a whole new agenda for her life.

"Which one is you, though?" asked the voice. "The one he married, or the one who hares off to London, poking and stabbing at a nerve you pretend you haven't got?"

"I'm ignoring you," said Justinia. "I'm not paying any attention."

"Okay," said the voice in a warm and friendly tone. "Go and buy yourself some pretties, Lydia's right, excellent way to cheer yourself up. Look, you've walked to the shop without realizing it. I won't go in there with you, I'll talk to you later."

Justinia dived into the shop, setting the delicate little Victorian bell with its neatly coiled spring clinking and clanking. There were two shop assistants in there today, the tiny one she had seen before, and a taller, very thin one with a deep red rosebud mouth.

"Ah, for the lover this time?" said the small assistant, recognizing her. "Something delicious, for a new man?"

"No, still just a husband, I'm afraid. I don't know what I want, I thought I'd try some things on."

The assistant pulled out smooth-running drawers hidden beneath the counter, and flung an array of shimmering, silky garments on the counter. "I remember your size, you see, all these are perfect for you, and you must try this, this pearly grey, so unusual, don't you think?"

The assistant with the rosebud mouth smiled her approval, and clicked in front of Justinia to the changing room, her body seamless in its close, short black dress, gleaming tights and high-heeled black shoes. She pulled back the thick silk curtain and ushered Justinia in.

Justinia sat down on the gilt chair, stretching her legs out in front of her, collecting her thoughts before reaching out for the armfuls of froth so deftly laid out by the assistant.

The shop was empty; she could hear the two assistants gossiping.

"Madame is very upset."

"I would be, too, imagine, someone dying like that on top of you."

"You don't know that he was on top."

"Madame's too discreet to say."

"Of course, it had been going on for years and years."

"Even when his wife was alive?"

"Did you ever see her? It's not surprising. I mean, Madame isn't young, but she does know how to look after herself."

"They say the Dean was very rich."

"I thought clergymen were against the rich."

"Not when it's one of them who has the money."

"He can't have got rich being a Dean, you hardly earn anything in the Church."

"Millions, they say."

"And all to Madame."

"Yes, but," and the voice sank to a thrilling and perfectly audible whisper, "but, Madame doesn't want the money."

"Why ever not?"

"She has enough money of her own."

"Nobody ever has enough money."

"Fact. She's made a fortune, ten shops she has now, and there's the export business she runs out of Harrogate."

"She isn't going to refuse it, is she?"

"She's going to give it away to charity."

"No!"

"That's what I heard."

The assistants jumped to attention as the shop bell gave a neat tinkle.

"Good morning, sir," said rosebud mouth. "How nice to see you again. What can we do for you?"

"I want something especially pretty today," said the voice.

Justinia's heart missed a beat.

It was Digby.

## 26

Justinia jumped to her feet, thinking how surprised he would be when he saw her there. Then she paused. It would spoil his pleasure in buying something for her if he saw her now, in the shop. Better to pretend, when he gave it to her, that she knew nothing about it. How kind he was, he must be missing her, buying her a present for when she came home. She listened, smiling, as Digby chatted to the assistant. Flirting, she thought.

"This is perfect," Digby was saying. "Size thirty-two A."

Ridiculous man, thought Justinia. He must know my size by now, I've never been a thirty-two A. I'll have to change it.

Then a chill little thought entered her head. He had bought her all kinds of things to wear since she had known him, and she had never had to change anything because it was the wrong size. Wrong colour, yes. Wrong style, often. But he always bought her the right size. She suspected he had her measurements written down in the little black notebook he carried everywhere with him.

Without meaning to, Justinia found herself standing on the chair. She could see into the shop in the gaps between the curtain rings and the thick pole above. Digby was holding up a pair of elegant camiknicks; what was he thinking of? Those would never fit her.

"And these, let me see, yes, exactly the right size." He reached into his jacket pocket.

"How would you like to pay, sir?"

"Cash."

Justinia slid down to the floor. More pleasantries were exchanged, the bell tinkled again as the door opened and shut.

Rosebud mouth appeared through the curtains. "You haven't tried anything on yet," she said reprovingly.

"No, I was trying to make up my mind. Do you know, I'm sure I heard a familiar voice in there just now. Was that, um, Walter Thring?"

"No, it's Mr John. He's in here ever so often, very fond he must be of his present young lady, he's been in here two or three times just these last weeks. She's very slim; petite, I expect. Now the one before, she was big, big all over. We carry quite a lot of stock for the bigger ladies, some of our customers always go for the more buxom type. Mr John is unusual, though, from large to small, just as the fancy takes him. I'm glad I'm not his wife."

"How do you know he's married?"

"Oh, you can always tell. You learn a lot about men in this line of business. They come in at Christmas to buy presents for their wives. Always black, and then a week later, the wives come in to change the items for something in a prettier colour. We call many of our black numbers the revolving stock, no sooner sold than back it comes."

"I thought men liked black. Don't they find it sexy?"

"It's strange, they think it might make their wives sexy, but when they're buying for their girlfriends, they go for white and pale shades. Classier."

"How surprising." Justinia managed a weak smile. "Look, I've just realized that I haven't got time to try all these things on today. Do you mind if I come again another day? It's my fault for daydreaming, but I've got a dentist's appointment which I mustn't be late for."

"Of course," said the assistant with quick sympathy. "Nothing painful, I hope, I dread the dentist, simply dread it."

Justinia let herself into Lydia's house with the key which Lydia had given her. She called Lydia's name; there was no answer, she must have gone out to do some shopping. Justinia didn't mind, she wanted to be by herself so that she could think. She didn't feel hurt, or stunned, or any of the things she might be expected to feel. On the contrary, she felt very cool and rational. She simply wanted to work out exactly what was going on.

There was a note on the table from Lydia. "Alban and Simon

caught earlier plane, gone to meet them. Sorry about lunch and cinema, another day, plenty of food in fridge. L."

I'll go home, Justinia decided. If Alban's back, Lydia will be okay. I'll have a look in Digby's desk, see if there are any clues to the identity of thirty-two A. . . . Or the previous, bigger lady. Might Digby have been buying a present for his secretary? No, that was what the Justinia of only a few weeks ago would automatically have thought. As it was, she knew perfectly well that Digby's secretary was a motherly woman in her fifties, and moreover Digby always gave her a handbag or an expensive scarf. Digby loved buying presents for people; now he had bought one present too many.

Could she face her mother?

She wouldn't have to, not until this evening. Celia was in Eyot, she knew, having her hair done and shopping. The house would be empty.

Justinia went out. No drooping now, there was determination in every line of her body. Flowers for Lydia, and some of those chocolates from Gumble's which she liked so much.

"The ones with real cream, please," she said.

"Indulging yourself?" said a voice behind her.

"Hello, Roxane. No, these are for Lydia. What are you doing here?"

"Ah, I'm on a sentimental journey," said Roxane.

"To Gumble's?" said Justinia doubtfully.

"Among other places," said Roxane dreamily. "Gumble's, and the rose gardens at Gossiby, and Hazlitt's Interiors . . . You don't know what I'm talking about, do you?"

"No," said Justinia. "I haven't a clue."

"It's all to do with my charity work," said Roxane. "When are you coming back to Unthrang?"

"Today. Later today, I've just got one or two things to do first."

"I expect Digby's missed you."

"I expect he's filled his time profitably," said Justinia, rather sharply for her.

Roxane raised one elegant eyebrow. "Hey, ho, all not so friendly in the FitzOdo household? Don't tell me the worm has turned, and you're going to take up singing after all?"

"Possibly," said Justinia.

"Make the most of the weather," Roxane called after her as she left the shop. "They say very warm tonight, and then later tomorrow an icy wind will come snaking down from Scotland, to blow our Indian summer away. There have never been such warm nights at this time of the year, did you know that? Not since records have been kept."

"I can believe it," said Justinia.

It was much later than she had planned by the time she left Eyot. She didn't need to hurry, though; her mother would go to the theatre or to the cinema before coming home with Digby after his lodge meeting.

As she swung the car round in front of the house, she felt she had been away for months, not days. Her mother had left some lights on, to warn the burglars away; what burglars, here in Unthrang, where life was so orderly?" She left the car in front of the house, she could drive it round to the garage later.

The kitchen was quiet and empty. She went upstairs to leave her bag, moving softly and humming under her breath, happy to be here alone. She took her music case out of the bigger bag and went back downstairs to put it in her room. How funny of her mother to leave that light on, she thought as she pushed the door open.

And that's a much bigger bum than Digby realizes, was her first, ridiculous thought as she came face to face with Genevra's rear end, which was dangled over the arm of the sofa.

She was naked, and so was Digby, wound around various bits of Genevra in a pose which Justinia didn't recognize, a man of parts, Digby, she thought grimly.

A surge of anger and indignation swept over her, as the scene before her fell into focus. "That's my sofa," she yelled. "How dare you, on my sofa!"

Digby untwined himself, stumbled to his feet, wilting before her scornful eyes.

"Justinia, I didn't expect . . ."

Justinia ignored him, she was advancing on Genevra with a look of menace that made her scuttle desperately behind the sofa. Then, to her own surprise, Justinia burst out laughing.

It was genuine, happy laughter, the laughter of relief and release.

"Oh, carry on," she said with a wave of her hand. "Take pictures of each other, and then you can see how ridiculous you look."

Digby was holding his trousers in front of himself.

"Don't bother, Digby," Justinia said. "I'm not remotely interested."

"No, Thomas," said Lily. "You are not going out for a picnic tonight."

Thomas slumped sulkily in his chair. "Everyone else is."

"Everyone else is what?" asked Sylvester, as he came into the kitchen.

"There's a picnic tonight. Up on the fells, because it's so warm and the weather's going to break tomorrow."

"A picnic," said Sylvester. "That sounds very innocuous. And no school tomorrow, because it's Saturday. Why not, eh, Lily?"

"Because not," said Lily inexorably. "When Magdalena and Val let Thomas come here for a weekend, they expect us to take care of him. Out on the fells in the dark is not taking care of him."

"But Lily, there'll be flares. It's all arranged, there'll be masses of people there, I'll be fine."

"No," said Lily, making an imperceptible gesture at Sylvester. He looked slightly taken aback, but reinforced Lily's veto as instructed.

"No, Thomas, if Lily says not, then not. I expect it'll mostly be the older ones, you might feel a bit out of it."

"Flora at the shop particularly asked me to come," said Thomas grumpily.

"Did she just?" said Sylvester with quickening interest.

"Another time," said Lily calmly. "Your time will come, Thomas, don't you worry, but not yet. Now take this tray into the dining room for me, and no arguing."

"I'm not going out on any picnic," said Sylvester. "So you can stay up and play a game. You choose, I don't mind what it is, as long as you don't cheat."

"Boys always cheat," said Lily, shooing them out of the kitchen.

Thomas had been looking forward to his weekend in Unthrang,

but it wasn't turning out too well. He had gone across to say hello to Justinia, but a tight-lipped Digby had told him that Justinia had gone out for a walk, and no, he didn't know when she would be back. He, Digby was about to leave for an evening in Eyot, so if Thomas would excuse him . . ."

Sadie wasn't her usual self, either, she seemed wrapped in thought, and rather vague. Issur had gone out, she said, probably to the picnic; she would be going out herself, later; no, she agreed with Lily, much better for Thomas to stay in tonight.

Thomas watched Pansy setting off towards the fell path. She was light-footed, almost dancing, pleased to be out in the warm night-time air. Lucius was coming over to go through some papers with Piers, Lily said. He and Merle had had their own picnic, she added with a wicked laugh, they had no need of darkness and the fells, although Merle had said she'd go up for half an hour. Marius was on duty with his goose, he would be back tomorrow.

Thomas didn't know what Lily was on about, he just knew he was being excluded, his blood was stirring, he wanted to be up and off. Lily wouldn't change her mind. "No way," she said, eyeing him. "It's not safe out there, whatever you may say. I'm locking up now, you go and join Sylvester."

"I don't want to play anything," Thomas told Sylvester in disgruntled tones. "If I'm not allowed out, I'll sit here and read."

"What are you reading?" asked Sylvester, as Thomas dragged a Penguin out of his pocket.

"The *Bacchae*. You know, Euripides," Thomas said.

"Are you doing that at school?" asked Sylvester, surprised.

"No," said Thomas. "Canon Feverfew said it wasn't suitable for us, and we weren't to read it, so I went and bought a copy at lunchtime."

"I see," said Sylvester.

Piers opened a small cardboard box. "More papers, I think." Inside were several black bound notebooks, neatly packed together. A sheet of paper and an envelope, unsealed, lay on the top. "They look like her diaries," he said, flicking through one or two of the notebooks. "They're written in Italian, I can't understand much of it."

"I can read Italian," said Lucius. "I'll have a look at them in a minute if you like. What's in that envelope? It looks quite new."

"It does, too," said Piers. He slid his fingers in, and drew out a thick sheet of paper. "Brilliant, Lucius, it's her will." He held up the paper, with Last Will and Testament written at the top in crinkly letters.

"It's just a will form from the stationer's," said Lucius, surprised. "How odd, when she had a perfectly good solicitor on call."

"That's why the solicitor asked us to look for another will," said Piers. "Auntie Zeph rang him up a few days ago, said she wanted to come and see them and change her will, but that they should know, in case anything happened to her meanwhile, that she had drawn up a new will, just in case."

"Almost as though she knew she wasn't going to make it."

"I think she'd been feeling pretty weak recently," said Piers. "I suppose you would, if your heart was running down."

"She should have gone to the doctors, they can give you all sorts of things these days."

"I expect she decided she'd had enough," said Piers. "Should I read it?"

"I don't see why not," said Lucius, who was consumed with curiosity. "The envelope wasn't sealed."

Piers looked up from the paper in astonishment. "I don't understand this at all," he said.

"May I?" said Lucius, looking over the top of his glasses at Piers. He took the will. "Pictures to Manchester, some bequests to some people, and to charity. Much the same as the solicitor said was in the previous will. Hello, she's left you a nice sum, Piers!"

"Yes, but look at the end."

"Good lord," said Lucius. "How unexpected, she hardly knew Justinia!"

Piers flicked the paper with his fingers. "She's left Justy this house and its contents – except for the pictures."

"How extraordinary," said Lucius. "And she doesn't give any reason why – there's no letter or anything else in the envelope is there?"

Piers shook the envelope. "No, nothing."

"It's a generous bequest, a house like this."

"Digby," said Piers crossly, "will be in clover. But why?"

"Do you know," said Lucius, "I think we may just find the answer to that in these diaries."

"They're ancient," objected Piers. "Look at the dates, fifty, sixty years ago. I mean, they might be of interest to a music historian, they must have been written at the time when she was still singing, but I don't see what they've got to do with Justy."

"I think she tucked the will in there on purpose," said Lucius. "I think she meant us to read these diaries when we found the will."

"I suppose so," said Piers, unconvinced.

"Do you mind?" said Lucius. "About the house?"

"No, not at all," said Piers, quite genuinely. "It would be a millstone round my neck, I'd have to sell it, and that would be a trouble. She's left me quite a lot of money, and since I'm going to make a great deal more in due course, I'm perfectly happy for the house to go where she wanted it to. I just wonder why Justy, of all people."

"Pour me another whisky," said Lucius. "And I'll see if these diaries throw any light on the mystery."

"Okay," said Piers obligingly. "I'll carry on with the other boxes."

He got up from the floor and went over to the table by the window to get Lucius his whisky. The windows were wide open, and the moonlight streamed in through the curtains.

"I can hear music from up on the fells," he said as he handed Lucius his glass. "Listen."

"Some of the locals are having an open-air frolic tonight, aren't they? I hadn't realized there was going to be dancing. That'll set the dinks quivering with fury as they try to get to sleep." Lucius tilted his head, listening hard. "It's very strange music. I don't recognize it."

"Haunting," said Piers with a shiver. "I don't like it. Roxane's gone, I wish she hadn't. I'm going to shut the windows, do you mind?"

"Go ahead," said Lucius, settling back into his chair and opening the first of the diaries.

Justinia heard the music, too, as she walked across Roxane's stable yard. A solitary light shone above the door, and she could hear the eerie sound of a peacock calling on the other side of the house. She felt as though she were in a dream. None of this is real, she told herself.

She pushed at the door which led into the swimming pool, half expecting it to be locked. It wasn't, and the door swung open. Inside, the pool glittered with a thousand broken fragments of light, as the moonshine poured in through the high windows. The statues gleamed palely; behind them were patches of deep purple shadow.

Magical, thought Justinia. She pulled off her clothes, letting them slide to the ground, and dived into the pool. She plunged to the bottom, running her hands along the mosaics there, before breaking the surface and taking a huge breath. She lay on her back, kicking herself slowly along the line of gods and nymphs. A figure, the naked figure of a man, stepped out of the shadows; Justinia's heart missed a beat. Then she saw who it was.

"Hello, Issur," she said. "What a fright you gave me. Of course, you would be here on a night like this."

Issur slid into the water. "Now, why do you say this?"

"You belong here, somehow," said Justinia, letting her head drift back as she paddled gently with her hands. "In the moonlight, and among these statues."

"Ah, now these statues. Some of them are very worrying. These muscles are not completely right, and one or two of the men are very over-developed."

"Hmm," said Justinia, thinking that Issur could hardly level any criticism on that count, not from what she had just seen.

Issur swam strongly away from her, turning and twisting like a porpoise. He relaxed against the side of the pool, shaking the wet hair out of his eyes, which were alight with laughter.

"I think you look very beautiful," he said. "It is very rewarding, you know, to make love in the water. Or there is a very comfortable place up there."

"Who said I wanted to make love?"

"I think you are in the mood for some madness," said Issur. "A little wildness, to take away the taste of your dull husband."

"Perhaps," said Justinia dreamily. "You've got a wonderful body, Issur."

"So," said Issur.

*   *   *

"Justinia, wake up! Are you all right?"

Startled, Justinia opened her eyes. Where was she? In the swimming pool, lying on the huge couch . . . of course. But the lights were on, and Gervase was standing, looking down at her, very concerned.

"Are you all right?"

Justinia seized a towel from the pile on the shelf behind the couch and scrambled to her feet. "Yes, of course I'm all right. I must have fallen asleep . . . Are you alone?" Her eyes flickered around the pool. No Issur to be seen. "Such a wonderful, magical night, don't you think?"

"You sound wild."

"I feel wild."

"I saw that Russian just now, I was on the fells. He was rather involved with two people. A man and a woman. There's a lot going on up there, rather surprising, actually."

"I'm not surprised," said Justinia.

"I never expected this kind of thing in the north of England," said Gervase, looking slightly ruffled.

Justinia gave a lazy smile and stretched her arms above her head. "Gervase, just enjoy it all. I don't suppose, as long as we live, we'll ever know such a night as this."

"Don't do that," said Gervase. "It's unsettling."

"Be unsettled, then," said Justinia.

"Justinia," he began, giving way to impulses he felt he should resist.

"Mmm," said Justinia, sinking back into the couch with him. "What a wonderful, wonderful night."

Thomas wasn't having such a wonderful night, nor were Sylvester and Lily having a peaceful one. Thomas woke up at one in the morning, crying and moaning, and when Lily, bundling herself into a red and pink silk wrap, burst into his room, he was sitting bolt upright in bed, staring at the moon and whimpering.

Lily sat beside him and hugged him. Sylvester, majestic in his dressing gown, and with his frizzy hair standing on end, patted the boy on the shoulder.

"What is it?" he whispered to Lily.

"It's that Issur," said Lily angrily. "Giving him ideas, a boy of his age."

Thomas caught the name. "Issur," he said, suddenly wide awake. "Issur was here. Dancing. He spoke to me, said not to forget him. But Lily, it was so frightening, not really like Issur at all. Much bigger, and I felt so cold and alone."

He broke into desperate sobs. "I think I want to be sick," he said suddenly, and dived out of bed to hurl himself down the two steps that led into the bathroom. Sylvester found him on his knees, pale and wretched, shivering with cold despite the warm night, and with beads of sweat prickling his forehead.

"Get him back to bed," said Lily, after she had wiped his mouth and hands. "Come along, poppet, you're safe now. Sylvester, tuck him up, give him an extra blanket from the cupboard, and stay with him."

She was back in a flash with a glass of brandy and water. Sylvester raised his eyebrows.

"It's what he needs," said Lily, supporting his back as she held the glass to his lips.

"After he's thrown up? Do you think it's food poisoning? What has he eaten?"

Lily looked at him reprovingly. "You know better than that. He wasn't sick, it was just retching, with shock and nerves. What he needs is to relax and go back to sleep. Look, his eyes are drooping."

She leant forward and kissed the by now very sleepy boy. "You go back to sleep now. I'll leave the landing light on, and the door open. Sylvester and I will be up for a while, so there's no need to worry."

Thomas gave a weak smile and snuggled down under his bedclothes, closing his eyes as though they were too heavy to keep open. Sylvester followed Lily downstairs.

"Well, that's woken us up," he said.

"We aren't the only ones awake, either," said Lily. "Did you hear that music?"

"I did," said Sylvester. "Shame Gabriel isn't here, he'd have been fascinated by all this."

"I shall be glad when it's over," said Lily. "Now, just this once, you can pour me a glass of wine."

Sylvester disappeared, his feet sounding softly on the cellar steps. He returned with a bottle and two narrow glasses.

"On such a night as this," he said, easing the cork out, "I think we should drink champagne."

"Wine of the gods," said Lily.

# Epilogue

The last chords of the organ voluntary echoed round the vault of the nave. The people in the congregation, a distinctly well-dressed lot, began to gather up their possessions and make their slow way out. Simon had decided to finish with a great flourish, let them know she's coming, he said, pointing upwards.

After a very quiet, private funeral for Zephania at St Quivox's, as she had requested, arrangements for the memorial service had been left to Justinia.

"Is there any point?" she said doubtfully to Sylvester and Lucius. "Nobody knew she was still alive, all her fame was in the past, will anyone come?"

"Leave it to us," said Sylvester and Lucius. "Of course they will."

In fact, since the discreet announcement of her death, there had been a flood of interest in Zephania. Valliaze's obituary had started it, and her life story captured the imagination of the general public as well as of the world of music. A publisher, hearing of the diaries, had been in touch with Justinia, and she, in a moment of inspired kindness, had passed the publisher and the diaries over to Merle.

"A marvellous story," said Merle. "And they're talking about a film."

The memorial service, originally due to take place in the choir of the Cathedral, had to be relocated to the nave when the cathedral authorities realized how many people were coming. The music alone would attract hundreds, and word was out that it was going to be a spectacular service.

"And it was," Justinia said to Sylvester as they made their way out through the great west doors, which were only opened on big occasions. "Wonderful music, Sylvester. You and Lucius really did pull all the stops out."

"She was a great singer and musician," said Sylvester. "Rare," he added, speaking with an instrumentalist's prejudice, "because they're so often one but not the other."

"I hadn't realized she'd taught so many big names," Justinia continued. "Quite a coup getting Maria van Marisco to sing. And Ferenc Latterly to play, I thought he never left Italy these days."

"Practically never, but he knew Zephania in America when he was a child, and he felt he should come to pay his last respects. And, good news, now he's decided he likes Eyot, and Lucius has persuaded him to give a concert at the Festival next summer."

Piers eased his way through the crowd to arrive slightly breathless at Justinia's side. "Do you know how many are coming back to the Manor?" he asked. "I'm sure it's going to be more than we reckoned on."

"Bound to be," said Sylvester cheerfully. "Don't worry, I put Lily on to it, she and Pansy really hit it off together. I told them to order extra from Gumble's if necessary, I expect you'll find their van in the drive when you get there."

Unthrang hadn't seen such excitement since Bert Toadflax's pig took first prize at the County show. Car after car drove through the market place, parked around the green and spilled over into the high street. PC Vibbs was pink in the face with the effort of directing people where to go. "Never seen owt like it," he said. "Bigger than a film star, she must've been, and living here all that time."

The Rev Wroot, clad these days in an elegant black soutane, popped into St Quivox to make a quick intercession for Zephania's soul, repressing the unworthy thought that perhaps she hadn't been a very devout Christian. "We all serve God in our own ways," he told the plaster statue of the Blessed Virgin Mary which had recently been installed above its own little altar. Then he hot-footed it across to the Manor, anxious not to miss a moment of the fun.

The cathedral had turned out in force, led by the Bishop, who felt he had a special role in all this, married as he was to

Faustina, a trained singer if not a professional these days. He found himself standing next to a suntanned Simon Praetorius, who was relishing the excellent champagne. He congratulated him on the service and its music. "Good to hear our own choir back in such good voice," he said. "I didn't see that new boy they made such a fuss about. Ill, was he?"

"No," said Simon. "He decided that the choir was too much like hard work, especially when I came back and they settled down to singing decent repertoire again. His parents have taken him off to a drama school in north London, a great career is predicted for him."

"Ah," said the Bishop wisely. "I don't pretend to know more than the average man in the street about church music, but Faustina assures me that the new arrangements for the choir are far better than those planned under the sponsorship scheme."

"More money," said Simon briefly. "Please excuse me, Bishop, I see my brother over there . . ."

"Of course, of course," said the Bishop heartily. "I must have a word with him myself in a moment, I want to tell him how much we're looking forward to the first performance of his new work, a privilege for the Cathedral to present it."

Justinia, looking flushed and singularly beautiful, was flirting with Valliaze. "Tell me how it's all going," he said, twinkling wickedly at her. "No problems with the husband?"

Justinia pulled a face. "Only financial ones, and the lawyers are sorting all that out."

Valliaze looked more serious. "How are you managing? Lessons with Yseult won't be cheap, and then there are other expenses, and living in London isn't easy these days."

"I've been very lucky," said Justinia. "Alexia Wryston is an old friend, and I have a room in her flat."

"The contralto; yes, yes, very good."

"And I'm doing freelance work for my old department and for some other people as well. I want to keep the house here, it's a link with Zephania. Pansy and Marius are going to house-sit for me, and I'll have to sell the jewellery to do some repairs which are needed, but I'll manage."

"Is it strange to discover that you had a grandmother you never knew about?"

Justinia looked a little sad. "I wish I'd seen more of her, got to know her better. And it'll be a long time before I forgive my mother for keeping it all secret."

"Did she know that Zephania Zouche was Stephanie Lucchesi?"

"No, no, she didn't. But she knew that she had been adopted, and she knew who her real mother was. She even knew what a very great singer she had been. If only she'd told me, I think it would have given me more faith in my voice."

"Because you might have inherited her talents?"

"No, because my grandmother had fought for her career, and it had mattered so much to her that she was prepared to make huge sacrifices for it. Of course, my mother wasn't really passing judgement on my voice when she told me over and over again that it was no good, that I didn't have the voice or the talent to succeed as a singer. It was the ridiculous sense of shame she felt about being illegitimate, and the feeling that being an artist automatically meant a life of utterly loose morals and no proper family ties."

"You mustn't blame her altogether," said Valliaze. "To her generation, illegitimacy was a stigma. Her adoptive parents were so very middle-class and respectable. I expect, without meaning to, they made it worse for her."

Justinia was unconvinced. Her mother had made one last desperate attempt to persuade her to give up any idea of becoming a singer. She urged her daughter to forgive Digby and to settle down and start a family. "It's the only lasting happiness a woman can know," she told Justinia. "Don't throw it all away for a dream, an uncertain future, no husband to support you."

When Justinia told her mother just how unsupportive Digby had been, Celia didn't change her mind.

"All men are like that," she said philosophically. "They stray."

"Digby didn't stray," said Justinia furiously. "He was screwing Genevra here, on my sofa, in my house. And she wasn't the first, either. I mean, she may have been the first on my sofa, but she wasn't the first fling that Digby's had since we got married."

"Take him away," advised Celia. "That's what I did with your father, and he became much easier to handle when I put temptation out of his reach."

"Might as well put Digby into a home," said Justinia, unimpressed. "or put a bromide in his tea. No, I'm not going back to him."

"He very much wants to have you back," said Celia.

"No, he doesn't," snapped Justinia. "He wants the Manor. And when I told him that I was leaving him for good, he made me an offer for it. And no, Mother, I am not accepting it; if I did have to sell it, which I don't, he'd be the last person on earth I'd sell it to."

Andrea and Ben, who was home from school, wriggled through to Justinia, followed by Thomas with a plate of tiny bouchées. "We're filling up the drinks," said Andrea importantly, slurping a generous measure into Valliaze's half-full glass. "Ben has got the red wine, but I don't see who'd want it when there's champagne."

"Have one of these, Justy," said Thomas. He turned politely to Valliaze. "And you, sir?"

Valliaze beamed as he took a bouchée. "Ah, it's Thomas, whose voice is dropping, and who hopes he will be a tenor."

Thomas grinned back at him. "Yes," he said. "Justy, did you hear about the choir?"

"I noticed they seemed to be back to normal today."

"Such goings-on." He lowered his voice to a conspiratorial whisper, after quickly glancing around to see if any clergy were in the vicinity. "You know the Dean left all his money, a terrific amount, millions, to his girlfriend."

"Yes," whispered Justinia. "I did hear."

"Well, she didn't want it, and she's given an awful lot of it to the Cathedral, for the choir!"

"As well as Digby's sponsorship money?"

"No, instead of. That's what's good about it. She said she liked the choir as it was, and that it had to go back to proper Evensongs and all that kind of thing."

"And money talks very loudly in the Church," said a carrying, adult voice.

"Hello, Alban," said Justinia. "You'll alarm the Bishop."

"They need livening up, dull lot," said another voice as Valdemar slid a practised arm round Justinia's waist and gave her a warm but not very cousinly kiss. "Magdalena's here, she was sorry she couldn't make the service, but she thought the twins might spoil the music."

"Are they here, too?" said Justinia.

"Yes," said Thomas. "Come on, I'll find them for you."

"I don't see that witless Succentor," said Valdemar, looking about the large, crowded room. With his height, he had an excellent view. "The place seems to be teeming with dog collars, but I don't see him."

"Ah," said Alban. "He's gone. They've sent him away, couldn't leave him here jeopardizing all that lovely money."

"I thought it was difficult to remove a canon from his perch."

"He's gone to serve the Anglican community in Iceland," said Alban.

Valdemar let out a crack of laughter. "What, a couple of Vikings and a shaggy pony? Oh, I like it!"

He caught sight of Lydia and beckoned to her. He lowered his voice, unusual for him, since he never minded what anybody thought of him; however, these were family matters. "What's the latest on Justy, Lydia? Virginia tells me that this Gervase fellow is very keen on her, think anything will come of it?"

Lydia shrugged. "I don't know. I think Justy likes him, but perhaps she isn't feeling very pro men at present."

"That's what Magdalena said. Oh well, anything's better than that Digby fellow."

Sadie had found Justinia with some difficulty. She gave her a warm hug, "Justy, I know it's all going to turn out well for you."

"Sadie," said Justinia. "Why is your house up for sale? I saw the sign as we came through."

"Went up this morning," said Sadie. "I hadn't told anyone, because you know how plans come to nothing, but I heard today. I'm off to South America; big expedition, I'm there for the parrots."

"Oh, Sadie, how wonderful," said Justinia. "I'm so pleased. But won't you want a house here for when you come back? And your children?"

"I've told them I'm leaving, and that they're old enough to

stand on their own two feet now," said Sadie in firm tones.
"I've done my best for them, I can't say they haven't been a
disappointment in many ways, but I don't care any more. For
the rest of my life, I'm going to do what I want to do. The house
is an encumbrance, and it has too many memories."

"Well, there'll always be a room here," said Justinia warmly.

"That's what Sylvester said, bless him. Plenty of room up at
Midwinter Hall, he told me. No, I'll be fine, but I'd rather be near
a university. Manchester have been making interested noises,
I've published a lot over the years, despite Charles's despising
my work so much."

"Any news of Issur?"

"He's in London," said Sadie. "Made it up with the management
at Rosebery Avenue, he'd walked out, you know, when he
went to Liverpool. Top of the bill, he's off to New York in the
spring."

"I wonder what the Americans will make of him."

"Plenty for him to do over there, I would imagine."

The two women smiled at each other.

"Mmm, yes," said Justinia.

"One thing," Sadie went on. "Jezebel."

"Of course, your parrot," said Justinia. "You can't take her
with you."

"No, and she needs a good home. Justy, I'd like you to
have her."

"Me?" said Justy.

"Please."


"Look at Piers and Roxane," Lucius whispered to Merle as he went
past with a tray. Merle tugged at his sleeve to make him stop.

"Roxane was just talking to me, Lucius. She says, do we want
to buy Juniper House?"

Lucius put the tray carefully down on a nearby window ledge.
"Say that again."

"She needs the money. You know her charity work?"

Lucius nodded. "Old ladies in Eyot, wasn't it?"

"Well, no, actually she was the charity. It was various men, of
course Roxane's very attractive. There was one for food – the man
from Gumble's, and a rose grower, who looked after her garden

for her, and the man who saw to the pool, and another man from that firm which does furniture and so on, Hazlitt's, you know."

Lucius's mouth twitched. "What a novel way of arranging your life. I wondered how illustration work could give her quite that standard of living. It must have been very tiring for her."

"No, she had a rota, regular days." Merle laughed at the expression on Lucius's face. "I think it shows enterprise," she said primly. "Anyway, she's stopping all that, because Piers doesn't like it."

"I'm not surprised," said Lucius caustically. "I don't think I'd care for it myself. I suppose he isn't prepared to join the list as resident musician every other Saturday?"

"No, he's not. He's put his foot down. Him or them."

"And she's chosen Piers? Wise woman, he's going to go far."

"   I think it may have been Issur who made up her mind for her, he seems to have done a lot of meddling in people's lives one way and another. So she'd like us to buy Juniper House. It will give her some money, pay off the last of her father's debts and leave a bit over, and she won't have to worry about upkeep. Oh, and she says we can still use the pool as much as we like."

"Good," said Lucius, "only we must make a contribution if her handsome pool man isn't coming every three weeks for nothing."

"She'll miss her charity work," said Merle.

It began to snow as they drove out of Unthrang. The windscreen wipers swished the fat flakes away with a steady thunk, thunk noise. Jezebel was muttering on the back seat, angry at being taken away from her familiar surroundings.

"What's Alexia going to say about that parrot?" asked Gervase.

"She likes parrots," said Justinia in a sleepy voice. "I expect she'll teach it lots of new words."

"Heaven help us," said Gervase. "It won't be fit for polite company."

"Nor is Alexia."

"Happy?" said Gervase, glancing sideways at her.

"I think so. Tired, it's been a tiring week."

"You can sleep in tomorrow."

"No, I can't. I've a lesson with Yseult at nine."

"You're settling in London for good, then, are you?" asked Gervase. He had been longing to ask ever since he heard from Virginia that Justinia had left Digby and had fled to London.

"Yes," said Justinia.

"To be with me?" said Gervase hopefully.

"To sing," said Justinia.

# Children of Chance
## ELIZABETH PEWSEY

In the sultry heat of an uncommonly hot English summer, young Prue Pagan heads north to take up a holiday job at Mountjoy Castle. Newly released from the confines of her convent school, she tastes the pleasures – and dangers – of her new position with innocent abandon. At nearby Midwinter Hall, Prue's more worldly friend Cleo is also working for the summer, in the employ of a famous cellist. While Prue is stalked by Lord Mountjoy's irascible heir, Cleo pursues her own quarry in typically uninhibited fashion. Nothing is quite what it seems, however, and many secrets lie hidden between castle, hall and village. By the time the summer is out so are most of the secrets, and Prue is not the only one wiser in the ways of the world.

'A deliciously wicked tale of the shedding
of innocence'
*Company*

'A witty, thoroughly English romp'
*Family Circle*

SCEPTRE

# Divine Comedy
## ELIZABETH PEWSEY

Late one night, a young girl running away from home tumbled impulsively off a coach in the cathedral city of Eyot, where she knew no one. Eight years later, Quinta is well established there, with a new identity. She has achieved an orderly life, balancing the demands of her daughter, her work as a violin maker, and the composer she lives with – until the unexpected arrival in Eyot of Lydia Holbeck, a friend from the past.

As Lydia draws Quinta out of her safe, careful ways, the cathedral community around them begins to ferment with scandal. A new Bishop is due, complete with a wife one member of the choir knows remarkably well, and by the time Quinta comes face to face with her past, no one's life is left unchanged.

'A light, entertaining tale, skilfully plotted, it achieves its uplifting effect by leavening realism with romance'
*Scotland on Sunday*

'Sharp, invigorating and enormous fun'
*Elizabeth Buchan*

SCEPTRE

# Volcanic Airs
## ELIZABETH PEWSEY

As fog rolls over the northern landscape of Eyotshire, the inhabitants of Mountjoy Castle are seized by an urge to escape south to warmer climes. First to go is 14-year-old Thomas, fleeing his boarding school to an island off the coast of Sicily, followed by his stepmother Magdalena, tired of her husband Valdemar's infidelities. While the tabloids latch on to the affair and blow it up into a scandal, one by one the Mountjoy family, its friends, a rather strange nanny and several musicians gather in the serene Villa Saraceno on the island of Aeolus, where there is more than one kind of slumbering volcano.

Only Valdemar is left behind, until he succeeds in tracking down his errant wife and children and joins a complex dance of love and betrayal in the heat of a Sicilian June.

**A Sceptre Hardback**

SCEPTRE